I0761810

PATH OF TERROR

LOGAN RYLES

Severn River Publishing
SevernRiverBooks.com

ISBN: 978-1-64875-690-0 (Paperback)

ALSO BY LOGAN RYLES

The Prosecution Force Series

Brink of War

First Strike

Election Day

Failed State

Firestorm

White Alert

Nuclear Nation

Fallout

Full Dark

Red Horizon

The Reed Montgomery Series

The Ian Hale Series

Line of Fire

Path of Terror

Price of Allegiance

Dogs of War

To find out more about Logan Ryles and his books, visit

severnriverbooks.com

"Better to fight for something than live for nothing."
—General George S. Patton

"Then said David to the Philistine, 'Thou comest to me with a sword, and with a spear, and with a shield: but I come to thee in the name of the Lord of hosts, the God of the armies of Israel, whom thou hast defied. This day will the Lord deliver thee into mine hand; and I will smite thee, and take thine head from thee; and I will give the carcasses of the host of the Philistines this day unto the fowls of the air, and to the wild beasts of the earth; that all earth may know that there is a God in Israel. And all this assembly shall know that the Lord saveth not with the sword and spear: for the battle is the Lord's, and He will give you into our hands.'"
—1 Samuel 17:45–47, King James Version

1

Western Equatoria, South Sudan
18:05 Hours, East Africa Time

They struck just after sunset, with a roar of engines and a chatter of gunfire. Four vehicles exploded out of a maize field, bearing down on the mud-hut village like streaking cruise missiles.

Two trucks featured swivel-mounted, Soviet-built DShK heavy machine guns. Nicknamed "*Dushkas*" by the militias who favored them, the guns opened fire as the trucks tore between mango trees, unleashing a deafening thunder of zipping death.

Yet the noise wasn't enough to drown out the screams.

Mothers cried for their children. Gunshot fathers writhed on the ground, scrambling to shield their families. The four vehicles encircled the village and two dozen men bailed from cabs and truck beds. AK-47s joined the assault, a ceaseless chatter that ventilated bodies as the invaders fanned out.

Swarming the village. Checking under bullet-ridden vehicles and shining lights into livestock sheds. Even kicking in the front door of a mud-walled church with a thatched steeple.

And still, the slaughter continued.

From the village outskirts, Lado Bakumba recognized the howl of approaching engines long before the gunfire began, and he knew what was coming. Lying on a cot in the back of a hut—the preacher's hut, actually—Bakumba was sweating off a nasty hangover. The day prior in a neighboring village, he'd stumbled into an open-air bar and dispensed a United States dollar from a roll of matching currency hidden in his canvas backpack. The dollar was enough to buy him a full five rounds of *kassese*, a local beer-like brew manufactured from sorghum by the woman who owned the bar.

As a lifelong alcoholic, Bakumba never refused any kind of drink, but kassese was a favorite. Five cups in, he was already inebriated and should have retreated to a shade tree to sleep off his buzz. He should have quit while he was ahead.

He didn't, and what happened next was predictable—even inevitable.

The kassese converted Bakumba into an amiable drunk, eager to make friends. He withdrew the roll of American currency—eighty-four dollars in total, nearly two months' wages for a working South Sudanese—and proclaimed his intention to buy drinks for everyone.

It wasn't a strictly selfless gesture. Bakumba had come to this place on a mission. Hired by a masked man in Juba who had supplied him with a hundred dollars and—most curiously—a digital video camera, Bakumba's object in journeying to Western Equatoria represented a vast improvement from his former life as a day laborer. Instructing him on how to use the camera, the masked man promised a ten-thousand-dollar payday—a literal fortune in South Sudan—if video tapes of certain "events" could be captured.

Bakumba only needed to know where to find those events. Perhaps his new drinking buddies, properly plied, could assist?

They'd beaten him and taken the cash, instead. Bakumba crawled much of the way to the next village, dragging a muddy backpack, which still contained the Sony RXO II digital camera. Apparently, the illiterate farmers had no use for it. Dehydrated, wounded, and penniless, he was at the mercy of the local minister, all concern for his journalistic ambitions long forgotten...

Until the gunfire began.

At the first bark of the Dushkas, Bakumba was on his feet. Scrambling across a dirt floor even as a stray bullet blew through the roof, he stayed low, heart hammering. He hooked the muddy backpack and scanned the room, desperate to locate a weapon.

There were so many in South Sudan—artifacts of one genocidal conflict after another. Yet there was no rifle to be found in the minister's hut. No pistol, no fighting knife, even. Only sagging furniture and a pair of dusty books.

Useless.

Another roar of gunfire, and a female wail as loud and long as a police siren pierced the night. Bakumba's body throbbed with pumping adrenaline. He clawed his way over a table, nearly tumbling to the ground again. He saw the window mounted high in the back wall—a square opening covered by cheesecloth to keep the mosquitos out. It might be just large enough to scramble through.

Bakumba went for it. He tore the cheesecloth away and shoved the backpack through, then began hauling himself up even as the shouts intensified. Bakumba recognized Zande, a Ubangian language spoken by the Azande tribe. It wasn't a surprise—the Azande had been involved with various militias all across the region for years.

What *was* a surprise were the next words Bakumba heard. They were English.

"Get the children!"

Bakumba hesitated, remembering the video camera. The masked man. The promise of ten thousand dollars for videos of *certain events*—specifically, events involving a man who spoke English.

But the camera was already outside, and the shouts drew nearer. There was no time for journalism. Bakumba would die if he didn't move quickly.

Grabbing the window frame, he hauled his body up and pushed his head through. On his stomach, halfway out, the gunshots rang even louder in his ears. He panted and kicked—he was almost ready to fall into the elephant grass growing outside the hut.

Then the next stray bullet zipped like an angry hornet and struck him in the back of his left arm just above his elbow. Bakumba choked on a scream and fell forward. He landed in sticky mud, pulsing waves of agony exploding from the fresh wound. With each thump of his accelerated heart, the misery came sharper than before, nearly overwhelming him.

Somehow, he found the backpack with his good arm. He entered the grass and scrambled on his knees for a thicket of wattle shrubs even as headlights swept the minister's house. Voices shouted in Zande. An AK snarled.

The gunmen were right on his heels. Bakumba could sense them, *picture them*, even as he zigzagged deeper amid the brush. He didn't dare stop until he'd progressed eighty yards or more. Gasping for breath, he finally risked a look back.

There were no gunmen chasing him. It was all in his imagination. But there *were* lots of gunmen gathered around a quartet of pickup trucks parked in the village's public square. Bakumba could see them through slits in the elephant grass—dirty, sweaty, and heavily armed.

Two groups of villagers joined the gunmen. Shoved over the limp bodies of their slain neighbors, they were herded into tight clusters, sorted not by gender but by age. Children in one knot—adults in another.

As Bakumba watched, heart thundering, a tall white man dropped out of a giant green military truck and stood between the two knots. Reaching into a pouch, the man produced a wad of something dark and packed it into one cheek. He chewed and spat brown saliva. His emotionless gaze swept the prisoners—some twenty adults, maybe two dozen children.

Bakumba's mouth went dry. Terror overcame him as every instinct of his overwhelmed mind screamed the same thing on silent repeat: *Run! Hide in the brush!*

But despite the merits of those arguments, another voice whispered promises of ten thousand US dollars stacked on a table. More money than Bakumba had ever *seen*, let alone dreamed could be his. Truly, a small fortune. Enough to buy his own bar in Juba. To be set for life.

The event. Bring me film of the event.

Bakumba fought through the pain of the gunshot as he tugged the Sony out of the backpack. He scrubbed dust from the lens and propped the camera on a lump of clay. He mashed the record button, mapping his point of aim through an LCD viewing screen.

The tall man, still chewing and spitting, approached the adults.

Bakumba followed him with the camera, squinting at a pitch-black tattoo that wrapped the man's muscled right bicep.

It was a snake—long and thick with its fangs opening across the inside of the man's forearm. Just the sight of it sent a chill up Bakumba's spine as the snake man snapped an unintelligible order to one of his men. The gunman translated the statement to the villagers, but none of the quaking prisoners answered.

Bakumba fought his own urge to hyperventilate, the fear growing so strong in his body that he couldn't have fled if he'd wanted to. He was frozen in place, transfixed by the horror that unfolded before him...

And knowing what came next.

The exchange between the snake man and the villagers continued. He squatted in the mud in front of a familiar face—it was the minister who gave Bakumba shelter. The snake man spat brown saliva between the minister's knees, and the minister mumbled desperate pleas in Zande.

Maybe the white man didn't understand. Maybe he didn't care. He stood and jerked his head. On cue, half the gunmen began hauling the children toward that monster-green truck.

The minister shouted. A woman screamed. Somebody broke ranks and fought toward the children.

Then, as Bakumba and his camera watched from one hundred yards away, the snake man jerked his head again. Atop a pickup truck a soldier pulled the charging handle on a Dushka, chambering a fresh round. The gunmen surrounding the adults retreated half a pace.

And the machine gun opened fire.

2

The Bob Marshall Wilderness, Montana
15:40 Hours, Mountain Time Zone

Ian Hale tracked his prey for thirty-one hours straight.

Beginning at the South Fork trailhead, where the confluence of the Flathead River and Meadow Creek marked the entrance of the one-million-acre wilderness, the party of two guides and four guests entered the mountains on foot.

With a layer of pre-Thanksgiving snowfall coating the earth, the average temperature inside "The Bob" never exceeded mid-thirties Fahrenheit, and rarely exceeded freezing. Frigid winds swept between peaks that towered thousands of feet overhead. Evergreen trees stood stoic alongside rivers choked by ice.

It was bitter. It was brutal. It was exactly what Hale wanted.

Loaded down with rifles and camping supplies, the hunting party was accompanied by one husky with booties on his paws. That dog stuck close to the lead scout—the introverted one, who was most annoyed by a chattering New Yorker dressed in a puffy luxury jacket.

Everyone was annoyed by the New Yorker. Two days into the trek, Hale wished the guy would take a tumble down a mountainside. But then at last the spike camp was reached—the position high in the mountains that the group would call home for the next five days. Scouts would assist in the erection of tents and the mapping of territories. Short- and long-range excursions would be scheduled. Mealtimes and emergency protocols were communicated.

But for Ian Hale none of that mattered. He'd only booked the scouting service because it was the easiest way to facilitate access to The Bob. Once the spike camp was established, Hale checked in with the introverted scout and briefly communicated his plans.

The guy was an ex-Army Ranger with a rippling shrapnel scar running down his neck. He didn't ask any questions or require Hale to jump through any hoops. He simply grunted an acknowledgment and passed off a sat phone.

Then Hale was off, hiking into the teeth of The Bob with only essential gear strapped to his back. The rifle itself rode in his arms—a bolt-action .300 Winchester Magnum equipped with a Leopold optic, and half a dozen two-hundred-grain hunting rounds. The weapon was loaded and ready to kill.

Hale only needed a target.

Hale found his target eighteen hours later—at least, he found his target's trail.

Six miles deeper into the Bob Marshall Wilderness, Hale deployed aluminum snowshoes and cinched the hood of his wool-blend jacket to fight the developing cold. Keeping his pace at a steady creep, he minimized his noise signature and breathed frozen air in regular cycles.

Conserving energy. Maintaining focus. Embracing the hostility of The Bob without fear, but with plenty of respect. It wasn't the first time men like him had braved this place. Decades prior, a detachment of Delta Force operators—the same famed Unit that Hale himself had once called home—had chosen these rugged mountains as a training site for future overseas activities.

Hale wasn't a part of that expedition, but ever since learning about it, he'd wanted to come here. He wanted to face the same mental, physical, and even spiritual tests of such an extreme environment—the combined confrontations of man versus nature, man versus other men, and most of all, man versus *himself*. The ultimate hurdle.

Hale would face that struggle for the rest of his life. For the moment his attention was fixated on an equally ancient conflict—man versus beast. Judging by the six-inch-deep tracks left in busted snow, the adversary in question was a bull elk. A heavy animal with broad antlers—broken branches marked the passages of those antlers as Hale squatted at the base of a tree, examining the tracks up close.

They wove between the evergreens, following a narrow mountain trail that wound toward a distant valley—a place where the elk might hope to find sustenance even as winter approached. Below six thousand feet, on south-facing slopes where the sun kept the snow at its thinnest, grazing could be found for weeks to come. Hale had studied topographical maps of the region and identified several such potential pastures deep inside The Bob—far beyond the range of most rational hunters.

Places where the biggest elk took shelter and only the hardest of men dared to follow. A *real* challenge.

Exactly what Ian Hale came for.

Still squatted in the snow, Hale deployed a bottle of talcum powder and twisted the cap. One squeeze ejected a feather-weight cloud of dust into the frozen mountain air, hanging for only a moment before blowing back across Hale's jacket.

The wind was in his face, carrying Hale's scent away from his quarry. With two hours of daylight remaining, there was time to reach the next peak. Maybe scope out the valley beyond using high-powered binoculars. Plot out a point of ambush and plan a stalking attack.

It would take hours. Maybe another day. In the near silent forest, Hale was on his own.

That was just the way he liked it.

3

Juba, South Sudan
14:35 Hours, East Africa Time

When Jaxon Wilks graduated summa cum laude from Harvard University with a master's degree in international affairs, his favorite professor warned him that being good is a blessing...but being *too good* is a curse that will lead you straight into an early grave.

Jaxon had no idea what the old man meant, and truth be told, he was having too much fun to worry about it. He loved studying shifting geopolitical landscapes, the tensions generated by ethnic polarities, scarce natural resources, and the ripple effect of global superpowers engaged in an endless tug of war.

His true dream? To be secretary of state. The youngest ever, ideally, which set him a hard deadline of appointment prior to his forty-first birthday. That was the bar he would have to reach if he would beat out John Quincy Adams, who held the record since 1817. It was *past* time for somebody to break it, and with an IQ of 128, Jaxon Wilks believed himself to be that man.

First, he needed to get to Washington, and he found his first opportunity as a research assistant for Maryland's senior senator. That old goat cared so little about anything that it was no trouble for Jaxon to manipulate his way into the title of "international affairs advisor," and from there Jaxon pretty much had free rein of the office.

He exploited it, identifying a prominent Maryland charity with ambitions of building a school in Africa but a lack of connections in the region. Jaxon, claiming to speak on behalf of the good senator, volunteered the assistance of his boss. He then proceeded to draft letters on *behalf* of his boss, forge a signature when nobody was looking, and dispatch them to every member of the Senate Committee on Foreign Relations.

Jaxon's sales pitch was compelling. Overnight, doors opened for the charity. The old goat was surprised to receive so many thank-you calls but was savvy enough to not look a gift horse in the mouth. Meanwhile, Jaxon parlayed his boss's golden hour into a lucrative position for himself at a prominent DC think tank, where his new title would be Advisor of African Relations.

In hindsight, that was the moment when Jaxon's well-laid plans started to go sideways. Up to that point, he was the go-getter. The smart kid with the sparkling résumé and quick wit. The wunderkind.

But he wasn't anything *specific*. He wasn't yet labeled, categorized, or pigeon-holed. If he'd been smart, Jaxon would have sidestepped the African Relations job for a more generic roll, or at least a roll involving a continent he remotely cared about.

For once, he wasn't smart. He took the job, he excelled like always...and just like that, he became *the Africa guy*.

Africa—really. That forgotten blob of earth where jungle and sand converge and shoeless hut-dwellers murder each other with sticks. Jaxon knew it was a politically incorrect viewpoint. He didn't care. He hadn't worked *this* hard for *this* long just to advise inconsequential policy on third world nations that half his bosses couldn't even spell.

He wanted to work on Europe, or maybe study the rising tensions in the South Pacific. *Real* problems. The kind that could catapult him to secretary of state status.

How was he ever going to be anybody while working on Africa?

Just breathe, he told himself. *You've got years to spare. Do the work, trust the process.*

Jaxon took his own advice. He gave everything to the think tank, pigeon-holed or otherwise. Eighty-hour work weeks and flawless execution at every turn. He trusted the process and owned his identity as the Africa guy. He gave it four hard years.

And then Jaxon was offered another unbelievable opportunity—a chance not only to escape the think tank but to actually *work inside* the US State Department. Yes, *really*. The role was advanced, placing Jaxon only three levels beneath the current secretary of state. A jaw-dropping offer.

The only catch? The job was Deputy Assistant Secretary of State...for *African Affairs*.

Jaxon finally understood what his professor had tried to warn him about. The curse had come back to haunt him. And yet he took the job, because what was he going to do? Refuse to work for the State Department?

No. He had to go, and he had to excel. Curse or no curse, it was his only path forward. Bouncing from one dusty African paradise to another. Dining on weird food and sleeping in aged hotels surrounded by cities full of barefoot locals, just like in his nightmares.

Nigeria, South Africa, Mozambique, Ethiopia, Cameroon. And now... South Sudan—the world's youngest country.

Over the last few years, Jaxon had become a soft expert of the gory conflict that had ripped Sudan in two, separating a predominantly Arab northern half from a predominantly African southern half. Armed militias, ethnic conflict, resource scarcity, and two very corrupt governments were all at play.

It was a story as old as time, a story Jaxon Wilks was sick of hearing. He'd been to Juba twice before and hadn't enjoyed it. Even less developed than most African cities, there was nothing good to eat and everything was dirty. The people always seemed to be hiding something. If you heard a distant pop, it likely *wasn't* a car backfiring.

For all that, Jaxon had never been so excited to board a plane in his life. He'd rushed to Juba, in fact—he couldn't get there fast enough. Because the opportunity that awaited him in South Sudan was the largest of his career. A monumental mission, entrusted to him based on all those years of miserable African study.

Exactly the kind of thing that could catapult his career straight to the top...but he had to *nail it*.

Debarking from the aged Boeing 737 that carried Jaxon out of Nairobi, he stepped into a blanket of heat and humidity that flooded his lungs like shower steam. Even in mid-November, it had to be ninety degrees in Juba. Jaxon was drenched in sweat long before he located his name printed on a cardboard sign.

But he hadn't felt this good in weeks.

"Deputy Assistant Wilks?"

The guy spoke clear English. He should—he was an American. The plain-clothed embassy security officer and driver of an armored SUV who was tasked with collecting Jaxon safely from the airport.

"That's me," Wilks said.

The guard took his bag and Jaxon slid into the Suburban's back seat alongside a man fifteen or twenty years his senior. Dark complexion, receding hairline, tight but genuine smile.

"Mr. Wilks?"

Jaxon accepted the handshake. "Ambassador. A pleasure."

The SUV rumbled away from the compact airport and into Juba's bustling outskirts—unique in its own way, but Jaxon had long ago stopped appreciating unimportant nuance. He was only thinking about the meeting ahead—about *nailing it*.

"We appreciate you being here on such short notice," the ambassador continued. "I expected to manage negotiations myself, to be honest. I guess Washington thought otherwise."

There was some disgruntlement in the ambassador's voice, but Jaxon doubted that this guy had any idea just how low his personal stock rated at the State Department. When it came to undesirable posts, Juba ranked near the top of the list—a place to park sloppy diplomats or those whose appointments involved little more than checking a box. Douglas Russell, the current Ambassador of the United States to South Sudan, was a long-time fixture of US diplomacy. He'd served as deputy chief of mission all around the world, and even briefly served as chief of mission—ambassador—in Italy.

It was in Rome that he imploded. Jaxon was unclear on the details, but he knew that Russell made a fool out of both himself and his country. Russell knew too much to be fired outright—so he was exiled instead. Parked someplace where he couldn't possibly do any more damage to Washington's sterling reputation.

That was the strategy, anyway. *And now this.*

"I'll be frank with you, Mr. Ambassador. I was sent with explicit orders to frontline negotiations. I'll handle all communication with the State Department and lead all discussions with South Sudanese officials. Your role will be to provide introductions and facilitate trust. That's all."

Russell tensed as Jaxon spoke, his stare turning cold. But for all that, he didn't pop back. He didn't challenge Jaxon's blunt declarations.

Maybe he was more aware of his eroded clout than Jaxon assumed.

"Can we get some more air back here?" Jaxon said, closing the subject.

The driver cranked up the AC. Jaxon watched the city roll by, noting a landscape of crumbling buildings, faded street signs, and dented cars. Kids ran half clothed through the streets. Dogs were so bone-skinny they looked like walking skeletons.

At every turn it was devastation. Destitution. Brokenness.

Sometimes Jaxon became so fed up that he stopped...seeing it. And yet he couldn't help but think: *All this could change overnight.*

The SUV finally reached the Ministries Complex—an ugly block building with armed guards standing out front and metal detectors at every door. The American party was expected, and Russell took the lead, his sullen disposition evaporating into a beaming smile. He introduced Jaxon to a smattering of irrelevant officials on their way down winding corridors to the Minister of Foreign Affairs office, where they were eventually ushered into a conference room.

Open windows. Blowing fans. No AC. Jaxon's suit stuck to his body from ankles to neck.

"Don't drink the water," the ambassador whispered.

Jaxon didn't need to be told. He remained quiet until the door opened again and a guy who could have been a pro football linebacker swept in. Tall and muscular, he moved easily, his smile revealing teeth so bright Jaxon wanted to blink.

Russell made introductions.

"Mr. Wilks, may I introduce His Excellency, Minister of Foreign Affairs Sebit Abiem."

"An honor, Minister."

"The honor is mine, Mr. Deputy Secretary. I trust your flight was pleasant?"

Anything but.

"Stunning views," Jaxon said.

Abiem laughed as though he knew what Jaxon *wasn't* saying. He took a seat and ushered the Americans to join him. A round of drinks was offered and politely declined. Jaxon shot Russell a sideways look, lifting one eyebrow.

Russell got the hint.

"Minister, the United States is enthusiastic about the opportunity to discuss a new, mutually beneficial trade agreement. Deputy Secretary Wilks has been authorized to speak on behalf of the State Department and offer terms for a contract."

"A contract?" Abiem lifted both eyebrows, feigning surprise. "My, aren't we forward? And I've barely met Mr. Wilks."

Stupid fool, Jaxon thought. But he remained calm. He had no choice. He needed ice in his veins. He needed absolute focus. Billions of dollars depended on it—his entire future might hinge on it.

Nail it, Jaxon.

"Minister Abiem," Jaxon said, his tone relaxed. "Let's back up. Tell me—what are you looking for in a trade partner?"

Abiem's mouth stretched into a greedy smile.

It was the right question.

4

The Bob Marshall Wilderness, Montana
17:04 Hours, Mountain Time Zone

There was something about the trail.

Hale wasn't sure exactly what, but it bothered him. Even as a gentle snowfall obscured many of the elk's tracks, those sheltered beneath tree limbs remained, and they didn't feel right.

Hale found the marks every few hundred yards as daylight faded, and it was one track in particular that caught his eye. He thought it was the right rear hoof, which seemed to drag instead of high-stepping through the snow like the others, almost as though it were a dead limb. Maybe the bull was limping?

Hale wasn't sure. Most of his skills involved stalking humans, which was much more a psychological practice than an ecological one. Still, he knew enough to fill in the gaps covered over by fresh snowfall. To find other indicators of the elk's passage—broken limbs, bruised bark, urine spots. By the time night fell he thought he'd gained on the animal. Some of those broken limbs were still sticky with fresh sap. The yellow spots of snow still smelled, however faintly.

The elk would bed down for the night. Hale had no choice but to follow suit. As the wind increased, bringing growing snowfall with it, Hale erected a one-man tent and heated water on a backpack stove to mix with freeze-dried beef stroganoff. The meal was eons ahead of the bland MREs Hale had consumed in the Army, so flavorful he would have eaten a second, but it was important to budget his rations.

Bedded down in a sleeping bag with wind beating against the tent and the distant howl of a wolf echoing from a faraway ridge, Hale closed his eyes and breathed deep. He ignored the cold, ignored the stiffness of tired muscles constricted around the titanium rod in his back. Most of all, he ignored the thoughts. Racing in the back of his mind, questions that played on repeat like the melody of a carousel.

Never ending. Never quite releasing him.

Is this what I've come to?

Hale awoke before the first light of day. He consumed a freeze-dried pack of oatmeal, stowed his gear, and sat quietly at the base of a tree just watching the first golden beams of the sunrise pierce the eastern horizon.

It looked to be a beautiful day in the making. As Hale sipped instant coffee, his mind drifted back to a Bible story his grandfather, Pat, used to read him as a child. A tale of long ago in a land far away. A war story, actually, involving a battle of the righteous versus the evil. The truth against deceit.

God stopped the sun in the sky that day. He granted the righteous army enough additional daylight to dispense absolute destruction against their enemies. A total, crushing victory—the kind military schools salivate over.

Hale believed that victory really happened, but he didn't believe that God would prolong the day ahead. It was his job to reach his target before the pitch black of Montana night closed over the mountains.

Back on the trail, the fatigue of three hard days hiking The Bob caught up with Hale. Toned muscles, trained by the Unit under the torment of endless days spent crisscrossing West Virginia mountains, were tested by the Montana ridgelines like they'd never been in Afghanistan. Hale was forced to pace himself to maintain effort throughout the day. He munched protein bars every two hours like clockwork and drank water even when he wasn't thirsty. He kept pushing, one ridge and peak after the next, keeping up with the continued broken limbs, torn bark, and occasional hoof tracks of the bull.

It was a mammoth—Hale knew that, now. On multiple occasions a thicket of evergreens had been plowed straight through, the elk using its antlers like the blade of a bulldozer and leaving a five-foot swath of destruction in its wake. In places where the snow deepened to two and three feet, the hoof marks of the elk plunged all the way to the bottom, leaving wide trenches behind.

And still, there was that uncertain lag in the animal's step. Hale detected it as an invisible subtext in the trail, a mystery Hale didn't yet have enough information to solve.

Was the bull injured? Did he suffer a birth defect?

Both options seemed unlikely. There was no blood trail, and if the bull was born with a defect that inhibited his ability to flee, he should have been long dead by now. Grizzlies roamed these mountains—many relocated by the state from more civilized regions where aggressive bears were a menace to soccer moms. Half a dozen times since leaving camp, Hale had found bear scat and paw prints. Once he even detected the silhouette of a grizzly about a mile away, strolling an adjacent ridge.

Savage, unafraid, and always hungry. A deformed elk would be easy prey—he would never be allowed to reach maturity.

So what, then?

Hale wondered, and he pressed on. Burning muscles, burning lungs, burning fingertips. Slogging on snowshoes, following the trail while keeping his eyes peeled for the same furry menace that threatened vulnerable elk. The Ruger Redhawk strapped to Hale's hip was loaded with five rounds of bear-stopping .44 Magnum, but he really didn't want to use it.

He only wanted to find his target. And he knew...he was close.

Another ridge, and Hale could finally see the valley below. A south-facing slope featured lighter snow than the north-facing trail Hale had just conquered. Sporadic trees gave way to patches of earth torn by previous grazers—elk, mule deer, maybe moose. A river wound between snowy banks, water gurgling past chunks of ice.

There wasn't a trace of humanity or human development. The air was clean, the sun bright from a cloudless sky. Hale fought to catch his breath, momentarily forgetting his prey and just savoring the magic of natural isolation. Of total loneliness so absolute it became its own form of company.

Silence. Stillness. Euphoria in its most subdued state. A perfect moment.

Then Hale saw it. He dug the binoculars out of his pocket and adjusted the focus, steady on his feet as he peered into the valley.

Two miles away. Edging close to the river, giant antlers drooping toward the water as it drank.

An absolute *monster*.

5

Hale approached from the south, keeping the wind in his face. Stalking the side of the ridge, he maintained the high ground for as long as he could, using thick timber and drainage ruts as visual cover.

Much more than their sight or sound, Hale knew that elks relied on their sense of smell for threat detection. Hale had plenty of time to close within killing distance, but if he rushed his approach and found himself upwind of the bull, the game would be up. The bull's long legs, deformed or otherwise, would carry him back into the mountains, out of range in seconds.

This would be Hale's only chance. He couldn't afford a single misstep.

No mistakes, Ian. Think and move.

Another half mile along the hillside, moving north. To obtain a clear shot, Hale would eventually need to descend to the valley floor, but he wanted to maintain the high ground as long as possible. As the sun crested mountain ridges, it created an upslope thermal—a current of warm air moving off the valley floor—and that kept Hale downwind of the elk.

It was a nifty trick, but Hale couldn't exploit it forever. Soon the real work began, only a hundred feet from the bottom of the mountainside. Hale entered a thicket of heavy timber, and his already crawling pace descended to a creep, one hand riding close to the Ruger Redhawk just in case of a grizzly.

Another half mile. Hale's last positioning of the elk put the bull only two thousand yards ahead, basking in the morning warmth near the river. With the precision shooting skills Hale had acquired in the Army, he was confident in his ability to drop the elk from half that distance. The rifle and the cartridge were both sufficient for the challenge.

But somehow shooting from that far away felt like cheating. Like hunting over bait or fishing with dynamite. At a thousand yards the elk's opportunity for escape was nearly zero. Most hunters couldn't hit from so far away—Hale's unfair advantage was well and good in war, but this wasn't war.

He decided on a final shooting distance of three hundred yards and kept moving. Deeper through the trees, stopping regularly to dispense talcum powder and double-check the wind. Weaving between entangled limbs, his body buzzing with adrenaline.

And then Hale broke through on the valley floor. Kneeling in the snow and lifting his binoculars, Hale steadied his breathing and focused...

He saw it. Eight hundred yards away, standing with its tail toward him. Bent and grazing, body rippling with muscle. It was *huge*. Twelve hundred pounds, easily—enough rich meat to fill Hale's freezer for a year.

A worthy target, but Hale wasn't home yet. He was still dedicated to his three-hundred-yard goal—fair play for the bull.

Descending to his stomach, Hale began the sniper's crawl. During his tenure in the US Army's 1st Special Forces Operational Detachment-Delta—known to its operators as "the Unit"—Hale hadn't been a sniper. He'd been what the Unit called a short-gunner—the guy who kicked in doors and nailed terrorists. As such, he'd spent most of his range time practicing with carbines, submachine guns, and pistols.

But he still trained with precision rifles, because in the Unit, every soldier was trained to perform every job. Hale had booked extensive time not only at the US Army's advanced marksmanship school but also at the US Marine Corps' Camp Lejeune Scout Sniper Course, where he'd learned to blend with the very fabric of the earth in his relentless pursuit of the target.

That was the Delta way—no bureaucratic squabbling, no tribal superiority. If the Marines did it better, then go learn from the Marines. Just be the *best*, no matter what.

Your country depended on it.

Seven hundred yards. Hale moved like a human snake, the rifle riding his back as his breath turned to steam. His chest constricted with the cold. His heart thumped a little harder with each passing yard.

He was tired—the cumulative fatigue of hiking The Bob was catching up with him.

He was hungry—the stalk had run long, and Hale was running short on food.

But if the next half hour was successful, none of that would matter. He would clean the elk where it fell. Build a fire and grill a fresh steak. Prepare the rest of the animal to be packed out in segments—a year's worth of protein properly earned.

Six hundred yards. Hale no longer needed the binoculars. He watched the elk as its antlers swung like the superstructure of a pivoting crane. Absolutely gorgeous—a spectacle of creation.

At five hundred yards Hale dispensed more talcum powder. The wind had nearly stopped, which was dangerous. A pause could precipitate a shift in direction. One whiff of Hale, and the elk would bolt.

Should he shoot from there? Five hundred yards was child's play. Hale could drop the elk with one twitch of his trigger finger. Over and done, a successful hunt.

No.

This wasn't about mission complete—not this time. Hale had made the elk a promise, even if the elk never knew it. He would give the bull every chance to escape. He would respect the game.

On the move again, now by inches, not feet. Measuring his breaths as the range finder on his binoculars measured his progress.

Four hundred yards, and the elk's head lifted. His nostrils flared. Hale froze, barely daring to breathe. He wanted to dust with the talcum powder, but what did it matter, if the wind had turned against him?

It would already be too late. Maybe the elk had detected something else—something interesting but not necessarily threatening. He hadn't moved from his grazing spot. His muscles remained relaxed even as he snorted.

Then he turned. He moved across Hale's path at an angle, approaching the creek, walking with a slight hitch in his back right leg. Hale couldn't tell why. The elk was moving too slowly to be sure.

Whatever the case, the bull was doing Hale's work for him. He was cutting yards. The range finder read 340 by the time the elk stopped to dip his mouth into the river. Hale covered the final stretch inside of five minutes, marking three hundred yards even and lowering the binoculars. Reaching over his back for the rifle.

It was already chambered. Hale used a frozen gopher mound as a shooting rest. He lifted lens caps and settled behind the rifle.

Under eight-times magnification, the elk loomed massive beyond the crosshairs. Hale could have dropped him with iron sights at this distance. He decreased the zoom and disengaged the rifle's safety.

The elk didn't notice the soft click. He kept drinking, his ears flicking in the morning sun. Hale took a moment just to admire the artful design of it all—the obvious beauty in every detail of the animal's biology.

Then he rocked his head. He lifted the crosshairs just an inch over the elk's heart and breathed deep. Exhaled half. Curled his trigger finger.

Then stopped.

There was something he hadn't seen before. Something he only noticed as the elk twitched, muscles rippling through his body but seeming to catch at his right rear hip—the top of that same leg that dragged when the bull walked. Hale pivoted his point of aim and increased zoom.

It was a scar. No—not just a scar. It was a *bullet* scar. A sloppy shot that landed *way* behind the vital organs, smashing into the elk's hindquarter. Decimating muscle, leaving him with the limp. Forever maimed, forever marked by a collision with the ultimate predator.

And yet he survived.

A lump rose in Hale's throat. He turned the rifle forward again, up the elk's graceful long neck to its massive face. A dark, sensitive eye. Lips dripping with icy water. An iron jaw and skyline antlers.

A warrior of America's forgotten frontier...and a survivor.

Hale reached for the safety. He held the rifle against his chest as he rose from the snow. Standing next to the same creek, three hundred yards from the bull, he watched the clueless animal for five long seconds.

Then Hale tore off one glove and put two fingers between his lips. He whistled, loud and high. The elk's head swept toward the sound. His wide eyes locked on Hale, and for a perfect moment, neither of them moved.

Then the elk's tail flicked. In a second he was on the run. Flashing across the snow, one leg semi-dragging. Headed toward the cover of the mountains. Already out of range—surviving once more.

Hale smiled.

6

Atlanta, Georgia
13:30 Hours, Eastern Standard Time

Laney Shaw loved "the A"—she always had.

Born and raised in the small Georgia town of Warner Robins, some of Shaw's best childhood memories involved pilgrimages to Atlanta, wrapped up in Braves gear during the summer and Falcons gear during the fall. At the top of the Westin Peachtree Plaza, Shaw used to stare wide-eyed over a city of glistening lights and polished stone—mile after mile of pure *excitement*.

Attending school in nearby Athens only inflamed her infatuation with Georgia's capital city. There were nights she and her sorority sisters spent in Midtown that she wasn't proud of. One particular SEC championship held at the old Georgia Dome involved security dragging her out by her Bulldogs jersey after *another* questionable officiating call.

Maybe she was a little proud of that one.

Whatever the case, whatever the occasion, Atlanta was in her blood. Since graduating college, Shaw had served in the US Army and worked as an executive for Sentinel, a private military contracting firm. She had traveled the world, and landed in Boston. She enjoyed dinners in Paris or Tokyo as much as margaritas on Caribbean beaches.

But nothing was like *the A*. Nothing hit as deep as that first sip of sweet iced tea flavored with fresh peaches.

Shaw only wished she was visiting under better circumstances.

Departing her terminal at Hartsfield-Jackson International Airport, Shaw waded through a swarm of offloading passengers. She had flown economy out of Boston, which was something she hadn't experienced in years. As a C-suite officer at Sentinel, she had enjoyed not only a healthy salary but unlimited first class flights, including for personal use.

That was then—back when Shaw had a job, a brand-new BMW, and a bright career ahead of her.

So much for that.

Outside, Shaw tossed her bag into the back of a waiting taxi. An Uber would have been both cheaper and cleaner, but she was in a hurry. Her flight had already been delayed and she was forty minutes behind schedule. The man she flew in to meet would wait—he would wait all day if Shaw needed him to.

But Shaw didn't *want* him to wait. The moment she received his phone call, she was booking the first flight out of Boston. She used in-flight Wi-Fi to coordinate meeting plans and to exploit her professional network in search of any intel she could scrounge.

She cursed herself, too. Not because she was so quickly engulfed but because she couldn't do *more*. If this was a year ago, back when Laney Shaw was still director of operations for Sentinel, this problem would have already been solved. A team of the most elite operators on earth would parachute straight into a combat zone, if necessary. James Thatcher, Sentinel's owner, would have performed the mission pro bono, because he was a good man.

Too bad he was also a conniving psychopath.

"Twenty bucks to step on it," Shaw said.

The cab driver snorted, and Shaw upped the bet to fifty. He accelerated along snaking I-85 to the heart of town, dropping her at the corner of Edgewood Avenue and Hurt Plaza, where an office high-rise towered over Woodruff Park.

At "only" eighteen stories tall, the Hurt Building had long since been eclipsed by an ever-expanding Atlanta skyline. Nonetheless, there was something about the Beaux Arts design that spoke to Shaw. It was old-school Southern prestige, featuring ornate scrollwork and a wedge-shaped footprint that resembled the Flatiron in New York.

It was a slice of home. It was also one of the cheapest places in downtown Atlanta to rent office space, a refuge for cash-strapped organizations that dared to defy the work-from-home revolution. Shaw passed the driver a hundred-dollar bill and retrieved her bag. She tilted her head and stared up at the Hurt's majestic profile.

She thought of Africa. Of a lonely little complex standing on the edge of an abyss...ready to be swallowed.

Shaw went inside. The directory listed Resurrection Mercy Ministries on the fourteenth floor—really the thirteenth, but superstition had overcome the Hurt Building's designers. She took the elevator and hurried past rows of empty office suites.

Shaw found RMM's name printed on a misted glass door at the end of the hall. When she knocked, a portly woman with a crown of white hair scurried to answer. Shaw introduced herself.

Hope flooded the old lady's eyes.

"Right this way, dear. Mr. Carpenter is waiting for you."

7

The Bob Marshall Wilderness, Montana
20:06 Hours, Mountain Standard Time

Hale reached the spike camp eleven hours after watching the elk sprint into freedom.

The return hike had been easier than the trek out. Free of the painstaking necessity to track his prey, Hale struck out using the overland navigation skills he'd mastered during Delta Selection, choosing the most direct course back to camp.

He wasn't hunting any longer. He'd already accomplished what he came for, challenging his body and knocking the rust off his tracking skills. He'd set his standards, and he'd achieved them.

He could rest assured, at least for a while, that he was still a warrior. For whatever that meant.

Half a mile from the spike camp Hale could already smell the fire—hear the laughter. His stomach growled as the scent of fresh meat blended with that of the smoke, the promise of his first truly hot meal in days.

Slipping out of the trees, Hale found exactly the scene he expected. Three urban sportsmen sawing into elk steaks while one of the guides tended a suspended grill rack. Despite the supposedly strict *no alcohol* policy, two of the guys were clearly inebriated, sharing an unmarked canteen.

Hale caught the eye of the introverted guide with the shrapnel scars, and the man simply shook his head.

"Hey, Lone Ranger. You made it back!"

It was the New Yorker who shouted, kicked back with elk grease on his lips and still wearing that stupid puffy jacket.

"You see anything?" one of the others asked.

Hale paused, his rifle held in low ready.

"Well?" the hunter prompted.

"Nothing to shoot," Hale said.

"Too bad, man. Benny shot a big'un. Nearly eight hundred pounds!"

"Nice," Hale said. He looked left and caught the guy with the shrapnel scars watching him. The man raised both eyebrows—Hale simply shrugged and pulled up a camp chair.

The second guide served him a steak—no sides, no sauces, no seasonings. None needed. The meat was cooked to perfection. Hale flicked open his Benchmade Adamas and used it as both carving knife and fork.

The steak was incredible.

"Hey, man, you got a call." It was the second guide.

Hale looked up. "What?"

"On the camp phone. Came in this morning."

"Who?"

"I forget her name. Some saucy chick—sounded like a country singer."

"Wait, what?" New Yorker broke in. "You sure she wasn't calling for me, bro?"

"Pretty sure," the guide spoke through his teeth. Hale wiped his mouth.

He knew who had called. A moment's consideration, and he also knew how she had found him. Before leaving his family farm back in New Hampshire, Hale had left his widowed grandfather with the name of the hunting company and a number to reach him at. Anyone who wanted to find Hale would call Pat. If Pat liked them, he might share the number.

That still didn't say *why* this woman had called.

"You want the phone?" the guide asked.

"Got one," Hale said.

"You want the number?"

"I know it."

"Aw yeah you do, you *dog*." The New Yorker again. Hale found himself stuffing the meat between his teeth a little faster. He cleaned his plate and drained a bottle of water before stepping fifty yards into the trees.

He dialed from memory...because he'd dialed that number maybe two hundred times over the past several years, and not at all for the reasons the New Yorker assumed.

Laney Shaw picked right up.

"Ian?"

Hale hadn't heard the voice in months. Not since the demise of Sentinel, where he and Shaw had both worked. Not since Maine, since a kidnapped congressman with a bag full of criminal evidence stapled to his chest.

Not since a lot of things.

"Yep," Hale said simply.

"Thanks for calling. Sorry to interrupt your trip."

"You called Pat?" Hale said.

"Yeah."

"So this is important."

Long pause. Shaw was laboring over something. Hale waited.

"I need a big favor," she said. "I wouldn't call if I could call anyone else."

That last line stung a little. Hale owed Shaw a favor or two himself. Big ones included. Maybe she was just being polite.

"When and where?" Hale said.

It was a blank check—because Laney Shaw was a fellow warrior, and Hale didn't believe in shortchanging brotherhood.

"Atlanta," Shaw said. "As soon as possible."

8

Juba, South Sudan
21:12 Hours, East Africa Time

The negotiations with Minister Abiem had not gone well.

Jaxon couldn't put his finger on the problem. He had probed Abiem, building rapport while also building a case for why the United States should be granted an exclusive contract to partner with South Sudan on a *massive* exploitation deal. The kind of deal which could lift the fledgling country out of obscurity, maybe even breaking its poverty cycle.

That was a clear win, right? Who better for Abiem to partner with than the world's greatest superpower?

But Abiem wouldn't commit, and wouldn't say why. He was ducking and weaving, making awkward jokes between irrelevant anecdotes. It was as though Abiem wanted Jaxon to woo him into a deal, maybe padding his personal pockets along the way.

That...or perhaps there was another deal with another interested party on the table.

Jaxon returned to the US embassy alongside a disgruntled Ambassador Russell, and neither of them spoke. On three occasions the ambassador had attempted to force his way into negotiations, nearly torpedoing the conversation every time.

No wonder he'd screwed up Italy—the guy was a brick.

Inside the embassy, a Marine guard led Jaxon to his private quarters, which featured a kitchenette and a bulletproof window overlooking the embassy courtyard/parking lot. Jaxon tugged his tie loose and drank bottled water from the TV stand. His laptop connected to embassy internet and Jaxon settled into a desk chair.

There was a phone next to the bed, but even within the security of a US embassy, Jaxon couldn't be sure who might be listening. He preferred encrypted communication via an internet call...not that he was looking forward to this conversation.

Jaxon ran his fingers through his hair before the video feed connected. The face on the other end was twenty-five years older than Jaxon's, wrinkled under a crown of gray hair. Assistant Secretary of State Paul Morris didn't look happy—Jaxon's boss never looked happy.

He looked like a guy who had given his life to diplomatic service and never landed a job title that didn't include the word *assistant* or *deputy*.

That won't be me, Jaxon thought.

"Well?" Morris barked.

"The meeting ran long, sir. We met with Minister Abiem—"

"We?"

"Ambassador Russell and I."

"I thought I told you to sideline that dingus."

"You did, sir. I informed the ambassador of his role, but I thought it best to include him in the initial discussion. I thought it could build trust with Abiem."

"Did it?"

It hadn't, not even a little. But Jaxon wouldn't admit to his own mistake.

"It was a difficult conversation. Abiem refused to get specific about a deal or even make an ask. I mentioned infrastructure support, medical aid, even energy technology. The only thing that seemed to hold his attention was defense."

"Weapons sales?"

"Maybe. He alluded to security concerns. The situation in Western Equatoria seems pretty bad. That could be holding him up, but..."

Jaxon hesitated. He knew what he wanted to say but he wanted Morris to ask—that would minimize the impact.

"Spit it out, Jaxon."

"I think we may have a competitor—somebody who hasn't yet clarified their offer. Abiem doesn't want to admit to their existence, so he's stalling. Keeping us on the hook while buying time."

"And you know this how?"

"I don't, sir. It's just an instinct. I felt like I was being strung along."

Morris considered that. He popped sunflower seeds into his mouth and chewed, sucked. Then lifted a paper cup and spat slimy hulls.

"Any idea who?" he asked.

"None, sir. Somebody big enough to offer legitimate competition, I would guess."

"Don't guess, boy. This is geopolitics—guessing isn't in our playbook."

It's the only thing in our playbook.

Jaxon kept the thought to himself. Morris spat more hulls.

"When do you go back?" he said.

"Tomorrow afternoon. The president will be joining us."

"Good. Leave that fool Russell in his office. Push until you uncover exactly what they want."

"That may be difficult, sir. He—"

"You heard me. Now get it done."

Morris hung up, and Jaxon simply cursed.

Halfway around the planet, Assistant Secretary of State for African Affairs Paul Morris stared at his computer and sucked sunflower seed dust from his teeth.

Thinking, and wondering who it was...but already having a pretty good idea. Because if Morris had learned anything during a thirty-two-year career in diplomatic service, he had learned who the major players were.

Who could be useful, who should be watched, and who could never be trusted.

In this situation? Morris's gut said China, not only because China had such a vested interest in Africa but because opaque negotiations were their trademark.

Glancing once to ensure that his office door was closed, Morris mashed a button on his phone for an encrypted line—the kind used for discussing classified matters with other diplomatic officials, but not this time.

This time Morris was calling outside the State Department. A rumbling voice answered.

"Go ahead."

"We have competition," Morris said.

Pause. "Details?"

"None. It's all hush-hush."

"China?"

"Seems like a fit."

Another pause, longer this time. Then: "What do you want to do?"

"I want to escalate," Morris said. "Get that ape on the phone. Tell him we need more action."

"That's..." Hesitation. "That's risky. This close to a deal, we need distance."

"But we aren't this close to a deal, are we? Abiem needs another push."

No answer. Morris gritted his teeth.

"Look, you coward. We're this close, okay? *This close.* I'm finished working the Africa beat. I've got my eye on the big job, and you're coming with me. Right?"

Silence. Then, at last, a grunt.

"I'll call."

The phone line disconnected.

9

Atlanta, Georgia
16:42 Hours, Eastern Standard Time

"As soon as possible."

Shaw had never before used those words with Hale, not even during their lengthy working relationship at Sentinel. He took them as literal. As soon as he terminated the call, he was checking out with the guides and solo hiking back to the base camp.

Ten miles. Straight through the night, guided by a headlamp and raw memory of the trail. It was a risky, maybe even stupid stunt. With steep slopes on either side, aggressive animals on the prowl, and the temperature dropping, a hike like this could easily leave even the most tenured outdoorsman frozen in a snowbank, not to be found until next summer.

But Hale went, because Shaw had called.

Sunrise crested the mountains just as Hale reached base. One of the guides was waiting in a truck to take him ninety-six miles southeast to Great Falls, a bustling metropolis of sixty thousand people.

Hale had the guide drop him at a UPS store, where he carried both the Ruger Redhawk and the .300 Win Mag inside. It would be too much trouble to fly with them, and neither weapon was particularly suited to a big city, anyway. He would ship both the firearms and his knives to an FFL dealer in New Hampshire and collect them whenever he could make time.

With his gear secured, Hale was back on the street. He consumed a diner burger in four minutes flat and took a bottle of water for the road. An Uber transferred him to Great Falls International Airport, where Hale bought a ticket for the next flight to Denver, his first stop on the route to Atlanta.

He slept the best he could in a compact economy seat with a twitchy hippy to his left and a babbling toddler three rows back. The plane touched down in Colorado around midafternoon and Hale ate again, killing a two-hour layover.

And thinking about Shaw. Thinking about the last time they interacted —an uncomfortable conversation outside a diner in Massachusetts. Hale had left on good terms with his old boss...at least, the best terms he could manage after destroying her career. Shaw seemed okay. Hale hadn't expected to see her again.

Why had she called?

Shaw hadn't said. Hale accepted that. He could wait another three hours, sleeping a little better on a quieter evening plane before the 737 began its final descent into Georgia's capital.

Hale had been there before, a few times. He knew Shaw loved it—he wasn't sure why. Dirty by appearance, congested to a degree even Boston couldn't rival, and boasting crime statistics that made Hale miss the comfort of the Ruger on his hip, Atlanta had always been a city that left him on guard.

Then again, Hale couldn't think of a city that *didn't* leave him on guard. Or a town. Or even a rural county. The Unit had done that to him. He wasn't convinced it was a bad thing.

At arrivals, Hale slid into another Uber—a Hyundai SUV with limited legroom. The driver played the blues and thumped the steering wheel as they crawled along I-85, consuming the better part of an hour to pass nine miles.

Their destination reminded Hale of the Flatiron in New York. Tall, stone, old. He stood a moment on the sidewalk, sweeping his surroundings. Noting the homeless guy on the corner whose shoes looked a little too clean. The cop parked illegally, apparently napping. The cab that circled the block twice with an empty back seat.

All items out of place, however insignificantly. All potential threats. Hale kicked himself for not dragging the Ruger through the hassle of air travel. It would be difficult to conceal, but at least he wouldn't be naked—

"Ian?"

Hale's gaze snapped left. Shaw stood at the tower's front entrance, dressed in blue jeans and a Georgia Bulldogs hoodie. Her hair was pulled back in loose pigtails. Her posture was almost as alert as Hale's.

And there was something else, also. Shaw seemed strained.

"Hey." Hale extended a hand, but Shaw bypassed it. She pulled him into a hug instead, quick and bro-like.

"Thanks for coming."

Hale grunted awkwardly. Shaw led him up the steps.

"You like Chick-fil-A? Of course you do, everybody likes Chick-fil-A. You know, it was founded here. In a mall, I think. They say they invented the chicken sandwich—talk about striking gold. They must have sold a billion of them."

Shaw was babbling, and that wasn't like her. She led Hale across a lobby and up an elevator. She shifted on her feet and popped gum. She checked her watch.

She still hadn't explained where they were going. Hale didn't ask questions as he followed her through a misted glass door that read Resurrection Mercy Ministries. Inside a small conference room, the furniture was old, the carpet worn. Narrow windows overlooked endless dirty towers, glowing in the late-fall darkness.

And yes, there was Chick-fil-A on the table. A pile of it in paper bags with bright red logos. Hale glanced around but saw nobody else. Shaw gestured for him to sit, and he took a chair with his back to the wall.

"Food?"

"Not yet," Hale said. He waited.

Shaw checked her watch again. "He'll be here shortly."

She hadn't explained who *he* was. Hale relaxed while Shaw dumped Chick-fil-A sauce over a boxed salad. She stirred with a fork. She slurped Diet Coke. She stirred some more.

She was coming out of her skin. Hale had never seen her this way—not once during their entire working relationship. Granted, most of their interactions back at Sentinel consisted of phone calls. He couldn't actually *see* her.

But Shaw had a reputation for a cool head. What had rattled her now?

The door opened, and a man entered. Late sixties, Hale judged. Salt-and-pepper hair and a suit that hadn't been in vogue since the mid-eighties. He glanced from Shaw to Hale, seeming confused.

Shaw dropped her fork. "Mr. Carpenter, this is Ian Hale. He's the one I told you about."

Hale stood and extended a hand. Carpenter accepted it, and Hale liked the shake. It was confident, but the guy still looked confused.

"You're...a soldier?"

Finally, Hale understood. He thought of his disheveled appearance. His uncut hair and beard. His *smell*, very likely. He looked more homeless than a warrior.

Wasn't that closer to the truth, anyway?

"No, sir," Hale said.

Carpenter frowned, but Shaw was already pushing the door shut. They all took their seats, Carpenter shooting Shaw a sideways look. Hale thought he might just as easily have said: *Seriously?*

Shaw simply nodded. Carpenter looked back to Hale.

"Ms. Shaw tells me you have a background in Special Operations."

Hale said nothing.

"She says you were the best private security operator she ever hired."

Again, Hale said nothing.

"I've known Ms. Shaw a long time, Mr. Hale. Since she was a child. She's not one to exaggerate. Is she exaggerating now?"

Hale cleared his throat. "I wouldn't know about being the best."

Carpenter smiled—just a little. "Spoken like the best."

Another long silence. Hale's protracted patience finally expired.

"Mr. Carpenter, I flew five miserable hours to get here. They have Chick-fil-A in New England."

He didn't have to say any more. Carpenter sat forward, interlacing worn fingers. Then he cut straight to the chase.

"Ms. Shaw tells me you're a traveling man. What do you know about South Sudan?"

10

The name rang like a gunshot through Hale's mind. His gaze snapped toward Shaw.

What did you tell him?

Hale didn't have to say it. Shaw knew what he was thinking. She shook her head, and Hale looked back to Carpenter, measuring the openness in his face. Searching for indicators of trickery. Wondering what this was *really* about.

Before Hale could decide, Carpenter sighed.

"Maybe I should start from the beginning. My name is Bill Carpenter, and I'm founder and president of Resurrection Mercy Ministries. Shaw tells me that you're a believer?"

"I am."

"Praise the Lord. I myself found Christ straight out of college. My girlfriend cheated on me—I freaked out and assaulted the guy. Spent a week in jail and lost my job. *Rock bottom*."

A short laugh—the kind that said Carpenter had gained some perspective and knew just how seldom *rock bottom* is really the bottom.

Hale didn't comment. Carpenter cleared his throat.

"Would you please eat, Mr. Hale? It's bad manners in the South to not feed a guest. Bad manners to refuse a meal, too."

A small smile curled Carpenter's lips. Hale gazed a moment longer and decided that he liked the smile. It reminded him a bit of Pat when Pat was feeling awkward...which was almost never. Regardless, Hale was hungry.

"Any spicy sandwiches?" he asked.

Shaw passed him a sack, and Hale dug in. Two sandwiches fully disassembled. Ranch spread on a bun. Two fillets packed inside with all the pickles.

More protein, less carbs. Hale took a big bite and couldn't resist a satisfied grunt. Carpenter resumed his explanation.

"After I met Jesus, I felt a call to enter ministry. That's when I founded RMM. We're an international nonprofit headquartered here in Atlanta. Most of our work focuses on serving impoverished youth across the developing world. Education, medical care—Gospel work, whatever it demands. Our proudest accomplishment is our orphanages—two in Southeast Asia, three in Africa. One of those African orphanages is in a place called Tambura. It's a small town in the Western Equatoria state of South Sudan."

Hale stopped chewing. He made eye contact with Shaw again—this time not because of the words *South Sudan* but because of *Western Equatoria*. It wasn't a place Hale had ever been, but he knew the name.

How could he forget it? What happened in Western Equatoria had nearly destroyed Hale's life.

"So you know it," Carpenter said.

Hale wiped his mouth. He didn't speak.

Carpenter sighed again. "Okay, so I'll do the talking. As you may or may not know, Western Equatoria is becoming an extremely dangerous place. Significant instability, horrific ethnic conflict. We founded the orphanage in Tambura specifically because of the instability. We first opened the doors two years ago, and it's quickly become our largest such facility. Seventy-seven children, by last count. Most orphans by death, some orphans by abandonment. It's a hard, ugly country, Mr. Hale."

Hale didn't need to be told. He'd been to South Sudan only once, and then for a short period. The mission placed him outside of Juba. The job was simple—hostage rescue.

Then the job went sideways. Local militia, hired by international puppet masters, ambushed Hale's team. He was the only survivor. He'd gone to war with those puppet masters, and he'd won.

But what motivated international interest in Western Equatoria in the first place still remained—an untapped wealth of recently discovered natural resources.

Could that have anything to do with present instability?

"Why am I here, Mr. Carpenter?" Hale didn't intend to be rude, he simply wanted to land the plane. He was exhausted, sore, and jet-lagged. He'd like to be home.

What was the punchline?

Carpenter opened his mouth, but it was Shaw who spoke next.

"I've called Bill *Uncle Bill* for most of my life. His niece, Mary Grace Dalton, was my best friend in high school. We were sorority sisters in college. Absolutely inseparable. After graduation, I joined the Army. Mary Grace joined RMM. She signed on for their international ministry program. It was supposed to be a gap year thing, but..."

"Mary Grace fell in love," Carpenter finished. "In love with the work, in love with the kids. She has such a big heart, and such a gift for working with children."

Carpenter stopped, but Hale could easily see where this story was headed—see why a man like him had been called.

"Mary Grace runs your orphanage in Western Equatoria," he said.

Carpenter nodded. "That's right."

"And there's been a problem?"

Shaw took that one. "The violence in Western Equatoria is spilling out of control. The government is losing ground to a warlord name James Wani —he's the leader of the White Nile Liberation Army, a splinter of a splinter that has somehow found footing. They've become a real threat."

"James?" Hale said, raising both eyebrows.

Carpenter waved a hand. "Christianized names are common in South Sudan. True Christian faith is...less common."

Hale nodded. Considered. Then repeated his question.

"So why am I here?"

"Ten days ago we deployed a resupply caravan to the Tambura orphanage," Carpenter said. "Three trucks, six personnel. It's a six-hundred-kilometer journey from Juba, and very difficult this time of year. We're still combating the rainy season—the roads are bad, but the orphanage's situation is serious. Too many mouths, not enough food."

"The caravan never made it," Hale guessed.

"No, they didn't. We lost contact about halfway, and South Sudanese military patrols located the scene two days later. It was a gun battle—all the supplies and vehicles were captured. The personnel were..."

Silence. Carpenter swallowed, his eyes watering. Hale got the message.

"The government in Juba is unable to secure Tambura. James Wani and his brutalist WNLA haven't obtained full control of Western Equatoria yet, but they've made resupply to our orphanage all but impossible. Mary Grace is running on borrowed time. We're working with some larger NGOs to airlift food directly into town, but that may be a temporary solution. There are concerns of Wani's troops firing on aircraft. We may not be able to resupply again, and in the meantime..."

"You need security," Hale said. "Boots on the ground who can advise you on exactly how bad the situation is."

"We do. And if the worst should be the case, I need somebody who can get my niece, and those children, *out* of South Sudan."

11

Western Equatoria, South Sudan
00:04 Hours, East Africa Time

Lado Bakumba escaped the village raid only to fall from the frying pan and into the fire.

Nearly two days had passed since the midnight attack that left adults rotting in the mud and children swept away in pickup trucks. Bakumba spent most of that time hiding in the brush looking out for African buffalo —arguably South Sudan's most dangerous wildlife. He had a little water in his pack and budgeted it the best he could. He had no food, and now his stomach was eating itself.

But worst of all was the pain in his arm. It throbbed, pulsing through his shoulder and into his skull. If he touched the wound, he could still feel the bullet lodged in the muscle, its conical shape deformed by previous contact with some hard surface.

Had he caught a ricochet? He might feel lucky for that—a direct hit from an AK-47 would have obliterated his humerus. But Bakumba didn't feel lucky, he felt *shot*. Alone in the middle of nowhere, seeing the burning huts and slaughtered villagers every time he closed his eyes. It was misery that wouldn't die as the sun disappeared, leaving him shivering in the sudden cold.

Ten thousand dollars.

It was the motivation that drove Bakumba into this nightmare. *Identify certain events, film them, and return to the masked man.* That was the mission. Bakumba had no idea what the masked man wanted with such videos...but what did it matter? He had money, and Bakumba dreamed of money. He dreamed of clean clothes and rich meals and a big bed on the top floor of the Radisson hotel in Juba—the pinnacle of luxury in his mind.

But what did such things matter if Bakumba died of infection or dehydration or the venom of a black mamba?

Black snake. He saw the white man again, and Bakumba's mind temporarily fixated on the spectacle. The bizarre appearance of a Westerner—an American, he thought—in the middle of an African civil war. Bakumba was plenty familiar with the scourge of James Wani and his White Nile Liberation Army. Mostly, the WNLB operated farther to the northwest, and Bakumba didn't know of any white man leading raiding parties. He hadn't heard of any...

Except from the masked man.

Juba. Get back to Juba.

It was Bakumba's only hope of survival. Nobody was coming to save him, and anyone who found him was just as likely to shoot him in the face as render assistance. He *had* to move, pain or no pain. He had to fight, or else give up and die.

Bakumba wasn't ready to die.

Back on his feet, Bakumba looked into a midnight sky plastered with brilliant stars. With ease he picked out the North Star, a skill his uncle had taught him as a small child. That reference point clarified the direction Bakumba would need to travel. Southeast, generally, until he hit a road or some landmark.

It was maybe three hundred kilometers to Juba, but that wasn't so bad, was it? Bakumba could walk. He was a Dinka, and the Dinka were seminomadic cattle herders who were used to walking long distances on foot. The pain was bad, but if Bakumba just pictured that giant hotel bed spread thick with ten *thousand* US dollars...

Bakumba fought his backpack open with one hand. He fished out a spare pair of pants and with effort managed to tie the ends of the legs together and loop them over his neck. It wasn't a perfect sling, but his arm felt better with the support. A little of his precious remaining water supply felt good on his throat.

Yes. He was ready. He was strong.

He could make it to Juba and the masked man.

12

Atlanta, Georgia
22:19 Hours, Eastern Standard Time

After mashing the elevator call button, Hale's thumbs jabbed across his phone screen while he waited for the car. A five-second Google search produced a litany of hotel options, all within easy walking distance. Hale wanted a shower before he slept. Eight, maybe nine hours, and he would be refreshed enough to brave the Atlanta airport a second time.

Back to Boston. Refit at Haleburg, the family farm. Then...

"Ian!"

Hale looked back just as the elevator dinged. Laney Shaw appeared, lifting a hand for him to wait. Her Bulldogs hoodie swished, pigtails bouncing. In another world, she might have looked like a late-in-life college senior. Maybe a research student pursuing a doctorate.

But nothing about the worry in Shaw's eyes spoke to the innocence of a college kid.

"Look," Shaw said, reaching the elevator. "I know it's last minute and really dangerous, but—"

"Shaw," Hale said.

She stopped, mouth open. The elevator timed out, rolled closed.

"I'll go," Hale said simply.

Shaw stood motionless a long beat, just staring. Then she threw both arms around his neck and pulled him into his second hug of the night. She squeezed this time instead of slapping like a bro. She held tighter, too.

"Thank you. Thank you so much."

Hale grunted, awkward again. Shaw withdrew and he adjusted his backpack. "Give me eight hours of shut-eye and ninety minutes to sketch an incursion plan. Do you still have contacts with charter flight companies?"

Shaw hesitated. "They all worked with Sentinel…"

"But they don't know we burned Sentinel down, so they shouldn't care."

Shaw tilted her head in a *fair enough* gesture. "I'll see what I can do. We fly out of Boston?"

"I do," Hale said. "You'll be staying stateside."

"What?" Shaw's voice was edged with indignation—maybe something closer to outrage. Before she could continue, Hale lifted a hand.

"It's a pit, Shaw. I've been to a lot of nasty places in my career, and South Sudan was one of the worst."

"You think I can't handle that?"

"I know you can," Hale said. "But you of all people should know how suicidal it is to go downrange without any support system. If you're in Africa, you can't be here in a big city to coordinate a Plan B in case things go sideways. That's a backstop I've depended on for years. You've never let me down."

It wasn't flattery. Everything Hale said was true. Shaw was a master at managing missions from afar, networking with obscure contacts and pulling rabbits out of hats to keep her people alive and on target. It was what made her such an exceptional operations director at Sentinel.

If Hale was going back to arguably the world's most dangerous country, he wanted somebody he could trust to know where he was. To monitor his situation and send help if necessary. Without Sentinel, Shaw lacked resources and heavy firepower, but she still had her contacts list and a near magical ability to make a lot out of a little.

Hale might need both.

"She's my best friend," Shaw said softly.

Hale nodded. He'd never really had a best friend in the traditional sense, but he'd had family. He'd lost most of them.

He knew what desperation felt like.

"I'll take care of her," he said. "Charter a plane and arrange a discreet flight crew. I'll be going in heavy."

"Local authorities?" Shaw questioned.

"I'll grease them when I arrive. A little cash works magic in a place like Juba."

Shaw said nothing. Hale could tell she was still hung up on the part where she remained behind, but his mind was already tumbling toward a question that had bothered him since his meeting with Bill Carpenter.

Hale lowered his voice. "Do you think..."

He trailed off, but one glance into Shaw's eyes, and he knew she was thinking the same thing—thinking about Hale's last mission to South Sudan. About what had been discovered beneath Western Equatoria clay.

A wealth beyond reason. A resource men might kill for.

And now? Men were dying.

"It's a heck of a coincidence," Shaw said.

"I don't believe in coincidences."

"Me neither."

Hale considered a moment longer and then shelved the thoughts—because they didn't matter.

Secure the orphanage. That's the mission.

"Book the plane," Hale said, mashing the call button again. The doors rolled open almost immediately. "I can fly out of Boston tomorrow afternoon. We'll talk before then—you'll know the plan."

"Ian." Shaw caught the elevator door just as it was rolling shut behind him. He turned back.

"This, uh, this ministry," Shaw began. "It's not a very large nonprofit. They pour most of their resources overseas. And you know, since Sentinel went under, I've been..."

She trailed off.

Hale squinted. "Are you talking about money?"

"Yeah..."

"You need money for the plane?"

"No, Carpenter can cover that. Just...your salary..."

Salary.

Just the thought of it was enough to bring a smirk to Hale's face. He shook his head. "Four years of six-figure earnings and all I bought was ribeyes and a motorcycle. Let's just say I need the exercise."

It was a poor joke. Shaw smiled anyway.

"Thanks, Ian."

Hale smacked the ground-floor button. "Boston. Tomorrow. Call me when you have the plane."

13

Juba, South Sudan
04:15 Hours, East Africa Time

He always rose early.

Since he was a child, since those brutal days at the orphanage in Hong Kong when he would slip out of bed before the sun crested the Pacific and wait by the kitchen door, hoping to be first in line for breakfast. It wasn't a natural habit, but a matter of personal survival. He ate while many of the other children went hungry precisely *because* he got up early. Because he traded sleep for opportunity.

He couldn't know it then, but the lessons learned in the brutality of that overcrowded children's home would stick with Wing-Kei Chan for the rest of his life...and serve him well.

Up early, every day. Before the sun reached the horizon, before the wolves reached the gates. It was a defense mechanism that became a weapon. It powered Wing-Kei through childhood years fraught with want into teenage years inflamed by an insatiable desire to conquer. He fought the other orphans—he rarely lost. Days before his sixteenth birthday, he was ejected from the orphanage altogether, thrown out to sink or swim.

Wing-Kei swam. Lost in Hong Kong he begged, scrabbled, stole, and *survived* until he was old enough to join the People's Army—free food, clothes, and lodging so long as he could rise to the challenge of life as a soldier.

But the military was no challenge for Wing-Kei. It was more opportunity. He rose early and worked hard every day for twenty-five years. He became talented in unique and useful ways. Offers of advancement presented themselves.

Wing-Kei walked through every door. No questions, no hesitations. He made friends in high places and executed on their specialized requests. They compensated him generously, but the money alone was little motivation for Wing-Kei. He already maintained a full belly and no longer had holes in his shoes.

What mattered most was the edge—the certain knowledge that he would never again depend on outside charity to thrive. He was in command now. That command began every day before dawn.

This particular day it began in Juba, South Sudan.

The hotel was a Radisson—one of the few name-brand properties in the city, but not the least bit fancy. Its primary perks included walls without bullet holes and a razor-wire enclosure that secured the property—both a significant plus.

As one of the planet's most violent countries, South Sudan was the furthest thing from a tourist destination. Bereft of the Western amenities that Wing-Kei had come to enjoy during his extensive travels, South Sudan looked nothing like Hong Kong, and yet it reminded Wing-Kei of his early childhood.

It was the scent of desperation in the air, of hunger and instability and primitive savagery just waiting to erupt. As a self-admitted racist, Wing-Kei blamed many of South Sudan's problems on her people. Ignorant, barbaric, and incapable of elevating themselves from this squalid pit, he saw them as little better than animals. Wing-Kei wasn't the type to empathize with animals—he was only interested in analyzing them.

In asking himself how he could exploit them.

Standing shirtless in front of filthy hotel windows, Wing-Kei stretched and touched the ceiling. He bent and touched his toes. He twisted until his spine popped.

Then he reached into a suitcase and produced a burner phone. Purchased locally with a local number and kept fully charged at all times, the device maintained impressive signal in the heart of town.

But it wasn't the heart of town that Wing-Kei was most concerned about. The text messages or phone calls he awaited would come from deep inside the African bush, far from the city. Even when his hired underlings —mud-brained locals easily bought with a flash of American dollars— wanted to call, they might have to journey for hours or even days to regain signal. Updates could be delayed.

Such was the case today. No calls or texts. Wing-Kei was disappointed but not surprised. He replaced the phone in his suitcase and withdrew another, this one paired to an Ethiopian phone number. Unlike with the first, a text message awaited him on this device. Printed in English, Wing-Kei nevertheless found it easy to read. He was fluent in five languages.

Two, 11/17. Net 31.

Wing-Kei scratched one cheek, decoding the message with ease and assessing its value. The second number was a date, written in American format—November seventeenth, which was the day prior. The *two* part would mean two targets.

And the thirty-one? A very nice haul.

Wing-Kei texted back. *Total?*

Pause. Wing-Kei waited patiently. Then a reply popped through.

116.

Phenomenal, Wing-Kei thought. There were almost that many in the dormitory he slept in as a child. Momentum, it seemed, was on his side. He could be patient with lack of updates on the first phone for a while longer.

He could keep this moving.

Proceed, he texted back.

Then Wing-Kei shut off the phone. He stretched again, arms lifted until his fingertips almost touched the ceiling.

Then he descended onto his hands and toes across the dingy carpet. Hands apart at shoulder level, his back arrow straight. Breathing deep, he dropped until his sternum almost brushed the floor, then powered up again until his elbows locked.

One.

Only 249 to go…all before sunrise.

14

Auburn, New Hampshire
08:12 Hours, Eastern Daylight Time

Hale tried to sleep. He booked a cheap room and showered before stretching out with the AC pumping. He closed his eyes. He breathed deep.

But sleep wouldn't come. The best Hale managed was a shallow dream state that felt like a loose hallucination, complete with visions of the past blended with those of the present and glimpses of what might have been the future. Hale saw a cabin in the woods surrounded by gunmen. A burning BMW and zipping bullets. A bloody knife and a face-off near a front porch.

Two snatching hands, two cracking shots.

But only one body dropped.

Hale buried his head beneath the pillows and fought for complete blackness. Not because of the nightmares—they weren't nightmares, really. Just vivid memories. Mostly Hale wanted to sleep because he wanted to *stop* thinking. To stop remembering, reviewing.

And wondering. Searching for the point.

At four a.m., Hale surrendered. He showered again and took a cab to the airport. This time the flight was direct. Hale folded himself into another economy seat and watched the sun rise over the 737's wingtips, a brilliant ball of blistering fire unblemished by haze or clouds.

Emerging out of Africa...and what hell it left behind it.

Touch down in Boston. Hale found his storm-green Ducati Streetfighter waiting in long-term parking, his helmet held in a nearby locker. He ignited the beast with a howl and gave it a moment to warm.

Then he was ripping up I-93. Crossing into New Hampshire and breaking toward Auburn. The gravel entrance of the family farm lay rutted by the heavy tires of Pat Hale's antique Ford Bronco. Hale was accustomed to wrestling the bike through those ruts, and broke out of the trees to the rich odor of sizzling eggs and bacon.

The family patriarch—and the only other surviving resident of this twenty-acre slice of heritage—was awake and working his best magic. Hale's stomach growled as he killed the engine and was immediately greeted by Trigger, Pat's blue-eyed border collie. All smiles and licks and muddy paws on Hale's already dirty hiking pants.

By the time Hale made it inside, Pat was already laying out another plate and dropping additional bacon onto the griddle. He didn't speak a word to his grandson—he simply wrapped Hale in a bear hug, then passed him a cup of black coffee.

Everything Hale needed.

They sat together at the worn kitchen table and packed down double portions of fried eggs with thick-sliced bacon and biscuits with apple butter. Trigger mopped up any scraps that fell. Neither of them spoke much, save for brief questions from Pat about Hale's hunt.

Hale knew why his grandfather was quiet. Pat had spoken to Shaw at least once, when she called to locate Hale, and whatever Pat didn't know he was smart enough to guess about.

"South Sudan," Hale said at last.

Pat grunted in way of response. Hale wiped bacon grease from his mouth and looked over a backyard of dormant grass primed for the first snowfall of the year. It would come at any time. At least a couple of inches. The yard would be stunning—fresh, cool.

So much unlike South Sudan.

"It's an orphanage," Hale said. "An Atlanta charity. They need security... maybe an extraction."

Hale shook his head, still fixating on the yard. He drew a fresh toothpick from a tray and slid it between his teeth. He thought he saw a chipmunk some sixty yards away, bouncing between uncut brush.

"You got something you need to say, son?"

Pat was as blunt as ever. Hale glanced sideways, suddenly on edge. The toothpick stuck in his mouth. His free hand flexed over the table.

But he didn't speak, because he didn't know what to say. He'd been fighting the same vague feelings ever since learning of Resurrection Mercy Ministry's problems.

Not doubt, and not fear...but anticipation. Almost excitement, and maybe that was what bothered him. Was he unsettled by how much he missed being downrange?

Or maybe it wasn't the action he craved. Maybe it was something deeper.

Pat slurped coffee and sighed. His cup landed on the table with a gentle thump. "Just keep it righteous, boy. The Father handles the rest."

Spoken like a man who knows.

Hale nodded. He withdrew the toothpick and sucked his teeth.

"Give me a ride to the airport?" he said.

15

35,000 Feet over the Atlantic Ocean
16:08 Hours Azores Standard Time

The Gulfstream G-IV collected Hale at eleven a.m. sharp.

A mid-eighties jet with plenty of miles beneath the wings, the aircraft was worn but in good repair. The pilots were middle-aged and friendly but didn't ask a lot of questions—certainly not about Hale's oversized and nondescript luggage.

With a one-armed hug for Pat and a scratch behind the ear for Trigger, who had accompanied them to the airport, Hale was off. The Gulfstream turned hard east, breaking straight across the Atlantic.

It was a *long* way to South Sudan. With a flight range of just under four thousand miles, the Gulfstream's first fuel stop would be in the Portuguese Azores, after which the pilot announced they would be stopping again in Ghana for a top off before the final sprint to Juba.

That was smart. Africa in general, but South Sudan in particular, was not the kind of place you wanted to get stuck looking for gas.

From New England to the Azores, Hale catnapped the best he could—he still struggled to fall fully asleep. After taking off again, he gave up the attempt and ate a cold lunch from an ice chest.

Then, at last, he turned to the iPad. Once issued by Sentinel, Hale had kept the device after the corporation went belly-up. It featured a waterproof, shockproof case equipped with a backup battery and the ability to be linked to an Iridium satellite phone for extremely limited internet use in extremely rural places—text messaging, basically.

It wasn't perfect. The backup battery was only large enough to recharge the tablet twice, and Hale knew from firsthand experience that a 9mm slug would shatter the case and decimate its contents.

Then again, the teammate who'd stood behind that iPad had walked away...so maybe the setup deserved a little more credit.

Hale fit noise-canceling headphones into his ears and cranked up a hard rock playlist fit to crack concrete. Classics, mostly. Led Zeppelin, AC/DC, Mötley Crüe, and a little Creed for a nineties flair. Then he accessed the files Shaw had emailed him.

Sentinel's shield-and-eagle logo was nowhere to be found on the PDF, but in every other way the mission brief was exactly like those Hale had reviewed as a private security contractor. A heading box listed all the summary information in a neat chart—destination, key personnel, mission objective, and mission parameters.

Much of that was blank. The only objective was to secure Mary Grace Dalton and her orphanage. Under *Parameters*, Shaw had written "use best judgment, communicate regularly," which was code for "just don't start a war."

Next came a rough map of South Sudan. The capital city of Juba, his first stop, sat in the south-central region of the country—Central Equatoria State, to be precise.

Tambura, where Mary Grace and her orphanage resided, lay some six hundred kilometers west of Juba, only a stone's throw from the border of the Central African Republic. Rural to a point of being absolutely desolate, it didn't take a regional expert to know that Tambura lay on the backside of nowhere. Juba, in fact, was the nearest major city, and the only South Sudanese city where any charter service would land.

That left Hale with the unfortunate task of reaching Tambura by road, and details of the route were almost nonexistent. Shaw, in fact, didn't know. When Resurrection Mercy Ministries had deployed staff to open the orphanage, they had hired a local guide to show them the way, but that was before the rise of James Wani and his White Nile Liberation Army. Finding a guide now might be a little more tricky.

Hale would confront that challenge if and when it arose. For the moment, he was more concerned about his primary—Mary Grace Dalton. Hale wanted to know as much about her situation and personality as possible, because if the situation turned ugly, he'd need to manage both. As any personal security specialist could testify, a reckless, obstinate, or stupid primary could be more dangerous than the enemy itself.

What kind of primary was Mary Grace?

Hale scrolled, then froze. Mary Grace's photo filled the top half of her page and for a long moment all he could do was stare. Something far beyond beautiful, Mary Grace was stunning.

Blond haired and blue eyed with high cheekbones and perfectly symmetrical features, she looked like something out of a catalog of runway models...except her natural beauty was where the glamour stopped. She wore ordinary clothes—jeans stained with red African clay, a shirt with the sleeves rolled up. Standing beneath a fig tree with a crowd of smiling children gathered around her, she appeared as comfortable in her own skin as Hale had ever seen anybody.

Like she was *born* to be standing exactly where she was, doing exactly what she was doing. Completely content to forget everything else on earth.

Wow.

Hale shook himself loose from the daze, glancing around to see if anyone had noticed, but both pilots remained in the cockpit.

Focus, Ian. Mission-minded.

He moved past the picture to Mary Grace's bio. It was extensive, written no doubt by Shaw herself. Born the same year as Shaw in the same town of Warner Robins, Georgia, Mary Grace came from money—a lot of it. Her parents were both successful partners at a regional law firm, and her grandfather owned a stake in a major hotel chain. She and Shaw met in high school and became fast friends as freshman. When they both graduated, they both attended UGA—Shaw on an ROTC scholarship, Mary Grace on her grandfather's hotel money.

A pre-law student, Mary Grace hoped to follow in her parents' footsteps and attend Emory University. She planned to marry some rich kid from Buckhead. She even hoped to open her own practice.

And then she was involved in a car accident. A nasty one, in her sophomore year of college. She was on bedrest for weeks and crutches for months. She fell behind in her studies. Her grades suffered. Mary Grace seemed to be losing it all—her entire identity. The rich boyfriend even dumped her. He couldn't afford to be "held back."

It was much more detail than Shaw usually included in a mission brief. Maybe she had simply been word-vomiting, distracted by worry. Maybe she was trying to sell him on Mary Grace, to build a connection in his mind to this person that Shaw loved so much.

Whatever the case, Hale didn't mind. He would approach the work the same regardless of any collegiate heartbreak Mary Grace had suffered. That was the job.

But he couldn't deny, the next part of the story landed hard.

Mary Grace went on a mission trip. Out of the house, out of Georgia, out of her comfort zone. Some place in Uganda—a Resurrection Mercy Ministries project. She spent three months in country...

And she returned a totally changed person. Completely disinterested with her previous goals, Mary Grace became obsessed with the RMM mission. Enraging her parents and perplexing her friends, she pivoted her studies at UGA from pre-law to international affairs. She graduated on a Saturday, and Monday morning she was on a jet headed back to Africa.

She almost never came back. A holiday here or there. A surprise visit for a big family event. But the rest of the time?

Mary Grace spent it in her new home. Uganda, then Ethiopia, and now South Sudan, where she directed her own orphanage. Living with those who needed her, serving them whole-heartedly. Learning the culture and the community and digging in for the long haul.

And smiling. Hale looked back at the photo and appreciated the radiance in a new light. He looked deep into her eyes and noted the resolution. The confidence. The dedication. Like an anchor in a hurricane, immoveable no matter the risk.

Exactly the kind of primary who would get *everyone* killed.

16

Atlanta, Georgia
11:20 Hours, Eastern Standard Time

Laney Shaw spent the night at the Westin Peachtree Plaza, the same hotel she had overnighted in with her parents so many times as a child. The next morning she walked down Peachtree Street to the Metro Diner, a local spot with great—if expensive—breakfast.

The coffee went down easily, but the pancakes were more difficult to manage. Shaw could barely taste the food as she fiddled with her fork, her mind wandering across the prior night's meeting. She had arranged Hale's charter before she went to bed, which was fortunate, because Hale texted her very early that morning, already back in New England.

Apparently, she wasn't the only one who couldn't sleep. Maybe for different reasons. As Shaw stared blankly at the wall and her food grew cold, all she could think about was Mary Grace Dalton.

Not the Mary Grace who lived in Africa, but the Mary Grace of before. The sorority girl at UGA, who partied hard and studied harder, fantasizing about the day she landed her first big law job and could buy her dream car —an Alfa Romeo 8C with a custom sky-blue paint scheme.

Yes, Mary Grace was a car girl, just like Shaw was a car girl. Shaw preferred the Germans, Mary Grace liked the Italians. In school she drove a used but well-loved Maserati Spyder—and drove it well. All the boys whistled. All the girls pretended to hate but were secretly jealous.

And wasn't that the point? Status. Recognition. Popularity.

Flash was the word Mary Grace used. Maybe *flash* was on her mind as she raced that Corvette down I-85, blazing around trucks and clipping along emergency lanes...

Then stopping. Suddenly, absolutely. Slamming against a dump truck, flipping the Maserati and flipping her world with it.

The trauma of that moment spread beyond her own life. Maybe her friends could be forgiven for struggling so hard to understand when she never really came back...

At least, not the way they knew her.

Shaw looked at her plate and the old lump returned to her stomach. That lump she first felt when she realized what a total heel she'd been—not only to MG but to her entire family. Shaw had told Hale that she and Mary Grace were best friends, and that was mostly true...

Shaw had just left out the part where she herself had shunned Mary Grace like the rest, disgusted by MG's disinterest in the old life. Uncomfortable with her new obsessions. No longer identifying or understanding.

When Shaw and Mary Grace reconnected some years later, it was only because one of Shaw's Sentinel teams were deep behind the wire in Ethiopia and Shaw needed somebody—*anybody*—to offer them food and shelter. Mary Grace was literally the last person Shaw wanted to call. She was also the only person Shaw could *think of* to call.

So Shaw did...and much to her surprise, MG couldn't have sounded happier to hear from her. She was also eager to help. Shaw's team was given a safe place to stay and medical care for a pair of bullet wounds. Full bellies and love from the children who marveled at the American's muscles. Sent safely on their way without questions or any concern for payment.

Shaw made a five-figure donation to Resurrection Mercy Ministries after that. She stayed in touch with Mary Grace, also. Shaw was able to render assistance now and then, usually with a phone call to some African contact.

But still, she carried the guilt. The sense that she'd never really squared with Mary Grace...and maybe the much greater sense that Mary Grace was winning at life in a way Shaw had never been selfless enough to experience.

Was that why Shaw had caught the first flight to Atlanta? Rushed to meet with Carpenter? Tracked down Ian and called in a favor that he didn't even owe her?

Now Hale was headed east—probably into legitimate danger. Where did that leave her? Sitting in a diner staring at cold pancakes, hating herself?

No freaking way.

Shaw dumped cash on the table and fast-walked back to the Westin Peachtree Plaza. American Express secured an open-ended reservation on her room. She locked the door and cranked the AC way down. She snuggled into her Bulldogs hoodie and opened her laptop on the desk. She logged into the Marriott's premium Wi-Fi and activated a VPN to secure her computer.

Then she fit a headset over her ears and accessed a digital call software. A holdover from her tenure at Sentinel, the subscription service now charged to her AMEX...but the digital Rolodex came free of charge.

Shaw selected a Washington, DC, number—somebody from the US Agency for International Development who owed her a favor—a clicked to dial.

It was time to find out exactly what was happening in South Sudan.

17

Juba, South Sudan
05:50 Hours, East Africa Time

The phone call woke Jaxon Wilks from a hard sleep.

It wasn't a good sleep. It wasn't deep. It was *hard*, reminding him of Sunday mornings at his University of Pennsylvania frat house. Even as a college kid, Jaxon was never much of a drinker—his ambitions for graduate school at Harvard were too important to risk. But there were those nights when peer pressure overcame him, and his lack of a drinking habit only served to get him hammered that much faster, leaving him sleeping all the harder the next morning.

That was how he felt waking up in Juba, and for the same reason. The night prior, Jaxon met with not only Minister Abiem but also with Abiem's boss, the president of South Sudan. What was meant to be a diplomatic discussion turned out to be a dinner party—emphasis on *party*.

They forced alcohol on him, round after round as music pumped. Visiting dignitaries and social elites strolled the pool deck of the president's mansion, and Abiem and his boss discussed everything *except* the details of a US–South Sudanese natural resources exploitation deal.

Jaxon tried to pivot the conversation. He tried to refuse the drinks.

Abiem and his cohorts maintained pressure, pouring Jaxon glass after glass of imported South African wine before rolling out a bottle of Johnnie Walker Black Label and fixing him a tumbler full.

That was the moment things really turned south. Jaxon managed to not make a fool of himself—he thought—and to return to the US embassy before blacking out. He'd saved himself from diplomatic embarrassment, but the meeting had been a total waste of time…and Jaxon had a strong feeling that was intentional.

But why?

Jaxon's brain was too cloudy and sore for him to wonder as he fumbled for the phone. He was going to silence it, but then he recognized the word "BLOCKED" on his phone screen alongside the location: *WASHINGTON, DC.*

Jaxon knew exactly what that meant. He knew he couldn't afford to ignore the call. He sat up and dashed water into his face, dabbing his skin dry with the same wadded-up dress shirt he'd worn to the party. A quick shake of his head, and then he finally answered.

"This is Wilks."

"How'd it go?"'

Assistant Secretary of State Paul Morris barked with traditional impatience, as though this conversation had already lasted hours too long. Jaxon squinted at his clock and calculated the time difference. It had to be about midnight in DC. His boss probably thought he was doing Jaxon a favor by waiting this late to call.

"It…" Jaxon hesitated, trying to decide how much of the previous night's embarrassment he wanted to admit to. Then he decided there was no use in lying. It could be a career-ending mistake if he was caught. "It wasn't really a meeting. More of a dinner party. Lots of visiting VIPs, lots of booze. I worked Abiem all night but couldn't get him focused on the deal."

Long pause. Jaxon braced himself for an angry explosion from the other side of the world, but it never arrived. Instead, Morris came back measured. Almost cold.

"What's your read?"

Jaxon rubbed his eyes, fighting through the headache as he unpacked what he could remember. He'd hoped to have a few hours of sobriety—and a greasy breakfast—to help him unravel his thoughts. Now he was forced to work in overdrive.

"He just..." Jaxon shook his head. "He doesn't seem to be taking me seriously. At the same time, he's keeping me close. It really feels like he wants to keep us on the hook while also stalling for time. Like he's got another negotiation underway."

It was pure speculation, and according to Paul Morris guesswork had no place in diplomacy. But Jaxon felt good about his assessment. Abiem had been charming the night prior. Engaged, hospitable, accommodating of anything Jaxon could possibly want *except* a discussion about contract terms.

It was exactly what Jaxon would expect if his assumptions about a secondary negotiation were true. Of course, the only way to be sure might be to wait around until that secondary negotiation was completed, in which case Jaxon might suddenly find himself facing a cold shoulder. If he was honest, Abiem had him over a barrel. The South Sudanese had all the power in this negotiation.

What was Jaxon going to do about it?

"We think it's the Chinese," Morris said.

"You mean the secondary negotiation?" Jaxon said.

"Right. That's the only player large enough to offer Abiem whatever infrastructure or technological resources he could want while also facilitating the mining operations. The Chinese already have a strong foothold in Ethiopia. They're crazy about Africa. It makes sense."

Jaxon didn't need to be told about the Dragon's exploitive obsession with Africa. He was an African expert, after all. He knew all about Beijing's relationship with Ethiopia, also.

So where did that leave them? Playing second fiddle to the Chinese, hoping that these hidden negotiations would fall through? If Jaxon knew Morris, his boss would never accept such a passive approach.

Jaxon was right.

"I want you back in touch with Abiem," Morris said. "Arrange a meeting today. I want you to push him on the benefits of American security assistance—that's our play here. Last night James Wani's White Nile Liberation Army hit Maridi. They sacked a South Sudan People's Defense Forces garrison, killed maybe thirty troops, raided a bank and then burned half a dozen buildings to the ground. It was brutal—I'm sending you photos."

Jaxon pivoted to his laptop. The email took a moment to load, but when it did his stomach turned.

Brutal was the right word. Wani's forces had completely obliterated the South Sudanese army garrison in Maridi, a mid-sized town in rural Western Equatoria. Bodies of dead government soldiers lay strewn across the street, two of them crushed by a truck. The photos were all taken by the light of nearby burning buildings, and in one place Jaxon thought he might be looking at a dead child.

He swallowed. Shook his head. "How...do we have these pictures?"

"Wrong question," Morris said. "The right question is *How quickly can we leverage them?* Look, kid. The South Sudanese government is getting manhandled in Western Equatoria, and Western Equatoria is where a billion dollars of strategic natural resources lay waiting for exploitation. They can't honestly pretend to sell those resources without first neutralizing Wani, and they clearly can't neutralize Wani on their own...so its *your* job to sell them on our assistance."

"You mean our military," Jaxon said.

"Is that what I said?"

It wasn't, but Jaxon knew what Morris meant. This wasn't a complicated problem. What lay buried beneath Western Equatoria was of tremendous value to the US government. He wouldn't be here nursing a hangover if it wasn't. He wouldn't have an opportunity to advance his career without it.

Why was he questioning anything?

"I'll arrange another meeting," Jaxon said.

"See that you do. Update me immediately after. And Jaxon?"

"Sir?"

"*Close the deal.*"

Morris hung up.

18

Juba, South Sudan
07:45 Hours, East Africa Time

The Gulfstream flew through the night, touching down in Juba with a scream of tires early the next morning.

There was only one airport in the city, and that airport had only one runway. It was paved, technically, but many of the planes that Hale observed parked alongside it featured tires caked in orange African clay.

They were NGO aircraft and a few bush planes. What was most ominous lay beyond the taxiway amid a tangle of brush. It was an aircraft wreck—a big one, only a hundred yards off the runway. Some kind of regional jet with about a third of the left wing ripped off. Run into the mud, maybe semi-stripped for parts...and then abandoned.

Because this was the third world, and the graveyards of this place rested right alongside the hospitals.

"Do you need any help offloading?" It was one of the pilots. He stood just outside the cockpit, his gaze darting between windows.

"Give me five minutes," Hale said.

He departed the jet with an HK VP9A1 pistol secured beneath his shirt in an appendix holster. His pockets contained a Benchmade Adamas knife in OD green...and hard American currency.

Hale advanced straight to the nearest officials—a pair of South Sudanese soldiers with cigarettes dangling from their lips. They addressed him in English to demand his business.

Hale wasn't surprised by the chosen language. English was common throughout South Sudan—in fact, it was the official language. Hale asked to see the customs officer, explaining that he was there on oil business and would like to fast-track his entry.

The soldiers knew exactly what that meant. They said nothing while Hale dealt one hundred dollars in small bills to each man—a generous sum for guys who made barely forty bucks a month. This wasn't Hale's first rodeo in the third world.

The cash was accepted without comment or gratitude. One soldier indicated a shack constructed near the airport's perimeter, and Hale headed that way. He could feel the pilots watching him, but their urgency added nothing to Hale's razor-sharp focus. From the moment they'd broken through the clouds above Juba, he'd swept the horizon. He'd monitored the distant hills, the sprawling brushlands, the syrupy-slow White Nile River lined by dirt roads and block after block of filthy concrete buildings.

Already Hale recognized the vibe. Deeper than depression, this sickened stillness reminded Hale of the cancer ward where his grandmother had taken her chemo treatments. It was the aura of a consuming disease that infected the very concrete beneath Hale's boots. It was corruption, deceit, greed. Less like a bullet to the face and more like a parasite that sucks away only enough life to bring an organism *near* death...but not quite over the edge.

It was pseudo death. A zombie state. A forever curse.

At the shack, Hale didn't bother to introduce himself. The "official" working the counter sat next to a whirring fan and flipped through a Ugandan pop-culture mag—South Sudan's comparably vibrant neighbor lay just a hundred kilometers to the south.

"I'm here for customs," Hale said.

The official jabbed a thumb over his shoulder. "The big building."

"Perhaps you misunderstand." Hale dispersed five hundred dollars over the shack's windowsill. The guy licked his teeth, casting a glance around the premises.

There was no one except the two soldiers, and they were quite literally looking the other way. The official took the cash and spun a keyring.

"Executive service for you, sir. Follow me to the side gate."

Hale walked both duffel bags through a chain link gate without the first sign of customs or security. No presentation of his passport, no questions about his origins or his business.

Just seven hundred bucks—*welcome to South Sudan*.

The jet streaked off the runway as Hale loaded his gear into the trunk of a taxi. He gave the driver directions for the Radisson Blu Hotel, a fourteen-story tower not far from the airport. It was one of the few chain hotels in the city, and the best option Hale could find online.

Ugandan pop played from the cab's stereo. Hale kept his hand near his concealed pistol as he surveyed passing streets, most of them paved but covered in potholes, all of them clogged with creeping traffic.

Everything was dirty. Everything looked hot. Most of the people didn't smile. The storefronts they passed were all in shambles, awnings sagging over windows so filthy they were practically opaque.

And then, in nearly an instant, everything changed. They departed the airport district and turned south for the river. The buildings grew taller and newer. The roads a little wider. They passed a soccer stadium—the White Nile River wound just beyond it.

This was the dressy part of town. The part most suited to hosting visiting dignitaries and anyone the government in Juba cared to impress. Hale had seen it before and none of the flash obscured the high concrete wall topped in curled razor wire that enclosed the Radisson hotel.

Again—*welcome to South Sudan*.

Hale booked a room and dropped his duffels onto the bed. He pulled back a curtain to look across the heart of sprawling Juba. Not a big city, but a dense one. Thin brown dust rose in a haze from the traffic churning through downtown. Hale's gaze caught on flags flapping over what might have been a government compound or a military base. In another place solar panels glinted, forcing him to squint. He noted markets and apartment complexes and tangles of squalid neighborhoods where too many people competed for too few resources.

It was an isolated metropolis trapped inside a corrupt, semi-failed state. Hale had seen it before and knew exactly how savage a place a city like Juba could be.

Checking his phone, Hale found two bars of international coverage. He shot off a quick text to Shaw, and the phone marked the message as delivered.

Arrived in J. Checked into temp hotel. Will update when have travel arrangements.

No immediate response from Shaw, which Hale expected. It would be after midnight on the East Coast.

Stepping to the hotel phone, Hale dialed for the concierge. A man answered in a distinct African accent.

"Hotel Radisson, how may I assist you?"

"This is room 312," Hale said. "I'd like to speak with a travel guide."

"You wish to view the local attractions?"

"Actually, I'd like to go on a safari."

19

Juba, South Sudan
12:02 Hours, East Africa Time

Wing-Kei took the call via an encrypted Chinese communications app similar to Signal—but funded by the Chinese Communist Party.

The number was location nonspecific, although Wing-Kei knew the caller to be dialing from only two kilometers away. It would have been easy for the two of them to meet in person, and maybe at some point they would, but why bother at this stage?

It was a needless risk of exposure. The app was secure. Whatever Wing-Kei's boss needed to say could be said from across town.

"*Zài tīng*," Wing-Kei answered. *I'm listening.*

"The Americans have requested another meeting with Minister Abiem. It is scheduled to occur later today. They may be ready to press their security offers."

Standing next to his hotel window, Wing-Kei watched battered cars rolling up and down an equally battered highway, a hazy sun hanging just over the eastern horizon. He accepted his boss's words without comment, knowing that orders would follow.

That was how it worked with Wing-Kei. He wasn't a mastermind, and he didn't want to be. He was an operator, thriving on the action and the execution, not the grand strategy.

"Last night James Wani's army sacked a South Sudanese military garrison," the boss continued. "The damage was severe. It may be that our hold on Abiem's attention will slip. You have to escalate your timeline."

There it was. The only thing in this entire spiel that Wing-Kei actually cared about. The mission.

"What do you want?" Wing-Kei said.

"Do you have the latest count?"

Wing-Kei didn't. He only had the count as of fifteen hours prior, but it should be close. His boss grunted.

"That won't be enough. Contact your operator and have him escalate his efforts. We'll need twice as many, at the least, and sooner than expected. The Americans have deployed a special negotiator—he's much more aggressive than their ambassador."

More extraneous detail. Wing-Kei simply spoke the obvious.

"My operator will want additional payment."

A snort. "So promise it to him. Wire no more than half. We'll erase him when we finish."

It was exactly the response Wing-Kei expected. Whatever funds his bosses lost in advance payments to the operator would be recovered ten-thousand-fold if this mission were a success.

It was a paltry price to pay.

"It will be done," Wing-Kei said.

His boss hung up without another word—the conversation was finished. Wing-Kei lowered the phone and rolled his neck until it crackled.

He was still looking out the window—now gazing into the parking lot. There was a man there whom Wing-Kei had seen twice before. Tall, muscular, white. He arrived in a taxi and came and went on foot. He didn't carry any visible military gear, but there was something about his bearing. Something about the way he walked.

He was military, Wing-Kei was sure of it. An American, perhaps? Maybe...someone like himself?

The white man disappeared through the hotel's gate, turning a corner. Wing-Kei blinked and shook his head.

What did it matter? There were killers crawling all over Juba. This man could be anybody—maybe another dog like the operator Wing-Kei had hired. Americans, in his experience, were all the same.

Easily understood, even more easily manipulated.

Wing-Kei lifted his phone and dialed.

20

Juba, South Sudan
12:45 Hours, East Africa Time

Nobody would go to Western Equatoria.

Hale spent the whole morning searching. First via the hotel's desk phone, and then on his feet actually working the streets of Juba. In a country boasting some of the most vibrant sub-Saharan terrain in Africa, Hale expected a horde of local businesses equipped with four-wheel-drive SUVs and babbling guides who would happily take a white man's money and show him the elephants.

Hale didn't care about elephants, and cared even less about a babbling tour guide, but he liked the idea of a knowledgeable local and a four-wheel-drive SUV. He consulted tour companies, transportation firms, and even a security service that offered armored vehicle transport.

In every case, the moment Hale mentioned the words *Western Equatoria*, he was shut down cold. No exceptions, no debate. The explanations were all the same—two words.

James Wani.

Hale crisscrossed the city. He killed time in a local cafe, striking up conversations with both a waitress and the sweaty guys seated at the table next to him—they had a truck. He was touring the country. Had they ever been to Tambura?

Both men smiled a lot when they talked, but when Hale asked about Tambura, those smiles evaporated.

"You're a dead man if you go," one man said.

That was the end of the conversation. Hale couldn't get anyone else to talk, and even the waitress turned cold. He exited the cafe and stood on a mud street, shabby homes built of blocks and tin packed tight together on every side. A moped rattled by, blasting blue smoke into Hale's face. He sipped from a branded bottle of water and checked the G-Shock strapped to his wrist, grimacing as he noted the time.

Four hours consumed and not one offer of guidance, or even a referral to somebody who knew somebody. News of the White Nile Liberation Army had swept the country, it seemed, and the terror of those rumors was enough to neutralize any desire for a quick buck from a cash-flush outsider. Even when Hale had literally flashed that cash, it wasn't enough to generate so much as a consideration of assistance.

The situation was worse than Shaw and Carpenter thought. A lot worse.

"So, man. You looking to go to Western Equatoria?"

The voice came from behind Hale, around the corner of the cafe where a dirt alley separated one shabby building from the next. Hale twisted, caught off guard. He'd passed the stack of milk crates twice without ever noticing the small black man who crouched at their base. In fact, had Hale noticed him, he would have thought the guy was a child. He was small, squatted with his bare feet bunched together, his knees rising up to his chest. Long fingers picked bits of coconut out of its shell and slipped them between dry and cracked lips.

He didn't look at Hale when he spoke. He focused on the coconut.

Hale narrowed his eyes. "Maybe."

The guy grunted, still fixated on his snack. For a moment, Hale thought he might be done with the conversation.

Then he said: "It's a bad place."

Hale glanced over his shoulder, suddenly wary of third parties—anyone who might try to sneak up while the little guy distracted him.

He saw no one. He stepped closer to the milk crates.

"You've been there?"

A dry laugh. "I was born there."

"You know a town called Tambura?"

No answer. The guy kept picking at the coconut. Something in Hale's gut told him to be patient. Finally, the guy looked up. Large black eyes swept Hale from head to toe as another finger passed between his lips—more coconut.

Deep in that gaze, Hale saw storm clouds. He saw pain.

He saw a lot of history.

"Why you want to go there?" the man said.

Hale squatted next to the milk crates, wondering how old this man might be. Maybe thirty—maybe fifty. There was nothing youthful about his unblinking stare, but gravity like that could be manufactured in an instant by sufficient trauma.

If that was true—if this man had experienced true pain—then he knew the difference between the truth and a lie. Hale decided to shoot straight with him.

"There's an orphanage in Tambura that's caught in James Wani's war," Hale said. "My job is to protect it."

A soft grunt. "Miss Mary Grace's orphanage."

"You know her?"

No answer. Hale was just about to speak again when the man said: "You are a soldier?"

Hale hesitated, fully aware of what connotation the term *soldier* might carry in a place like this.

"I used to be," he said.

"And you go to help Miss Mary Grace?"

"That's the plan."

Another slow nod. The face dropped, and the man resumed picking at his coconut. "In the Konyo Konyo market there is a man named Bol who sells trucks. Find one owned by the UN or a charity—they take better care of the motors than the militias do. Buy plenty of fuel, also. It is a long way to Tambura, and supplies will be scarce. Tomorrow morning at sunrise I will meet you here, and I will show you the way. It is not safe to travel at night."

Hale squinted. "You're a guide?"

"No. But I know the way to Tambura, and nobody else will take you. James Wani has terrified them all. I will show you the roads to avoid his territories."

"Why?" Hale said.

He couldn't help it—it was the logical response. All day long he'd fought to find somebody willing to take money for the trip. Now this guy was volunteering.

"Why does it matter? You need the help. I am offering."

"So how do I know I can trust you?"

Dark eyes fixed on Hale's, unblinking and focused. Hale had the sudden sensation that he was the one being evaluated, not the other way around. The moment lasted for nearly a minute, and Hale didn't look away.

At last the man said: "Because I know war."

Another long beat, then the face dropped. The coconut picking resumed.

"Buy the truck. I will be waiting."

21

Atlanta, Georgia
07:05 Hours, Eastern Standard Time

Avril Lavigne woke Shaw.

She hadn't even realized she'd fallen asleep. Flopped out over the hotel room's desk with hair wadded beneath one ear, she must have passed out sometime after midnight.

Shaw sat up with a jerk, the chorus of "Sk8er Boi" blaring from her iPhone—a high school anthem that never failed to startle the mess out of her.

She *really* needed to find a new ringtone.

Checking the screen, Shaw recognized the sat phone number and took only a moment to scrub dried saliva from her cheek before swiping to answer.

"Ian?"

From the far side of the world, Hale's voice sounded only a little distorted—satellite phone technology had really come a long way in the decade-plus that Shaw had spent in the military and working in private security.

"Did I wake you?"

There was no way Shaw was admitting to being woken, let alone woken with drool on her face. She chugged water and grunted a negative.

"Where are you?" Shaw said. "You make it to Juba?"

"Landed seven hours ago. Checked into the Radisson to store my gear. I just bought a truck."

Shaw squinted. "What?"

"Nobody's running transport to Western Equatoria. I spent the whole morning looking. This place is scared out of their minds."

Western Equatoria. The name was enough to clear the cobwebs still clouding Shaw's mind. Hours of research from the night prior returned in a rush—the content of the phone calls, emails, and web chats. Dozens of them.

"We need to talk," Shaw said. "They're right to be scared."

From the far end of the line, Shaw heard gears grinding. The phone thumped against some hard surface, and a horn blared.

Hale returned a moment later. "Sorry. Stick shift. Hit me with the highlights."

Shaw did, jumping headfirst into a facts-only summary. "The short answer is that Western Equatoria has become a total war zone. It's much worse than Mary Grace indicated, maybe worse than she realizes. Since 2021, ethnic clashes between rival Azande and Balanda communities have sponsored a vicious cycle of retaliatory raids and revenge murders that have thrown tens of thousands into homelessness and starvation. These are mostly non-military groups, but you wouldn't know the difference. They're heavily armed with all the usual Russian and Russian knock-off hardware, including machine guns and shoulder-fired rockets. Torched villages, stolen cattle, and massacred communities are all commonplace. It's guerrilla war on steroids...hence all the orphans, I guess."

Shaw paused to chug more water. Hale was ready with the right question.

"Where does James Wani fit in?"

"Wani and his White Nile Liberation Army arrived on scene maybe eighteen months ago—not long after Resurrection Mercy Ministries founded their orphanage in Tambura. The situation at the time was unstable but mostly contained between rival factions. Like gang violence in a big city—if you're a third party and you keep your head down, you're mostly okay. But then Wani shows up and declares an alliance with the Azande. As a former officer in the South Sudan People's Defense Force, Wani is a seasoned military strategist and understands how to organize ground troops. He managed to unify fragmented Azande militias and build them into a more legitimate army—legitimate enough to wipe the Balanda out of Western Equatoria and even seize significant territory along the South Sudan/Central African Republic border. Entire villages in that region are under complete WNLA control."

"And Juba is just allowing this?"

"Of course not. The SSPDF has engaged Wani's forces on multiple occasions. Some of those fights have been really nasty—casualties in the triple digits, with the bulk of that bloodshed falling on the government's side. Wani's soldiers are heavily armed and much better trained than the militias Juba is accustomed to fighting. Nobody seems to know how, but they've acquired some really nasty equipment—armored trucks, mortars, anti-aircraft and anti-tank guns, even a captured government helicopter, although that may be a myth. The standing narrative in Juba is that the government will not be intimidated by 'marauding thugs'—their words, not mine. But the reality remains that James Wani is all but a king. His ranks are swelling, and my suspicion is that Juba is scrambling. In another six months, their hold on Western Equatoria could be all but gone."

In other words, Hale thought, *this problem isn't going away. It's only getting worse.*

"When did all this escalation begin?" Hale said.

Shaw didn't immediately answer. She didn't want to answer at all. What was the point?

"It's a messy place, Ian. This stuff comes in waves—it's like chasing the wind. You can't—"

"Answer the question, Shaw."

She breathed deep. "Like I said, Wani founded the WNLA just under two years ago. But the fighting has really intensified over the last six months. Juba seems to be making a concentrated effort to...push him out."

As soon as she said it, Shaw regretted it. She knew it would only be fuel on Hale's mental fire, even if the information she communicated was accurate. What did that help? The core realities of Mary Grace's situation in Tambura remained the same.

"Look, it's probably just a coincidence. Like I said, this stuff comes in waves—"

"Western Equatoria, Shaw. Exactly where a businessman I was sent to rescue from contract kidnappers claimed to have discovered a mass deposit of a rare natural resource. The kind of thing any developed country in their right minds would scramble to recover."

"And that could be a coincidence. Even if it's not, how is that your fault?"

More silence. Brakes squealing. Whatever Hale drove chugged as it idled.

"Ian..." Shaw started. Stopped. She thought of Mary Grace—of all the combat reports she'd read of James Wani's attacks against government positions. Whatever villages or communities stood in the way were flattened—smashed by falling mortars while bullets whizzed as thick as locusts, bodies torn and left to rot.

Ugly business. Some of the worst she'd ever encountered.

"I can't ask you to go ahead with this," Shaw said. "It's not what I thought it was. We can figure out another way...maybe an airlift."

"You said Wani's guys have anti-aircraft guns?" Hale said.

"Possibly."

"So you think anybody wants to fly out there?"

Shaw didn't. She'd already considered that angle. She just couldn't cross the hurdle of sending Ian Hale into a death trap—not again.

"If half of what you say is true, that orphanage needs help more than ever," Hale said. "I found somebody who claims to be from Tambura. He's offered to guide me."

"You said you couldn't find a guide."

"He's not a guide, he's just a local who needs cash."

"Do you trust him?"

"He knows Mary Grace. He named her without prompting. I think he's had some interaction with the orphanage."

"And...you just stumbled into this guy?"

"There's no perfect solution, Shaw. It's six hundred klicks to Tambura and I don't know the terrain. There's no opportunity for this guy to sell me out if nobody even knew I was coming."

Fair point.

Shaw's mind spun only a moment longer before she realized that it didn't matter what she thought. This was Hale's decision. He was the one charging headlong into the unknown. She only wished she was there with him, that she could offer Mary Grace more than the promise of *somebody else.*

At least if it had to be somebody else, it could be Ian Hale.

"Call at any time," Shaw said. "You need cash for the truck?"

"I got it covered. I'll keep you posted as we move. And Shaw?"

"Yeah?"

"I know you were sleeping."

Hale hung up. Shaw rolled her eyes and flung the phone down. She ran both hands through her hair and breathed deep once more. Her gaze settled on her laptop, the screen covered in pictures from Western Equatoria battlefields. Bodies torn and mutilated.

And she hoped Mary Grace was right about an all-powerful God—because a very powerful devil had declared residence in South Sudan.

22

Western Equatoria, South Sudan
13:48 Hours, East Africa Time

There were 215.

Muddy. Slender. Many with ribs showing and eyes sunken into their heads. Some scarred from previous combat, and two even bearing the tattoos of crossed AK-pattern rifles—no doubt the symbol of some splinter-cell militant faction that didn't last long enough to be remembered...yet their mark remained.

It was in the eyes of those with the tattoos that Marc Harden saw the most death. While many of the children barricaded inside a ten-foot stockade recoiled from the presence of the muscled South Carolinian, those with the tattoos didn't give an inch. They stared through gaps between the logs, meeting his gaze and not so much as blinking.

Harden didn't think they were brave, or even defiant. He thought they were empty. Like the lights were on but nobody was home; those two boys existed as zombies. Breathing, eating, but rarely speaking and never reflecting any emotion.

Drones. Automatons.

Cannon fodder.

Packing tobacco into his cheek, Harden returned their gazes without comment, relishing the rush of nicotine even as he ignored the current of sweat slipping down his back. The mosquitos buzzing around his face. The steam that hung in the air hours after the sun rose, a cloud that made it difficult to breathe.

What a pit.

It was a lot like Jasper County, really. When Harden closed his eyes, the mud squishing beneath his boots wasn't orange African clay but brown Carolina sludge. It surrounded a thousand fragmented streams, many flowing into saltwater marshes and freshwater swamps.

He could still picture that mud caking his hands and knees as he scrambled through wax myrtle and button brush. Desperate for cover, ignoring the mosquitos that threatened to eat him alive.

The drunken voice from not far behind was the real threat. Marc Harden's old man had beaten his wife to death, escaping prosecution on a technicality. He'd broken his daughter's leg, and she never reported it—or walked the same again.

Now he was coming for his youngest. The liquor rage had overcome him. He'd already bruised flesh and blackened eyes—tonight he looked ready for murder.

But Marcus Garrick Harden wasn't born to go down easy. Not like his mother, not like his sister. He would hide in that brush, enduring the mosquitos and biding his time. Waiting for his old man to pass out cold in the living room of their dilapidated trailer home. Creeping like a swamp rat between the trees, right to the edge of the river where that plastic box lay.

Heavy. Damp. And when he lifted it, something moved inside.

Harden opened his eyes, his heart rate thumping a little faster with the memory. He spat more tobacco juice and advanced to the palisade. He tugged the short sleeve of his shirt up his right arm, exposing an iron bicep…and the tattoo.

"You see this?" Harden said, addressing the nearest automaton kid. The boy didn't answer but Harden knew he understood because his gaze switched to the tattoo.

A black snake. As thick as a hand grenade, it was wrapped around

Harden's bicep and curled to his forearm where the triangular head opened to expose bloody fangs and a white mouth.

"Come on," Harden encouraged. "Come have a look."

The boys exchanged a glance. Then one of them took a half step forward. He licked his lips and peered at the snake. He looked back to Harden.

"Black mamba," he whispered.

Harden laughed. "No, kid. *Cottonmouth.*"

Harden winked. The boy's empty eyes turned colder than before. His jaw locked and the muscles trembled, but he didn't say anything.

What was he going to say? He was on the wrong side of the fence.

"Only two kinds of animals in this world," Harden said. "Hunters and prey. Which one do you think I am?"

Again, no answer. The boy glared while his compatriots cowered in the shadows. Mostly boys, but not all. Harden's employer allowed for girls, also. In fact, he didn't seem overly concerned about *who* the children were...

Only that they were children. No older than fourteen, the rest should be shot on sight. The younger ones should be brought here, barricaded and fed and kept healthy.

For now.

"Hey, boss."

The voice was heavy with an African accent—Dinka, Harden thought. Not that he cared. The guy was a thug, just like all of Harden's men. He liked booze and pork and women, when he could get them. He was cheap to hire and did what he was told.

That was good enough for Harden.

"You gotta call on your mobile," the man said.

The soldier extended a hand, offering a chunky satellite phone. Harden took the device and turned away from the fence. He hadn't tired of staring the boy down, but he'd certainly tired of smelling the children and their open-air lavatory—a facility that only some of them used.

Animals.

Harden redialed.

"What is the count?"

That was how the employer answered the phone. Customary bluntness communicated in English tinged with an Asian accent—Harden wasn't enough of a linguist to know *which* Asian accent, and neither did he care.

"Two-fifteen," he said. "Another six on the way."

Silence. Harden waited, because he'd once read in an article entitled "Five Negotiation Tactics to Get the Salary You Deserve" that you should never be the first to speak in a negotiation. Never be the first to make a demand.

He knew the number was low. He knew the employer wanted more. He wouldn't be the one to volunteer a solution to that problem.

"It must be more," the employer said. "Twice as many—and soon. By next week."

Harden snorted, spraying tobacco juice. Whatever demand he expected, this far exceeded it.

"Two hundred in one week? Are you insane? It took me the better part of a month to catch these. The little turds are fast—like swamp rabbits. Then some of them croak before I can get any food in them. They're mostly skin and bones anyway."

Harden feigned obstinance, but in truth he'd already moved past the outrageous demands and was already calculating how much he could extort for the additional work. Because be it Jasper County or Iraq or some CIA black site in Asia or even here, in South Sudan...*money talked.*

"How much?"

The employer was as smart as Harden thought. He cut right to the chase. Harden appreciated that—but he also remembered the Five Negotiation Tactics. Two of the five were variations of the same principle.

Don't speak first.

Don't name a number first.

"What's it worth to you?" Harden shot back.

He heard the employer mutter a curse. Harden didn't care—he only wanted to hear a number. Something he would counter by 20 or 30 percent. Maybe demand some money up front—

"A hundred thousand dollars," the employer said. "Fifty percent now. Fifty percent on delivery."

A hundred grand.

It was the same amount Harden had signed on for in the first place—the full volume of his contract, instantly doubled.

Not bad for swamp rabbits.

"Done," Harden said. "Wire the first half. We'll begin immediately."

"See that you do. Also, on the next raid, it's time for your men to wear the uniforms."

The uniforms. Why did this guy care about uniforms?

It was a stretch to even call them that, honestly. What his employer had sent looked more like tattered, mismatched rags, but all with that same symbol on them. Some long-legged bird standing atop curving palm limbs that surrounded a star, a crescent moon and...Harden couldn't remember what else. It was too complicated.

But he was kind of curious.

"What's this Lord's Resistance Army, anyway?"

"What?" The employer's voice snapped, just a little.

"This LRA thing on all the uniforms. What's up with that?"

Silence. Harden squinted, ready to probe further—then he was cut off.

"Two hundred grand," the employer said. "Half of it now. I want you finished by this weekend. And Harden?"

"What?"

"*No more questions.*"

The employer hung up.

23

Juba, South Sudan
06:10 Hours, East Africa Time

The truck was a 1999 Toyota Land Cruiser Model 79—a four-door pickup equipped with four-wheel drive, a diesel engine, a brush guard with a winch, and an expanded fuel tank offering a total capacity of 150 liters.

Imported from Kenya, the Cruiser was a right-hand-drive model and had seen heavy use. The AC system didn't work and the speedometer never rose off of zero. The odometer displayed 260,000 kilometers, but it didn't spin when Hale drove.

Yet the vehicle ran well, because that's what Land Cruisers do. Through war zones and natural disasters and some of the most punishing terrain on the planet. Hale had encountered them in Afghanistan, Africa, and Southeast Asia, and he trusted them as much as any man could trust anything man-made.

Bol the car dealer knew what he had and wanted fourteen grand—Hale haggled him down to eleven and filled the Cruiser at a roofless South Sudanese fuel station. Assuming five kilometers per liter, 150 liters of diesel should be enough to get Hale to Tambura.

Should be.

From the fuel station, Hale drove to the Radisson. Alone in his room he conducted a full inventory of his gear, double-checking each item for function before repacking them in the duffels.

His primary weapon—always a rifle—was an HK416 carbine chambered in 5.56 NATO. Designed with a piston recoil system in place of traditional direct impingement, the 416 was a favorite of Delta Force and Hale had learned to trust it through mud, blood, snow, and sleet. The Trijicon MRO optic, paired with a swing-mount magnifier and a SureFire weapon light only enhanced its performance, while seven fully loaded magazines stood ready to keep the rifle fed.

For a side arm, Hale had the HK VP9 with three seventeen-round magazines. Another Trijicon red dot rode the top of the pistol's rail, along with a weapon light mounted to the accessory rail.

Then there were the knives. In his pocket, the Benchmade Adamas. Locked horizontally in a Kydex sheath across his chest rig, a TOPS Knives Dawn Warrior with a razor edge. For emergency medical, Hale kept a trauma kit packed in the cargo pocket of his left leg. His backpack was loaded with survival supplies, dry food, a water filter, and the same camp stove and binoculars he'd used in The Bob.

It was a full combat load-out. Everything Hale needed and very little that he could live without. Enough to survive in the brush while unleashing limited but lethal force. Hale felt good about his gear—he knew it, understood it, and trusted it.

So why couldn't he shake the uneasiness eating at the back of his mind?

Hale repacked the gear and laid it by the bed before stretching out with the VP9 close to hand. He stared at a hotel ceiling speckled by water damage and breathed in easy cycles to prompt sleep.

To *stop* thinking—at least about how he felt. With barely nine hours remaining before Hale was scheduled to meet his coconut-eating guide, he needed to sleep. He needed to reset his mind and hone his focus.

Closing his eyes, he embraced the black.

Cannon fire rippled across the horizon.

Not artillery. Not rockets. Real cannons, slinging solid shot low and slow across packed New York farmland. Morning mist, fading under the autumn sun, couldn't obscure the crimson line. It broke through the haze at two hundred yards, a wall of blazing red marching in perfect unison, muskets gleaming.

"*Fix bayonets!*"

The order roared from the end of a shabbier line of men gathered just beyond the trees. Mismatched uniforms and boots with holes in them. One man wore a scarf wrapped around his skull, already stained in blood. Half the weapons weren't even military grade.

But the musket riding in Hale's hands was clean and loaded. He measured its weight while his heart slammed in his chest, flinching as a cannon ball slammed into a nearby oak. Limbs and splinters rained over the line. Somebody screamed. Hale got the bayonet out of its scabbard but couldn't get it locked onto his muzzle. Every time he rammed it down over the musket, his hand went right through as though the weapon had suddenly become an illusion. A mirage. The bayonet itself shattered under Hale's grip like a champagne flute dropped onto concrete.

"What are you *doing*?" the man next to him screamed.

"*Ready!*" The next order echoed down the line. Hale released bayonet shards and lifted the musket—it was solid again. He got his thumb on the flintlock hammer and cocked it. That wall of red was barely eighty yards away.

"*Aim!*"

Muskets locked into shoulders. Hale's head rocked behind his sights—little more than a brass pin at the tip of the muzzle, and the muzzle danced like heat waves in the desert. The wall of red stopped and the enemy made ready to fire. Hale blinked, searching for a target. Everything was blurry. He couldn't force his eyes to focus.

"*Fire!*"

Muskets rattled. Hale pulled the trigger but nothing happened. The musket turned to vapor again, his hands clamping around nothing. From fifty yards the enemy returned fire—all around Hale men pitched to the ground. The vapor musket slipped from his hands and Hale scrambled to collect it only to become tangled in a mass of American bodies.

Then horse hooves danced around him. A saber flashed. Hale looked into the eyes of a tall rider dressed in muddy blue, his bare head damp with sweat, his face...so familiar. He glared at Hale, teeth clenched. He spoke in a growl.

"*Useless!*"

And Hale fell. Straight through the ground, straight through the dark. The next thing he tasted was salt—it dripped from his face in a torrent, not sweat but ocean spray. Covered in sand, Hale was soaked to the bone, dressed in soggy green fatigues with a Browning 1911 pistol clutched in his right hand.

On every side was nothing but noise—men shrieking, guns thundering. Hale looked up a torn and bloody beach to a wall of sand dunes speckled with pill boxes. Between them, enemy soldiers dressed in dark gray rushed behind curls of barbed wire. He blinked and when he opened his eyes his face was drenched in blood—an American GI struck the ground next to him, his body shredded by bullets.

"*Hale!*" somebody screamed. "Hit that nest! Shut 'em down!"

Hale's gaze snapped left. An Army sergeant, dug into the sand along with half a dozen infantry, jerked his arm in a throwing motion. Hale followed the gesture and found the source of the emergency—a blazing machine gun with three gray uniforms gathered around it. Sandbags protected them. Hale saw little more than helmets. He fumbled with the 1911's safety, and the sergeant shouted again.

"*Grenade! Throw a grenade!*"

The words pounded in Hale's head as the pistol fell through his fingers. He slapped his chest and found a single fragmentation grenade clipped to a gear strap. Hale fumbled to unclip it as the machine gun swept again. Bullets tore the sand, zipping right over his head before ripping into the sergeant's position. One slug struck a soldier in his helmet and blew right through, hurling him back. The others pressed themselves closer into the ground but there was nowhere to hide.

"Throw it! Throw it *now*!" the sergeant screamed.

Hale yanked the pin, rising out of the sand. Winding back his arm just the way Uncle Sam had taught him. Estimating the range, releasing the spoon and hurling...

The grenade left his hand—and then stopped. Caught by the wind, it appeared suddenly weightless, just like the musket. It hung in midair just out of reach. Hale stared, transfixed by horror as the grenade blew backward—not toward him, but toward the sergeant. The machine gun snarled and another soldier hurtled to the ground, spraying blood. The grenade fell, landing at the sergeant's feet.

But the sergeant didn't reach for it. He looked straight at Hale instead—their gazes locked, and Hale's heart stopped. He recognized the face. He *knew* those eyes. They turned hard and angry just as Hale launched himself toward the grenade, ready to fall on it himself.

"*Useless!*" the sergeant shouted.

The grenade detonated. Screams and smoke blanketed everything. Hale was still diving and never stopped falling. He pitched through emptiness, the guns fading behind him as thunder took their place, a churn of rotors over a racing jet engine.

Hale hit the floor on his chest, the breath exploding from his lungs. Already he was sliding, flailing for something to cling to as the Black Hawk helicopter pitched and rolled beneath him. Hale tasted burning jet fuel. From the cockpit, alarms buzzed and an Army pilot shouted into his radio.

"*Down, down. Echo Niner-Eight is going down!*"

Black sky swirled. Hale's boots flew through an open side door as his hand caught on a tie-down ring. He was clinging to the spinning bird by only three fingers—he was losing his grip. Hale looked back into the chopper and suddenly the roar of the crashing bird vanished from the night.

Faces surrounded him. Battered and bleeding, some framed by helmets and others by a tricorn or kepi hat. All dirty, all blackened by smoke—and all with the same eyes. Passed from generation to generation, a heritage as violent and proud as the country they loved.

"Hale!" the nearest shouted. "Why are you so *useless*?"

It was the last question, the last word. Before Hale could even think to answer, his fingers broke from the floor of the chopper. He hurtled into the night.

The dark swallowed him once more, and the helicopter struck the ground in a starburst of flame.

Hale sat upright in bed, chest heaving and arms shaking. He blinked and the chopper was gone. The faces were gone. The Radisson Blu Hotel took their place, beige walls and a bed covered in tangled sheets. Hale looked to his hands and half expected to see blood—smoke stains and grit.

His palms and fingers were clean, but trembling. He closed them and swallowed, still panting. The dream had been so vivid that he could still smell the crisp New York air at the Battle of Saratoga—the salt spray at Normandy. The burning jet fuel as Echo Niner-Eight pitched to the ground...

All gone in a moment. None of it real, at least not the way he'd seen it.

But the screams? The desperate orders? Those were real.

Why are you so useless?

Hale closed his eyes and clenched his teeth. The question echoed in his mind, but it was no longer his ancestors who asked.

It was Hale himself.

24

Juba, South Sudan
06:00 Hours, East Africa Time

Hale's guide was as good as his word.

With the sun cresting the African horizon, Hale found the little man standing beside his milk crates, worn sandals strapped to his feet and a faded Nike backpack printed with "NEW ENGLAND PATRIOTS—SUPER BOWL LII CHAMPIONS" slung over one shoulder.

Hale stopped the Cruiser, and the guide climbed in. He placed the backpack in the floorboard, but instead of sitting, he squatted in the seat just the way he'd squatted next to the milk crates the day prior, his knees drawn up to his chin and one long finger scratching behind his ear.

"I never got your name," Hale said.

"I am Tito."

"Like the vodka?"

"The what?"

"Never mind. Do you have everything you need?"

Tito's only reply came as a grunt. Hale sighed, resting a hand on the shifter. "Well, don't you want to know *my* name?"

Tito appeared half asleep with his eyes closed. "I already know your name, Kawaja."

"Kawaja?" Hale squinted. "What does that mean?"

Tito smirked just a little, his eyes still closed. "White guy."

Hale stared, not sure whether to laugh or roll his eyes or eject Tito back to his milk crates on reasons of insanity.

In the end he only sighed—because what else was he going to do? He still needed a guide. Tito was still his best option.

And Hale was, in fact, a white guy.

"Okay, Tito. So which way?"

"West, Kawaja. When you reach the grasslands, wake me."

They barely made it out of Juba before the rain began.

At first it was barely a shower, but Hale's first warning that something worse was in store came from Tito, who wound up his window without comment or explanation. Minutes later, the deluge arrived.

Pouring down. Pounding on the Cruiser's roof and flooding cracks in the busted pavement. Hale wound his own window up, half his body already soaked, and leaned low to squint down the highway. The windshield fogged, and without climate control, Hale was left to use a spare T-shirt to clear it. He wrestled the Cruiser around ruts and potholes, the traffic around him rapidly fading as Juba vanished.

They rode along the A43 Highway, northwest to Kenyi. Clusters of slouching shacks were quickly replaced by rolling fields covered in thick grass and sporadic brush. Hale saw cattle—knots of them, grazing beneath the rainfall with tails flicking and horned heads occasionally shaking like dogs. The highway, once a four-lane, tightened down to a two-lane as its surface worsened by orders of magnitude.

Potholes the size of small cars. Ruts so deep Hale worried about scraping the Land Cruiser's undercarriage. Chunks of broken asphalt just begging to pierce tires. Visibility reduced to barely fifty yards.

It was a mess, and just when Hale thought the highway couldn't get any worse...it turned to dirt.

"You will want the four-wheel drive," Tito said.

He remained squatted in the passenger seat, moving easily with the jolts of the road, his eyes usually closed. Hale shot him a sideways look, but didn't argue. The Cruiser's transfer lever shifted with a satisfying *chunk* of shifting metal, and then they were off again, slower this time.

Passing onto the mud, all four tires grabbed as the diesel engine strained. Hale downshifted as necessary to manage the ruts with increased torque, jarred from one side of his seat to the other. Feeling like they were crawling, barely inching westward.

Would it be *this* bad the entire way?

"Did you go to the game?" Tito said suddenly.

"What?"

Tito shook his backpack by one strap. Hale's gaze settled on the Super Bowl logo. He shook his head.

"No."

"Did you watch it on TV?"

Hale frowned, trying to remember which game Super Bowl LII had been. As a Patriots fan, he remembered many Super Bowls...He just couldn't keep up with the Roman numerals.

"Who did they play?"

"The Eagles?" Tito said it like a question.

Hale scratched a cheek—then he remembered. "Yeah, I watched it. New England lost...Thanks for reminding me."

"Lost?" Tito reached for the backpack, examining the Patriots championship design.

Hale sighed. "They print gear for both teams ahead of time so they can sell it immediately after the game. The loser's gear goes to...well."

Hale didn't have the heart to say *places like this*, even though that was exactly the truth. Tito studied his backpack a moment longer, wiping smudges of dirt with wide thumbs. Then he replaced it in the floorboard and folded his arms, as though Hale's claims personally offended him.

Surveying the sky through his window, Hale found swirling gray clouds so thick that only trace amounts of sunlight filtered through. Barely enough to see by.

"I thought the rainy season ended in November," he said.

Tito grunted. "I thought the Patriots won the Super Bowl."

Hale wasn't sure what to say to that, so he said nothing. Forced to downshift yet again, they slowed to barely thirty kilometers an hour—a snail's pace.

"We should make good time today," Tito said. "It is two hundred kilometers to the start of Western Equatoria. The roads are good that far."

"Good?" Hale said. "This is *good*?"

Tito only smiled—a tight, humorless expression. Outside, lightning flashed, and Hale saw another pothole coming. Ten yards across, already flooded. There was no way around it—existing tire tracks appeared on the far side.

Hale dropped another gear and plowed ahead.

25

Western Equatoria, South Sudan
12:15 Hours, East Africa Time

Lado Bakumba was ready to drop.

He had walked all night—slept all day curled beneath an acacia tree, sweating and panting and thirsty...and then walked all night again.

At first his progress was steady. His empty stomach bothered him, but he found a wild mango tree with a couple of late-season fruits undiscovered by birds or monkeys. The mangos were mushy, verging on rot, but they were better than being hungry.

His real problem was hydration. After emptying the water bottle in his backpack, Bakumba had no choice but to refill it from a muddy stream, and that was dangerous. There could be diseases in the water. Bacteria, perhaps parasites. Bakumba wouldn't know for hours or days after drinking, but what choice did he have?

If he didn't drink, he'd die for sure. The water tasted bad, but he got it down. He kept moving, fighting past the growing agony in his arm as his skin turned purple and swelled. The smell was terrible, and Bakumba worried about infection.

If he could just make it back to Juba, everything would be okay. He could collect his money and see a doctor. It would all be worth it.

Then the storm arrived. Sometime just after sunrise, it began as a shower and then it became an hours-long torrent. At first refreshing, it cooled Bakumba's skin. He held his mouth open as he walked, savoring the naturally clean water. When lightning startled him from not far away, he dashed for cover beneath an acacia tree...

Only to have the next flash of lightning literally strike the tree. An ear-piercing blast temporarily deafened him, timber cracking as Bakumba scrambled to escape. His right foot sank into a collapsing mole-rat tunnel, and he nearly fell. He pulled his leg free just as the next detonation of thunder shook the earth.

Then he *did* fall. Toppling sideways, sliding through grass and landing on a hillside. Bakumba rolled over the pack and over his makeshift sling, pain exploding through his unprotected arm as mud coated his face and hands and he just kept falling.

Down—hundreds of meters right to the bottom of the slope where Bakumba crashed headfirst into a riverbed. It was already flooded by the storm. Water surged over his head and Bakumba went under. He gasped for air as his face broke the surface, only to be sucked down once more.

Bakumba was swept downstream—way downstream as periodic lightning revealed open brushlands on every side. He saw antelope sheltering beneath trees. They stared at him as he rushed past, flailing with one arm and diving toward the bank.

But he carried on. Another kilometer, maybe more, *knowing* that he would die. That after everything, this was the end.

Then Lado Bakumba was thrown onto a muddy bank. Ejected like a bent soup can that a child had tired of kicking, he landed so hard that the breath rushed from his lungs. Staring at a sky thick with clouds and still cracking with thunder.

But no...

The thunder Bakumba heard was sharper than the voice of the thunderstorm. It was closer, also...and constant. Mixed with faint screams.

Bakumba rolled, landing on his wounded arm and fighting back a scream of his own. The world danced around him—he vomited up river water and smashed his face into the mud. When he lifted his head, he heard the thunder again, a constant roar.

It was the voice of a Dushka heavy machine gun.

Panic took over—all Bakumba could think about was finding a place to hide. With rain splashing on all sides, it was impossible to tell where the gunfire originated. It felt like it was all around him, like at any moment hot lead would tear through his body. Blackness would overcome him.

Focus, Lado! Find cover!

He ascended the riverbank. Clawing through mud and brush, dragging his swollen arm. The backpack caught on passing thorns, and not for the first time since being shot, he wanted to abandon the camera and forget about the entire mission.

But if he did that, all this misery would be in vain.

Bakumba reached the top of the bank. A wall of elephant grass greeted him, offering concealment. Bakumba wriggled inside, spitting blood from a busted lip. He thought the thunder of the Dushka had faded...

Then Bakumba broke through the grass, and immediately froze. Lying on his stomach, he looked down a gentle slope to a clearing obscured by smoke—despite the rain, a half dozen huts burned. Bakumba smelled gasoline and smoldering tires. Fresh panic rushed his chest as he saw the bodies...

And the soldiers.

26

Western Equatoria, South Sudan
12:28 Hours, East Africa Time

Hale and Tito crossed into Western Equatoria after six hours of slogging along flooded roads.

Twice, the Cruiser got stuck. The first time, Hale managed to reverse his way out. The second time, he had to deploy the winch, lashing it to a roadside tree and fighting the driving rain. Back on the road, he avoided ruts by rolling right down the middle, riding at barely twenty KPH with Tito still squatted in the passenger's seat, calling out occasional turns but otherwise remaining silent.

As the clock reached noon, the rain finally slackened. Hale surveyed sweeping vistas of rolling bushland—just like a postcard photo, but so much more raw. It reached straight to the horizon, tall grass and low scrub brush beaten by the wind, sporadic clusters of acacia trees sheltering herds of white-eared kobs—antelope—and occasional knots of buffalo. Once, Hale even saw a pair of elephants strolling with ears flapping, impervious to the storm.

It was picturesque, but Hale didn't trust the serenity for a millisecond. Occasional abandoned vehicles, left beside the road with flattened tires and shattered glass, told a more sinister story of this place. There were villages, also. Compact settlements with only three or four huts each, usually constructed near streams or patches of forest.

But the villages were empty. Many of their huts were burned. Others stood with doors open to vacant blackness, and most ominous of all, some were scarred by bullet holes.

While passing one such village, Hale noticed Tito surveying the spectacle. He looked unbelievably somber.

"Dinka," Tito said.

"What?"

"It is the Dinka who do this," Tito clarified.

The Cruiser jolted, drawing Hale's attention back to the road. He wrestled the vehicle through another rut, adding power as a cascade of muddy water crashed over the hood.

"Is that a militia?" Hale said.

"They are a people," Tito clarified. "Cattle herders from Sudan. They take what is not theirs, and the government protects them. It is because they are rich. Because cows are *money*."

Tito's voice turned cold as he spoke—as cutting as a surgeon's scalpel.

"Do the Dinka fight for James Wani?" Hale said.

Tito snorted. "They fight for whoever will make them more rich."

The conversation died as the Cruiser rounded a curve, and Hale identified a Y-shaped intersection in the road ahead. He slowed, waiting for Tito to indicate a turn, but his guide wasn't looking at the road. He was looking off into the hills, his eyes suddenly squinted, his nostrils flexing.

"Which way?" Hale said.

Tito didn't answer. Hale brought the Cruiser to a stop while Tito fixated on the hills, his body perfectly still.

"What is it?" Hale pressed.

"Smoke," Tito said. "Fresh."

Hale didn't smell anything. He bent his head and looked out Tito's window. All he saw were trees, tangled brush, some good grazing land but no wildlife…

Then Hale heard it. A faint snarl, too sharp to be thunder. It came and then it faded and then it returned again. Short bursts, classic technique.

Hale killed the engine and listened again, wondering if he'd imagined the sound.

When the snarl resumed, he was certain. Even over the rattle of rain on the roof, he made out the measured *thump, thump, thump* of large-caliber rounds erupting from a wide muzzle—brass casings falling in a shower.

Heavy fire.

Hale fired up the Cruiser and wrenched the shifter into reverse. Four tires spun as they bounded backward, heading for the shelter of overhanging acacia limbs. It wasn't perfect cover, but it felt better than the open road. Hale backed the Cruiser beneath the umbrella limbs of the acacia and cut the motor once more. For twenty long seconds he heard nothing but rain and the distant roll of thunder—real thunder.

Then another burst. Not the heavy machine gun fire of before but a shorter, sharper pop of an AK-47. From someplace to the north beyond a range of low hills, a scream tore the air.

"Dinka," Tito said. Hale glanced his way and found the little African squatting rigid in the seat. He didn't appear startled, but laser focused.

"We should go," Tito said. "They may flee by the road."

Hale had already thought of that. Pushing the door open, he landed up to his ankles in thick mud. The air, nearly sauna-like with humidity, was so still that Hale felt like he was underwater. The gunfire was fading, shorter bursts growing more sporadic.

The scream had faded, also.

Reaching the Cruiser's rear door, Hale snatched the zipper on the first of his duffel bags. The contents, already organized for quick access, deployed in two segments.

First was his plate carrier/chest rig. Loaded with spare magazines, the TOPS Dawn Warrior, and a SureFire Tactician handheld light. It slammed against Hale's chest and he affixed the side straps.

"What are you doing?" Tito hissed. "We should go!"

Hale heard him, and Hale knew better. The road wasn't safe while any sort of firefight roared nearby. It was the first place fleeing militia would run to, and anyone they encountered would be sitting ducks.

Hale reached back into the bag and produced the HK416 rifle. One pull of the charging handle pumped a green-tipped round of 5.56 ammunition into the chamber.

"Stay here," Hale said. "Lie low and don't make a sound. I'll be back."

"*Kawaja!* This is not a good idea—"

"Stay here!" Hale repeated.

Then he seated the rifle into his shoulder and sprinted up the first hill.

27

Hale tasted diesel fumes first.

Oily and thick, they reminded him of tank or heavy truck fumes as thorn bushes dragged against his tear-resistant combat pants. Hale's face dripped with sweat as he ran. Humidity hung around him like a cloud—every passing branch was heavy with water. In mere yards Hale was soaked, his breath coming in damp gasps as he crested the hill and shrank into a crouch, surrounded by elephant grass.

Spread beneath him were miles of brushland/forest blend, vacant of wildlife and feeling completely hollow...except for the village that burned alongside a distant winding river.

Four huts, all on fire. Hale deployed the three-times magnifier behind his red dot optic and settled his head against the HK's stock. He steadied the rifle and softened his breathing, sweeping the village...

And almost immediately finding the bodies. Maybe twenty in total, twisted and bloodied on the ground, apparently shot to death. One of them lay with his arm nearly blown off, no doubt the work of the heavy machine gun Hale had heard—sweeping and then re-sweeping its targets.

But these were no targets at all. They were civilians, unarmed and helpless. They lay abandoned in the mud while in the distance, driving away from Hale, two vehicles bounced along a rough trail.

The first was a heavy truck, rolling on six wheels with a canvas-covered bed. Even at a thousand yards Hale easily identified it as a Ural-type general purpose military vehicle—the Russian equivalent of the American deuce and a half. It wasn't the first time he'd seen such vehicles in use outside the Russian military. They were prevalent across war-torn nations like South Sudan—Russia would sell to just about anyone.

Pivoting the magnifier one inch, Hale settled over the second vehicle. It was a Land Cruiser pickup, but to Hale's mind it was a "technical"—a civilian vehicle modified for military use, and often mounted with a weapon system. In this case the weapon was a heavy machine gun, probably the same heavy machine gun that had mown down those villagers.

Hale watched the two vehicles fade, blowing sweat and rain from his lips. In another few moments they would be out of sight, lost in a thick patch of forest.

A lightning attack. Bodies left to rot. Trucks hurtling into the early afternoon haze.

Why?

Movement caught Hale's eye before he could generate a hypothesis. It came from about fifty yards east of the burning village. He recentered the magnifier and recognized the silhouette of a man crawling out of the grass, headed toward the village. He moved in little jerks, like a wounded animal clawing its way out of the mud. Hale couldn't tell where he was headed, or if he was armed. He seemed to be carrying something...maybe a bag?

Once again Hale's thought process was derailed by fresh activity. This time not from the crawling man but from the forest beyond the village. Hale swept the rifle toward the horizon...

And found the enemy technical. It was returning to the village.

28

Western Equatoria, South Sudan
12:58 Hours, East Africa Time

Bakumba filmed the entire attack.

Nestled in the grass, he panned the Sony camera as the gunmen split the villagers into two groups—children and adults, just as before. The huts were already burning, the women sobbing and screaming. One of the men fought back with his bare hands and was beaten to death with rifle butts.

The gunmen laughed. They jeered. They looked exactly like the crew that had assaulted the village where Bakumba was shot...except these guys all wore jackets with patches on the arm. Some kind of insignia?

Bakumba couldn't tell. He guided the camera, heart pounding, as the children were thrown into the back of a six-wheeled truck. A mother made a desperate lunge for her daughter—then the soldiers opened fire. AK-47s and the machine gun mounted over the bed of the second truck poured lead while screams ripped the air. A few victims tried to run.

None escaped. Bakumba filmed it all, raw adrenaline masking the misery of his swollen arm. He was terrified, frozen, panicked, *thrilled*. He focused the camera on faces, both those of the gunmen and those of their victims, ignoring a flashing *low battery* alert.

The attack was already over. Children screamed for their parents, but nobody answered. Two gunmen climbed into the cab of the six-wheeled truck, and two more climbed into the back with the children. The final four soldiers loaded into the pickup. Tires spun and engines raced. Bakumba filmed their retreat, his heart still hammering from the demonstration of unthinkable violence.

Now that it was over, he felt pretty amazing. It was kind of a rush.

The camera beeped, jarring Bakumba out of his survivor's high. The battery was on its last leg, but that was okay. Bakumba had more than enough footage—he should get back on the road.

But then again...the masked man wanted journalism. That was what he claimed, right? He wanted *the truth*. Bakumba had filmed the attack from a hundred yards and the picture seemed clear enough, but why not get closer now that the gunmen had cleared out? Why not film the bodies?

That might be worth something extra—*a bonus*.

Bakumba sloshed through a muddy ditch, still enjoying the pain-muting benefits of adrenaline. He mashed the record button as he reached the first body. It was a woman, and she was a mess—the Dushka had chewed her from head to toe. He focused on her lifeless eyes, then moved to the next victim, his own body alive with nervous energy.

He could barely believe what he was looking at. What he was doing. How *insane* this all was. Stepping over bodies, Bakumba breathed in shallow cycles, his eyes burning in the smoke. He'd almost reached the center of the village.

Then he heard it. Low over the horizon, at first obscured amid the crackle of a burning hut, but then clarifying. It was the rush of a surging engine. Bakumba's face snapped up, his body freezing in sudden panic.

The Toyota pickup with the swivel gun exploded over a hilltop, headed straight for the village. Bakumba saw it, and he knew the gunmen saw him.

He threw himself toward the brush just as the machine gun opened fire.

29

Western Equatoria, South Sudan
13:06 Hours, East Africa Time

Hale sprinted.

Down the hillside and through the brush. Carrying the rifle across his chest and tracing the path of the technical as it descended toward the burning village.

Whoever the survivor was, his luck had run out. Long before he saw the oncoming truck, Hale watched him enter the village. Standing over bodies, he seemed to examine them. He swept them with some handheld device. A camera?

It didn't matter. The disaster was already unfolding. Hale hurtled down the hill even as the survivor finally saw the oncoming truck. Through passing acacia limbs Hale watched the muzzle of the Dushka turn. A burst of angry fire ripped across the torched village.

The bullets missed. The survivor, temporarily sheltered by smoke, was lunging toward the brush, but the technical had almost reached the village. Hale sprinted another eighty yards, legs stretching as his heart hammered. Sweat streamed down his face and smoke stung his eyes. He ground to a halt at the tree line and braced the HK against the trunk of another acacia.

The technical stopped also, sliding in the mud. Forty yards from its target, two hundred yards from Hale. Everyone on board was shouting. The gunman was loading a fresh ammunition belt, working the bolt. Sweeping his gun.

Hale breathed. Slow and steady, flicking the 416 to semiautomatic mode. Closing his left eye and leveling the red dot under the aid of the magnifier. Selecting his target, curling his trigger finger.

The gunman wrapped his hands around the Dushka's twin grips. He bent forward as he fought to look through the smoke...

Then Hale sent a bullet tearing through his right temple—just behind the eye, straight into the brain. The body pitched sideways and the Dushka went off, hurling rounds into empty air.

Hale's finger had already relaxed just enough for the competition trigger to reset. He was pivoting for the next target, squinting through the haze.

Then somebody—probably the driver—realized what had happened. The engine surged and the technical disappeared behind a burning hut. Hale jerked away from the tree, on the move once more. Grass tore at his chest rig as he ran stooped, the HK held at eye level. He couldn't see anything but smoke and the burned-out hulks of huts. The gunmen couldn't see him, either. He was confident of that.

But they engaged anyway. Somebody regained control of the Dushka, and no doubt judging by the angle from which the last operator had been shot, they picked a direction of fire and clamped down on the trigger.

Hale hit the mud. Thorn brush tore at his sleeves as heavy Russian rounds split the air. The thunder of the gun was ceaseless. With no concern for overheating the weapon, the new operator poured rounds through the brush and trees seemingly at random, most landing yards from Hale's position.

Hale didn't wait for the shooter to adjust fire. He scrambled on his stomach, tacking northwest toward the nearest burning hut. The smoke it belched would obscure his position until he was nearly on top of the technical. If the driver had any sense at all, he would move.

He didn't. Hale closed a hundred yards and returned to his feet with the rifle at the ready. Circling the burning hut, he gained speed, still closing on the technical. He could make out its rear bumper through the smoke. He traced the outline of the machine gunner and lifted the rifle.

Pop, pop, pop!

The HK barked and the guy pitched forward, shot through the head, neck, and spine. The Dushka fell silent and the technical's engine roared, reverse lights glaring. The driver cut the wheel hard to the left, swinging the passenger's side window around—already Hale could see the AK muzzle poking out.

Hale opened fire. Bullets broke through the pickup's rear glass and blew out the windshield with a spray of crimson. The truck kept coming even as the rifle fell from the window—only the driver was still alive, and he kept his foot jammed into the accelerator. The technical shot behind another burning hut, gone before Hale could identify a target. His eyes streamed under the sting of the smoke. It burned his lungs.

Keep moving.

Hale sprinted again. Not deeper into the village, but back into the grass, conducting a combat reload to lock a full thirty rounds into his rifle.

The truck was still running but no longer moving. It sat obscured by smoke and dwindling flame. Hale could make out the muzzle of the Dushka pointed toward the sky, one bloodied body overhanging the side of the truck bed. He thought the driver's door might be open...

Then the AK opened up. From beyond the technical, firing over its hood. The blink of muzzle flash was lost in the hut fire, but Hale could map the sound of each ear-splitting crack. He dashed deeper into the brush, conscious that the moment the shooter detected movement he would adjust his point of aim. He would sweep left, turning toward the open brushlands...

Hale beat him to it. He reached the back of the truck just as the shooter saw him. The AK withdrew from the pickup's hood. The shooter snatched it right—already too late.

Hale fired as he ran, driving rounds to center mass before stitching upward—collar, neck, face. The guy fell even as Hale continued firing. By the time he reached the truck the gunman lay lifeless with six different holes drilled through his torso, wide eyes staring up to heaven.

Hale cleared the truck's cab, sweeping the blown-out rear glass, then the side window—also shot out. One body lay inside, and two more lay in the truck bed. All three were bloodied and lifeless. Mounted above them, the Dushka was still piping hot, the midsection of its barrel cherry red.

But nobody was left to fire it. Even as Hale's ears rang, the battlefield around him grew still. Smoke boiled from the burning huts, but the core of the village was silent. Everywhere he turned, bodies lay twisted.

And yet, Hale could feel it. He could sense life, somewhere in the haze. The lone survivor was still a survivor.

Hale edged through the muck, identifying a trail. It led him to the edge of the village. Another ten yards, and he found a bush broken on one side. A shadow that shouldn't have been there.

Hale spoke in calm English. "Show yourself, or I'll shoot."

It was a promise, and it was received as such. A silhouette moved. Slowly, a figure crept out of the shadows, one hand raised. He was tall, black, and his left arm was held in a makeshift sling rigged out of a pair of pants. A backpack rode his good shoulder. A sweat rag wrapped his skull. Hale saw no weapons on him.

He was quaking, dark gaze flicking from the bodies to the still-chugging technical, and at last to Hale.

But it was Hale who spoke first.

"Who are you?"

30

Atlanta, Georgia
05:38 Hours, Eastern Standard Time

This time the call didn't wake Shaw—she had been up since four thirty sharp, running six miles on a hotel treadmill before showering in cold water and chugging a protein shake.

It wasn't her regular morning routine—the calisthenic torture that kept her body pounded into shape despite her proclivity for ultra sweet drinks. But given the circumstances, it would have to do.

At the first chime of the phone, Shaw reached for her cell before Avril could really get going. It was Bill Carpenter calling—Shaw didn't hesitate to answer.

"Hello?"

"Laney, sorry to call so early. I hope I didn't wake you."

Shaw chugged water, wishing it were an iced coffee. "I was already up. What's going on?"

"Mary Grace emailed. She wants to discuss further aid drops. Of course she knows that we've deployed a security professional, but based on the tone of her email, she's no more interested in evacuating than before. We've scheduled a call. I thought, maybe..."

Carpenter trailed off. Shaw filled in the gaps.

"You want me to join."

"She trusts you, Shaw. An outside voice might be helpful."

Shaw wasn't sure if Mary Grace trusted her or not—nor could Shaw blame her. Shaw's stomach still squirmed when she thought about the car wreck, the fallout…her abandonment of the "new" MG.

But that wasn't the point. Carpenter had asked for help, and Shaw would do what she could. She would do anything to help protect Mary Grace.

"When's the call?" Shaw said.

"Half an hour."

"I'll see you then."

"Thank you, Laney."

Shaw hung up, running the math to consider what time it must be at the orphanage in Tambura. Nearly two p.m., right? Early afternoon.

And what about Ian?

Shaw reached for her laptop to see if Hale had transmitted any updates via his satellite-phone-linked iPad. The last she had from him was a brief "*headed east*," time stamped for seven hours prior. She shot off a quick "*sitrep?*" then reached for her shoes.

Just before her gaze left the computer screen, it snagged on an incoming email from an address she recognized. An old contact from her Sentinel days—a "regional affairs analyst" for the Central Intelligence Agency.

Shaw had long suspected that Nolan O'Rourke's actual role wasn't limited by region and had nothing to do with affairs—at least, not the public relations kind. Their paths first crossed while Shaw was scrambling to mitigate a mushrooming disaster in Ho Chi Minh City—a four-man Sentinel team that had inadvertently collided with a heavily armed Vietnamese crime ring.

The bloodshed was monumental. One of Shaw's guys was killed in action, and the rest couldn't stack bodies fast enough. On the run through the city, kicking down doors and terrorizing civilians, Shaw was 98 percent sure that the Ho Chi Minh mission might be the end of her career—if not the end of Sentinel.

Then O'Rourke called. Out of the blue, just a calm voice on the other end of a blocked number. He introduced himself as a regional affairs analyst and offered to assist with "the situation." Shaw was just desperate enough to agree, and what happened next was both totally unexpected and totally unexplained.

The Vietnamese gang bangers pulled back. An unmarked SUV screamed into the parking garage of the abandoned hospital where her men were hiding out. Twenty minutes later they were outside the city and boarding a King Air 350—also unmarked—for the sixty-minute flight to Phnom Penh, Cambodia.

No questions asked, no payment requested. According to her men, the pilots never spoke, and nobody from Vietnam ever came knocking at Sentinel's door. The body of their slain operator was even returned... draped in an American flag.

Shaw owed Nolan O'Rourke. She wasn't sure what he'd done or why, but she was confident her men never would have escaped Vietnam without him. She and O'Rourke never spoke of the incident, but they did speak—semi-often.

O'Rourke would call Shaw asking about ongoing Sentinel missions around the world. He always seemed to know as much about the placement of Sentinel operators as Shaw herself, and he almost never attempted to interfere. He just wanted to know things—often odd, seemingly irrelevant details about local governments, militias, warlords, or anybody else Shaw's teams might have encountered. O'Rourke was a curious fellow, and he wasn't stingy with his own knowledge. He often returned the favor, assisting Shaw with details of operational zones from the Arctic Circle to Madagascar.

Were they friends? More like symbiotic organisms swimming in the same putrid petri dish. Shaw never pressured O'Rourke on his true status with the Agency, and he never volunteered the information. When Shaw began her research on the situation in South Sudan, Nolan O'Rourke was one of the first people she contacted.

Inside her email, she found only two words: *Signal, call.*

No surprise. This was O'Rourke's usual method of communication. The messaging and calling app, Signal, was far from perfect but it was unquestionably superior to naked wireless communication.

Shaw found the contact and dialed.

"Shaw. What's kicking?"

Despite never meeting O'Rourke in person, Shaw had a picture of him based on his rumbling voice. She thought he was probably big, probably an ex-football player. He kept his hair short but not necessarily in a crew cut. She didn't get ex-military vibes from O'Rourke—she thought it more likely that he was a bright student at a good college and got picked up by the Agency right after graduation. With some special talent that landed him in the operations directorate, who knew how his career had blossomed from there.

"I'm good, Nolan. Thanks for calling."

"Sure. What's up in South Sudan?"

The question came a little more abruptly than Shaw expected. She leaned back in her chair, debating how many cards she should hold...then deciding that there was no reason to hold any. This wasn't a covert operation. This was a rescue op—something that any human being with a heartbeat should support.

"I'm helping a friend," Shaw said. "She runs an orphanage in Western Equatoria. It's gotten hot. I sent an old colleague of mine from the private security industry to offer her some aid. Now I'm trying to unpack exactly what's going on and whether I should pull them both out."

A grunt. Shaw thought she heard traffic. O'Rourke was driving.

"Let me simplify the debate," O'Rourke said. "Get them out. Both of them. Right now."

Shaw sat up, her spine tingling. It wasn't just O'Rourke's tone, it was his directness. She never recalled him offering such blunt advice.

"What do I need to know?" Shaw said.

"Just what I told you. Pull your people out and send nobody back in. I'd recommend an air lift, if available. At worst, try to get them into Uganda."

"Wait," Shaw squinted. "*Uganda?* What are you talking about?"

Brakes squealed. Somebody honked. At last, O'Rourke sighed.

"Look. This is off the record, okay? After you emailed I made some phone calls. Western Equatoria is on fire. I'm talking masses of civilian refugees crossing the border into the Central African Republic and Congo. Widespread tribal violence, mostly at the hands of some upstart warlord. James Wakki...Wunki..."

"Wani," Shaw said.

"Yeah, that prick. He's made a mess, and it's only getting worse."

"Worse how?" Shaw pressed.

"Worse like he'll burn the whole place down to get what he wants, and what he wants is total control of Western Equatoria. More, if he can get it. He's got a real bone to pick with the government in Juba—the usual freedom fighter nonsense. *You're corrupt, so move over and let me be corrupt instead.* That kind of thing."

Shaw knew—she'd seen it all around the planet, including in her own backyard. It wasn't news that Wani was a problem. Still, O'Rourke's abruptness was unsettling, to say the least. It left her wondering what was really going on. How an entire region, unstable though it may be, could have turned nuclear so quickly.

"Hey, Nolan," Shaw said. "You hear anything about coltan in Western Equatoria?"

Short pause. "Col-what?"

"Coltan. It's a metallic ore—pretty valuable, apparently. They use it in computer components or something. Anyway, a large deposit of the stuff was apparently discovered in Western Equatoria earlier this year. I just wondered if that might have anything to do with the spike in violence."

Shaw didn't specify that the discovery of aforementioned coltan had been the first domino to fall in a chain that had nearly gotten both herself and Hale killed. A chain that had run from South Sudan and across Serbia to Berlin and eventually right back to Boston.

A chain that resulted in Sentinel's ultimate demise...to say nothing of the demise of Sentinel's owner. That was information O'Rourke didn't need.

"First I've heard of it," O'Rourke said. "You say it was just discovered?"

"Uh-huh."

Pause. O'Rourke muttered a curse about another driver. Then: "Listen, Shaw. These people are always killing each other. That's why they have so many orphans. All I can tell you is that it's getting worse, and if you don't get your people out of there, you might bring them home in body bags. Sorry to be so macabre, but that's how it looks."

Shaw considered for another moment, then sighed. "Thanks, Nolan. Call me if you hear more."

"Sure thing."

O'Rourke hung up. Shaw blinked and her computer clock clarified. It was fifteen minutes until the scheduled call with Mary Grace—no time for an iced coffee on the way. Barely enough time to run the three blocks to the Hurt Building.

With a fresh Braves T-shirt and Bulldogs ball cap, the laptop folded beneath one arm, Shaw headed for the elevator.

31

Western Equatoria, South Sudan
13:48 Hours, East Africa Time

Staring up the length of a black rifle into the dark eyes of the white man who held it, there was zero doubt in Bakumba's mind that one wrong word would be the end of his life.

"I asked you a question." The soldier's voice remained calm. Bakumba thought his accent was American, but he couldn't be sure. The man hadn't asked if Bakumba spoke English—even now he was assuming. In fact, Bakumba did speak English, just like most South Sudanese who had ever lived in Juba. He could play dumb, and maybe that could be helpful...

Or maybe he shouldn't test the patience of a man who had effortlessly destroyed *four* militiamen.

"Lado," Bakumba choked. "My name is Lado Bakumba. Please don't shoot."

The guy didn't move, he didn't relax. He kept the gun zeroed on Bakumba's forehead.

"Why are you here, Lado? Why were they trying to kill you, and what's in the bag? Answer quickly."

"They're raiders," Bakumba said. "They wanted me dead because I'm a journalist. I have a camera!"

It was the first explanation that came to him—something that should generate sympathy. Didn't all Americans love journalists? It was mostly journalists who visited South Sudan—people to take pictures of suffering Africans.

Bakumba reached for the backpack, ready to prove his story with the revelation of the camera. The muzzle of the rifle nearly rammed his eye out.

"*Stop.*"

Bakumba froze, that gaping hole of death hovering millimeters from his face.

"One hand only," the man said. "Open it up."

The man named Bakumba trembled as he followed Hale's command.

The bag was filthy, stained with mud and traces of blood. It wasn't heavily loaded, but still might contain a handgun or a grenade. Even a knife could be a problem—Hale was uncomfortably close to his subject. Ideally, he'd stand back.

But something in his gut told him that this guy needed to be watched like a hawk. Up close, not allowing him any breathing room.

The zipper slid. Hale instructed Bakumba to dump the bag. One water bottle joined a muddy pair of socks wrapped around...

A camera. Compact, robust, built for filming outdoor adventures. It was covered in mud, like everything else.

"Give it to me," Hale said.

Bakumba passed off the device—Hale accepted it with his left hand, keeping his right wrapped around the HK's pistol grip. He mashed buttons, but the camera's screen remained black. Maybe the battery was dead.

Hale turned back to Bakumba. "Do you know who they were?"

He tilted his head toward the still-chugging technical. Bakumba shook his head.

"You filmed them sacking this village?" Hale continued.

A nod.

"And they shot you?"

Hale jutted his chin toward Bakumba's swollen arm. Bakumba swallowed.

"In another village."

"You filmed that, also?"

Another nod. Hale measured the depth of his gaze, searching for indicators of deceit. Bakumba looked sincere enough, but Hale had been fooled before.

Slowly, he stepped back. He lowered the rifle and glanced around the village. It still swirled with smoke. The bodies of the men Hale had shot lay limp alongside the villagers they had murdered.

A slaughter-fest…and yet something was missing. Many of the villagers who lay twisted and mangled around their burned-out huts were middle-aged—child-rearing age.

And yet there were no children. Not anywhere.

"You move, and I shoot," Hale said.

He kept Bakumba in his peripheral as he returned to the bullet-ridden technical. There were glass bottles on the floor. Lots of empty AK-47 brass. Blood that had drained from the gunshot passenger. Nothing else of note.

Hale inspected the bed, sweeping each body…and stopping.

There was something on their arms—both of them. The jackets didn't match but the cloth patches stitched to their sleeves did. The design featured some kind of long-legged bird with one foot lifted. It stood atop twin palm fronds that bent around a star, a crescent moon, and a heart.

Above the fronds was stitched the word: *Lord's.* Beneath the fronds the patch read: *Resistance Army.*

Digging into his pocket, Hale produced his cell phone and powered it on. There was no signal, of course, but the camera still worked. He snapped a picture.

Then he turned back for Bakumba, squishing through the mud. He stopped directly over him, lowering the rifle's muzzle over Bakumba's chest.

Then he said: "What was in the other truck?"

32

Hale walked behind Bakumba on the way back to the Cruiser. The rain had finally stopped, but the ground was pure muck. It sucked around Hale's boots as he held the rifle in low ready, still watching Bakumba like a hawk.

One glance over his shoulder was enough to confirm that the technical was history. A column of smoke marked the gasoline fire that Hale had used to torch it. The truck would never see combat again, and the machine gun mounted in its bed would be super-heated and warped beyond use.

Another piece taken off the board. But what was the game?

The rain-soaked acacia tree appeared a hundred yards ahead, still sheltering the Cruiser. They reached the outstretched canopy and Hale whistled.

He didn't see Tito. The Cruiser sat right where he'd left it, its windows rolled up. Another whistle, and still no response.

"Tito!" Hale hissed, lifting the rifle.

Bakumba stood frozen, wide eyes sweeping the grass. The road. Turning back toward Hale.

Then a sudden shriek broke the stillness, and a flash of red exploded from Hale's left, bounding toward Bakumba. Long before Hale could adjust his point of aim, the red flash hit Bakumba broadside and bulled him straight to the ground. A scream broke the air and in an instant the two figures were locked in a death tangle, legs thrashing and arms flailing.

Hale saw the rock just as it rose in a clenched fist—long fingers, a skinny arm.

"*Drop it!*"

Tito wasn't listening. Bakumba jerked his head sideways just as the rock smashed past his face, clipping his ear and earning a shriek. Hale grabbed the adjustment strap on his rifle sling and snatched it, securing the weapon close to his body. He tore through trampled grass even as Tito prepared to swing again, still aiming for Bakumba's head. The rock reached its apex—the blow began.

Then Hale rammed Tito. Two hundred twenty pounds of solid American muscle sent the little man flying. The rock went with him—Tito landed with a thud, breath hissing between his teeth.

Then Hale was on him, clearing Bakumba's body and drawing his pistol as he planted one boot into Tito's sternum.

"*Drop it.*"

Tito didn't respond. Crushed to the ground, helpless to break free, his wide eyes fixated not on Hale or the pistol but on Bakumba. He looked crazy—consumed. A total departure from the ultra-calm, half-awake squatter Hale had found picking apart a coconut with his bare fingers.

"He is Dinka," Tito growled. "He did this! He burned these villages!"

Through his peripheral vision, Hale could still see Bakumba laid out on the ground—skinny legs splayed, one ear bleeding. In just a matter of moments Tito had done a number on him.

All with a rock.

"Give me that," Hale snarled. He tore the rock from Tito's grasp and hurled it into the brush. Then he lifted his boot.

"*Up.*"

Tito was quick to oblige, his burning eyes fixed on Bakumba. He looked ready to pounce.

"I will shoot you," Hale said, pointing the gun. "Don't budge."

"Check his forehead," Tito said. "You will find the truth!"

Bakumba began scrambling backward at that, kicking at the dirt. "Please! I didn't kill anyone!"

"*Stop*," Hale said. "Lie still."

Bakumba saw the HK pistol and he obliged. Hale squatted alongside him and tore the sweat rag away from Bakumba's head...

Exposing three slender scars, shaped like chevrons with their wings curving upward toward his scalp. Barely perceptible, but highlighted by gleaming sweat.

Hale looked to Tito.

"*Gaar*," Tito spat. "Dinka facial scars, this happens when they become a man. I told you before—*he* is your killer."

33

Atlanta, Georgia
08:45 Hours, Eastern Standard Time

The call with Mary Grace Dalton did not go as planned—at least, not if the plan was to have her agree to an evacuation.

They spoke via video call, not sat phone. Thanks to the marvels of modern satellite internet, the challenge in Western Equatoria wasn't connection so much as electricity to power the laptop. Mary Grace had to charge it using a generator, and fuel was limited—she preferred not to power on the laptop at all.

But Bill Carpenter wanted to see her face. More importantly, he wanted her to see *his* face, and Shaw's. He wanted Mary Grace to understand just how dangerous the situation had become, and Shaw was fully on board with that priority.

The call with O'Rourke, however nonspecific their discussion was, had chilled Shaw. If James Wani's White Nile Liberation Army was half so committed as the CIA believed...

Well, suffice it to say that Shaw was ready to pull whatever strings she could to facilitate an air lift out of South Sudan for both Mary Grace and

Hale—the kids too, if possible. Moving children out of their home country might prove to be a legal nightmare.

One step at a time.

Mary Grace came on screen. She sat in a dimly lit room with stucco walls, her once manicured face now suntanned and relaxed. Her hair was corralled in a loose ponytail. Her smile as bright as the noonday sun.

And Shaw felt terrible. Like a vagabond—a street urchin. Mary Grace looked *amazing*. Even after all these years, all that time overseas in such harsh environments, she looked healthier and brighter than Shaw had ever seen her, even in college.

She looked *alive*, delighted to see her uncle, surprised but equally delighted to see Shaw. Eager to discuss logistics, security measures, additional supplies for the children.

All that enthusiasm vanished when Carpenter made his request. Radiance turned to indignation and a flat refusal. Mary Grace was *not* coming home. She was *not* abandoning the children.

The remainder of the call was spent discussing what Mary Grace wanted to discuss—airdropped supplies, regional coordination with other NGOs, and a corporate strategy to lobby for a United Nations peacekeeping coalition. No admission of personal danger, zero discussion of admitting defeat.

Then the call ended, leaving Shaw to only shake her head in semi-amazement, semi-irritation. Mary Grace Dalton hadn't changed a *bit* since college. Yes, she'd grown up. Yes, her values had been reborn.

But at the end of the day? She was still a queen, and she still got what she wanted one way or the other.

"You're gonna have to drag her out," Shaw said.

Carpenter exhaled a long sigh. He rose from the conference table and walked to the window, overlooking downtown Atlanta. Tense as a bowstring, shaking his head at nothing.

Then he simply turned for the door, leaving Shaw just as her phone dinged. The notification was from Signal. The contact was encoded, but instantly recognizable.

Hale.

Shaw didn't bother checking the message. She dialed his sat phone instead, and Hale answered.

"Shaw?"

"Ian, thank God. Where are you?"

There was more strain in Shaw's voice than she expected. She'd spent the last half hour so focused on arguing with Mary Grace that she'd almost forgotten how worried she was about Hale and the storm she'd sent him barreling into.

"About two hundred klicks northwest of Juba," Hale said. "Progress is slow. The weather is bad—the roads are worse."

"But you're safe?" Shaw said. "No sign of conflict?"

The pause from the other end of the line unsettled Shaw. When Hale next spoke, his voice had lowered.

"I picked someone up," he said. "Local guy—claims to be a journalist. My guide says that he's Dinka, whatever that is. I found him getting chased through a burning village by four guys in a technical. They were about to blow him in half."

Shaw's chest tightened. She didn't need to ask what had become of the four guys. The fact that his newcomer was still alive told the story.

"That village was wasted," Hale continued. "All the adults killed, all the children missing. The new guy says they were kidnapped. He filmed the whole thing."

"*Filmed it?*"

"That's what he said."

"You saw the tape?"

"The camera is dead. I don't have a charger. Tito doesn't believe him, for whatever that's worth."

"Tito?"

"My guide. He blames the Dinka for all the local destruction—we passed more than a few burned-out villages on the way here."

Shaw assimilated the information in silence, chewing her lips and trying not to fixate on the word *technical* and the images of unchecked guerrilla warfare it generated.

"Does the new guy speak English?" Shaw said.

"Yep."

"And he said he's a journalist?"

"Yep."

"Did he say who he works for?"

"Freelance. He claims that he's under contract to document the conflict."

"So he knows who the tangos were?"

"He has no idea."

"Were they wearing any uniforms?"

Pause. "Actually, yes. Not matching uniforms, but they all wore matching patches. I'm gonna try to send a photo...Stand by."

Shaw switched back to the Sentinel app. It took fully five minutes for the message to come through, and when it did the picture was grainy—Hale must have scaled the size and quality way down for the Iridium phone to manage the transmission. The photograph was of a man's bloodied arm, and Shaw zoomed in on the patch stitched to his sleeve. It was only barely readable.

"Lord's Resistance Army..." she said.

"You heard of it?"

Shaw thought she had, but she couldn't recall any details of the memory. She squinted, considering, and then shelved the question for later research.

Hale didn't need to be kept on the phone. She had other information to communicate before cutting him lose.

"I'll look into it. Listen, Ian. I spoke with a contact in the intel sphere. He has information on the conflict in Western Equatoria. No great specifics, but it's worse than we thought."

Hale listened quietly while Shaw hit him with the highlights—everything O'Rourke had communicated about James Wani's reign of terror across the region. His expansionist plans, his ambitions against Juba. The tens of thousands of civilian refugees that were fleeing his war zone, pouring into neighboring countries.

A total nightmare.

When Shaw finished, the question Hale asked wasn't what she expected.

"Does Wani kidnap children?"

Shaw considered, reviewing everything she'd dug up about the warlord over the past three days. It wasn't a heck of a lot—he was still pretty new on the scene. She didn't recall anything about kidnapping children.

"Not that I know of."

"And he doesn't operate a militia known as the Lord's Resistance Army?"

"Again, not that I know of."

"Then it's possible we've got two bad actors at play, and at least one of them is snatching kids. There's a whole crowd of kids sitting defenseless at that orphanage. The mission continues."

Shaw closed her eyes, breathing through clenched teeth. She wanted to kick herself.

Of course Hale would say that. What did she expect him to say?

"We're getting you out, Ian. We're getting everybody out. I'll burn down every phone line on the planet if I have to—I'll find transport."

"Works for me. Until you do, I'll lock things down here on the ground. Take a breath, Shaw. You sound stressed."

Maybe it wasn't a joke, but Shaw couldn't help a dry smirk. She rolled her eyes.

"Thanks, doc. That's good advice."

"The only kind I give."

Awkward pause. Shaw cleared her throat.

"Message me updates as often as practical, okay? And...keep your head down."

"Good copy. Minuteman *out*."

Hale hung up. Shaw lowered her phone and chewed a thumbnail, staring at the desk. Contemplating the puzzle at hand.

And somehow feeling...she was missing something huge.

34

Western Equatoria, South Sudan
15:50 Hours, East Africa Time

The Ural truck returned to base. The Land Cruiser technical never did.

Standing by the gate posts of the old Sudanese army outpost—now long abandoned with roofs caving in and the perimeter fence semi-collapsed—Marc Harden looked down a winding forest road and listened. When one of his men approached from behind, already mumbling a question, Harden shot up a hand to silence him.

He focused on the squawks of gray parrots. The occasional barks and growls of Colobus monkeys, high in the trees. The scratch and rustle of monitor lizards as they navigated dry leaves and scrambled over rotting logs. All the jungle sounds.

Well, not *real* jungle sounds. Technically, the ecosystem in this part of Western Equatoria was more of a lush, dense forest. To Harden's redneck mind, it was all the same, and what mattered more than correct nomenclature were the sounds he *didn't* hear.

There was no chug of a distant engine, no splash of tires through flooded ruts. No shouts from his men, late but returning.

The Ural sat behind him, offloading its catch of sobbing children. But the Land Cruiser *still* didn't appear.

"Hey, boss." The soldier spoke again, a little impatient this time. "You good?"

Harden looked back, the tobacco packed into his mouth swelling one cheek. He'd stopped chewing while he listened. Nicotine-laced saliva now pooled on his tongue. He spat.

"What happened?"

He'd asked already. He wanted to hear it again, just to check for consistency.

"I told you. We gathered the kids and departed the village. Everyone dead, everything burning. Some ways down the road the pickup turned back, just to surprise any survivors. Like you ordered."

It was true, Harden had ordered that. In the chaos of lightning attacks, villagers sometimes managed to hide or play dead. Doubling back eliminated the chance for anyone to trail his men.

"And?" Harden prompted.

"I thought I heard the machine gun. I don't know. We kept going."

"And when they *didn't* catch up?"

A shrug. "We did what you said. We returned to base. Now we are here."

Everything about the soldier's body language screamed of irritation, like a sulky teenager forced to state something he found perfectly obvious. Harden would like to have gut-punched him, maybe even shot him in the head, but there were others watching, and besides...

He might already be four soldiers short.

"Get the kids in the cage," Harden snapped. "Refuel the truck and reload for another raid."

The soldier squinted. "Without the pickup?"

"Take the Jeep." Harden jabbed his chin toward a dusty white Jeep Wrangler. The letters "UN" were still barely visible on the driver's door.

"There is no machine gun," the soldier said.

Harden drew to within inches of the soldier, forced to rock his head back to make eye contact, but not the least bit intimidated. He spoke through his teeth.

"*Then carry extra rifles.*"

The soldier got the message. His gaze fell and he headed for the Ural. Harden watched him go, then slipped outside the fort. He stood in the road, chewing and spitting. He unclipped his sat phone and dialed a number by memory.

The masked man in Juba would not be pleased by the news, but he needed to know. That technical might still turn up, but if it didn't...

It meant someone had returned fire.

35

Washington, DC
13:13 Hours, Eastern Standard Time

Assistant Secretary of State Paul Morris didn't bother with cursing his deputy out.

What was the point? Jaxon Wilks could be obnoxious and arrogant, too confident in his own abilities and too obsessed with his own future. In that way, Morris would be a fool not to admit that he and Wilks only butted heads because they were so much alike. Morris was only too happy to leverage Wilks's aggression for his own benefit—he couldn't afford to dump cold water on it.

But there was a bigger reason Morris didn't explode when Jaxon reported the latest round of failed negotiations with the South Sudanese, and that was a pure and simple truth. Something Morris was smart enough to understand and savvy enough to accept as the focus of his ire.

It wasn't Wilks's *fault* that negotiations had failed. Wilks was correct in his assessment that Minister Abiem was stringing America along. Despite the pressure, despite the aggressive promises of security support and enough fresh asphalt to keep the sitting South Sudanese regime in power for decades, Abiem was refusing to bite. Refusing to commit.

He was attempting to play both ends against the middle, possibly with the Chinese or maybe with the freaking Slovenians for all Morris knew. What did it actually matter?

This deal was too big for Morris to let slip away. Wilks believed it could be the kind of win that could catapult him to the top—he was right.

But not before Morris had his turn.

Activating another private line, Morris dialed from memory. He tapped one polished dress shoe over worn carpet, picturing Abiem—a third world pig playing games with the greatest super power the world had ever known. *Daring* to refuse their generosity. Daring to toy with America's nerves.

He would learn the cost of defying Washington. Before this was over, he might pay with his entire career.

"Hello?"

The rumbling voice answered without identifying itself. The speaker already knew who was calling. He probably knew why.

"Stalemate," Morris said. "Juba won't commit."

"Still playing for time?"

"Feels like it."

"You still think it's the Chinese?"

"I think it doesn't matter."

Silence—nearly a full minute of it. Then: "What do you wanna do?"

"I want to drop a bunker buster on their heads."

"Meaning?"

"Meaning I want an escalation. Something bigger than before—something the whole world can't ignore."

"That's…risky."

"It's our only play. Abiem thinks he can stall on security while angling for a better deal. Let's make him believe that if he doesn't sign on the dotted line *tomorrow*, he'll have a thousand UN peacekeepers crawling across his backyard by next month. How's *that* gonna play with the Chinese? The last thing those little wontons want is international oversight."

Another lengthy break in conversation. Morris knew his partner was calculating, maybe sketching out a loose plan. Whatever it was, it had to be bloody. Morris was okay with that.

Was his partner?

"I'll make the call," the voice said. "Do you want details?"

"Only when I read them in *The New York Times*."

Morris hung up.

36

Western Equatoria, South Sudan
20:36 Hours, East Africa Time

The sun set, but Hale didn't stop.

With the Cruiser's headlights set on low beam, providing barely enough illumination to keep him out of the ditches, Hale rode with his rifle resting on the dash and his pistol holstered close to hand.

Tito rode next to him, squatting sideways in the seat so that he could monitor Bakumba. After concluding his call with Shaw, Hale had attended to Bakumba's gunshot arm and found a wound rank with the onset of severe infection. He dispensed peroxide, and Bakumba screamed like a gut-shot pig, thrashing against the tailgate of the Cruiser.

There was no point in attempting to recover the bullet still lodged in Bakumba's arm. The flesh was too swollen, too sensitive. Hale administered oral antibiotics and ordered Bakumba into the left rear seat, where Hale could keep an eye on him in the rearview mirror. He was bringing the wounded Dinka for two reasons.

First, Bakumba needed more than meds. His best shot at keeping his arm was the orphanage doctor in Tambura. Hopefully, the infection would calm by then and surgery could be performed.

Second, Hale wanted Bakumba close because he didn't trust the newcomer for a moment. If Bakumba was what Hale thought he was—some kind of bounty-hunting videographer—he would be only too happy to sell Hale out to the highest bidder.

The thugs Hale had killed at the burned-out village might have friends.

Whatever the case, it was dangerous to drive in the dark, but Hale could feel the pressure of passing time bearing down on him. At some juncture, speed itself was his best defense, even if *speed* came as a slog through axle-deep ruts.

One kilometer, then ten. Then fifty.

Even with the storm gone, standing pools of water cascaded over the Cruiser's hood every few yards. Bakumba groaned in the back seat, begging for painkillers. Tito snarled at him, advising him to shut up. Hale just focused on the road, managing the accelerator to keep all four wheels biting the mud as best they could.

It was hot inside the Cruiser. Hale rolled his window down and directed Tito to do the same—then quickly rolled them up again as a swarm of mosquitos penetrated the truck. They bounced down a hill, curving along the road and nearly crashing headlong into sudden, rushing water.

Not a puddle—this was a river. Sandy brown and flooded above its banks, the current moved in a gargling rush, tearing past draping tree limps and torn clumps of elephant grass. Hale would have heard it several hundred yards back if not for the chug of the Cruiser's diesel engine. As it was, he slammed on the brakes only just in time.

The Cruiser slid to a stop. Hale sat with the truck in first gear and glanced upstream and down. In either direction it was too dark to see more than a few yards. He risked the brights, but they didn't help much. He saw the far bank, maybe twenty yards away. The road resumed there, climbing up another rutted hillside choked by brush...then disappearing into the dark.

Hale glanced at Tito. The African's bony knees rose nearly to his chin, wide and dark eyes sweeping the path ahead.

"Have you been here before?" Hale said.

A grunt.

"Is it safe to ford?"

No answer. Hale shook his head and wrenched the parking brake. He bailed with his rifle in hand, boots squishing through the muck as he approached the bank.

It was a *lot* of water, and Hale had no way of knowing how deep it was. Equipped with a snorkel that raised the engine's air intake to roof level, the Cruiser was built to cross rivers like this.

But if the current pushed too hard, if the truck lost its footing and rolled...

"Kawaja!"

Tito's voice hissed from the still-open driver's door. Hale looked back, squinting into the glare of the headlights.

"Come back." Tito beckoned.

Hale took one more look at the river and then returned, finding Tito squatted in the driver's seat, leaned out through the open door and looking back the way they'd come.

"What?" Hale said.

Tito lifted a hand. As Hale watched he peered up the road, nostrils flexing like a bloodhound struggling with a scent.

"*What?*" Hale repeated.

"Diesel fumes," Tito said.

"We're in a diesel truck, genius."

Tito's gaze snapped toward Hale. From the back seat, Bakumba moaned and mumbled about morphine, but Hale ignored him. There was something in Tito's face that he didn't like—something he'd seen before.

"Not our diesel," Tito said.

Hale didn't have time to reply. Even over the rush of the river, he felt the vibration. It rumbled up through his mucky boots, like the faintest hint of a distant earthquake. A split second later, he smelled what Tito had smelled —thick, greasy exhaust.

Hale flicked the safety off his rifle and reached to extinguish the Cruiser's lights. He'd barely flicked the switch before a matching glow silhouetted the top of a hill two hundred yards behind them. The rumble in Hale's boots grew sharper.

And then a white Jeep Wrangler, open-topped and loaded down with passengers, exploded into view...followed almost immediately by a Russian-built Ural truck.

37

Hale didn't have time to think. The moment he saw the Jeep he also saw the four heavily armed men packed inside, silhouetted by the Ural's headlights.

"In!" Hale shouted.

He shoved Tito just as the first shout carried from the distant hilltop. It was spoken in a language Hale didn't recognize, but even at two hundred yards he didn't need to be a linguist to catch the gist. Landing in the driver's seat, he dropped the rifle onto the dash and dumped the emergency brake. Even before the Cruiser was in gear, it was rolling into the river. Water exploded against the brush guard and then the tires caught. Hale mashed the gas.

He didn't upshift. He needed the torque.

Both Tito and Bakumba had seen the distant vehicles. Bakumba was rambling in his native tongue and Tito was snapping back in the same. Hale didn't understand a word and didn't care. The Cruiser's back wheels were fully engulfed now. The water rose almost to the side-view mirrors and they were barely twenty feet off the bank.

Then the first gunshot popped. An AK round, rushed and random. The bullet pinged off the Cruiser's cab and whined as it ricocheted into the darkness. Tito shouted but Hale remained calm.

Two hundred yards was a long shot in the dark. If the gunmen wanted to close the distance, they'd have to descend their hill, temporarily losing sight of their quarry as the road curved.

Just get across the river, Ian—then you can run.

Water covered the Cruiser's hood, sloshing against the windshield. Hale's boots were wet—water rushed in from beneath the dash, also. In the back seat, Bakumba shouted and thrashed. Hale glanced over his shoulder to check on the enemy.

The Ural truck was still there, parked at the top of the hill. But the Jeep had disappeared.

Faster. Move!

Hale mashed his foot deeper into the accelerator, and the submerged engine rumbled. They were almost to the middle of the river, moving at barely a crawl, but as Hale attempted to upshift, the Cruiser's wheels broke traction. It was too much force—the riverbed was too loose. He *had* to crawl. They only needed another hundred feet.

Then the Jeep arrived, its headlights blazing through the Cruiser's rear glass.

"*Down!*" Hale shouted.

The gunfire ignited in a storm. AK rounds tore into water, sending geysers erupting on all sides as the Cruiser reached the midpoint of the river. Other bullets struck metal—one shattered the Cruiser's rear glass and zipped right through the windshield, blowing the rearview mirror away.

Hale scrunched his shoulders together and dropped his head. The tires were slipping again—the engine strained but they weren't moving any faster. The weight of the river's current crushed against the body panels and rushed over the hood.

They were sliding *sideways*. Downstream. It was exactly what Hale had feared. He could see the far bank but was no longer drawing toward it. All four wheels spun and the truck shuddered...then Hale felt the back end begin to turn.

No, no, no!

Hale fought for the clutch. The water rose up to his knees and the gunfire redoubled from behind. Two more rounds tore through the back window and then the glass shattered. A tidal wave rushed in—Bakumba screamed and Tito clung to the passenger seat, turning his face into the glare of headlights before shouting in instant panic.

"*Rocket!*"

One glance was all Hale needed to confirm the truth. He saw the soldier, and he saw the RPG launcher settling onto his shoulder.

No more time.

Hale snatched the shifter into reverse and dumped the clutch. The engine surged under full throttle—the front tires spun backward, no longer fighting but now aiding the pressure of the river.

And the guy with the RPG fired.

38

It all happened at once.

As Hale mashed the accelerator, the force of the river finally had its way with the Cruiser. The back end broke free and the truck swung in line with the current, lurching downstream only a millisecond before the rocket-propelled grenade streaked across the water.

It didn't hit the truck. It blew past the windshield with barely six inches to spare. The grenade hit the far bank, ten yards to Hale's left—and detonated.

A concussive blast drove mud and shrapnel against the passenger's side windows. Glass cracked and the truck heaved. Hale yanked the shifter into first gear, already knowing he was too late.

They left the riverbed. Hale actually felt the moment all four tires broke free, allowing the current to surge beneath them and eliminating any hope of regaining control. In a split second, they were spinning—he saw the lights of the Jeep and the Ural, mixed with distant muzzle flashes, and then everything went dark.

Water rushed through the shattered back glass, rising up to Hale's chest. He fought the submerged controls and slammed on the accelerator, hoping for the tires to grab once more, but the engine only coughed—then the entire gauge cluster went black.

The engine was dead, and Hale couldn't see a thing. Water reached past the steering wheel and up to his chest. He thought they were still spinning but in the dark it was impossible to tell. He tasted the mud—behind him Bakumba gargled and to his left Tito thrashed.

Light, Hale. Find light before this thing flips.

Hale slapped his chest rig and located the SureFire. One click and hot white glare blazed against the water. He saw Tito first, clawing at the pickup's door handle. The latch clicked but water pressure held the door closed. Hale twisted to try his own door—and ducked just in time.

The storm must have felled the tree. It was a mahogany, maybe a teak. Something tall with a high canopy. It lay across the river with one jagged limb pointed straight at Hale's window, visible under the glare of the SureFire.

Hale dove face-first a split second before the Cruiser collided with the tree. Glass shattered, audible even through the water. Metal crunched and the truck came to a jarring halt, pinned by the current.

Hale attempted to lift his head but never made it out of the water. The back of his skull smacked the underside of the penetrating limb. It hovered just above the water line, holding him beneath the surface while the steering wheel, door, and seat boxed him in.

Panic rushed Hale's body. He twisted and choked, fighting the urge to inhale water. The flashlight still clipped to his chest rig blazed into his face. Hale blinked on grit and felt a hand on his arm—Tito's hand, maybe, fighting to pull him free.

But that would never work. Hale couldn't wriggle past the limb and his door was held closed by the tree.

The seat.

Hale jammed his right hand between his leg and the door. He found the seat's recline lever but his fingers slipped—his heart hammered harder. What little oxygen remained in his lungs was burning quickly. He was almost spent, almost out of time.

He found the latch a second time and yanked. The seatback popped beneath him. Hale rammed his feet against the lifeless pedals and shot backward, beneath the limb and out the back side of the driver's compartment. He surfaced with a heave, exploding into barely twelve inches of breathable space remaining inside the pickup's cab. Muddy damp air flooded his lungs and Hale almost went under again, but bounced off the reclined seat back. His head smacked the ceiling and water rushed across his face.

Only ten inches remained. With the Cruiser trapped by the tree, the cabin was taking on more water than it could empty.

"Kawaja!" Tito shouted. "Kawaja, *do something*!"

Hale didn't need to be told, and he already knew what to do. With two doors pinned by the tree, two others held closed by the current, and the back window too narrow to scramble through, there was only one option. Hale wrapped both arms around the tree limb still jutting over the driver's seat and hauled his body upward. He hung there, still gasping and suddenly aware that Bakumba no longer screamed.

Was he dead?

It didn't matter. They would all be dead if the situation didn't change.

Hale shoved his legs over the steering wheel and on top of the dash. With thigh muscles bunched and his face hovering just above the water line, he clung to the limb, then rammed with everything he had. Once—twice. Boots slammed into the interior of the busted windshield, and he thought he felt something give.

The water rose another inch. It splashed over Hale's mouth and ran into his nose, burning and choking him. He wanted to let go, to claw at his face and to sit upright. He didn't allow himself.

He kicked again. Once, twice—everything he had.

39

The Land Cruiser's windshield collapsed on the final blow.

Exploding out of its frame, cracked and shattered, it was instantly smashed against the tree by the current. Hale released the limb and went under. He reached for Tito but couldn't find him. There was no chance to reach for Bakumba. He had to get *out*.

Hale rotated beneath the limb and pulled his body forward, over the wheel. He briefly clawed for the HK416 he'd left on the dash, but the river must have already swept it away. Hale exploded through the open windshield cavity. The current slammed him against the tree, but his face cleared the waterline.

Hale gasped, clawing against bark and nearly falling. With his knees planted on the Cruiser's submerged hood, the water still boiled up to his shoulders. He thrashed and turned back, grasping at stray limbs with one arm and flailing beneath the water with the other.

"*Tito!*"

Nothing but the rush of the river answered Hale. He reached back into the truck, touching the wheel and the dash but not feeling skin. Hale drew another breath, ready to plunge back in.

Then a hand closed around his wrist—long, skinny fingers and a bone-crushing grip.

Hale hauled. With one arm hooked around the tree trunk, he planted a boot against the Cruiser's submerged door pillar and pulled with everything left in him.

It was Tito. His head broke the water line and wide, crazed eyes locked with Hale's. Then Tito went down again. He released Hale's arm. Hale felt a leg kicking beneath the surface.

Tito was headed *back* into the truck.

"*Tito!*"

Hale dove again. Back beneath the surface, he barely caught Tito's leg as it thrashed past his face. The rest of Tito's body was buried in the truck. Hale grabbed the leg and pulled, his boots sliding over the truck's hood. He broke the surface just long enough to gasp another breath.

Then Tito exploded through the windshield cavity again. This time, he wasn't alone.

Lado Bakumba was limp and unconscious as Hale hauled both him and Tito to the surface. Two heads emerged under the glare of the SureFire, Tito's jerking and shaking, Bakumba's not moving at all. The pair of them went under again, but Hale had his arm hooked around the tree again.

He pulled, kicking off the nose of the truck. The water was too deep for Tito—Hale's toes barely scraped the bottom. It didn't matter. The tree served as a lifeline. Hale dragged them along until he could find traction in the mud. Another long stride and the river dropped beneath his armpits. He could stand. Hale turned and dragged.

They reached a clay riverbank in a heap, Bakumba landing on top, either unconscious or dead. Hale hit the ground with his stomach convulsing. He puked up river water and fought to shove Bakumba off Tito—the Dinka struck earth with a meaty thud.

"You good?" Hale choked.

Tito only coughed. Hale moved past him and went straight to Bakumba. He grabbed the man by the face and parted his lips. Four compressions of his chest, then forced air transfer through his mouth. Hale repeated the process in the dark, the glare of the bouncing SureFire useless to him. Checking for a pulse against Bakumba's neck, he thought he felt one, but Hale's own heart was slamming so fast it was difficult to tell.

"Is he dead?"

Tito spoke in a hiss. Without answering, Hale snatched the light from his chest rig and passed it off. Tito directed the beam onto Bakumba.

Another six compressions. Hale bent and forced air. Six more compressions. One more lung full of air. Two more compressions...

Then Bakumba jerked. He spat up water—a lot of it. Hale twisted Bakumba's head to keep him from choking, and Tito lowered the light. In the intervening seconds as Hale caught his breath, he looked to Tito.

Tito's gaze fell. Hale cocked an eyebrow.

"Dinka?" Hale said.

Tito spat into the grass.

"Human," he muttered.

Fair enough.

Bakumba regained full consciousness, immediately kicking his way backward from the river. Hale took the light and scanned it toward the truck.

The Cruiser was right where he'd left it, pinned against the tree, its cabin flooded with boiling water.

Trapped. Wrecked. Ruined. And Hale's gear?

Mostly gone.

Hale swept a hand over his body, checking for what had survived. His rifle magazines were there, now worthless apart from the HK416. The TOPS Dawn Warrior and his pistol, while waterlogged, were still strapped to his body. All that remained in his pockets was a Benchmade Adamas and a flooded emergency lighter.

His sat phone, iPad, food and fresh water were all gone. Swept away by the river.

Bad.

And as soon as the thought rang in his mind, Hale felt something. Starting in his boots, rumbling up his legs. It was a faint shudder, like a very distant earthquake.

Tito's wide eyes snapped upward. "*Diesel!*"

40

Western Equatoria, South Sudan
23:35 Hours, East Africa Time

Matt Kirby was born in Vancouver, but he hadn't lived in Canada for so long that he barely remembered what it felt like to be cold. Southeast Asia was never cold—neither South America nor Africa. Occasionally, when Kirby piloted a United Nations Humanitarian Air Service turboprop across mountains during winter months, he experienced a little of that hometown chill. He didn't enjoy it.

The sweat was what Kirby was born for. Piloting small bush planes between African villages and across South American jungles was what brought him to life. Kirby had wanted to be a fighter pilot, but colorblindness crushed that dream before it started. He next turned to the airlines, intoxicated by the dream of career flight...until he actually landed a job as first officer aboard a twin-engine commuter jet. It was only then that Kirby understood why airline pilots were sometimes mocked as "bus drivers."

The light trainer aircraft Kirby learned to fly on were fast, agile, and *fun*. The bulky commuter jets, by contrast, were slow, lumbering, and regulated on every level. Operating one felt less like flying and more like...well, driving a bus. Pushing buttons. Following protocols. Killing time on autopilot while streaking back and forth, back and forth over the same dirt.

Sure, the money was good. But Kirby hadn't fought his way past color-blindness and into the cockpit for the money—he craved adventure.

That was when the United Nations' World Food Programme came knocking with an opportunity Kirby would have seized *without* a salary.

"Come fly for a cause," they said. "We'll give you a little plane and some dirt runways and wish you luck."

The sales pitch wasn't far from the reality. Within Kirby's first year he flew to more countries than he'd flown to *states* during his entire career as an airline pilot. Moving food and medical supplies, volunteers and United Nations officials, he bounced across three continents in half a dozen different aircraft—all small, single- or dual-engine turboprops with a lot of wiggle in their controls and a lot of vibrations in their seats.

It was *real* flying. The kind that sent your heart into your throat when turbulence shook you like a rag doll, or a wet mud runway grabbed your tires and threatened to flip you on takeoff. It was adventure, it was thrill. But it also *mattered*. Kirby could see, firsthand with every flight, how he was making an impact. Hungry children were fed, sick parents were treated, and evacuees were removed from war zones. All in a week's work, serving some of the most challenged corners of the planet.

At present, that particular corner was South Sudan. Kirby had arrived only three days prior, and his mission was simple. As the rainy season faded across middle Africa, a predictable outbreak of cholera was sweeping along the border of South Sudan and the DRC. The UN was responding accordingly by deploying shipments of vaccines—first to a regional distribution center in Wau, and from there across the region to every point of need.

That was where Kirby came in. His Cessna 208 Grand Caravan, capable of transporting thirty-five hundred pounds of cargo, nine people, or a mixture of the two, was the perfect tool for final-leg delivery. Already he'd flown two flights into Yambio, delivering crates of supplies and vaccines. For the next twelve hours he was scheduled to be off, but upon landing back at Wau, Kirby found a crew of two aid workers, a doctor, and one translator eager to get to work assisting with the outbreak. Kirby knew from firsthand experience how badly they were needed.

So he refueled and loaded up again. The Grand Caravan climbed into a clear night sky speckled with stars—not a cloud in sight. They banked south and Kirby set the autopilot. He didn't *like* using the autopilot, but he couldn't deny that fatigue was setting in. Technically, this trip would require him to exceed his daily flight limit. He would need to fudge some numbers on his paperwork when he returned—get himself just under the eight-hour cap.

It would be worth it. The people of Yambio needed the help.

While the two Spanish aid workers and the translator slept, the doctor sat wide-eyed directly behind Kirby, trembling with every patch of turbulence. Kirby looked over his shoulder and grinned.

"Don't like to fly?"

The doctor forced an awkward laugh but didn't otherwise answer. Kirby found himself wishing one of the Spanish girls were awake—they were both cute, and he was getting sleepy. A little conversation would be nice. Maybe he could brush the dust off one of his aviation-themed pickup lines.

So how do you like flying here on earth?

Apologies for the turbulence—my heart hasn't calmed since you stepped on board.

Hop into the cockpit, ma'am. Supermodels fly first class.

Okay, so they weren't *great* pickup lines. But Kirby's extensive research on the subject indicated that the magic was in the execution, not the substance. A winning smile paired with the liberating effects of an adventure buzz could be a powerful cocktail.

If only it was the doctor who passed out cold.

"Hey. Is that thunder?"

Kirby twisted in his seat, jarred from his musings. The doctor's accent was Italian, his voice strained.

"Say what?"

"I thought I heard thunder," the doctor said.

"Ah. No." Kirby winked. "Clear skies. We're good!"

Then Kirby heard it too. Low on the horizon and rumbling like distant fireworks, the sound was just audible over the roar of the turboprop. Kirby's gaze swept the instruments, searching for alarms of abnormalities. He took his gaze off the windshield for only a second.

Then the doctor shouted—loud into the headset, something panicked and unintelligible. Kirby's gaze snapped up just as the first flash of hot orange fire ignited the night two hundred yards to their left. This time the thunder was neither distant nor subtle—it boomed as the Cessna dipped sideways.

Now it wasn't only the doctor who shouted—one of the Spanish girls screamed. The next two blasts detonated within spitting distance of their right wingtip, and shrapnel peppered the Cessna's fuselage. Kirby's gaze snapped in that direction as his mind, supercharged by adrenaline, finally made the connection.

Anti-aircraft fire.

The thought cleared his brain. His right hand dropped to the dash and killed the autopilot as his left hand yanked on the yoke. The Cessna nosed up, hard. Kirby planted both feet into the pedals to control the tail as he applied more throttle. They were climbing, as fast as possible. They were headed into a midnight sky speckled with stars. From the back, the doctor mumbled prayers in Italian and the aid workers babbled in Spanish. The translator, a South Sudanese, called Kirby's name but Kirby couldn't make out the rest of what he said.

"Just hang on!" Kirby said. "We're pulling out of—"

Then the next shell hit. Not a near miss this time, but a direct strike. Kirby felt it from somewhere behind the cockpit. The ensuing blast was so loud, so close, that it deafened him. In an instant the throb of the turboprop vanished into a low ringing. Hot African air ripped over Kirby's shoulder as both pedals turned slack beneath his feet. He looked back, panic rushing his chest as the Cessna stalled in midair.

The tail was gone. He could see straight through the fuselage and out a gaping hole, all the way to the ground some six thousand feet below. For a split second, all was still, and he looked dead into the eyes of the nearest aid worker.

She was maybe twenty. Perhaps taking a break from college to do some good in the world. Young and healthy with her whole life ahead of her—and truly, very beautiful. Her dark Mediterranean eyes locked with

Kirby's. He saw the terror, the absolute fear. He knew she didn't deserve to die.

But that decision had already been made. In the next moment, a second shell hit, blasting right through the fuselage. The Spanish girl was thrown against a wall, blood spraying Kirby's face.

And then they were all going down.

41

Western Equatoria, South Sudan
23:41 Hours, East Africa Time

"*Diesel!*"

Hale's pistol cleared its holster even as the single word left Tito's lips. Looking upriver, he caught the first glare of flashing headlights just as he recognized the rush of a Jeep's engine.

"*Move!*" Hale hissed.

Tito scrambled up the riverbank, half dragging Bakumba. Hale rushed past them both and reached a low clay cliff, about four feet tall, where flood waters had carved away the bushlands. Above the cliff, elephant grass bent in the night breeze, and to Hale's left, maybe a hundred yards away, the headlights blazed toward him.

"In the grass," Hale said. "*Go!*"

Tito scrambled up the cliff with the agility of a mountain goat while Hale kicked and clawed his way up more like a cow. They both turned back to haul Bakumba up. Grass closed around them. To their left, the snarl of the vehicles grew louder, joined by shouts.

The truck, Hale thought.

These guys had come looking for the Land Cruiser, and they would find it pinned against the fallen tree. A white roof like a neon sign under the glare of headlights, and muddy tracks leading up the riverbank.

From there the next play was obvious.

"Hurry," Hale hissed. "Try not to break the grass. Follow me."

Tito seemed to understand. He tugged on Bakumba's arm, and Bakumba scrambled to his knees, ready to follow.

Hale turned straight ahead, weaving through the grass, leaned low to keep his head concealed, the HK pistol held close against his leg. He'd already worked the slide to check for obstructions, and the weapon appeared operational, but he couldn't help remembering how many AKs were visible inside that Jeep, let alone whatever resided in the bed of that Ural.

Why did they want us dead?

The thought flashed through Hale's mind, barely recognized before being shelved. It didn't matter. Maybe they thought he was the man who attacked and killed those four thugs in the technical. Maybe these were just the kind of men who shot whatever they saw.

Regardless, Hale's best option remained concealment. Put some distance between himself and the river, get lost in the darkness—and cross all other bridges when he came to them.

Fifty yards. The headlights turned away from Hale, but that wasn't a good thing. The soldiers had found the sunken Land Cruiser. Hale could tell by the shouts, by the glare of a spotlight mounted to the roll bars of the Jeep. He looked back and lifted a hand, looking down the trail they had left.

No, not *they*. Hale glided like a shadow and Tito was almost as stealthy. But Bakumba? He moved like an elephant, crushing grass and leaving no doubt of where he had been and where he had gone.

All three men stood motionless, holding their breath. Hale fixated on the spotlight and prayed that their trail would be lost in the shadows. That the gunmen would think their quarry had drowned. That they wouldn't turn inland—

No such luck. A shout rang from the riverbank, and the spotlight pivoted. Then the hunt was on. A chorus of voices joined the first, and the Jeep's tires spun.

"They see us!" Bakumba cried. "They'll kill us!"

Hale turned straight to Tito and pushed him from behind.

“Run,” he said. “Don’t stop unless I call for you. Okay?”

Tito didn’t argue. He grabbed Bakumba’s arm and yanked. The two of them, bent and stumbling, vanished into the grass. Hale gave them five seconds to disappear. He swept an arm to obscure their path.

Then he turned for the oncoming Jeep.

42

Hale didn't wait for the gunmen to find him.

He marked the still-chugging Russian Ural a hundred yards off his right shoulder, a pair of soldiers wielding AK-47s standing alongside it. The Jeep bore down from directly ahead—the last place he wanted to be was caught in between the two vehicles, taking fire from both sides.

Hale chose his own battlefield and split left. Crossing the path of the bouncing Jeep only yards ahead of the spotlight's beam, he placed the vehicle between himself and the Ural. Three tangos rode inside—one behind the wheel, one manning the spotlight, and a third leaning out the passenger's side door with an AK pointed ahead. Three more advanced on foot, trailing the Jeep by some fifty yards.

Targets acquired.

Hale waited until the Jeep ground to a stop at the end of Bakumba's elephant trail, the soldiers pausing to unravel the mystery of Hale's rushed concealment. He gave them not more than ten seconds before they were back on the move, and he hit them in eight.

Hale closed to within twenty yards, waiting until the last possible moment to rise, aim, and shoot—all in one motion. The HK cracked and the soldier behind the spotlight took a bullet straight to his skull. Hale was already back on the move, lost in the brush as the body pitched sideways.

Somebody shouted in surprise, maybe panic. Orders snapped and an AK shredded empty grass.

Hale never stopped. He wove left, breathing gasoline fumes as he hooked directly behind the Jeep. The three advancing soldiers, now only thirty yards behind, stalled amid the gunfire and chaos. They missed him—Hale made it to the driver's side and was still moving. The driver's body rose through the Jeep's open top as he pointed into the brush, screaming at his men.

Then Hale exploded out of his crouch and the HK spat fire. Six rounds were stacked so close together that they sounded like full-auto fire, each stitching holes through necks and faces, dropping the driver and his shotgun-seat gunner almost on top of each other. As Hale squeezed off the last shot, he passed the HK into his left hand and hooked his right through the open rear of the Jeep. He got a hand on a blood-spattered AK, snatching and running. Diving for cover around the Jeep's nose.

Hale hit the dirt—then every survivor was firing at once. AK-47s barked and bullets blew out the Jeep's windshield. Everyone shouted—nobody seemed to know what they were aiming at. Safely sheltered behind the Jeep's engine block, Hale reloaded the pistol and holstered it, then rocked out the AK's magazine to check the load.

The bullets looked clean, and the magazine felt about two-thirds full. He latched it in place and pulled the bolt just far enough to ensure that the weapon was chambered. Then he seated the rifle into his shoulder and measured the tempo of the incoming fire. Bullets blew away both mirrors and pinged off the roll cage—some even landed with meaty thuds, zipping into dead bodies. There was no discrimination, no strategy to the fire. It was wild and desperate, undisciplined and unchecked.

And that worked to Hale's advantage. Sheltered at the Jeep's nose, he could afford to wait. He also knew that AK-47s heat up fast. Even with wooden hand guards to insulate the shooter from the barrel, the cumulative effect of thirty or more rounds dumped in rapid succession was impossible to ignore. Pretty soon, the rifles would be difficult to control. They would need to be reloaded. There would be a break in the fire.

Then it came. Two of three rifles choked. Shouts grew louder. Hale exploded from in front of the Jeep and swung directly over the hood, aiming through the shattered windshield.

Three targets—all fully exposed. Hale popped off a string of shots and dropped one man like a tree. The second he winged. The third leveled his weapon.

Hale scrambled to the Jeep's passenger side as fresh gunfire opened up from the Ural. Maybe four gunmen remained—the winged one, his surviving buddy, and two more at the truck. This was still a long way from over.

Hale reached the Jeep's rear bumper, the rifle riding at eye level as he tracked movement in the grass. Both survivors had vanished into ground cover, but neither of them had frozen the way they should.

Hale fired again—somebody screamed and the grass jerked. He squeezed off four more shots and the movement ceased.

Then muzzle flash lit the night to his left. A bullet pinged off the Jeep. Another whizzed past his head. Rushed, emergency shots.

Hale swung, aimed, and fired, all together. The muzzle flash vanished. Blood sprayed the elephant grass, and bullets poured from the Ural. It wasn't aimed or measured, but panic fire. The spaghetti-on-the-wall approach of men who knew they'd stumbled into a hornet's nest.

And yet, despite the chaos, there was a certain effectiveness to their strategy. Unlike the three corpses in the grass, these guys were smart enough to alternate their reloads—the storm never ceased, and Hale thought he heard gears grinding.

They were running at whatever speed the hulking Russian truck could manage.

Not a chance.

Hale scrambled along the sheltered side of the Jeep, reaching the passenger's side door and clawing it open. A dead man fell out. Hale fished through the floorboard looking for a spare magazine. He found nothing except a pool of blood and an empty RPG launcher.

Shrinking back, Hale winced as a near miss cartwheeled over his head, buzzing like a wasp. He risked a glance over the Jeep's hood, then dove for cover again as the next burst nearly erased his face.

Only one guy was shooting. The other sat behind the Ural's wheel, grinding between reverse and first gear as he fought through a multi-point turn, redirecting the truck away from the river.

Ten seconds more, and the truck would be gone. Hale, his hapless guide, and his wounded stray would be left stranded—the Cruiser was flooded beyond use, and Hale could tell by the smell of gasoline fumes that the Jeep's fuel tank had been shot. Raw fuel poured out...

Raw fuel.

Hale dipped his head beneath the Jeep. He found the stream splashing off the undercarriage and soaking the dirt beneath—several gallons of unleaded gas.

Good enough.

Hale dug into his pocket and found the emergency lighter—a compact, electric unit that generated a sustained arc, not a flame. He mashed the button and the cap flipped open, exposing a crackling blue line.

More gunfire from the Ural. Another grind of gears. Hale rushed, bent over, twenty feet into the elephant grass with the lighter still buzzing.

Then he turned and flung it, straight beneath the Jeep.

43

Hale hit the deck only a split second before the gasoline detonated.

Heat boiled down his legs and singed his exposed arms, brilliant orange light illuminating the bushlands as bright as day. Hale scrambled another forty feet into the grass before the rest of the fuel tank could detonate.

He barely made it. The Jeep exploded, torn body panels ripping through the air. Hale smelled burning flesh and torched grass. The glare was blinding as he looked back.

But he could still see the Ural. The truck sat motionless some hundred yards behind the Jeep, both the driver and his sidekick no doubt transfixed by the sudden explosion...just as Hale expected.

Back on his feet, Hale circled the blaze, monitoring the Ural's position by its headlights. It still hadn't moved. He couldn't see either survivor—he assumed they were inside the cab, watching the fire.

Hale accelerated. Another ten yards, then he was dead in front of the truck. He turned toward it, keeping the rifle up. The grass stood undisturbed all the way to the Ural. Eighty yards, then sixty. The Ural's engine rumbled as the driver let the clutch out. The vehicle began to turn.

Forty yards. Hale slid to a stop and stood upright. The rifle, already riding at eye level, locked into his shoulder. He looked past blazing headlights and over a sloping camouflaged hood to a split windshield—two heads silhouetted behind. Dark eyes locked on his, turning wide.

Hale fired. Four shots in two stacks—the AK slammed and glass shattered. Blood sprayed the truck's cabin. Bodies slumped and the Ural growled, bouncing ahead as a foot rammed harder into the gas. With its wheels still turned, it was headed on a curving path for the river, nothing but brush standing in its way.

Hale sprinted, crossing ahead of the truck and spinning just in time to catch the driver's side door handle. The Ural rumbled at fifteen or twenty miles per hour and yanked him from the ground. Hale dropped the rifle. He got one foot on the running board and jerked the door open. The river was barely a hundred feet away and the truck was still surging under the pressure of the dead guy's boot.

Hale ignored the body and went for the ignition switch. One solid click and the motor died. The transmission locked up the drive shaft, and the Ural lurched to a halt, throwing Hale from the running board.

He didn't fight—he landed on his feet, breath exploding from his lungs. One hand dropped to his side and the pistol cleared its holster once more. Hale swept the cab, but neither occupant moved.

They were dead, shot through the head. In the sudden stillness, only the crackle of the Jeep fire broke the silence. The crackle and...was that a voice? A whimper?

Hale put his back to the engine block and listened for a repeat of the sound. He thought he heard it.

Soft, nearly indiscernible. A distressed voice.

Hale crept along the truck's side, his body still supercharged by adrenaline. Keeping his head safely beneath the bottom of the canvas top that covered the Ural's cargo deck, he noted the voice growing louder as he neared the truck's rear.

The canvas cover opened in a slit, two flaps held closed by knotted rope. Hale could see nothing through that slit, but as he squatted, a creak of shifting floorboards signaled movement inside.

Hale lifted the pistol. Another shift from inside was matched with a repeat whimper. Then one half of the canvas door shuddered under pressure. A hand appeared—small and searching, locating the rope.

Hale barely breathed. He waited as the hand found the knot. Another few seconds, and the flap slackened. The outline of a figure appeared, a long arm reaching out.

Hale hit the switch on his weapon light. He swept the gun up, pouring illumination into the truck. Somebody shouted and put up a hand. Hale's trigger finger constricted.

Then he stopped cold. His heart slammed. For the first time, he could see clearly into the covered cargo deck.

They were children.

44

Tambura, South Sudan
07:55 Hours, East Africa Time

Joseph wasn't his real name.

Born Biel Gatdet in the mid-eighties and growing up in a Nuer community of what was then a united Sudan, Joseph's family was wealthier than most. They didn't have a car, or even very many cattle, but they had enough income to keep three square meals on the table each day, which was more than many Nuer could claim. Perhaps it was the luxury of a full belly that allowed Joseph time for his imagination to wander.

From his earliest years, he craved adventure. Somewhere beyond the mud and heat of Jonglei State, maybe in some big city like Khartoum, Kampala, Cairo or—just maybe—beyond Africa?

It was a big world, and the one-room schoolhouse where British missionaries taught Joseph to read featured a map of that world. Biel used to stare—he used to dream.

When the Sudanese Civil War, which had raged in other parts of Sudan since before Biel's birth, spilled across Jonglei, those dreams of adventure became harsh realities. Biel watched his community succumb to the carnage of South Sudan's struggle for independence from Khartoum. He was only seventeen when a midnight raid by the Sudan Armed Forces left both of Biel's parents shot to death and his sister hauled off screaming in the back of a truck.

That was when he ran. All the way to the nearest encampment of the Sudan People's Liberation Army—the military organization most directly engaged in challenging the SAF. They handed him a rifle and he fought. Across Jonglei and north into enemy territory. Dodging bullets and taking lives and becoming so angry. So cold and ruthless. No longer the son of his mother, or the student of those loving British missionaries.

Biel became the monster he swore to destroy...and then, he became a prisoner.

Just eighteen months before the 2005 Comprehensive Peace Agreement which would lead to South Sudan's eventual independence, Biel was captured by the SAF. They imprisoned him, beat him, starved him. Left him teetering on the edge of death by dehydration. Tormented him with shrill music blared into his cell.

And eventually...they set him free. The war was over. Biel was literally kicked out of the back of a moving truck, left in a ditch with no food, no water, no identification or money, and only threadbare clothing. He would have died there...but the missionaries returned.

Not the British. These were Americans from some place called Atlanta. They lifted him out of that ditch and treated his wounds. They fed and cared for him for months. While Biel wrestled with the demons of the battlefield, the servants of Resurrection Mercy Ministries never ceased to love him, opening the Scriptures to offer him hope.

That was where Biel Gatdet met Joseph. The eleventh son of Israel, the patriarch of the nation by the same name. A favorite son, in fact, born into a good life. But then that life was taken from him—he was imprisoned. He suffered for many years.

But in the end? He became like a king, because God had a purpose for him.

"God is not finished with you, Biel," the missionaries said. "You are the son of a King...if only you will follow Him."

Yet again adventure had come knocking. This time, Biel would answer that call as Joseph, and he would answer it without a gun. Signing on with

Resurrection Mercy Ministries, he traveled from Uganda to Kenya to Ethiopia and eventually home to South Sudan. He met a kind woman named Mary Grace Dalton, and together they opened an orphanage in Western Equatoria—a haven for children whose parents had been claimed by violence. Joseph spent his days maintaining the facility and sharing stories of his namesake with the children.

He wasn't a king—but Joseph Gatdet felt like one. And if it weren't for the dust rising over the eastern horizon, the smile he wore like a favorite T-shirt would yet again have stretched his face...

But the dust was there.

Standing atop the flat-topped, three-story orphanage, Joseph held binoculars to his eyes and squinted at that dust. It rose from the road leading east to the village of Tambura, which was some three kilometers away. Only barely dry from the storm of the day prior, that route was narrow and winding and heavily rutted. It was used only by light-duty pickup trucks that delivered airdropped supplies from Tambura's dirt runway. Usually, those trucks came at about this time of day.

But they never created this much dust. The column was fully a hundred feet high, churned by heavy tires and carried by a lazy breeze. It reminded Joseph of years gone by—days he tried to forget.

Times of war.

"What is it, Joseph?"

Diko, a seventeen-year-old Nuer, waited anxiously at Joseph's side. Every few seconds, he twisted and spat over the roof's edge, a nervous habit that annoyed Joseph, but Joseph said nothing.

He just watched the dust, the tension in his stomach escalating as the column grew taller. Low hills covered in thornbush and elephant grass still obscured the source, but soon...

"Have you prayed today, Diko?" Joseph said it as much to distract himself as his young associate.

Diko didn't answer, and Joseph withdrew from the binoculars.

"Well?"

"I was busy. The well pump wouldn't start."

"Hmm," Joseph grunted. "Too busy digging for earthly water to ask your Maker for living water. Disappointing."

Through his peripheral, Joseph watched Diko grow still. He resisted a smile and refocused the binoculars. The column of dust was still coming, its source only just out of sight. Soon, he would know...

"Is it military?" Diko asked.

Joseph didn't answer.

"Should I get the guns?"

This time Joseph withdrew fully from the binoculars, his gaze turning hard. Diko cringed, and Joseph lifted his canteen from a belt pouch—an Army surplus canteen still stamped with the emblem of the SAF.

It used to bother him to drink from it. He refused to throw it away. Every time he lifted that canteen it was a reminder—*forgive much, for you have been forgiven more.*

Joseph drank. He passed the canteen to Diko. He lifted the binoculars once more.

Then he saw it. Lumbering like a bull elephant on six giant wheels. Painted green with a canvas-covered bed and a jutting front bumper. It was just over a kilometer away, but even at that distance, Joseph could tell that the Russian-built Ural truck had its windshield shot out.

His stomach tightened. Joseph deliberated for only a moment.

Then he said: "Go and get Miss Mary Grace. Quickly!"

45

Tambura, South Sudan
08:15 Hours, East Africa Time

Hale was ready to drop.

For ten hours straight, he had wrestled the monster Russian truck through ditches and across streams. Over hills and around them. Following Tito's directions through dense forests with roads so narrow that tree limbs dragged the Ural's sides.

Straight through the night, he pushed the truck as hard as it would go. The vehicle was a behemoth, built for durability and strength, not speed. Technically, it was ideally suited for this environment.

But the body count Hale had accumulated during only days in South Sudan hung over his mind like a cloud, reminding him that he had made enemies he still didn't understand. The men he had shot alongside the river all wore the same bird-and-palm-frond arm patch as the men he had killed while rescuing Bakumba—*Lord's Resistance Army*.

Perhaps Hale had exterminated the whole of that militia, but he doubted it. Whatever survivors remained would be unlikely to forgive or forget. They would want their truck and their kidnapped children back.

Hale had half a dozen AK-47s and a few hundred rounds of ammunition, but his best defense by far was to *keep moving*...until, at last, Tito lifted a hand.

"There! It is the orphanage."

The building was three stories high, built of dirty concrete blocks and surrounded by acacia trees. Hale noted the glint of glass from the building's roof—maybe binoculars, possibly a rifle scope. It concerned him, but one glance at Tito put his mind at ease. Riding squatted in the seat next to him, a broad smile stretched the little man's mouth like Hale hadn't seen before. It extended across his entire face, even penetrating his eyes. They forded another stream, and Hale slowed on the far side.

Somebody was headed their way. A tall man dressed in desert tan with a floppy safari hat. A canteen bouncing on his hip, his posture stiff and semi-defensive. Hale couldn't see any weapons, but at fifty yards he ground to a stop anyway.

"You recognize him?" Hale said.

By way of answer, Tito pushed half his skinny body through the open passenger's side window of the truck and lifted a hand.

"*Joseph!*" He called. "Joseph, it is me!"

Tito shouted and all the tension evaporated from the stranger's posture. He broke into a run and circled straight to the Ural's passenger side, jumping onto the running board and pulling Tito into a hearty, backslapping hug.

"Tito! Praise God. Where have you been?"

Tito mumbled an answer, but Hale couldn't understand it. The hug persisted another few moments until at last Tito was released. He slid back into the cabin, allowing Hale a clear view of the guy in the safari hat for the first time.

Middle-aged, heavily weathered, but smiling ear to ear. Hale cleared his throat, and Tito remembered his manners.

"Kawaja, meet Joseph," he said simply.

Joseph's gaze swept across the cabin, catching momentarily on the AK sandwiched between the seats, and the pistol mounted to Hale's hip. When his gaze locked with Hale's, the smile was all but gone, replaced by tense uncertainty. He extended a hand anyway.

"Welcome, friend. I thank God that you arrived safely."

Hale looked into Joseph's steady gaze and liked what he saw. He accepted the offered handshake—the grip was good.

"Is Mary Grace Dalton here?" Hale said. "I need a sat phone. We have a problem."

46

Atlanta, Georgia
00:36 Hours, Eastern Standard Time

Shaw never returned to her hotel suite. She worked from the Hurt Building, a laptop computer and empty coffee cups spread across the same conference table where she and Bill Carpenter had met with Hale.

Following her last phone call with Hale, her first order of business was to research on this so-called LRA, or "Lord's Resistance Army." It took all of five minutes and one Google search for Shaw to be snatching up her phone, redialing Hale.

He didn't answer. Bill Carpenter entered the room and happened to look over her shoulder. His face blanched at the sight of the LRA's Wikipedia page, and from that moment, Shaw knew she was on the clock.

Hale, Mary Grace, the orphanage staff, and *all* the children had to be removed from Western Equatoria—immediately. It was priority number one for Shaw, and as soon as she updated Carpenter on Hale's engagements with presumed LRA fighters, it was priority number one for Resurrection Mercy Ministries, also. All other operations would cease—all staff would be focused on the single objective of arranging air transport for the orphanage.

As a former operations officer for a prominent private security firm, Shaw's contacts list included a long list of regional airlines, air freight companies, and private contractors who owned planes. She thought it might take her a few hours—and more than a few thousand dollars—to book contract flights.

But then she learned of the United Nations Humanitarian Air Service flight from Wau to Yambio. The aircraft was a Cessna 208B Grand Caravan. The night previously, it had carried five persons, including a Canadian pilot, two Spanish aid workers, an Italian doctor, and a South Sudanese translator. Additionally, two ice chests full of cooled cholera vaccines were destined to combat a growing outbreak along the South Sudan/DRC border. The plane departed Wau at 23:35 hours local time and was scheduled to land in Yambio sixty-four minutes later.

It never arrived. Panicked radio traffic from the pilot reported anti-aircraft fire from a point near South Sudan's Southern National Park...then the radio went dead. The US military provided satellite imagery of the wreckage to the United Nations eleven hours later.

The plane was little more than blackened scrap—no survivors were visible. And the bullet holes still visible in the wings? They looked like the handiwork of a ZU-23-2—a Soviet-built, 23mm anti-aircraft gun in common circulation amid militias around the region, particularly the larger ones... like James Wani's.

Shaw was behind the curve on the facts, but the rest of the South Sudanese regional world was *not*. Everyone with a jet, a turboprop, or so much as an experimental aircraft knew all about the shocking demise of the UNHAS flight, and *nobody* was interested in flying into Western Equatoria. Not for Ian Hale, Mary Grace Dalton, or a thousand orphans.

It wasn't happening. The airspace was dead.

Shaw completed call after call and hung up with a slam after each one —shot down as surely as a plane load of cholera vaccines. As if that defeat wasn't bad enough, there was one more development that stressed her more than details of the LRA and news of the downed plane combined—the fact that Ian Hale had completely disappeared.

He missed his first check in four hours after their last conversation at

0900 hours the previous morning, and every call Shaw dialed since then had resulted in nothing save endless ringing.

Four hours of silence became eight. Then twelve. Now *fourteen*.

Shaw was reaching panic mode. She kept telling herself that Hale was probably fine. That maybe his sat phone and tablet had been lost or run out of battery. That Hale was a competent operator, qualified to survive in any environment on planet earth. He was well armed and laser focused. He *would* be okay.

So why hadn't he checked in?

Shaw gulped cold coffee. It wasn't *iced* coffee, it was just old. Stretching her legs beneath the table, she gazed through rectangular windows at the geometric mass of Mercedes-Benz Stadium one thousand yards away. Illuminated in trademark Atlanta Falcons red, the structure was beautiful. Striking.

Shaw still missed the Georgia Dome—the previous headquarters of Georgia gridiron glory. All those SEC championships and bowl games. Fall afternoons with her father, cotton candy and too much soda and *so* much shouting.

It was Shaw's childhood, demolished for the sake of bigger and better. She understood it. She still hated it. Life could suck.

Where was Hale?

No longer able to distract herself, Shaw was just returning to the computer when the door burst open. Bill Carpenter, looking every bit as exhausted as Shaw felt, stuck his head inside.

"You awake?"

Shaw looked over her shoulder. "What's up?"

"Mary Grace is calling. She's got Hale."

Shaw exploded out of her chair, energized for the first time in hours. She followed Carpenter—practically *pushed* Carpenter—down the hallway to his office. Dusty and packed with books, the room lacked a view of the new stadium but boasted a stunning vista of commercial air conditioners mounted to the roof of the Natural Sciences Center next door. Carpenter took his seat behind an outdated computer and Shaw joined him. Internet in Atlanta was lightning fast, but internet in rural Africa, modern miracle though it was, took its time loading.

Mary Grace appeared first. Sweaty, red-faced, but smiling. She sat with a South Sudanese child in her lap. The girl wore a grin the size of Texas and played peek-a-boo with the computer screen, causing Mary Grace's laptop to shake.

"MG?" Shaw said. "Are you okay?"

"Fine, Laney. Fine. Just finished lunch. Our cook barbecued us a nice goat. Wasn't it a nice goat, Tereza?"

More giggling from the child. It was a sound like gurgling water in the desert, and yet Shaw found herself wanting to put hands through the screen and throttle Mary Grace. For four solid days Shaw had drowned herself in reports of escalating violence. She had deployed an old friend—she had cashed in favors and stressed herself out of her mind. She *knew* how bad the situation was.

And yet here was Mary Grace, as relaxed as a half-drunk sorority girl on a Caribbean cruise.

"Where's Ian?" Shaw said.

Mary Grace's smile faded. "Mr. Hale arrived an hour ago. He...brought some children."

"Children?" Shaw and Carpenter said it in unison.

"Orphans...probably. We really don't know. They won't talk."

"Where did he pick up children?" Carpenter said.

Shaw thought she already knew the answer. Mary Grace simply shook her head. "I don't know. I haven't talked to him yet. There are two men with him, also, and a lot of guns. Look, I appreciate your concern, but you know how I feel about bringing weapons onto the property. We can't fight fire—"

"Mary Grace," Shaw snapped, cutting her off. "Do you still have a sat phone?"

Pause. "It's in my office."

"Get it, and get Hale. I want him on the phone."

47

Tambura, South Sudan
09:03 Hours, East Africa Time

The truck smelled of death.

Standing at the back of the Ural, Hale overlooked a wooden bed scarred by use…and stained with crimson. AK-47 brass lay scattered beneath metal benches, and handcuffs dangled from the tubing that supported the canvas cover.

It wasn't difficult to guess how this truck had been used. The story was written in the eyes of the nine children Hale had rescued.

Total terror.

"Mr. Hale?"

Hale turned, swigging from a bottle of water the man called Joseph had brought him. It tasted a bit muddy, but was cool on his throat. He felt like he needed a gallon of it.

One glance at Mary Grace Dalton, and all thoughts of water or food or even his own exhaustion took a back seat. She approached from the orphanage dressed in a swishing patchwork skirt that was clearly hand-stitched. Her hair was tugged back into a ponytail, her skinned tanned by the African sun. Moving light and easy with a subdued smile and not a trace of makeup, she was somehow even more radiant than she'd looked in her college snapshots.

Aged since then, certainly. Weathered, also. But still the kind of woman who could derail thought.

"Miss Dalton," Hale managed.

"Please, call me Mary Grace." A broader smile. "I see that Joseph brought you a drink. We draw the water from our Hawkeye well."

"Hawkeye?" Hale wasn't sure why he said it. He was suddenly awkward, not sure where to look. Her eyes, a color somewhere between sapphire and polar ice, seemed to look right through him.

"Over there." Mary Grace gestured. "It was built with donations from a small farming community in Iowa. That's why we call it the Hawkeye well."

Hale nodded absently, still unsure what to say. His mind, now kept awake for thirty-plus hours, felt like it was mired in quicksand.

"I appreciate you coming," Mary Grace continued. "I'm glad you brought the children. We may not have enough beds but...we'll fit them in."

Again, Hale remained silent, and this time it was Mary Grace's turn to shift. She lifted a sat phone.

"Laney asked for you to call her."

"Laney?" Hale squinted.

"Laney Shaw?"

Dummy.

Hale took the phone and turned away, feeling a little like he was floating. Like his feet didn't touch the ground.

"Mr. Hale?"

Hale looked back. "Yes?"

Mary Grace stood tall, chin lifted. Her smile had faded. She didn't look harsh, just...focused.

She was looking at the rifle that hung across Hale's chest, a captured AK-47 with a two-point sling.

"The weapons scare the children, Mr. Hale. I recognize that you're here to protect us, but if there's any way that you would consider leaving your guns in the truck..."

Hale squinted, identifying the words but not quite sure what he was hearing. He waited, wondering if Mary Grace was joking or might clarify.

She didn't, and Hale simply turned away again. He walked thirty yards to an acacia tree that stood between a mechanical shed and a Mitsubishi bus. The bus appeared to be broken down, its hood propped open on a stick of wood.

Hale passed into the acacia's shade and dialed from memory. Shaw answered immediately.

"What happened, Ian? Are you okay?"

Shaw's energy reminded Hale of a yapping Chihuahua—which was ironic, because Shaw hated little dogs. He rubbed his face and cracked his neck and wished he had three fingers of just about anything poured over ice.

"Complications," Hale said. "We lost our equipment during an engagement. We captured a vehicle and made it to the orphanage. All's well that ends well. How are you?"

Shaw wasn't in the mood for jokes. She wanted details—she wanted a full engagement summary. Hale leaned against the tree, replaying the events in his mind and finding that they all blurred together.

He recounted the incident the best he could, focusing on the key points—tangos appearing, tangos engaged, tangos biting the dust. And then...the children.

"How many?" Shaw said.

"Nine, none older than fifteen."

"Not the kids, the tangos. How many did you kill?"

Hale squinted. "Eight...I think."

"And their uniforms?"

There was something in her voice that bothered Hale despite his exhaustion. An edge—like she was just now driving to the heart of her concern.

Of course he remembered the uniforms. He remembered the patches.

"More LRA," Hale said. "Speaking of which, did you learn anything?"

Pause. "Yeah. I did. You're gonna want to be sitting down for this."

"I'm already sitting down."

"Right. So—it's not good. The Lord's Resistance Army was originally a Ugandan militia formed by a guy named Joseph Kony back in the late eighties. He was a religious extremist with a revolutionary agenda. Over the nineties and the early two thousands, Kony's influence spread over swaths of east and central Africa, including Uganda, the Central African Republic, Congo, Sudan, and South Sudan. His many alleged atrocities include murder, mutilation, sex slavery—including that of minors—and, most notably...the kidnap of children to train as child soldiers."

A cold chill rippled up Hale's spine, defiant of both his exhaustion and the sticky African heat. He stat up.

"You said this Kony operates in South Sudan?"

"He used to. According to rumor, he may still be hiding there. But the LRA has been largely destroyed by combined efforts of government militaries and international pressure. As of today, the organization is thought to be practically defunct..."

So who did I kill?

Hale rolled the thought in his mind without needing to voice it. He knew Shaw was already thinking the same thing.

"I spoke with Bill Carpenter," Shaw said. "He remembers the LRA from his mission trips back in the nineties. The look on his face said it all. He referred to Kony's militia as total savages. Trust me, Ian. Bill Carpenter doesn't talk that way about anyone."

Hale believed her, and he also believed Carpenter. Not because he knew Carpenter but because he'd witnessed firsthand a truck full of dried blood and imprisoned children. He'd walked over the bodies of slain parents. It was total savagery beyond question.

So was the LRA resurging? Was this Kony guy back? Or maybe...

Maybe it doesn't matter.

"I killed a dozen people to get here, Shaw, and it wouldn't take a genius to know where we went. If there's any organization in the region, LRA or otherwise, interested in kidnapping children...well, I'm sitting at an orphanage full of them, and I'm not such a badass as to hold off an army. Where are we with the evac?"

Hale didn't like the pause that followed his question. He liked what Shaw said next even less—all about a Cessna Grand Caravan shot down in Western Equatoria and a state of aviation panic that had swept the region.

"I'm doing everything I can, Hale. I'll keep beating down doors until we find a solution. In the meantime...you sound wrecked. Try to get some rest.

Inspect the facility and prepare a defense report as soon as you're able. We'll take this one step at a time."

It wasn't what Hale wanted to hear, but Shaw's measured calm was exactly the approach that had saved Hale's neck more than once. Without Sentinel's resources to fall back on, Shaw wasn't so well equipped as times past, but if Hale needed somebody to haul him out of a mess, he still liked his odds with Shaw better than most. She'd never let him down before.

"James Wani unleashing terror," Hale said. "The LRA resurging out of nowhere. A UN plane shot out of the sky. All of this on the heels of a discovered coltan deposit that we both know half the planet would kill for. You can't tell me that's a coincidence."

"I know," Shaw said, her voice softening. "I'm thinking the same thing."

The line fell silent for a long moment. Hale blinked heavy eyes and sipped Hawkeye water. Then he nodded, accepting the situation and ready to run with it.

What else was he going to do?

"Give me a few hours to reset," Hale said. "I'll call with a defense plan."

"Good copy," Shaw said. "And Ian?"

"Yeah?"

"I'm really glad you're okay."

Hale didn't know what to say, so he simply grunted and hung up. He laid the phone in the grass and relaxed against the tree. The bark was rough but felt like an absolute cloud. Each muscle group in his battered body relaxed in sequence, and he allowed the AK to rest across his lap, still dangling from its sling.

He closed his eyes, for just a moment. He breathed deep.

And then he was gone.

48

Western Equatoria, South Sudan
09:22 Hours, East Africa Time

They were dead—every one of them.

Strewn across a field of crushed elephant grass, Harden's latest raiding party was shot to pieces. While most of his soldiers lay twisted and growing stiff, the two inside the torched Jeep Wrangler were identifiable only as blackened skeletons.

The rest? Consumed by fire.

Harden swung from the passenger's seat of a Toyota Hilux pickup, his boots landing amid ashen grass stems as he spat tobacco juice. He pushed the sunglasses up his nose and unsnapped the retention strap on his hip holster, easing access to the Glock 17 mounted there.

The field around *tasted* of death—a cumulative flavor Harden had encountered so many times in his life.

None of the six African militiamen who accompanied him said a word as Harden walked across the field, still chewing and occasionally spitting, one hand resting on the pistol. He reached the Jeep and stopped, staring at the human skull that rested in the driver's floorboard. There was a bullet hole in the side of it—drilled by a 9mm, he thought. Strong enough to punch in but maybe not strong enough to punch out.

More than enough to extinguish life.

A dry, lifeless smile stretched Harden's lips as he looked to the ground and found a bent metal water bottle. It was contorted by the heat of the fire but still bore the engraved logo of the Los Angeles Lakers, a hugely popular brand in a country full of the world's tallest people.

The South Sudanese *loved* basketball. Harden had bought his men a TV and a DVD player to view recorded NBA games. The guy who carried the bottle, a treasured possession, was one of his best captains.

Shot through the head.

Harden laughed. Dry and soft, the sound was barely audible. He fixated on the bottle. He chewed.

He snapped.

One boot struck the bottle like a soccer ball. Harden threw his head back and screamed, spraying tobacco juice. Cursing. Turning to find his men cowering near the Hilux.

Dogs.

Harden expelled the tobacco in a wad and reached the truck. Tearing through the glove box, he found his sat phone and mashed the power button. He looked across the field, past the bodies and the burned Jeep to what was *not* there.

A Russian Ural truck.

"What is your update?"

The Asian voice was as calm as ever. Harden packed fresh tobacco into his cheek before answering.

"I found the site. All soldiers accounted for, all dead. Looks like an ambush."

Silence on the line. Harden knew what his employer was thinking—the same thing he had been thinking ever since receiving the panicked midnight phone call from his Lakers fan captain.

"We're under attack!" the captain had shouted. *"We need backup!"*

Then the line went silent, as though the phone was shot right out of the guy's hand, and all Harden could think was: *What?*

"The children?" the voice said at last.

Harden swept the battleground once more, maybe hoping to find smaller bodies.

There were none.

"Gone," he said. "The Ural is gone, also. We found a Land Cruiser in the river not far away. The water has receded but was high last night. Looks like it got stuck...I don't know."

"Did you search it?"

Harden had. He'd waded up to his stomach in the river, and inside the trapped Land Cruiser he found a number of things. Waterlogged, mostly ruined, but all of it top quality combat gear. The kind a hardcore killer might use.

"They were pros," Harden said. "I found American gear—the good stuff."

The employer considered in silence, and Harden let him. He already knew where the conversation was headed. There was only one logical conclusion.

"We cannot allow witnesses," the employer said.

"I know."

"And now we are down nine children."

"I know."

"How many men do you have left?"

"Seven—not my best."

"Equipment?"

"One Hilux, two older Land Cruisers. One needs a tire, neither have machine guns. I'm down to small arms."

It wasn't enough to finish the job—Harden knew that without needing to be told. But that was his employer's problem.

"There is a splinter unit of rogue militia camped about forty kilometers northeast of your base," the employer said. "They used to be members of James Wani's crew. They split away and now they're just...roving thugs."

"How many?" Harden asked.

"Fifty, maybe sixty."

"Equipment?"

"I do not know."

"Are they...*flexible*?"

The employer knew what Harden was asking. It was the single most important question.

"They're accused of gang-raping children," the employer said.

Harden snorted. *Pretty flexible.*

"I'll need money," he said. "And not just for them. We're dealing with professionals now. The risk has increased—I expect my compensation to increase with it."

The employer didn't hesitate. "I'll double your fee."

Better than I hoped.

"Done," Harden said. "I'll update you tonight."

He hung up, still staring at the toasted Jeep and the fragmented skeleton crumpled inside. He could still hear his captain screaming at the TV as the Lakers defeated the Miami Heat for the 2020 NBA championship—their third "consecutive" title.

The captain didn't know that Harden had hand-selected the Lakers most dominant seasons and assembled them on the DVD to appear successive. A happy militia was a deadly militia, right?

Stupid fool.

Harden swung aboard the Hilux.

49

Juba, South Sudan
09:30 Hours, East Africa Time

Wing-Kei ended the call with Harden and stood silent in the Radisson hotel room, staring at the satellite phone.

And thinking.

Nothing about the slaughter of Harden's men particularly surprised him. They were soldiers in name only, mostly untrained, universally under-equipped, and not particularly intelligent. Wing-Kei himself could have killed a dozen of them single-handedly given the element of surprise and a reliable handgun.

No—it wasn't their deaths that bothered him. With heavily armed units of James Wani's White Nile Liberation Army swarming Western Equatoria, momentary misidentification could have been all that was needed to touch off a massacre.

But where were the *children*? The WNLA wasn't known to employ child soldiers, and they weren't known to build orphanages, either. With their parents slain, the kids would have likely be transported to the nearest village and dumped.

Was that what happened? Had Wani's men kept the Ural as a war prize?

Maybe. But how did that explain the Land Cruiser abandoned in the river, stocked with American gear?

Wing-Kei didn't like any of it. He was starting to get a bad feeling, and he knew why. He'd let this operation run too long. He'd gotten greedy, pushing Harden for more when he should have made what he had work. One anonymous phone call to the nearest United Nations field office would be all it took to touch off the investigation. Two hundred kids was *plenty...*

But the tape.

Wing-Kei still needed the tape. In his gut he knew that no volume of print journalism, however graphic, could take the place of ten seconds of real-world footage. A single clip, shot from the right angle and capturing the right details, could make all the difference. It could push the entire world over the edge.

Where was the tape? Had his journalists died, also?

Wing-Kei had sent *six men* into Western Equatoria, and not one—

The sat phone trembled with an incoming call, jarring Wing-Kei from his thoughts. He checked the screen and swallowed—he couldn't help it.

He recognized the +251 Ethiopia calling code. The boss was calling.

"What is the status?"

The voice made no attempt at warmth. In turn, Wing-Kei made no attempt at avoiding the difficult.

"The children are assembled. Less than I had hoped for, but enough. News of the village strikes and kidnappings are running wild throughout the region. I've sponsored rumors of an LRA resurgence here in Juba, also. The context is established."

"And documentation?"

Wing-Kei hesitated. His boss gave him no chance to evade.

"You have nothing."

"I still have locals in the field," Wing-Kei said. "I may have something."

The response sounded even weaker coming out of Wing-Kei's mouth than it had in his mind. He waited while the line remained silent.

At last, the boss said: "The Americans are adding pressure. We have no choice but to proceed. Have you made plans for the main event?"

"Nothing final—my contractor is short on troops. I have arranged for him to meet with a local rogue militia. They should be easily bought. From there, we only need a target."

"Word must leak *beforehand*, Wing-Kei. This only works if it occurs in the correct order."

Wing-Kei knew that better than anyone. This entire operation was his own brainchild, after all. He was *this* close to landing a massive success that would launch him all the way to the top...

"I'll make it work," Wing-Kei promised. "You have my word."

"Update me," the boss said flatly. Then he hung up, and Wing-Kei ran a hand over his bald head. Stepping to the window, he looked across a dusty and semi-crumbling city, straight west into the rolling brushlands.

Toward Western Equatoria. Toward miles and miles of ungoverned wasteland...and a billion dollars of untapped natural resources, waiting to be claimed in the name of China.

50

Western Equatoria, South Sudan
17:14 Hours, East Africa Time

Hale awoke with a start.

Eyes popping open, he clenched his hand around the AK's grip as pressure bounced off his cheek. Come and gone, the tap was followed by a sound like soft wind chimes. Hale snatched the rifle into his shoulder and the wind chime sound cascaded into a chorus of higher-pitched squeals just as his vision finally snapped into focus.

Context returned—a dusty yard overhung by the sprawling limbs of the acacia tree, and a three-story building turned amber by the glow of a late afternoon sun. Hale saw dust in the air and the gunshot Ural still parked where he'd left it.

And he saw children. Four of them, hiding behind the nose of the Mercedes bus—the one with its hood open. From twenty feet they peeked out, eyes wide and alarmed. In another blink, Hale realized he was pointing the rifle at them—realized that the wind chime sound he'd heard was children giggling.

Then screaming.

Hale lowered the gun, flicking the safety on with his right index finger.

It closed with a metallic snap and one child jumped. All four kept their gazes frozen on them. The oldest couldn't have been more than ten, the youngest maybe six. They were black, small, skinny, clothed in mismatched T-shirts and pants with tears in their legs. Hale could see only one foot, but that foot was bare.

Slowly, Hale released the rifle with his left hand. He waved, forcing an awkward smile.

For a split second, nothing happened. Then one of the children giggled and babbled something. All four of them vanished behind the bus, gone in the blink of an eye.

"They like you."

The voice sounded from somewhere to Hale's right. He twisted, looking back toward the mechanic's shed. The man called Joseph stood just inside, scrubbing his hands with a greasy towel. Behind him an engine block lay torn apart on a workbench, tools scattered around it.

Hale blinked, still struggling to bring his mind back to the present. He thought of the amber-colored concrete blocks and twisted his wrist to check the time. The G-Shock read 17:20—hours after he'd settled beneath the tree.

"You slept like a log, my friend," Joseph said, emerging from the shed and drawing his canteen. He took a long draw, then offered the canteen to Hale. Still seated at the base of the tree, Hale didn't hesitate. He tasted the same muddy water from the Hawkeye well as he had before—only this was further flavored by the smell of sunbaked aluminum.

"It's good, right?" Joseph said.

Hale could only grunt. He returned the canteen empty and wiped his mouth.

"I'm sorry about the gun. I just...reacted."

Joseph waved a dismissive hand, leaning against the tree and looking across the compound. Hale couldn't see them, but he could hear children playing. Joseph smiled as he watched.

"There is no greater joy than the joy of a child. It's like sunshine in a bottle."

Hale didn't comment, still extricating his mind from a web of unconsciousness. Now that a perceived threat turned out to be nothing more than a playful child tiptoeing up to poke him in the face, adrenaline faded quickly. He was coming back down to earth, taking inventory of his mind and body.

He was sore and stiff. His ears rang, and his neck ached. But for all that, he felt rejuvenated for having slept against a tree, much more so than he would have expected.

"I always said that nobody sleeps better than a soldier," Joseph said. "On rocks or dirt or leaning against a tree. A soldier can sleep anywhere."

Hale squinted in a ray of unfiltered sunlight, looking up at Joseph. For the first time since meeting the man, he took his time surveying large, dark eyes. Searching their depths. Evaluating what lay behind.

Joseph looked...like a very deep lake. Still at midday, without a breath wind to disturb the surface or a trace of guile to cloud metaphorical water. He was calm in the way only a man who is at peace with himself can be.

And yet...

Hale extended a hand and bit back a grunt as Joseph helped him off the ground. His thighs were both asleep and buzzed as blood flow returned. It felt a little funny to stand.

"Do you speak from experience?" Hale asked.

Joseph laughed. "Experience sleeping on rocks and dirt?"

"Experience as a soldier."

This time there was no laugh, and something stirred beneath the lake in Joseph's eyes. It wasn't deception, but it wasn't transparent, either.

"You must be hungry," Joseph said. "Ajok, our cook, has prepared lentil soup with flatbread—we have Skittles for dessert."

"Skittles?" Hale said. "The candy?"

"Indeed! They were sent from Atlanta with the last air drop. One thing you will learn about our little ones—they *love* candy."

Joseph started toward the orphanage, but Hale hung back. Rotating away from the compound with the rifle riding its sling, he looked east toward very distant Juba.

Rolling hills and tangles of trees obscured his view at barely a hundred yards out. Even from the vantage point of the orphanage roof, three stories off the ground, Hale doubted he could see more than a mile—less with morning fog.

It was a bad situation. A tango, or even a hundred tangos, could slip within sniping or shelling distance and nobody would know anything about it until the gunfire began. With the bulk of Tambura three kilometers away, whatever petty security forces the South Sudanese government kept there would be useless in the event of a raid. Likewise, fleeing to Tambura for shelter would be a fool's errand. As the Ural passed along the outskirts of town, Hale saw nothing more than a cluster of shabby houses.

No safe place to hide. No high ground from which to stand and fight.

"It's okay," Joseph said, looking back. "We're safe."

Hale stared Joseph down a long moment, resisting the urge to state the obvious.

If you were safe, I wouldn't be here.

"Will Mary Grace Dalton be at dinner?" he said at last.

"Of course."

"Good." Hale rotated the rifle to hang at his side and started toward the building. "We'll be holding a security conference over our Skittles."

51

Washington, DC
10:30 Hours, Eastern Standard Time

Morris had been hyperbolic when he said that he would read details of his partner's efforts in *The New York Times*—he didn't expect that to be literally the case.

The headline an aid sent him was only available online, not in the printed edition, but it was still the *Times* and that meant it was being read by who knew how many thousands of people. Alongside photos of one Canadian, one Italian, one South Sudanese, and a pair of young Spanish girls, bold text declared: UN RELIEF FLIGHT SHOT DOWN OVER SOUTH SUDAN—JAMES WANI TO BLAME?

Morris shoveled sunflower seeds into his mouth, nervously chewing and spitting while he speed-read the column. He skipped past details of the victims and focused on the location. The international reaction and response. Statements issued by the UN about their growing concern of Wani's aggression—their demands for Juba to take action or else allow a peacekeeping coalition to deploy into Western Equatoria.

Unbelievable.

Morris's fingers jabbed at his desk phone. The private line rang only once. Morris barked before the rumbling voice on the other end could speak.

"Are you out of your *mind*?"

Pause. A chair groaned as its occupant reclined.

"You wanna rephrase that question? Because I'm not hearing any gratitude, and I should be."

"A *UN flight*. That ape shot down a *UN flight*. Four nationalities on board. Do you know what that means?"

"It means we're done fooling around," the voice snapped with uncustomary impatience. "It means Abiem has a choice—US Marines or an international coalition. Either way, somebody is parachuting into his backyard. I've done my part, Morris. *Do yours*."

The call ended with a slam. Seated behind his computer, Morris blinked, both caught off guard and instantly indignant. He wanted to curse as he smashed the handset back into its cradle. He wanted to throw something.

And yet...wasn't his partner right? Morris had pushed for a trump card. What could be better than direct outrage from the United Nations?

Morris sucked sunflower seasoning from his teeth, ignoring the chime of an incoming email. Feeding fresh seeds between flabby lips, he chewed and calculated. Envisioned the angles.

And then reached the obvious conclusion. The *only* conclusion.

Lifting the handset, he paged his secretary. She connected him with the American Embassy to South Sudan, and he waited in silence until Jaxon Wilks took the call.

Morris's young protégé sounded exhausted, maybe a little frayed.

"Mr. Assistant Secretary—did you hear?"

Morris ignored the question, diving straight ahead into one of his own. "When's your next meeting with Abiem?"

"Meeting? Sir, I'm talking about—"

"That smoked UN flight," Morris cut him off. "I know."

"They think it was James Wani," Jaxon said. "The South Sudanese are in panic mode. I can't get through to Abiem's office—they say he's managing the crisis."

Morris snorted, not buying the explanation for a millisecond.

"He's stalling, same as before. Only now he's *out of time*."

"Sir?" Jaxon sounded confused—Morris wanted to strangle him.

"Get back in the car and get over to Abiem's office," Morris said. "He *will* see you, like it or not. I want you to inform Mr. Abiem that the United States has grown weary of his delays. The situation in South Sudan is of grave concern. He will either accept our generous offer of security assistance...or we will back a mandatory deployment of UN peacekeepers, and there will be *no* mining in South Sudan—not by anybody. Understand?"

Silence. Then Jaxon said, very slowly: "Are you sure you want to exploit this, sir? That could backfire—"

"I know what I'm doing," Morris snapped. "Do you understand your orders, or should I replace you?"

Another hesitation. Then: "I understand."

"Excellent. *Get it done*."

Morris slammed the phone down a second time and glanced back to his computer. He scanned the faces of the five victims. He imagined those images playing across the screen at the next meeting of the United Nations in New York.

Playing across the screen...and then being swept right under the rug.

It was time to make a deal.

52

Western Equatoria, South Sudan
18:20 Hours, East Africa Time

Every room in the three-story complex featured a low ceiling and painted plywood walls—many decorated with children's artwork drawn in crayon. The ground level was the most developed, with a cluster of classrooms on one side, a small medical center, and a kitchen stocked with stainless steel cook wear.

There were no interior doors, only curtains or open frames. Box fans drew damp African air through open windows. Sanitary services consisted of three outhouses mounted over pits at the back of the complex. Joseph explained that floors two and three were both dormitories—one for the girls, one for the boys. Cots, hammocks, and pallets served as beds.

It was the very definition of rudimentary living, not quite primitive but rougher than any Army barracks Hale had ever slept in. The floor creaked as he stepped inside, the chatter of children bouncing through the halls growing suddenly quiet as dark eyes fixated on the newcomer.

There were children *everywhere*. Mostly elementary age, but Hale noted two toddlers and a couple others that appeared closer to adulthood. Mostly barefoot, all clad in multicolored hand-me-down clothes with their hair cut short and their skin clinging tight to slender frames.

"How many?" Hale asked.

Joseph smiled—but it wasn't a happy smile.

"Seventy-three, before you came. Eighty-two now. Twice as many as six months ago."

Hale looked to his left, locking gazes with a six- or seven-year-old girl dressed in pink. She huddled behind a door curtain, only half of her face visible, but that half was more than enough to tell a story. Thick scars swelled from her chest and proceeded up her neck, an irregular mass that converged just above her jawbone.

They were burn scars, a whole nest of them. Maybe an accident, but judging by the way the girl's one visible eye locked on the AK riding at Hale's side, he didn't think so.

"Joseph," he said.

"Yes?"

"You gotta safe place to store this?"

Joseph took the rifle, and Hale extended empty hands toward the doorframe as he descended into a squat. He offered a smile, his voice just loud enough to carry.

"Hi, I'm Ian. What's your name?"

The girl blinked. She remained frozen behind the curtain, dead still for a moment, then trembling as the whites around her irises turned red.

Then she vanished in a chorus of thumping feet, leaving Hale with his hand outstretched...something like a cloud of dread closing over him.

53

Dinner was served behind the orphanage in an open-sided pole barn stocked with picnic tables.

Hale scrubbed his face and hands in a bucket of well water before circling the building in time to find all eighty-plus of the children gathered around one particular table at the back of the pavilion. A chorus of laughs and shouts exploded from the crowd, matching a heavy *thump* of flesh against wood. Hale stepped into the barn, lifting a hand to block the setting sun.

Then he found Tito, squatting on the table exactly the way he had squatted next to his milk crates, with his knees rising up to his ears. He drew his arms and legs so close to his body that he looked ready to be packed into a whiskey barrel. Slowly, his arms extended outward, elbows locking. The children grew perfectly silent, every eye fixed on the spectacle.

Then Tito exploded off the table. Launching himself fully a yard into the air, he completed both a backflip and a full 360-degree spin before landing precisely where he'd started, his bare feet slapping the tabletop. The children roared, a tidal wave of grinning faces crowding toward the table as Tito beamed.

Hale smiled also. The children chanted, and Tito performed the trick on repeat, never seeming to grow tired as he effortlessly launched his skinny body—always landing right back where he started.

"Simple joys," a voice said.

Hale twisted, finding Mary Grace Dalton standing just behind him, a sheen of sweat coating her forehead. She watched the children with a subdued smile, much like the one Joseph used. Very contented, very sincere.

Also a little sad.

"Back at UGA, a brand-new Mercedes wouldn't have generated that much joy," Mary Grace said.

Back at UGA, you wouldn't have been shot at over dinner.

It was another thought Hale kept to himself. He looked back to the children and lost himself for a moment in their shouts.

"Higher, Tito! Go higher!"

"How do you know him?" Hale said.

"Tito?"

Hale nodded, arms folded. The sigh Mary Grace exhaled was a lot sadder than her smile.

"Tito was...a friend from the start. His family lived in a village some ways north of here. Their makeshift orphanage was the inspiration for our permanent installment here in Tambura. Tito and his family helped us restore this place. They were carpenters by trade."

Were carpenters. Hale couldn't help but notice the past tense. He shot Mary Grace a look.

"Ethnic cleansing," Mary Grace said, her voice barely above a whisper. "Dinka militia raided Tito's village. Everyone who lived there was a member of the Zande tribe—sworn enemies of the Dinka. Supposedly it was a revenge strike...who knows. Sometimes vengeance is an explanation, sometimes only an excuse. Tito was the only survivor, but he suffered a severe pelvic injury after being run over by a light truck. The bones never fully healed, and there was nerve damage. That's why you never see him sitting—he can walk and squat and flip...but he can't sit. Not without tremendous pain."

Mary Grace finished the story, and Hale's gaze traveled back to Tito. He remembered the first time they met—the deep pain in Tito's eyes. That pain had only faded once in Hale's presence—the moment burning hatred took its place.

And yet Tito had volunteered for this trip without any request for compensation and at great personal risk to his own life.

Why?

"You saved his life," Hale said. "Didn't you?"

"Tito was dying of infection," Mary Grace said. "We flew in a doctor from Uganda...We treated him just in time."

"*I know war.*"

Tito's words echoed in Hale's mind, suddenly landing so much deeper than before. But the context of grace—of a real-life miracle—explained something, also. It explained why a man who couldn't even sit would willingly ride for hours across torturous terrain, and into a war zone.

Because he owed his life to these people.

"We should eat," Mary Grace said.

At a table near the barn's perimeter, the portly local cook, Ajok, ladled lentil soup into shallow bowls, each with a chunk of flatbread. Her assistant was a teenage kid called Diko, who scurried to follow Joseph's every direction as the children were herded to the tables.

There was also an old man named Wal, who served as the orphanage's doctor. He wasn't actually a doctor, but he'd once been a medic in the Sudanese Armed Forces. A land mine had all but decimated his back, leaving him useless to the SAF and to much of African society.

Like so many in his position, the orphanage became a home for Wal, and because he could read, Wal was able to sharpen his medical knowledge by extensive study of what textbooks RMM could supply. Now he administered the vitamins and soft medications stored in the orphanage's infirmary, occasionally performing stitching jobs or minor surgeries.

"I was able to remove the bullet from your friend's arm," Wal told Hale as they slid onto bench seats. "The muscle damage was not bad, but the infection is severe. I gave him morphine and the strongest antibiotics we have. He is resting in our clinic."

Hale nodded his thanks, though in truth, he'd barely thought of Bakumba since arriving. At least the guy wouldn't die of an infection, rotting in some ditch outside a torched village.

"My small ones! Quiet now, quiet. It sounds like a herd of monkeys in here!" Joseph shouted across the pole barn—by way of response he received nothing but laughter.

"Monkeys don't live in herds, Joseph!" a young voice, heavy with attitude, retorted.

"What's that? I didn't know we had a scientist in the room. What *do* monkeys live in?"

The laughter died. All eyes turned toward the outspoken child. She giggled, then shouted: "Your house!"

Fresh laughter. Joseph feigned outrage, shaking his head. Mary Grace allowed twenty seconds of chaos, then clapped her hands.

That brought calm quicker than a shotgun blast. She directed them to bow their heads—Joseph prayed. Solemn but not heavy, the tone was that of a man speaking to an old friend. When he finished, the children all shouted an "amen," and then the clamor resumed as Ajok and Diko dispensed the food. The head table was last to be served, and Hale's stomach growled by the time a dented steel bowl landed in front of him.

It smelled amazing. It tasted just as good.

"Tell us about yourself, Mr. Hale."

Mary Grace's voice sounded like gentle music, and Hale wiped lentils from his lips, suddenly self-conscious. Everyone at the table was looking at him, including Tito, who squatted not far away.

Hale wound his mind through the usual—career highlights, technical certifications, skill sets ranging from *mastered* to *good enough to be dangerous*. What did Mary Grace really need to know?

"I was in the Army—Delta Force. I trained in personal protection and hostage rescue, among other things. I have extensive expertise in site security—securing buildings, in other words. I'm not a miracle worker, but I'll do my best to improve your situation until RMM arranges a long-term solution."

Hale finished, and the table remained quiet. Tito chewed, smacking his food. Everyone else just started.

Then Mary Grace laughed. "My goodness, Mr. Hale. I was asking about you *personally*."

"Oh." Hale swallowed soup. "I, uh...I'm from New Hampshire."

"I'm so sorry," Mary Grace said.

Hale squinted. She blushed.

"It's a joke."

Hale nodded. "Sure."

"So...you were born in New Hampshire?"

"I was."

"And after that, what did you do? Besides securing buildings, I mean."

A playful light twinkled in her eye. Hale scanned back behind his Army days, all those years ago to a childhood that now felt like a black-and-white movie played on the other side of a cloud. He couldn't hear anything. The pictures were obscured.

And maybe that was a blessing, because the highlights weren't pretty. What was he going to tell Mary Grace, anyway? About the father who reenlisted in the United States Army following 9/11 and never came home? About the mother who grew distant and depressed, burying herself at work until the night she fell asleep behind the wheel, surviving a crash only to become a vegetable?

Or maybe he could tell the table about what happened *after* the Army. A bloody story about Sentinel, a private military contracting firm—an opportunity for a fresh start, until Hale himself left its treasonous owner lying shot through the head.

No. None of that was dinner talk.

"I grew up on a small farm," Hale said. "So mostly...I secured barns."

Dead silence again. Then everyone laughed together—including Tito. Mary Grace's laugh was the loudest of all, rolling and smooth and genuine. Hale could imagine what it must have sounded like when she was a sorority girl at UGA—the very life of the party.

It was a nice image.

"I tell you what, Mr. Hale," Mary Grace said. "You're a tough nut to crack, I'll give you that."

Hale dipped his head. Mary Grace lifted her water cup.

"Here's to Mr. Hale, and the Lord's provision. We're thankful to have him...and pray that we won't need him."

Hale touched cups with Mary Grace and enjoyed the mud-flavored well water. She held his gaze for a long moment as she sipped, blue eyes sparkling. The stare quickened Hale's heart rate and left him awkwardly looking away.

His gaze landed on a child at the end of a long table. Small, slender. Clad in pink. She watched him through one eye...not because the other eye was hidden behind a door curtain, but because the other eye was missing. In its place was a black patch. The scars Hale had seen before, now exposed to the sunlight, glistened with sweat.

She stared, unblinking. Unsmiling. Her food was untouched.

Hale glanced left and found Mary Grace watching him. The smile had left her lips, and the sparkle had left her eyes. She swallowed soup, glanced to the child, and then calmly returned to her meal.

Hale did the same even as his appetite evaporated. He stared into the dented soup bowl and couldn't help but think...

You're going to need me.

54

Western Equatoria, South Sudan
20:12 Hours, East Africa Time

Lado Bakumba was in agony.

The bullet wound had hurt before, certainly. It stung like fire when he was shot, it throbbed as it swelled, and it seared like a hot iron when Ian Hale poured peroxide on it.

But after a while, it sort of numbed. It became background noise, his body muting the worst of the burn as he learned to overcome. So long as the arm remained motionless, unused and undisturbed, Bakumba could manage the misery. The heavy painkillers Hale gave him helped a lot.

But then came the orphanage, and that fool doctor.

No, not *really* a doctor. The stooped old African was something closer to a demon. He had poked and probed the arm, unleashing bloody pus as Bakumba howled and Diko, Wal's young assistant, held him down.

The bullet had to come out, Wal said. If it wasn't removed immediately, the infection could turn lethal. Petrified of the pain, Bakumba refused to cooperate, demanding morphine. A little was administered—just enough to calm his quaking body.

Wal spoke gently. He promised a smooth operation. Bakumba

continued to fuss, but eventually he let Wal talk him into it. He even allowed Diko to secure his arms and legs to the operating bed—a mere precaution, Wal assured him. The morphine would erase all pain.

It did not. It helped, maybe, but as Wal rooted through the bullet channel, Bakumba screeched. Diko shouted for Joseph, and Joseph arrived to cover Bakumba's mouth—he was scaring the children. The operation lasted for what felt like hours, and Bakumba longed to pass out.

Finally, Wal got the bullet out. It wasn't a rifle slug, as expected, but a pistol bullet. Joseph pronounced it to be a 9mm and seemed to think that was somehow a blessing.

Bakumba demanded more morphine. They gave him some, but not nearly enough. They actually left him strapped to the bed under accusations of being "obstinate." Bakumba cursed them, but what could he do? The hours slipped by as his bandaged arm throbbed. He banged his head against the bedframe and howled, but only Wal responded, advising Bakumba to "control his tongue" and "try to rest."

Bakumba imagined what it would sound like to split the old man's head with a brush knife. The thought was satisfying enough to bring a smile to his face, but it didn't last. The pain returned. He gritted his teeth as a dinner bell rang. Sunlight faded and Bakumba lay sweating and cursing himself.

He shouldn't have come here. He should have dropped off the Land Cruiser when nobody was looking, slipping into the brush long before he was nearly drowned. With a stolen sat phone, he could have turned east. He could have called the masked man. He had the camera.

The camera.

Bakumba's gaze ran down his leg to a bulging pocket. The camera, tucked inside not long before Hale drove the Land Cruiser into the river, had survived the flood and traveled with Bakumba all the way to Tambura. He hadn't checked to see if it was busted or otherwise destroyed—it was supposed to be waterproof, right?

If Bakumba could just get the device charged, he might still have something to sell—something to justify all this insane suffering. More than the video, the bullet wound *itself* might be worth something. As a bona fide war journalist, couldn't he claim a bonus?

The pain faded as Bakumba's mind raced with the possibilities. For the first time in days, greedy anticipation outweighed his discomfort. He thought of ten *thousand* US dollars—unimaginable wealth. All he had to do was get back to Juba...

Or maybe he didn't have to. Maybe all he really needed was a satellite phone. The masked man had urged him to call if he needed assistance. Bakumba had his number written down in permanent marker on the inside of his shirt. If he could just get free of the restraints...

Footsteps padded across linoleum, an awkward shuffle instantly recognizable as that of the depraved doctor. Bakumba forced himself to relax, adopting a makeshift plan. The strategy wasn't difficult—Bakumba had charmed people his entire life.

Sure enough, Wal appeared, his wrinkled, sweaty old face looming over Bakumba. Wal smiled and lifted a bowl.

"Hungry?"

Bakumba *was* hungry. The smell of whatever Wal carried reminded him of home-cooked meals from a childhood long forgotten. Bakumba tried to sit up—the restraints caught him, and he cursed.

Wal settled onto a stool with a sigh and a weary shake of his head. He did not reach for the restraints.

"We don't allow profane language, Mr. Bakumba. It's not good for the children, and truly, it's not good for you. Has anyone spoken to you about the future of your immortal soul?"

Bakumba wanted to throttle the man—clamp down on his throat until his eyeballs popped out. Make *him* scream.

Instead, he breathed deep. He focused on the problem at hand...and lowered his voice to something just pitiful enough to evoke emotion.

"I'm very hungry."

Wal nodded. He rose with a grunt and put hands on Bakumba's restraints.

Then he hesitated. "I have your word?"

Bakumba said nothing. He merely stared, unblinking, and nodded once.

Wal bought it. He unbound Bakumba and helped him into a seated position. The pain was back, pulsating into Bakumba's very skull. His vision wavered, and he steadied himself on his good arm. Sweat ran down his face, but he was okay.

He was free.

"Here," Wal said. "Lentil soup."

Bakumba used his good hand to operate the spoon. One shaking mouthful, and he closed his eyes.

He saw Juba. That Radisson hotel he'd always dreamed of. A suite on the top floor, bucketloads of cash spread across the bed. Hookers and enough dope to silence the pain. Plans to leave South Sudan in the dust. To start a new life in a better, brighter place.

Maybe as a full-time journalist, even. Why not? He'd have experience.

"Is it good?" Wal asked.

Bakumba smiled, lentils sticking to his teeth.

"So good."

55

Western Equatoria, South Sudan
21:33 Hours, East Africa Time

Marc Harden had visited some terrible places—hellholes on six out of seven continents, and the only reason he'd never parachuted into the seventh was because penguins have nothing to steal.

From cutting his teeth in the deserts of Iraq to refining his skills across Agency black sites around the globe, Harden was no stranger to mortal danger. He'd stared death in the face a dozen times, barely escaping on each occasion. He knew what terror felt like—the slow-motion dread of walking a knife's edge.

That was the feeling Harden experienced as he and his men closed on the coordinates provided by his employer. Deep in a sub-Saharan forest not unlike the one where Harden kept the children imprisoned, the first thing that he noticed was how dead quiet it was.

No birds chirping, no monkeys barking. No pigs rustling in the bushes. Harden stopped the Hilux, his gaze sweeping beyond the headlights into inky black shadow.

He didn't have night vision, and even if he did, he wouldn't have worn it. He wasn't trying to sneak, and wearing NVGs would put the militia on edge

—Harden didn't want to be shot in the face before he even had a chance to voice his proposal. Riding with their weapons concealed beneath blankets, and the LRA uniforms left behind, neither Harden nor his two recently promoted captains looked like soldiers.

They looked like wandering fools, bumping down a rutted forest trail in a vehicle so battered it was hardly worth stealing. If the employer's intel was correct, and that rutted forest trail led past a splinter-cell militia's forest hideout, Harden and his men *might* be allowed to pass. It was late, after all. The militia might be sleeping off a bender, too lazy to bother with three men and a battered truck.

Alternatively, they might unload on the Hilux just for the fun of it. There was no way to be sure, which fueled Harden's anxiety. Within minutes, maybe seconds, he could be *lights out* without warning. Worse still he might be taken hostage, held for ransom or sport. Carved apart one piece at a time, just as Harden himself had carved apart swamp rabbits in Carolina and human beings in pits around the globe.

Really, there was no point in worrying about it. The next phase of the mission was clear. The compensation had been doubled. Harden hadn't come to Africa to play it safe.

So he drove on—another two hundred yards with both captains sitting silent and tense alongside him. Harden wrestled the truck into a turn and reached for his chewing tobacco. He touched the pouch...then his hand froze. His left foot smashed down on the clutch, his right foot on the brake. The Hilux slid to a halt, headlights bouncing. One captain gasped, but didn't move.

Nobody moved. It was far too late to run. Sitting at a full stop halfway through the turn, Marc Harden stared down the muzzle of a Russian Dushka heavy machine gun. Mounted to the bed of a Nissan Patrol pickup, the weapon jutted over the cab, one man standing behind it while two more sat behind the windshield. As the Hilux slid to a stop, the Patrol's headlights flashed on, blinding all three of them in an instant.

Harden lifted a hand to shield his eyes as shouts rang through the woods. Boots squished in the mud and Harden attempted without success to track the movement of shadows beyond the glare.

Then a harsh click from his own window sent him jumping. Harden spun to find the slanted muzzle break of an AK-47 hovering only inches from his face, a soldier standing behind.

"Stop engine," the man said. His English was abrupt, crude. Harden cut the Toyota's motor off and lifted both hands. Turned sideways, he could see shadows in the forest. Maybe half a dozen of them, moving just behind the trees. They were all armed, all full-grown adults.

Safe to say he'd located the militia.

"Out," the man with the AK said. He stepped back, and Harden unlatched the door, immediately returning both hands to head level as he landed in the mud.

"Turn," the man demanded. Harden complied, and he and his captains were rammed against the bed of their own truck, legs kicked apart as gunmen swarmed from the woods. Wallets, pocketknives, and a flask of good Kentucky bourbon from Harden's back pocket all landed in the dirt. A gunman opened it and sniffed, wrinkling his nose in disgust. Harden might have laughed if he weren't so focused on staying alive.

"Who are you?"

The question was barked as the search was complete.

"My name is Harden."

"Why are you here? Where are you going?"

More angry questions, but Harden could already tell that his captor was getting bored. Another sixty seconds, and Harden might get shot through the head.

"I'm looking for Thon Jok," Harden said.

The gunman perked up at the name. He prodded with the AK. "Why you want to see Thon Jok?"

Harden shoved the rifle away, growing impatient. The gunmen on every side tensed. Harden kept his tone even.

"I have a business proposition," he said.

"Proposition?"

"Opportunity," Harden clarified. "*Deal*. I want to make a deal."

The gunman knew that word. He clucked, wrinkling his nose.

"What do you offer?"

Harden turned for the truck bed, and guns snatched toward his head. He froze, lifting his hands.

"*Relax*," Harden said. "Geez. Don't you people have a chill mode?"

"Slow," the gunman said. "Move *slow*."

Harden did. He wrapped his fingers around the hard plastic edge of the bed liner. It rattled to the touch, already loose. He tugged it away from the truck's cab, exposing a cavity.

Everyone waited, the guns still brandished. Harden's hand emerged from the cavity holding cash—a whole *wad* of American dollars.

"Here," Harden said, tossing the money. The gunman nearly dropped his AK trying to catch it. He rolled the wad in his hand, eyes growing wide. Everyone around him was equally transfixed.

Harden grinned. "So *there's* the chill mode."

The gunman shoved past Harden and dug behind the bed liner. Two more rolls emerged—just fifteen grand in total, but a small fortune in South Sudan.

"You have more?" the gunman demanded.

Harden scooped his flask from the mud and relaxed against the truck bed, taking a long swig. He smacked his lips.

"Call your boss, big dog. Let's make a deal."

56

Western Equatoria, South Sudan
22:12 Hours, East Africa Time

After dinner, Hale took stock of the orphanage's defensive equipment—and he didn't like what he found.

As head of maintenance and security, Joseph was in charge of the weapons stash, which was kept in a locked metal case at the back of the mechanic's shed. The lock stuck—Joseph had to lubricate it before the key would turn. Hinges groaned. Oily rags covered the contents.

Hale swept them back and found...almost nothing. Two handguns, both outdated Russian Makarovs mottled by orange rust, with only nine rounds of ammunition between them. One sixteen-gauge break-action shotgun of unknown origin, and one bolt-action Lee-Enfield rifle chambered in .303 with a ten-round magazine and a hand guard that extended the length of the barrel.

No optics. No modern battle rifles. Not more than a handful of shells for the shotgun and maybe forty rounds for the Enfield.

Unbelievable.

Hale slammed the case shut and followed Joseph around the perimeter of the property, questioning the use of each building, learning the orphanage's daily routines, and reviewing what current security measures were practiced.

The short answer? Nothing but a lot of prayer, which Hale personally believed in, but the abject lack of contingency plans stunned him. Joseph had constructed thick wooden doors and shutters for all the ground level doors and windows of the main building. In event of disaster, the children and staff could be barricaded inside.

But then what? The guns were all *outside*, in the shed across the property. The building was block, but there were no shutters on the second-floor windows, and many of the floors and interior walls were constructed of bone-dry plywood. All it would take was a well-aimed incendiary grenade to flush everybody out again.

Worst of all, there was currently only one operational vehicle on the entire property, and that was the Russian Ural Hale had arrived in. The bus had thrown a rod and needed a full engine rebuild. The tractor hadn't run in living memory.

"We survive on faith."

Joseph said the words as he and Hale stood on the roof of the main building, overlooking darkened bushlands. Even in the cool of night Hale sweated. The gentle croon of Ajok singing the children to sleep joined the chatter of insects in the nearby elephant grass, a symphony beneath ten million brilliant stars.

It was beautiful. As wild as the Bob Marshall Wilderness, as serene as Haleburg. Yet Hale had never felt more exposed in his life. Like a bug on a cookie sheet...just counting the hours until the oven clicked on and roasted him to death.

"I'll see you in the morning," Hale said bluntly. He descended through a hatch in the roof, taking stairs to the ground floor. Diko swung in a hammock near the building's front door, one leg dangling out as he snored. Hale hadn't seen Wal, Tito, or Mary Grace since dinner—he hadn't seen Bakumba since arriving.

That was okay—he wanted to be alone. He took his AK, a large bottle of Hawkeye water, and the orphanage's lone satellite phone—another problem—into the tall grass alongside the disabled bus. Hale settled onto the ground and rested the rifle across his legs. He cracked the water open and drank. He inhaled clean air and marveled at how much better it tasted than the air in Boston—or even urban New Hampshire.

This was wild. Pure. And dangerous.

Hale dialed Shaw.

"Mary Grace?"

"It's me."

"Ian, finally. What have you got?"

"You want the bad news or the really bad news?"

Shaw groaned. "Hit me where it hurts."

"This place is a death trap. The whole thing. They're exposed, immobilized, and way under-prepared. If two dozen gunmen attacked tonight, you'd be watching CNN report the massacre tomorrow morning. There wouldn't be a thing I could do about it."

Silence. Hale wasn't sure if he'd stunned Shaw or if she was just taking time to think.

"Mary Grace said they have a local security team," Shaw said.

Hale snorted. "One middle-aged mechanic and a barefoot kid with a handful of rusty surplus firearms between them—maybe enough bullets to hold off an invasion of groundhogs. I wouldn't call it a security team."

This time Shaw swore. Hale simply chugged water. It still tasted like mud, but the flavor was growing on him. Maybe there were some kind of beneficial minerals involved.

"You said they're immobilized?"

"Yep. We've got the Russian Ural I arrived in, which isn't nearly big enough to hold everyone. They've got an old Mitsubishi bus—it might hold fifty kids, if you really squeezed. There's eighty-two children on sight, plus the staff, but it doesn't matter either way, because the engine is blown. Mary Grace's 'security team' is working on it."

More muttered profanities. Hale rocked his head, trying to get his neck to crack. The muscles were as tight as banjo strings—his whole body felt that way. He was still tired and should probably sleep.

The way this thing was unraveling, he might not sleep again for days.

"What else?" Shaw said.

"Well, in the *pros* column we've got plenty of food and fresh water. The infirmary is reasonably well stocked and there's a guy on site who knows a little more than me about emergency medical care. Undisturbed, we'll be good for weeks."

"But?"

"But the moment some jackass with a private army decides to make this place a target, it's over. I'll take ten or twenty with me, but there's no way I can protect this place, let alone the kids. It's simply not defensible. Even standing on the roof thirty feet in the air, I can't see more than a few hundred yards. We're sitting in a bowl surrounded by hills and trees, with no walls and no methods of suppressive fire. I really couldn't think of a more vulnerable position."

A moment's pause. Then Shaw asked the only question that mattered.

"Recommendation?"

"The same as before—evac, as soon as possible. With the Ural I can ferry everyone to the nearest airport. We'll be exposed while moving, and whoever I leave behind will be sitting ducks, but it's the best I can manage on my own. I just need you to find a plane."

More silence. Hale sipped water and a dribble of it ran down his neck, cool and refreshing. It made him want to dump the entire canteen on his head.

"Well?" Hale pressed.

"I'm still hitting a wall on that, Ian."

"What does that mean?"

"It means that Wani's little stunt with that UN plane has every bush pilot and charter flight service hugging the ground. I can't find anyone willing to fly, no matter the price."

Hale poured a palmful of water into his hands and wiped down the back of his neck. The cooling effect was miraculous—he finally got his neck to crack.

"What are you telling me, Shaw?"

No answer. Hale gritted his teeth.

"Hey, hotshot. I'm the one on the ground. If you've got an ask, at least do me the courtesy of making it clear."

"I need you to hunker in place," Shaw said. "Secure the site the best you can and remain in contact until we can figure something else out. I know it's not ideal. If you want to withdraw, I would understand—"

"Okay," Hale said.

"Okay?"

"Okay. I'll figure it out."

Long pause. Hale could feel the tension on the line, and he wished Shaw would get over herself. He wasn't making this hard on her—she wasn't making it hard on him. It was a nasty situation, however you sliced it.

"I owe you one," Shaw said at last.

Hale only grunted. "I'd like to say I'm not keeping score...but maybe you do."

A tense laugh. Hale breathed deep and noted his eyelids were yet again growing heavy. His mind spun with preparations for increased security—small changes that would make little or no impact on the big picture but might give the orphanage a fighting chance against a small attack.

Maybe.

"Get some rest," Shaw said. "I'll have my phone on me. One day at a time, right?"

"Good copy." Hale hung up. He leaned against the bus and noted that it was every bit as comfortable as the acacia tree earlier that day.

What more could he do in the dark?

The sunrise would bring the truth.

57

Western Equatoria, South Sudan
22:42 Hours, East Africa Time

Bakumba lay awake on the infirmary cot, waiting for the orphanage to fall asleep.

Wal and the fat cook were up the latest. Even after the kitchen was clean and the children shooed into their dormitories, the two of them sat at a table in the hallway and played round after round of mancala with a series of small dishes and a handful of dry beans. With each round the beans rattled against baked clay and Bakumba wanted to throttle them both with his bare hands. The cook would laugh, Wal would hiss like a rabid animal, and the game would begin again.

For hours. Bakumba monitored the time by the ticking hands of a clock mounted on the infirmary wall. Probably, Wal and the cook thought he was asleep. The rest of the orphanage was asleep. Bakumba hadn't seen Tito or Hale or the pretty white woman in hours.

He'd like to see the woman again. Alone in some desolate place with nobody else around, he might like to see a lot of her. Why wait for the payout and the Radisson?

But he couldn't allow himself to be distracted. First, he needed the sat phone. He needed an isolated place to make the call. Already he had memorized the long number written on the inside of his shirt. Now, if those old fools would only go to bed…

Finally, they did. The game was packed up. Wal and the cook prattled at each other in what sounded like Murle, but Bakumba only caught fragments. The lights switched off, and footsteps shuffled down the hall.

Both away from Bakumba…and toward him. Wal entered the infirmary, sweeping the curtain door aside. Bakumba closed his eyes and lay still as Wal switched on a light, then grunted to himself and switched it back off. Wal shuffled some more. He crossed the room.

Then a second cot creaked, and Bakumba wanted to scream.

Seriously?

Another ten minutes crept by. Then fifteen. The doctor began to snore, sounding like a sleeping elephant with a muddy nose. Bakumba waited another five minutes…then he rotated on the cot. It groaned beneath his weight, but the snoring didn't stop.

The doctor lay still. Bakumba padded with ease to the curtained door and slipped into the hallway. He looked both ways, listening for a disturbance. He heard nothing save cicadas buzzing like machine guns in the grass outside. The orphanage itself was fast asleep.

Bakumba crept toward the front door, moving only on the balls of his feet. He already knew where to go—he'd seen the sat phone resting on a desk in the orphanage's small office. It was the first door on the right, just inside the main entrance.

Was the phone charged? Bakumba hoped so. With a full battery, he could take it with him. Maybe even leave that night—vanish into the brush and rendezvous with the masked man to collect his payout.

But Bakumba was getting ahead of himself. First, he needed the phone.

At the end of the hallway, he found a drawn curtain blocking his path. Bakumba slowed and listened for the creak of a chair or the rattle of fingers on keys, sounds he associated with office work from the hours he'd slaved in a textile factory. The boss man had sat in an elevated booth, typing and relaxing and mostly doing nothing.

Another fat fool.

There was no sound beyond the curtain. Bakumba curled is fingers and drew it back. He looked past the chair and beyond stacked books and papers. He didn't see the phone, so he eased inside. The curtain closed behind him. He twisted to survey the desk.

Nothing. Bakumba tugged a drawer open. It was loaded with pens and notebooks, but again, no sign of the phone. He tried another drawer and found charging cables. The third and final drawer contained files. Bakumba whispered a curse and straightened. He turned toward the back wall, ready to search battered bookshelves.

And nearly jumped out of his skin. Squatted in the corner with his knees drawn up to his ears, his body as still as a statue, was Tito. The little man's eyes were open, locked on Bakumba even as his hands wrapped tight around his own knees. He didn't blink, didn't budge, didn't speak. He just stared as Bakumba's heart hammered in his chest, tidal waves of stress hormones cascading through his body. Bakumba was also frozen, locked in place, terrified.

Then he snapped. He spun and raced through the door, back into the hallway. In another moment he reached the infirmary and slid inside. Wal lay snoring right where Bakumba had left him—moonlight illuminated Bakumba's cot, and he eased into it.

Looking back to the curtain, he saw Tito's glowing eyes, like the eyes of a jungle cat, watching him. Bakumba blinked and the eyes were gone—Tito was gone. He hadn't followed.

But Bakumba could still see him, and the surprise was enough to terminate any future plans of searching the office or the orphanage that night.

The phone call would have to wait until morning.

58

Western Equatoria, South Sudan
07:41 Hours, East Africa Time

It took all night, but Marc Harden got the deal done.

The gunmen in the woods took over the Hilux, loading Harden and his men into its back and blindfolding all three. The road was rough and rutted, and with their hands bound, the three of them were left fighting to stabilize themselves in the bouncing bed.

A large part of Harden wondered if they were being taken to their deaths. If these thugs would content themselves with the Hilux and fifteen grand worth of cash, not bothering to risk their lives for more. All Harden could really count on was greed, but greed in his experience was a powerful motivator.

Hadn't it motivated *him*?

They drove for nearly an hour before brakes squealed. The engines continued to hum as a conference was held in some local dialect that Harden couldn't differentiate from pig latin. He waited, forcing himself to remain calm. The engines surged again. Water splashed beneath the Hilux, some of it washing through cracks in the battered bed and soaking his feet.

Five minutes later they arrived at their destination amid a clamor of voices, a blaring stereo, and the smell of roasting meat. The truck stopped. The tailgate dropped and Harden was hauled out—he didn't know about his men. He submitted himself to being marched across sticky mud and into some kind of building.

He knew he was inside because the mud turned to packed earth, and the air grew thick. Across the room somebody smacked as they ate. Harden was shoved into a kneeling position and the blindfold was yanked off his eyes.

He was indeed inside. It was a one-room hut with plank walls and a tin roof. A cot stood in one corner—no other furniture. Only one other person occupied the room, and he was a stocky black man with a bald head and wide, pale eyes. He sat cross-legged on a rug, eating pork from a metal plate. Gnawing the meat off the bone.

He didn't so much as look up for several minutes, leaving Harden to kneel and wait, his knees aching but his mind relaxed. This wasn't his first third world rodeo.

Finally, the pale eyes swept Harden. The guy burped as he flicked a rib bone into a nearby bucket, then picked his teeth with a dirty fingernail. He didn't blink—he didn't seem particularly interested in what he saw.

From somewhere behind Harden a voice spoke in that same unfamiliar tongue. Something flew over Harden's shoulder and landed next to the stocky guy. It was a small canvas bag—from inside, the stocky guy withdrew Harden's cash. Thumbed through it. Grunted as though it were useless paper, and turned back to Harden.

"What do you want?"

The accent was rural African, but the English was clear enough.

"I want to make a deal," Harden said.

A snort. "A deal for your life?"

"No, a deal to hire you."

That brought on a dry laugh. The guy muttered something and one of his men brought him a glass bottle full of brown liquid. Homemade beer, probably. He chugged, then wiped his lips.

"I work for no man—not even God. Why should I work for you?"

Harden shrugged. "Because I'll pay you."

"I already have your money."

"Some of it. You think I was dumb enough to bring everything? There's fifteen grand there, and I'll pay you another thirty grand for three days' work."

A pause. The pale eyes squinted as one jagged fingernail tapped the bottle.

"That's a lot of money in South Sudan."

Harden said nothing.

"Just what kind of work are you hiring for, Mr...."

"Harden."

"Ah, yes. Mr. *Harden*."

"I'm raising an army. I believe you have one."

"Do I?"

"So I'm told."

"Told by who?"

Harden shrugged. The pale eyes narrowed.

"Did the government send you?"

"No."

"The United Nations, perhaps? The African Union?"

"No."

"And I should believe you because..."

"I'm telling the truth."

"The certain truth?"

"Is there any other kind?"

Harden was weary of the games but knew better than to expose his impatience. He lifted both eyebrows, waiting for the smile to return. It did not. The stocky man's face grew harder. Suddenly, he snapped his fingers and barked a command.

Harden's body tensed, red flags popping in his mind as fight-or-flight hormones rushed his system. Before he could budge, an AK-47 muzzle jabbed into his back. Two powerful hands shoved him down by the shoulders. A door flap snapped, and a panicked shout rang through the room. Harden turned his head in time to see one of his men dragged in. A heavy boot landed in the guy's spine, pinning him to the dirt even as he fought to break free.

"Silence!" the stocky guy barked. "Shut him up!"

The next boot struck the guy's head. He choked and spat blood. Harden's heart hammered and he wanted to lunge—not to save the guy, but to save himself. Run like wildfire into the forest.

But it was way too late for that.

"Now," the stocky guy said, turning to the cot and reaching beneath the pillow. He drew a polished Colt single-action revolver—old-school, with a six-inch barrel. The hammer snapped at half-cock and the cylinder spun like a roulette wheel. Then the muzzle leveled over the pinned soldier's head.

"I ask again. Who sent you here?"

"My boss," Harden said. "He needs an army."

"Your boss the UN? The AU?"

"Not hardly."

"Not hardly," the guy repeated. "So your boss is a savage?"

"As savage as you."

"How do I know?"

Harden's mind spun. He felt this game winding down fast. The guy's patience might break at any moment...Why not push him over the edge?

"Shoot him," Harden said.

"What?"

"Shoot him," Harden repeated. "Is that what a UN agent would say? Blow his head off. I came here for fifty soldiers, not one."

Eyebrows rose over pale eyes. The guy looked from Harden to the pinned soldier, who was once again thrashing to break free.

Then the stocky man grinned. He de-cocked the revolver. "*You* shoot him."

"What?" Harden feigned surprise. He wasn't.

"You prove what you are."

Whatever, dude.

Harden extended a hand. The stocky guy passed him the revolver, butt first. Harden felt the weight of it, admiring the smooth craftmanship. The pearl grips. The historic styling.

Then he cocked the hammer and blew his captain's brains out. One thunderous shot, the gun bucking in his hand. No more screams. Harden lifted the muzzle and blew smoke from the barrel.

"Nice gun," he said. He flipped it around and offered it back to the stocky guy. The eyebrows remained frozen in an arch as the gun was accepted, silence hanging for another long moment.

Then they all laughed at once. The body was kicked to the side. A chatter of jungle dialect summoned more glass bottles. One was thrust into Harden's hand, and he was invited to drink.

And keep drinking. All night long. With music pounding and bad booze flowing and roasted pork lifted straight from the spit, he made friends with Thon Jok, the amateur warlord. He negotiated a deal. He went to bed late and awoke the next morning to find his second man also dead—tied to a tree with a bullseye painted on his bare chest and hatchet marks perforating his rib cage.

So much for him.

Harden puked behind his hut and wiped his mouth with the back of his hand. He tugged on his shirt and circled to the barbecue pit out front to find Thon waiting—still pale-eyed, still stocky, and not the least bit hungover.

"Good morning, my new friend. I trust you slept well?"

Harden hadn't, but he merely grunted. Thon passed him a bottle of water and Harden drank some and dashed the rest over his face. He was hungry—he smelled more roasting meat.

But Thon didn't lead him to eat. He gestured him down a short trail instead, winding through trees before opening, all at once, into a clearing. Torn grass and high-canopied trees with a field of small huts packed to one side, a parking lot full of vehicles on the other.

And weapons. Weapons *everywhere.*

"Behold!" Thon said. "Your army."

59

Western Equatoria, South Sudan
09:15 Hours, East Africa Time

Hale found Joseph at the Hawkeye well just after sunrise.

A diesel engine operated the main pump, but there was also an auxiliary hand pump that Joseph used to draw a pail of drinking water. The two of them passed a dipper back and forth in silence, then Joseph ducked his head and turned for the brushlands.

Hale dashed the remainder of the water over his face, scrubbing with his bare hands. It was a poor excuse for a shower, but the best he could manage. Glancing toward the horizon, he found a distant silhouette now resting on its knees, hands lifted toward the sunrise. Joseph stayed like that a long time, and even though it felt like an intrusion, Hale couldn't help but watch.

The scene reminded him of Afghanistan, of the Army. Of the Bible he always carried and the mornings when he would pray in some desolate place. The many days, many months, when Hale's faith was the only thing that kept his sanity intact. Even as he flew from the side of a spiraling helicopter, he never lost that faith. He maintained it during all the surgeries and straight through his medical discharge.

Maybe it was during his tenure with Sentinel that he just became so... worn out.

I should join him.

The thought had barely cleared Hale's mind when the kids exploded out of the orphanage's front door. Not some, but all. Apparently it was bath time, and bath time was held outdoors under the spray of the diesel pump. Hale stepped awkwardly back while Mary Grace and Ajok shepherded the girls and Diko and Wal managed the boys. Then everyone assembled under the same pole barn, and while Ajok cooked breakfast, Mary Grace delivered a Bible lesson.

Standing in the back with the AK-47 slung over his shoulder, Hale expected the children to be restless. They weren't—they listened with calm focus, taking their turn at asking or answering questions. When the discussion finished, Joseph prayed, and breakfast was wheeled out. Hale sat at the head table as before, but managed to avoid a personal interview with Mary Grace. In fact, she had notably cooled toward him since the evening prior, and Hale thought he understood why.

She kept casting icy glances toward the muzzle of the AK, visible as it protruded over Hale's right shoulder. Hale ignored her, finishing a bowl of maize porridge and remained seated as Ajok, Diko, and Mary Grace cleaned up. Joseph was trying to explain the concept of the sea to a small child. It was referenced in that morning's Bible lesson, and the girl had never seen a body of water larger than a pond. Joseph gesticulated with his arms thrown wide, and the girl shook her head in disbelief.

"Ask Mr. Hale," Joseph said. "He's seen it."

The girl turned, the question ready on her lips. She froze when their eyes locked, seeming to freeze for a long moment. Then she scurried off without a word, leaving Hale with something like an artillery shell smashing through his chest.

"Don't take it personally," Joseph said. "You're new."

Hale watched the children spread across the grass behind the pole barn, apparently segmented in preparation for morning school lessons. There was a lot of laughter, a lot of smiles.

But not all smiles. Scattered here and there, Hale found wide eyes and blank faces. Children sitting with their arms and legs drawn in, looking shaken and defensive. He watched them for several long minutes, then spoke softly enough that only Joseph could hear.

"Would you do me a favor?"

"Mr. Hale? *Mr. Hale!*"

Mary Grace Dalton marched from the back of the orphanage, another patchwork skirt swishing around her legs. One glance and Hale thought she looked ready to rip him limb from limb—he had a pretty good idea why.

Across the yard beneath another acacia tree, nine children sat alone in a knot. Joseph was there, squatting and smiling as he spoke to them. Nobody seemed to be speaking back.

"Just what do you think you're doing?"

Mary Grace reached him, and Hale sighed. Resting one hand on his sidearm, he turned to face her. The AK was gone—Joseph had secured it. Probably the pistol should be gone, also. It wouldn't make his job any easier, but Hale felt naked enough.

"I'm doing my job, Miss Dalton."

"*Children?*" Mary Grace snapped.

"Witnesses," Hale said. "The only ones I have."

He turned back for the tree. Mary Grace swished alongside.

"They're *terrified*. Do you understand that? Half of them haven't spoken since you arrived. This isn't the time."

Hale ignored her, and Mary Grace caught him by the arm. The grip was tighter than he expected, hauling him to a stop.

"I won't allow this," Mary Grace said.

Hale waited a long beat, staring unblinking into those bright blue eyes. Waiting for her to calm down, if only a little.

"You see those kids?" Hale tilted his head toward the children dispersed for school, and Mary Grace looked, despite herself.

"Imagine them stacked in a mass grave," Hale said. "That's what I'm trying to prevent."

He pulled free without another word and proceeded across the field. Mary Grace followed, but Joseph intercepted her, speaking in a soothing voice. Hale ignored them both and offered his kindest smile to the cluster of nine kids.

They were all staring at him—none spoke. They huddled like herd animals, packed together for protection from a predator. In their eyes, Hale knew that *he* was that predator.

"Hello." Hale settled onto the grass. He was several yards back—far enough for the children to be comfortable, he hoped. He wished he'd unstrapped his chest rig before approaching.

He hadn't taken it off in two days.

"I'm Ian," Hale began. "What are your names?"

No answer. Hale expected that—this wasn't his first time attempting to pry battlefield intel out of terrified children. This sort of thing was almost routine in Afghanistan.

"I saw you playing basketball earlier." Hale tilted his head toward the wire hoop mounted to a utility pole across the yard—no net or backboard. In truth, it was the other children who played. These children shrank back in their nervous herd.

But all children love sports, right?

"You ever watch the Celtics play?" Hale asked, miming a seated free throw.

No answer, but they were watching him closely.

"I got to see the NBA semifinals a few years ago," Hale said. "Celtics versus Nets. Two seconds on the clock, all tied up at one-oh-seven each. Then Jayson Tatum takes the pass, runs inside and spins—shoots with one hand!"

Hale mimed the motion, remembering the moment in vivid detail. His gaze swept the knot of children, a smile stretching his face.

Nobody answered, or even flinched. It was though they didn't speak English, but Hale knew they did. They were stonewalling him—likely out of fear. Maybe out of simple mistrust.

Hale shrugged a little sheepishly. "Maybe you had to be there."

From somewhere behind him Hale was conscious of Mary Grace's stare boring into his back. Gently, he swung off his butt and onto his knees. He closed half the distance to the children and settled into a seated position again.

None of them had run. They still sat frozen. The girl with the burned face was there—no longer dressed in pink, but now in a fresh flower print. Hale smiled.

She did not smile back.

"Look," Hale said. "I could really use your help. I'm here to keep you safe from bad men—like the men who took you from your homes. I need to know who they are. I'm hoping you can tell me what happened."

More silence. Hale studied each face, taking his time. He was most interested in the older two children. They were both boys in their tweens or early teens. Both lithe and healthy.

Suitable soldiers, Hale thought—and hated himself for thinking it. But that was why these children were targeted.

"Tell me about the men who took you," Hale said. "What were they like?"

Still, no answer. Hale remained patient. He plucked a long stem of grass and wrapped it around his finger. Just buying time, just being calm.

"They won't take you again," Hale said, staring not at the kids but the grass. "I promise. You're safe here. We'll take you back home, if you want—"

"No," a weak voice murmured from the crowd.

Hale's gaze snapped up. One of the smaller boys was crying—he might have been eight years old. The two older boys glared, but the younger didn't stop.

"Don't take us back. There is nothing. They killed *everyone*."

"I'm sorry," Hale said.

The boy's face fell. Once again, silence blanketed the group. The younger kids avoided Hale's gaze while the older boys glared at him—unblinking. Like he was the enemy.

What am I missing?

"These men who burned your village...did you see them?"

No answer.

"Did you see who they worked for?" Hale said. "Who the boss is?"

"He was like you," a soft voice answered.

It was a girl who spoke, small and skinny, and the moment she did, one of the older boys shoved her.

"No," Hale said. "Let her talk."

The girl remained silent.

Hale leaned forward. "How was he like me? Was he tall? Did he wear this?"

Hale tapped his chest plate.

Before the girl could answer, one of the older boys spoke for the first time. His voice was low and cold, little more than a snarl.

"She means he was *white*," he said. "She means he was *American*."

60

Western Equatoria, South Sudan
12:02 Hours, East Africa Time

Bakumba's next opportunity to search for the sat phone didn't arise until after lunch.

The orphans and staff gathered as before beneath the pole barn. Leftover lentil soup and flatbread was served. Bakumba hadn't enjoyed it the night before and didn't want any for lunch, but Wal didn't give him a choice. He was dragged out to the head table, plumped down between Wal and the boy called Diko, and scolded by Ajok when he attempted to eat with his hands.

The white woman was there—and yes, she *did* look fine. Bakumba had never been with a white woman before. He couldn't deny that the prospect excited him, but before he could get too deeply lost in his own fantasies, Ian Hale appeared—and with him, *the phone*.

It was clipped to Hale's belt alongside his gun. He sat and ate with the others, talking with Joseph and Mary Grace. The three of them seemed mildly distressed about something, or at least preoccupied. They didn't engage with anyone else at the table. Bakumba watched while shoveling lentils with a bent spoon, his gaze bouncing to the sat phone as his mind spun.

How was he going to get it? Hale was armed, and Bakumba had seen him fight. There was no option to take the device by force. Maybe if Hale was sleeping...

The meal concluded. Hale and his comrades fell into distracted silence. The children helped Diko and Ajok to clear the tables. Wal called after Bakumba, asking about his arm.

Bakumba merely grunted in response. He wasn't paying attention—he was fixated on Hale. As Mary Grace said something, Hale reached to his belt and unclipped the sat phone. He passed it to her. Mary Grace rose and headed for the building, dialing as she went.

Bakumba's heart rate quickened. He rose from the table and scooped up his dishes, pretending to head for the kitchen. Mary Grace made it inside and Bakumba sidetracked to dump the dishes. He hurried back into the hall just in time to see Mary Grace slip into the orphanage office.

He couldn't follow her, but he didn't need to. He only needed to wait for her to emerge, and see if she had the phone with her. If she left it behind...

"Why do you watch her?"

Bakumba spun at the sudden voice to find Tito standing only inches behind, his arms loaded with dishes. He stared at Bakumba, suspicious and cutting. Not budging from the hallway.

"Who do I watch?" Bakumba snapped. It was the first thing he thought to say.

A column of boisterous children barreled past, forcing them both to step aside. Tito never took his eyes off Bakumba the entire time. He didn't so much as blink. When the hallway grew quiet again, Tito's voice grew quiet with it.

"Some men," he said, shaking his head. "No matter how many people believe in them, no matter how many second chances they take...they never change."

There was something in his tone that cut like a knife. Bakumba felt it, slicing right through his chest. It enraged him—it turned his skin hot. He pushed Tito with his good arm, sending bowls clattering to the floor.

"What do you know, small man? Stay out of my way!"

Before Tito could respond, the next column of children crashed in, separating the two men. Bakumba took the opportunity to make his exit, joining a growing throng of orphans at the well. Their voices clamored together, a song about living water and the loving God who gave it.

Stupid fools.

Bakumba's heart was still thumping, his face flushed and warm. He imagined himself tearing out Tito's judgmental eyes, leaving him to squat blind for the rest of his miserable life, able to watch *nobody*.

It was a thrilling thought, enough to soothe the fire burning in Bakumba's chest. But what happened next made him forget about Tito altogether. Mary Grace appeared from the office at the end of the hall, just a few yards away. She joined the children in song and stepped into the front yard.

She did not have the phone.

61

Juba, South Sudan
12:47 Hours, East Africa Time

It was the call Wing-Kei had waited for—the call he'd almost given up hope of receiving.

Ringing into a burner phone that he had purchased precisely for this occasion, the caller ID displayed a prefix of +8816, which indicated an Iridium satellite phone. It wasn't a number Wing-Kei recognized, but that wasn't a surprise. The contracted "journalist" may have needed to improvise.

Wing-Kei took the call. He listened in silence as the caller babbled—a long, meandering story full of irrelevant details. The only ingredient that mattered was the recording. The caller had it—he claimed it was crystal clear.

And did it depict a white man with a snake tattoo?

Indeed it did.

Wing-Kei advised the contractor to stand by—the contractor didn't like that. It was only after another babbling outburst that Wing-Kei finally placed the voice in his mind, identifying the speaker from his lineup of recruits.

Of course it had to be *this* fool. To complicate matters, the caller explained that he was hiding at an orphanage near Tambura, some town Wing-Kei had never heard of. He couldn't talk long, and he might not be reachable at this number. Wing-Kei shut him up long enough to call up a satellite map of Western Equatoria on his laptop. He found Tambura with some difficulty. It was little more than a speck, just some huts gathered along a pair of muddy streets. The orphanage was someways to the north.

But there *was* a dirt airstrip.

Wing-Kei returned to the phone. He told the caller to calm down and listen. Wing-Kei would meet him at the Tambura airport that night. The caller should bring the camera and tell nobody where he was going.

Would Wing-Kei bring the cash? the caller pressed. *Of course* he would. The caller needn't worry about that. Just bring the camera, and don't let anybody follow. They would meet at ten p.m.

Wing-Kei reinforced the details until he was convinced the caller understood. He hung up and wiped sweat from his forehead, returning to his laptop to launch an encrypted messaging software.

The Juba airport wasn't far away. Finding a local bush pilot willing to fly into Tambura so soon after the UN relief flight was shot out of the sky would be nearly impossible, but if anyone had connections amid the grimy African underworld, it was China. Wing-Kei himself didn't need to stress over the details. He only needed to type his request into the message box and hit send.

Ten minutes later, he had a time and a place to meet a pilot. They would leave after dark to increase security. The flight to Tambura would take about two and a half hours. Wing-Kei would have the pilot refuel while he met with the caller—Lado Bakumba.

If all went well, he could declare mission success by midnight.

62

Atlanta, Georgia
07:14 Hours, Eastern Daylight Time

Shaw didn't know what to make of Hale's report.

It came in the middle of the night, which was fine, because Shaw wasn't sleeping anyway. She'd catnapped between phone calls and emails but really couldn't remember the last time she'd slept for more than an hour straight. With pressure building in Western Equatoria, and Hale's initial estimation of the orphanage's risk level confirming what Shaw already suspected, there was really only one course to take.

Resurrection Mercy Ministries had to get their people out. No debates, and no delays. Somebody—be it the LRA or a poser, it didn't matter—was kidnapping children. Barely a hundred miles northeast of Tambura, a warlord had declared independence and was shooting down aircraft. The government in South Sudan seemed incapable of responding.

Shaw and RMM were on their own, and what they needed was a *plane*. An aircraft large enough to carry a hundred people and a pilot bold enough to fly it through a potential anti-aircraft storm. It was a lot to ask, but this couldn't be the first time this situation had occurred, right? There had to be a protocol.

But there wasn't. Nobody Shaw spoke to seemed to know anything about emergency air crews or protection forces available for loan. The UN wasn't returning her calls. The African Union literally laughed her off the phone the moment she spoke the words *Western Equatoria*. The American government was hands-off and disinterested.

And then Hale's second report arrived. Not the initial security briefing, but the phone call that followed his interview of the children he had rescued on the way to Tambura.

"He was white...He was American."

The words landed like bombshells, leaving Shaw squinting and confused. *An American?* How could dazed and terrified children possibly know that?

But they did know. Apparently this guy had become something of a nightmare across the region—a child-snatching monster who emerged from the dark, slaughtering parents and dragging their little ones off to no one knew where. His description had circulated in whispers, originated by the rare survivors of his attacks, and perpetuated by the raw terror his threat promised.

He was tall—built like a mahogany tree, one child said. Short-cropped pale hair and an iron face. He always wore military gear, like Hale's. He wore sunglasses, they said, and spat a lot. Nobody knew why—Hale guessed the man chewed tobacco.

But the feature every child agreed on was too striking to be myth or legend. It was a snake, thick and black and tattooed around the American's right bicep. Its head appeared on his forearm, fangs bared. One of the children compared it to a black mamba—a viper domestic to Africa and feared by locals for its fast-acting venom.

"They were certain about the snake," Hale said. "Right arm, jet black."

Shaw could hear the anger in Hale's tone even as he tried to mute it. She thought he understood—although perhaps Hale was jumping to conclusions. This guy might be American, he might be former military or even spec ops. He might be ex-Delta Force, for all they knew.

Or he might be just another thug with a rifle.

Shaw promised to investigate and hung up, chewing her lip. Her eyes burned to the point that no amount of blinking could clear them. She desperately needed a shower—a change of clothes. A hot meal.

But first, she wanted answers about the snake man. Because even as she told herself that Hale was jumping to conclusions, her own mind fought to do the same.

"Shaw?" Nolan O'Rourke answered in his trademark rumble—he did *not* sound happy to hear from her.

"Yeah, it's me." Shaw ran sticky fingers through her hair, remembering too late that she'd just finished a chocolate bar. *Fantastic.*

"Listen, I got something out of Western Equatoria. I'm looking for an ID on a Caucasian male working the region—possibly American, possibly ex-military. Definitely a problem child."

O'Rourke breathed a curse. She heard feet tap on a floor, then an office door closed.

"Maybe you missed the memo, Shaw. I'm not your personal government Google. I told you before, I don't have time for—"

"He's kidnapping children, O'Rourke. Massacring their parents and torching their villages. If there's even a chance an American is leaving fingerprints like that, don't you want to know?"

Long pause. O'Rourke's chair creaked. At last he said: "You know this how?"

"Because my guy shot up one of his raiding parties and rescued nine victims—all children, all witnesses. They've got quite the story to tell. They described a big hunk of a guy, white with blond hair and a full suit of battle rattle. Oh, and a snake tattoo. Jet black and wrapped around his right arm, baring its fangs."

"Wait, what? What kind of tattoo?"

"A snake tattoo. Some kind of viper."

"You say these kids saw this guy in person?"

"Two of them did. The rest of them knew him by rumor, but the descriptions were all the same."

"Right or left?"

"What?"

"The tattoo. What arm was it on?"

"Right arm."

Silence again. Shaw's eyes narrowed.

"You know this guy, O'Rourke?"

"I'll call you back," O'Rourke said. "*Don't* mention this to anyone."

He hung up. Shaw withdrew her phone and stared at the screen. That bad feeling that had spawned the moment Hale made the report about the snake man was only growing. It was developing into real unease. She blinked, and almost imagined she could picture the guy, even though she'd never seen him. Almost imagined that he was there, in the room...

Another blink. Shaw shook her head.

Get yourself together, Laney. You need a coffee.

Shaw locked her computer and pushed off her chair. She took her purse and turned for the door.

She would get the coffee, but she'd start with a shower. A change of clothes. A fresh Bulldogs hat.

And then she'd get back on the grind, because Shaw wouldn't rest until Hale, Mary Grace, all her staff, and every one of those kids was out of Western Equatoria.

63

Western Equatoria, South Sudan
17:48 Hours, East Africa Time

Hale spent the entire day doing whatever he could think of to give the orphanage its best possible chance of survival.

It wasn't a lot—there was little to work with. Hale coordinated with Joseph to have the Ural's diesel tank topped off from the reserves used to operate the well pump. He had every available water jug filled and packed into the back of the truck, along with dry food stores and blankets. He spread maps of the region across an outdoor table and searched the hills and forests for a haven—better yet, a stronghold.

The closest thing he could find was a South Sudanese military garrison located nearly a hundred kilometers northeast, deep into the brushlands near the town of Nagero. Joseph warned that the area was infested by James Wani's troops, and the garrison might be abandoned—nobody knew for sure.

The only other options were Tambura, which was no better a defense than the orphanage itself, or the slightly larger town of Yambio, nearly two hundred kilometers farther south.

In other words, there was no option. This orphanage sat on the edge of the universe, and while raiders could be fast and agile, moving eighty-plus children would be anything but. Their best defense was really no different by sunset than it had been at sunrise: A lot of prayer. A lot of hope.

"God presides in the great assembly; He renders judgment among the 'gods.'"

Joseph spoke at Hale's elbow as the two of them stood once again on the orphanage roof, watching the blazing African sun sink into the horizon.

"'How long will you defend the unjust and show partiality to the wicked?'" Joseph continued, his body relaxed. "Defend the weak and the fatherless; uphold the cause of the poor and the oppressed. Rescue the weak and needy..." Joseph turned to Hale, his dark face glowing under the last rays of the sun. "Deliver them from the hand of the wicked."

Hale stared back, nodding slowly. He recognized the words—they were from the Psalms, although he couldn't recall exactly where. It was a prayer, echoed through the ages, whispered in a primitive and barbaric time.

And here, in the twenty-first century, as relevant as ever. Because technology rises and empires are built...but people are all the same.

"Amen," Hale said simply. He slung the AK over his shoulder and surveyed the distant horizon, a cloud-like darkness closing on their position with every passing minute. He breathed deep, and one final time, he rehearsed the plan.

If given time, they would run. South to Tambura or west into the brush. Whatever made sense in the moment.

If they didn't have time, Hale would barricade the children in the main building and leave Joseph in charge with a handful of AKs. Hale himself would ascend to the rooftop and engage targets at distance. If—*when*—things got close, he would fast-rope to the ground and just...

Do what he could.

We aren't there yet, Hale reminded himself. *Shaw is still working*.

"Do you play puppets, Ian?"

Hale squinted, twisting. Joseph lifted a hand, snapping his fingers and thumb together as though they were a mouth.

"Puppets—there are some downstairs, mostly made of socks. The children love them. After dinner we can sit on the roof and have a show. Laughter is good medicine."

Hale forced a smile. His gaze drifted back to the horizon, and the image of dirty socks with patchwork eyes faded from his mind as thoughts of the firefight near the river returned. Nine children in the back of the truck, dead gunmen everywhere.

How many remained? How long before their boss, the man with the snake tattoo, located the orphanage?

We aren't there yet.

"Let's eat," Hale said.

64

Western Equatoria, South Sudan
19:51 Hours, East Africa Time

Bakumba could hardly believe his luck.

All afternoon he'd plotted his escape from the orphanage. It wasn't like they were holding him hostage, but he didn't want anyone to know when he left, because he didn't want to answer questions—and he really didn't want to be followed.

What Bakumba needed most was a moment of distraction when he could slip through a door and fade into the brush, preferably with a backpack full of food and water slung over one shoulder. The obvious opportunity would be bedtime, but there was a problem, and that problem's name was *Tito*.

The flat-footed little troll wouldn't leave him alone. Indoors and out, at mealtimes and while Bakumba pretended to rest beneath an acacia tree, any time he turned around, Tito was there. Usually a ways off, but always staring right at him. Whenever Bakumba got near the children or Mary Grace, Tito got closer.

It was like he was attached to Bakumba. Like he was a horsefly buzzing just out of reach, but always there. It was infuriating—it made Bakumba want to fly off the handle.

But what was he going to do? Bash Tito's head in? The idea was to slip away *without* drawing attention...and that was when Bakumba got lucky.

There was going to be a party. Something about puppets and pudding—Bakumba didn't get details, but the children were excited out of their minds. They rushed up and down the hall while Bakumba sat alone on his bed, ignoring the ache in his arm and fixating on his problem. Wal stuck his head in, asking if Bakumba would like to join. The pudding was chocolate—didn't that sound nice?

It did, very much. Bakumba was tempted to partake right up until the moment Wal mentioned the party's location.

"The roof?" Bakumba questioned.

"The stars are lovely at night," Wal said. "And there's room for everyone to spread out."

Everyone.

Suddenly, Bakumba forgot about chocolate. He wasn't interested in puppets, but he *was* interested in everyone else being on that roof. He faked a stomachache, and Wal advised him to get some rest. Bakumba stretched out and listened as tiny footsteps faded upstairs. Through the open window he could still hear the laughter—children giggling, adults gesticulating in cartoonish voices.

He checked the wall clock. It was eight thirty—just ninety minutes to spare. He could make it three kilometers in ninety minutes, easy. He could even run if he had to. There was nothing wrong with his legs.

He just needed some basic provisions in case the masked man was delayed. Bakumba might lack a formal education, but he knew what it took to survive in a place like this. He wasn't a fool—he would hit the kitchen first.

Bakumba rolled onto his butt, moving slowly to mute the creaking of the cot. He placed both feet on the floor and listened. All he heard was more laughter from two floors overhead.

Where was Tito? Upstairs with the others...or lurking in the shadows below?

It didn't matter—it was time to go. Bakumba double-checked his pocket for that precious cargo. He padded into the hallway, checking both ways before orbiting toward the kitchen. Nothing but a curtain hung in his way. Inside he found bottled water and flatbread wrapped in cloth. He crammed both into a canvas bag, just turning for the exit when the rich scent of sweetened chocolate flooded his nostrils.

It was the pudding pot, resting forgotten on the stove. A walking snack would be nice, wouldn't it? Bakumba hadn't had any pudding in years. He slipped closer and found an inch of sticky goodness left in the pot's bottom. This wasn't the cheap, instant stuff. This was homemade, prepared by the fat cook.

Bakumba dipped a hand in. He sucked a heavy blob from his fingertip.

It was *divine*. Rich and thick and very sweet. It tasted like real sugar, a luxury where Bakumba grew up. Why not take some?

He scanned for a dish or a cup but found only spoons and a kitchen knife. He turned the opposite way, back toward the door.

And then ice flooded his lungs.

Standing just inside the door, flat-footed with narrowed eyes, was Tito. He was barely three feet away, but Bakumba hadn't heard him enter, hadn't heard him *breathe*. He was like a ghost, piercing Bakumba with dark, cutting eyes.

"What are you doing?" Tito demanded.

Bakumba deadlocked. His heart hammered. For a split second he considered running—sprinting for the door…

But no. Tito knew nothing. Why panic?

"I'm hungry," Bakumba said.

Tito's eyes narrowed even further. "Why do you have the bag?"

Bakumba glanced down before he could stop himself.

"Where are you going?" Tito demanded. "What did you take?"

"Nothing," Bakumba said. "Get out of my way."

Tito didn't. He took a step closer instead. He was fully a foot shorter than Bakumba, but he didn't look intimidated. He reached for the bag.

"Come with me," he said. "We're going to see Kawaja."

"Hands off." Bakumba grabbed Tito by the wrist, pushing back. Tito didn't give ground—he was stronger than Bakumba expected. He got his fingers around the bag's strap and jerked.

Then Bakumba hit him—straight in the jaw, one lightning right hook. Tito's head snapped back, and Bakumba saw red. His body snapped into autopilot. He struck again just as Tito slammed into the stove. The pudding pot fell. Spoons rained across the floor. Tito clawed for Bakumba's face, desperate and flailing and badly outgunned.

And then Bakumba found the kitchen knife.

65

Western Equatoria, South Sudan
20:44 Hours, East Africa Time

Hale heard the scream first.

It was almost lost amid the children's laughter. Hale twisted at the edge of the roof and looked down—into the front yard.

Then he heard the crash. Metal cascading across a floor, followed almost immediately by another shout—and then an ear-piercing shriek.

Hale exploded off his chair and tore across the roof, reaching the hatch just as Joseph emerged from behind a row of upturned tables. Mary Grace called after him, but Hale didn't wait. He reached the third level and his boots thumped against plywood. The HK VP9 cleared its holster as he spun for the stairs.

The screams had turned to muted groans. He could barely hear them—he thought they came from the ground level. Another four steps and then he was at the second floor. He bypassed the girl's dormitory and hit the next flight. The VP9 rose to eye level, Hale's offhand index finger hovering over the weapon light pressure switch.

The stairs let out near the back right corner of the building. The rear door opened to his right, the main hallway to his left. No further screams ripped past the plywood walls, but in their place Hale thought he detected a choking gurgle.

He cleared right—nothing. He spun left and activated the light, blazing white-hot glow down the hallway, and immediately located the tracks. They were crimson red, leading out of the kitchen and directly to the front door.

Hale ran. He reached the building's exit and swept the light over the yard—he saw nothing. He spun back just as Joseph reached the bottom of the stairs, Diko in tow.

"Kitchen!" Hale shouted.

Hale tore past the curtain, his finger curled around the trigger, ready to fire. He found the blood trail. He turned right, toward the stove.

And then he found Tito—seated on the floor, leaned against the oven with one hand clutched around his stomach. There was blood *everywhere.* It soaked the floor and drenched Tito's shirt. Lying on the floor next to him lay the weapon—a kitchen knife, stained up to the hilt.

"In here!" Hale shouted.

He killed the weapon light and holstered the pistol. Joseph reached the kitchen just as Hale landed on his knees in the blood. He ripped the Sure-Fire light off his chest rig and clicked it on. Joseph caught it as Hale peeled Tito's arms away from his stomach.

The little man quaked. He was turning pale, his eyes wide. Sweat ran down his face and Hale leaned sideways to allow room for the flashlight beam.

It didn't take long to find the source of the blood. Not one wound, but several. Deep stabs across Tito's stomach and into his chest, savage and merciless strokes that sliced flesh and decimated organs. Hale slid his hand behind Tito's back and felt more blood.

Some of the strokes had penetrated all the way through. Hale glanced once to Joseph, then pulled Tito off the oven. Tito quaked. Hale spoke softly in his ear.

"Stay calm...we're right here with you. I'm going to lay you down, okay?"

Hale got him stretched out and called for a towel. Diko handed it off just as Mary Grace and Wal appeared in the door. Mary Grace gasped, standing frozen. Wal barged in while Hale pressed the towel onto Tito's stomach. Tito groaned, eyes widening. He was crying.

And he was dying.

"The children," Joseph hissed.

Mary Grace was in shock, but she got the message. She turned, snapping the curtain door closed behind her. Joseph dropped to one knee, still holding the light. Wal pressed in alongside him, quickly displacing Hale's hand and lifting the towel.

His face blanched. He swallowed and looked to Hale. One glance into the old man's eyes, and Hale knew exactly what he was thinking. These injuries were beyond both of them. Tito needed immediate, major surgery.

"Let's get him to the infirmary," Hale said.

Wal nodded, and Hale slid one arm beneath Tito's neck. Tito grabbed Hale by the sleeve and shook his head, mumbling weakly.

"We have to move you, Tito. We've got to stop the bleeding."

Tito blinked back tears and tugged once more on Hale's sleeve. His lips parted and he hissed something, spraying blood.

Hale hesitated. He looked to the towel, already saturated, and knew it wouldn't matter if he could wheel Tito straight into the trauma center at a major American hospital. The damage was done. Too much blood was lost, too many organs shredded.

Hale leaned close, bringing his ear inches from Tito's lips.

"What is it?"

"Ba...Bakumba," Tito hissed.

"Bakumba did this?" Diko asked, his voice trembling.

Hale snapped his fingers, shooting a glare. He leaned close again.

"I'm listening, Tito."

"Bakumba...ran out," Tito hissed. "He's going..."

A pause. A wet, heavy rasp. Tito was swallowing back his own blood—his teeth were crimson. Hale looked into his face and his own eyes stung.

"...tell them," Tito choked. "Tell them where to find...the children."

Hale's blood ran cold. He leaned close, squeezing Tito by the shoulder.

"Tell *who*, Tito? Who's he going to tell?"

Tito's eyes watered. He tugged on Hale's sleeve one more time.

"Don't let these children…know war."

The words landed like cinder blocks against Hale's chest. He wrapped his hand around Tito's and squeezed. The little man squeezed back. He smiled.

And then he died.

66

Atlanta, Georgia
14:19 Hours, Eastern Daylight Time

O'Rourke never called Shaw back—so she called him. Three times in between hounding a Ugandan NGO to lend her a pair of Twin Otter aircraft to fly the orphans and Mary Grace's staff out of Tambura in batches. She lied and said she had pilots on standby, ready to make the flights through the night.

In truth, pilots and planes were a chicken-and-egg problem, and Shaw figured that if she could get one, it would be easier to find the other. The Twin Otters were nineteen-seat, turboprop aircraft capable of cruising at 170 knots with a range of just under eight hundred nautical miles. It wasn't an ideal solution, but Shaw figured that two small children equaled the size and weight of a full-grown adult, so three flights should be enough—four at most.

But the Ugandan NGO was *not* playing ball. Good aircraft came at a premium in East Africa, and no NGO on the planet was flush with cash. Even if they believed her story about stranded orphans and a possible resurgence of the Lord's Resistance Army, they weren't willing to risk their own hardware to bail her out.

This was Africa, they reminded her. Everyone had problems.

Shaw swore and smashed the phone into its plastic cradle. It had been six hours since she showered and changed, and she needn't have bothered. Stress unleashed waves of nervous sweat. It didn't help that the Hurt Building's AC struggled to keep up even in late November.

"Anything?"

Bill Carpenter leaned into the room. Shaw shook her head.

"Nobody with a heart."

She twisted to her keyboard, rattling off a follow-up email to a follow-up email—another contact, this one working with the World Health Organization. Anybody with a plane, right?

But nobody was responding. It was as though nobody took her seriously...or maybe didn't *want* to take her seriously. Suddenly, she understood why so many fundraisers and champions of third world causes could come off as so caustic, so pushy.

They were fed up with apathy.

Shaw cracked an energy drink and chugged. The sugar and caffeine landed in her gut like a hand grenade, supercharging her system. She drank half and was just turning back to the computer when her phone buzzed.

It was O'Rourke—*finally*.

"What have you got?" Shaw barked. There was no humor in her voice, no patience. She didn't care how that landed.

"Did your guy ever get a photograph of the snake man?"

It wasn't the question Shaw expected. She rotated her chair away from the table, squinting.

"What?"

"The guy with the snake tattoo. Did your guy ever get a picture?"

"Of course not. I told you, the kids reported it. If my guy saw him, Snake Dude would be fertilizing elephant grass by now."

Long pause. Shaw's patience snapped.

"*Hey*. What did you find?"

"I can't confirm positive ID without a photo," O'Rourke said. "I can't tell you who he is."

"I didn't call for positive ID, jackass. I called for an *idea*. I've got two

Americans and nearly ninety South Sudanese pinned in a corner with God knows what breathing down their necks. Do I really need to beg?"

Silence.

"Nolan." A trace of disbelief dampened Shaw's tone. "Come on, man. How far do we go back?"

"The Agency has no involvement in Western Equatoria," O'Rourke said. "That's really all I can tell you."

"The Agency? Who said anything about the Agency? I'm talking about *my people*, Nolan. I need to know what's coming for them. Better yet, I need two or three planes and some fearless pilots. Is loyalty a dead currency in Virginia?"

More silence. Shaw wondered if she'd pushed too far.

No, forget that. She'd push harder. Her *people* were up the creek without a paddle, and—

"I can't help you, Shaw. The Agency has no involvement in Western Equatoria. That's all I can say."

Then O'Rourke hung up. Shaw removed the phone from her ear, squinting at the receiver. Barely believing what she'd just heard.

Was this guy for real?

She slammed the receiver home, so hard she busted plastic. Shaw screamed. She shoved the phone away, running both hands through her hair.

She had *nothing*. Nothing at all. All those years of connections made and favors issued, all those networks built and relationships forged. Shaw built her *career* by fixing things. By bailing hard men out of ugly situations with phone calls and "pretty please."

And now, when it mattered most?

She was three-and-out. Worse, she was losing yards. She was backed into her own end zone, scrambling for a Hail Mary and facing a safety.

What was she going to do?

Before Shaw could answer her own question, the door blew open again. It was Carpenter—Shaw lifted a hand.

"I'll replace the phone."

"What?"

Shaw turned. Carpenter scanned the table, then shook his head.

"I need you in my office. Hale lost somebody."

Nestled in a cubical at the back of CIA headquarters, Nolan O'Rourke sat with his hand on his desk phone, the call with Laney Shaw just completed.

But his mind was far from finished with its subject.

Spread across O'Rourke's computer screen, the personnel file was stamped in bold red with the words TERMINATED WITH PREJUDICE—Agency speak for *blacklisted*. Just beneath that label, the name *Marcus Garrick Harden* was written above a date of birth, height and weight, eye color and ethnicity, blood type and place of origin. Like a supercharged driver's license, it was everything anyone inside the CIA might need to know about Harden in a glance...but the true story of his life was so much deeper.

Born in Jasper County, South Carolina, Harden enlisted in the United States Marine Corps straight out of high school and served seven years. First infantry and then MARSOC, five deployments and a *lot* of action—more than most in his boots. Harden discharged from the Corps under questionable circumstances. Rumor had it he'd evaded a potential court-martial only by virtue of his expiring contract. Nobody knew exactly *what* the potential investigation was about. The inquiry was never documented, and therefore practically did not exist.

Whatever the case, Harden wasn't finished pulling triggers. The next door he knocked on was the Agency's. With the Islamic state running wild across the Middle East, Africa, and Southeast Asia, and cartels dominating Central America, the Agency needed security contractors in a bad way. They were willing to overlook petty rumors of misconduct, and it just so happened that "Marc" Harden aced his tryouts.

Seriously—he placed top three out of a recruiting class of over two hundred. Ice cold and laser focused, Harden was the perfect operator...

Or so the Agency thought. For two years everything went swimmingly. Then the rumors resumed, and this time, they weren't entirely unsubstantiated. Harden worked black site security, rotating across three continents and perfectly content to remain overseas for years. He didn't have a family. He didn't have a house or any friends back home.

What he *did* have was a hobby—and that hobby was murdering people. Terrorists or suspected terrorists, cartel soldados, and warlords. Anyone who the CIA kidnapped to "interview" was likely to disappear. Because so many of Harden's associates shared his distaste for America's enemies, they looked the other way at first.

But then it got bloody—really, really bloody. Harden got bolder and rarely bothered to cover his tracks. He was becoming a real liability, but because the black sites he guarded were already off the books and questionably legal, it wasn't like Langley could prosecute him openly.

So they did the other thing. They cut him a six-figure check, terminated his employment with prejudice, and strongly advised him to get lost—permanently. That was four years ago, and nobody at the CIA had seen or heard from Harden since. O'Rourke himself, familiar with the case, assumed Harden to be camping out in some third world megacity, boozing his life away and—probably—murdering the occasional nobody just to scratch the itch.

At least he was *gone*. At least he wasn't Langley's problem.

Until...

O'Rourke stared at the personnel photo. Harden looked straight into the camera and...there was nothing. Lifeless eyes, a total zombie. Wrapped around his right bicep, curling to his forearm and baring bloody fangs, was a brown-black snake. A cottonmouth viper, common in Jasper County.

Snake man.

O'Rourke's jaw tightened. He debated only a moment longer, wishing he could ignore it all...but knowing he couldn't. He lifted the phone and dialed. A receptionist picked up and O'Rourke identified himself. He was transferred right away.

"Yeah?" Assistant Secretary of State Paul Morris answered with traditional abruptness.

"It's O'Rourke. We've got a problem."

67

Western Equatoria, South Sudan
22:06 Hours, East Africa Time

Hale trailed Bakumba for three hundred yards beyond the orphanage.

At first it was easy. Hale implemented short bursts from his weapon light, tracing blood into the brush. The trail led generally southeast—maybe toward Tambura.

But the farther Hale progressed, the less blood he found. Bakumba, he concluded, wasn't bleeding himself. This blood was from Tito, tracked on Bakumba's sandals, and fading within a few hundred yards.

In broad daylight there would still be signs—bent and broken bushes, disturbed grass. But in the dark and moving in a hurry, those more subtle marks would be difficult to find, and Hale was already five to ten minutes behind his target. Finding him now was like finding a needle in a haystack while blindfolded.

More importantly, every step Hale traveled away from the orphanage left vulnerable children and unprotected adults at his back. It was a classic case of *mission-centric mentality*. Hunting Lado Bakumba mattered.

Securing the orphanage mattered more.

Hale stopped at the crest of a hill and scanned the horizon for 360 degrees. He saw the orphanage—a black blob lit only by intermittent flashlight beams. To the west the bushlands opened toward the Central African Republic. To the north and east, forest took over. Someplace to the south, Tambura slept.

Lado Bakumba was out there, on his way to exposing their position. Alternatively, maybe he already *had* exposed their position. As Hale departed the orphanage, Mary Grace had shouted from her office.

The sat phone was missing.

Hale bit back a curse and spat. He didn't know why Bakumba wanted to sell them out. Maybe just to spite them—maybe the threat was nothing more than empty words.

But if there was a chance, however slim, that Bakumba was in earnest...

Hale jogged back to the orphanage, circling the mechanic's shed just in time to find Diko emerging from the back of the Ural with an AK-47. Joseph, crossing the yard to meet Hale, saw it also. He shouted in something other than English, his face consumed by storm clouds.

"They're coming!" Diko protested.

Hale ignored them both and reentered the orphanage. The hallway smelled of blood, Bakumba's murderous footprints marking a trail to the kitchen where Hale found Mary Grace.

She kneeled beside Tito's body, a bloodstained sheet now draped over it. She was crying.

Hale hung back, a little awkward. He was angry, also. He could still picture Tito squatted next to his milk crates, picking apart coconuts. Just struggling to get by, like so many others.

And yet only Tito was brave enough to go with Hale into Western Equatoria.

"I'm sorry," Mary Grace said. A tear trail stained her cheek, half her face illuminated by the bloody SureFire that still lay on the floor.

"Do you have another phone?" Hale said, his voice subdued.

"We used to—it broke. They were supposed to air drop us a spare, but in all the chaos..."

"What about video calls? Don't you have satellite internet?"

"It's spotty at night. Something about air moisture content. I can try."

"Please do. I'll be right there."

Back outside Hale found Joseph tying off the ropes that secured the Ural's cargo area. Diko now stood empty-handed, shifting on his feet and obviously scared, but trying not to show it. Trying to be a man.

"Mary Grace is contacting Atlanta," Hale said.

Joseph finished with the rope. He swept the safari hat off and mopped sweat from his face. "And then?"

Hale didn't answer. He was staring across the bushlands again, measuring the odds and reaching one crushing answer, every time.

"Come on," he said.

The three of them reached the orphanage office just as Mary Grace's laptop connected with RMM headquarters. The picture lagged and the speakers crackled.

"Switch off the video," Hale said. "The audio may clarify."

Mary Grace clicked her mouse and tapped a key to increase volume.

"Mary Grace?" It was Carpenter.

"I'm here. I have Joseph and Mr. Hale with me."

"What happened? Why didn't you call on the sat phone?"

"We lost the phone," Hale cut in. "Somebody was killed. Get Shaw."

"Somebody was *what*?"

"*Get Shaw*, Carpenter."

The audio went quiet and Mary Grace looked up. She was chewing her lip.

"Did you find him?" she said.

Hale shook his head, and nobody else spoke until Shaw's voice burst through a moment later.

"Hale?"

"I'm here."

"What happened?"

Hale summarized to save time. Shaw listened without interruption. In the background Bill Carpenter whispered, "God save them."

"Are the children okay?" Shaw said.

"They're scared," Mary Grace said. "They heard the scream. We put them to bed."

"And your staff?"

"Unhurt," Joseph said.

"Okay," Shaw said. "Clear the room. I want to talk with Ian alone."

Nobody moved. Mary Grace leaned toward the computer.

"Laney, I'm not comfortable—"

"*Do it*, MG." Shaw's voice popped like a whip. "I don't have time to argue."

Mary Grace flushed, but Joseph put a hand on her shoulder. He gave her a gentle squeeze.

"It's okay, miss. Let's get you and Diko some water."

That was enough. The curtain swished closed behind them, and Hale settled into her chair. He found a pair of wire earbuds curled on the desk and plugged them into the computer. The sound quality was still poor, but Shaw's voice was intelligible.

"What's your read?"

Hale knew what she was asking—not about what had happened but about how he would respond.

"As he was dying, Tito claimed that Bakumba was going to 'tell them' where to find us. I assume that *them* means the child snatchers...whoever they are."

"You think its true?"

"It doesn't matter if it's true. This place is still a death trap—we've just added one more reason to worry. Where are you with transport?"

"It's...it's not good," Shaw said. "I've hounded everyone from the UN to the WHO to small-time NGOs across East Africa. Nobody is touching Western Equatoria—especially by air. That downed UN flight has got everyone rattled."

Hale gritted his teeth. He wanted to lash out—he wanted to ask whether those bleeding heart NGOs would prefer to read about eighty kids kidnapped and pressed into military service, or else shot to death and left to rot.

It didn't matter. The anger wouldn't help him. He needed to focus.

"Best-case scenario," Hale said. "When can you get us out of here?"

Shaw didn't answer. A long moment ticked by.

"Well?"

"I...I don't know, Ian. I don't know who else to call."

Hale closed his eyes. He breathed deep—once, twice, three times. He counted to ten just like his grandfather had taught him as a small child.

Focus on the facts, Ian. Think rationally. Then make a call.

"I'm going to move them," Hale said. "I'm not sure how, but we can't stay here. We'll update you on departure—stand by your computers."

Before Shaw could answer, Bill Carpenter broke in.

"Mr. Hale, you *can't* move them. There's nothing within fifty miles of Tambura except empty bushland and forests infested with militia. You'd be stripping them of the only protection they have."

"This orphanage is no protection, it's a trap. A dozen men could pin us down with minimal tactical acumen. Any heavy machine gun or shoulder-mounted rocket system could punch right through these walls. That's game over in minutes, not hours. Now you trusted Shaw's judgment when she recommended me—this is where the rubber meets the road."

"He's right, Bill," Shaw said. "They may not be safe on the road but they're certainly not safe at the orphanage. You gotta trust him."

"And where will you go?" Carpenter demanded.

Hale had been wondering the same thing. He'd come up with only one answer—maybe not a good one, but it was the best he had.

"There's a South Sudanese military outpost just west of the Southern National Park. Joseph knows the way."

"Wait," Carpenter said. "You mean the garrison outside of Nagero?"

"Yeah."

"Ian. That's *ninety miles*. The road is little more than a track, and it'll be completely washed out this time of year. You'd do well to make twenty miles an hour—*if* you had something to drive in the first place. Isn't the bus broken down?"

It was. Hale didn't need to be reminded what his problems were.

"I'll *handle it*, Mr. Carpenter. That's my job. If we can reach that base, the South Sudanese army will secure the children and buy Shaw a little more time to arrange transport. It's not a perfect solution—just the one I have."

No answer. Hale gritted his teeth, ready to hang up. He didn't need anyone's permission—he was well aware of the responsibility crushing down on his shoulders.

"You can trust him, Bill," Shaw said. "He's the best I ever had."

Another long break. Then Carpenter said: "We're praying for you, Ian."

"Thank you, sir."

A door closed. Shaw returned to the line.

"I'm alone. Anything else?"

Hale considered, looking through the office window. He saw the bus—he saw the Ural. He thought he had an idea.

"We'll leave just before sunrise," he said. "That'll leave us with minimal time in the dark."

"Sounds good. What else?"

Hale's mind switched back to the unknowns—particularly, to whoever might be coming after them.

"Did you learn anything else about the snake guy?"

"I...called the CIA."

"And?"

"And they emphasized that they're *not* operating in South Sudan."

"What does that mean?"

"I don't know. I pushed—they pushed back. It makes me wonder..."

Shaw trailed off, but she didn't need to finish. Hale could connect the dots.

"I'll call you before we leave, Shaw. Stay after those aircraft."

"Good copy...and good luck."

Hale returned to the hall. Mary Grace was gone but Joseph was there, a bloody towel in one hand.

"Over here," Hale said.

Joseph joined Hale at the door. He lifted both eyebrows in question.

"Just before dawn," Hale said. "All the kids, and enough supplies for three days. We're moving to the army base."

Joseph glanced toward the stairway and the dormitories. Hale could see the strain in his eyes—the doubt. He turned back.

"They won't all fit in the Ural," he said. "I still need parts for the bus..."

Hale looked back into the yard—first at the broken Mitsubishi, then at the Ural...and its solid-steel bumper.

Hale said: "Do you have a heavy chain?"

68

Western Equatoria, South Sudan
22:32 Hours, East Africa Time

The contract journalist was late.

Wing-Kei stood on the dirt runway a few yards down from the Cessna 206 Stationair that had flown him into Western Equatoria. The flight had been long and rough—they skirted south of the most direct route to avoid airspace controlled by James Wani's militia—but Wing-Kei had left on time and he'd arrived as scheduled. He carried a backpack loaded with a sat phone, a computer to read the memory card from Lado Bakumba's camera, and two bottles of filtered water for himself.

There was also a pistol—a Glock Model 26 equipped with a suppressor—but Wing-Kei had removed that from his pack and tucked it into his pants instead. He ignored the impatient glances of the pilot, his gaze fixed on the nearby lights of Tambura.

There weren't many of them. The village was small, its main street running only a little longer than the airstrip. There was a church with a tin roof, and a general hospital that was the largest in the region—and still barely larger than a medium-sized aircraft hangar.

All the streets were dirt, all the houses huts. The air smelled of cow dung, mud, and despair—odors Wing-Kei had inhaled all around the planet and wouldn't bother trying to escape now.

He only waited, sipping water, until at last a figure emerged from the shadows.

Lado Bakumba walked with one arm held in a sling, although "walk" was a loose term—his stride was closer to a stumble. With worn sandals dragging the earth and sweat streaking his face, he looked like he'd just walked right through a war zone.

In fact, he had.

As Bakumba approached, Wing-Kei lifted a neck gaiter up to his nose, obscuring his face. Then he stepped into the light, lifting a hand.

Bakumba grinned—actually grinned—when he saw Wing-Kei. He dug a black device from his pocket and lifted it like a trophy. Wing-Kei simply tilted his head to one side, directing the limping Dinka toward an empty lot surrounded by a broken fence. Wing-Kei had already scoped it out and knew it would be private, concealed from both the town and the airstrip. He turned the corner and Bakumba followed, placing one hand on a fence post and wheezing like a wounded elephant as he stopped.

"I…I had to walk," Bakumba gasped in English. "They tried to kill me!"

Wing-Kei noted splashes of blood on Bakumba's arms and pant legs. His right hand was literally stained with it, and yet Bakumba's only apparent injury was his bandaged left arm—not bleeding.

"Let me see it," Wing-Kei said.

Bakumba passed him the camera—it also looked like it had been through a war. The lens and control screen were filthy, but the robust little unit seemed to be intact. Wing-Kei got the connector cover open and dispensed a micro SD card. The little chip slid easily into the reader built into his laptop. He held the computer against his chest while accessing the video files.

"It's good footage," Bakumba said. "I was so close I almost died. I was shot! That's got to be worth a little extra, huh?"

Wing-Kei ignored the comment as the computer loaded the first video clip. He watched in silence as the images flashed. The camera shook a lot—Bakumba must have been panting, or maybe just shaking with fear. That was okay, because he got the job done. The video captured every crucial point.

A heavy Ural truck. A small army of gunmen herding children into its bed. A machine gun cutting their parents down like dead grass.

And one man who didn't look like the others—a white man with a thick snake tattoo wrapped around his arm.

"You like it?" Bakumba asked, grinning again.

"It's good," Wing-Kei said simply. He shut the laptop and replaced it in his backpack along with Bakumba's camera. Then he turned for the airplane.

"Wait!" Bakumba called.

Wing-Kei looked over one shoulder, eyebrows lifted in a question.

"My…my money," Bakumba said, his brow furrowing in confusion.

Wing-Kei rocked his head back, grunting as though he'd forgotten the obvious. He dropped a hand to his shirt. Bakumba's gaze illuminated with hope.

Then Wing-Kei drew the Glock and shot the Dinka right between the eyes. A crack like the sound of hands clapping—no louder. Bakumba's body flinched…

Then he hit the ground like a dead tree, and Wing-Kei simply holstered the pistol. He tugged the neck gaiter down and picked his way through the grass back to the airstrip. He paused halfway to the plane, inputting a lengthy number into his sat phone. It range twice.

Then Marc Harden picked up.

"Yeah?"

"I have your next target. It's an orphanage near Tambura—about eighty children and a few staff. I want you to hit it immediately."

A soft whistle. "Eighty kids? You…want them all?"

Wing-Kei considered. "Take half. Kill the rest."

Silence. In the background Wing-Kei thought he heard laughter and the clink of beer bottles. Harden must still be in camp with the militia. If they were up this late, they were likely drunk. That would delay their deployment—it was over a hundred kilometers from the camp to Tambura.

"Is there a problem?" Wing-Kei pushed.

"No," Harden said, a little too quickly. "You've just...never asked me to kill them before."

"Now I am."

Another pause. A slosh of liquid courage. Then Harden grunted.

"Yeah, okay. We'll leave first thing in the morning."

"You'll leave tonight. Combine Thon's forces with your remaining troops. I want everyone to wear the uniforms I sent."

"That LRA stuff?" Harden sounded confused again—maybe a little wary.

"It's a disguise," Wing-Kei said. "Extra precautions."

It was a logical explanation. Wing-Kei hoped Harden was drunk enough to accept it.

"I'll talk to Thon. We'll leave as soon as we can."

It still wasn't the answer Wing-Kei wanted, but maybe the best he could get.

"When you finish at the orphanage," Wing-Kei said, "burn it to the ground."

Then he hung up, proceeding to the Cessna's starboard door. The pilot, still waiting in the cockpit, leaned out to looked down the runway—toward the fence where Bakumba had disappeared. *Maybe he heard the shot*, Wing-Kei thought. *Maybe he recognized the cough of a suppressed handgun.*

So what?

Wing-Kei climbed in. He rested the backpack in his lap and shut the door.

The pilot still hadn't moved. He shot a sideways glance at his passenger.

"Juba," Wing-Kei said.

The pilot hesitated only a moment longer, then he looked away. He started the engine and completed his preflight while Wing-Kei sat with his hand on the backpack, picturing the footage. Picturing Harden, framed front and center—an ex-CIA operator, caught red-handed sacking villages.

The burned and bullet-ridden orphanage would be just icing on the cake.

69

Atlanta, Georgia
17:01 Hours, Eastern Daylight Time

Bill Carpenter was ready to drop.

He'd hadn't spent this much time on his feet since he was a soccer star at TCU. He hadn't spent this much time on his knees...maybe ever.

It felt useless, and he felt like a traitor for admitting that. As a man of ministry, he *believed* in the power of prayer.

So why did it feel like he was talking to the ceiling?

Carpenter blinked at his desk, and when he opened his eyes, the clock read eighteen minutes later than it had the moment before. He was literally falling asleep sitting up—he couldn't remember the last time he'd been home, the last time he'd showered, or the last time he'd eaten anything that didn't come in a bag.

All he could think about were the innocent lives trapped in South Sudan. Eighty-two kids, three staff members, his own niece. And one American warrior that *he*, William Stills Carpenter, had deployed straight into the jaws of death.

God, get them out. Just get them out.

Carpenter rocked his head back and breathed deep. He was so, so tired...

Down the hall a door closed, jarring Carpenter. Footsteps thumped on the carpet. The pace sounded too angry to be his secretary's.

Shaw?

Carpenter stumbled into the hall and looked right. Laney Shaw stood waiting for the elevator, one foot tapping. Then checking her watch.

"Laney?"

Shaw glanced over her shoulder but didn't say anything. She turned away again and Carpenter started down the hall.

"Laney. Where are you going?"

Shaw didn't answer. The elevator opened and she stepped inside. Carpenter blocked the door, and their gazes locked.

"What are you doing, Laney?"

"What do you think?"

"This won't help."

"So what will?"

Carpenter didn't have an answer. Nobody had an answer.

"I sent him in there, Bill. He went for *me*. Mary Grace depended on *me* to protect her. This is my mess."

"It's nobody's mess, Laney."

"Yeah? Well, somebody's still got to clean it up."

Shaw slapped the ground-floor button. The door attempted to close, but Carpenter still blocked it. He looked into young and angry eyes...and he saw himself. Maybe thirty years ago, back when more piss and vinegar ran in his veins than blood. Back when he was wild and reckless and yes... still used by God.

Carpenter stepped into the car. The elevator started down and he rode with his eyes closed, praying once more. By the time they reached the ground floor, his spirit had calmed. They entered the lobby, and then Shaw faced him again.

This time her eyes were rimmed red, but her chin held high. Despite the disheveled hair, the wrinkled and stained Bulldogs hoodie...she *looked* like a soldier.

"I gotta go, Bill."

Carpenter pocketed his hands. “Do you need a charter?”

“I got a commercial flight to Kampala. Maybe it’ll be easier to negotiate air transport in person. Mary Grace can only shelter at that garrison for so long.”

Carpenter nodded slowly—then he extended both arms and Shaw hugged him.

“If I was ten years younger…” Carpenter whispered.

“You’d still be old as dirt,” Shaw retorted.

Carpenter smiled wide. He smacked Shaw on the back. She withdrew.

“God be with you.”

“Yeah, Bill. You too.”

Then Laney Shaw jogged to the door.

70

Western Equatoria, South Sudan
04:45 Hours, East Africa Time

It was a terrible idea—and it was the best idea Hale had.

An hour before dawn, he emptied the orphanage. Shepherded by Mary Grace, Ajok, and Wal, eighty-two children split into two groups. Thirty-two gathered at the back of the Russian Ural. The other fifty clambered aboard the Mitsubishi bus—the same bus with a blown engine and no parts to fix it. Only now that bus was connected by two heavy chains to the Ural.

Hale wasn't sure what the tow rating of the Russian monster was. He didn't know for sure what the bus weighed, either, or how well the aged tires on the Mitsubishi would hold up against washed-out roads. He planned to place Diko in the bus's driver's seat and have him steer around the ruts as much as possible, but without power steering that would be difficult at best.

As for brakes…well. Hopefully Diko wouldn't need them.

"Mr. Hale?"

It was Mary Grace calling—and Hale didn't want to answer. Standing at the back of the Ural, he was busy lifting small children onto the cargo deck.

They were all lighter than they should have been. Most of them smiled. A few avoided his gaze. They all looked scared.

"Mr. Hale."

Mary Grace was right behind him, her voice firm. Hale stopped and braced himself. He turned.

But Mary Grace didn't say anything. Dressed in jeans and a T-shirt, she wore a floppy safari hat that might have belonged to Joseph. It was stained with sweat, drooping down to her neck but stiff over her sparkling eyes. She stared at Hale without blinking, and he didn't see any of the defiance or challenge that he expected.

Only a lot of grit.

"I just wanted to say thank you," Mary Grace said. "We...we trust you."

Hale didn't know what to say, and before he could decide, Mary Grace leaned close and curled a hand around his neck, lips pressing against his cheek. A quick kiss, and then she was gone, spinning in the dirt and headed for the Mitsubishi. Hale stood frozen, watching her go and blinking like a fool. He caught Diko standing next to the bus's open doors, gawking at Mary Grace and then turning a big grin and a double thumbs-up on Hale.

Hale flushed and hurried to lift the last five children. There was dry food and jugs of water in the truck, also. Medical supplies were packed into the bus.

All the weapons would ride in the Ural's cab.

"All ready?"

It was Joseph. Hale looked to the eastern sky.

It was still dark, but not so perfectly black as before. The stars had disappeared, and the distant horizon appeared faintly gray. Hale gave it another half hour before that gray turned to orange.

Yes...they were ready.

"Ian."

Hale glanced sideways. Joseph was watching him.

"Second thoughts?" Hale said.

"No. I was just going to say...there's lipstick on your cheek."

Hale's hand flew to his face before he remembered that Mary Grace hadn't been *wearing* any lipstick—or makeup at all. He shot a glare at the bus and found Diko falling over the steering wheel laughing.

Joseph laughed too, and swung into the back of the Ural. He seated himself on a bench alongside a row of children and promptly burped. The children laughed. Hale tugged the tow chains and inspected their hookup on the Ural's bumper one last time. He walked a circuit around the Mitsubishi, kicking tires and double-checking the door.

Everything was tight. The rig was as ready as it was ever going to be. And yet...

Hale felt the eyes and turned. He looked into one of the Mitsubishi's rear windows and found the swollen face of the little girl with burn scars staring at him. Still dressed in flower print, still not blinking. Like a ghost, but when Hale blinked, she was still there.

And so was that feeling.

"All ready?" Joseph called again from the back of the Ural. It was enough to snap Hale back to the present. He slogged through the mud, pointing at Diko on his way past. The kid shot him a salute, and Hale reached the Ural's cab. The engine started with an angry growl, and he gave it a moment to warm.

Then he found first gear. He checked the map taped to the dash, a route leading north for ninety-odd miles. The transmission caught with a shudder, and the chain snatched tight. Hale added gas and the 6x6 drivetrain dug in.

Then they were off—lurching and grinding toward the promise of safety.

71

Western Equatoria, South Sudan
07:12 Hours, East Africa Time

Marc Harden hadn't recruited an army—he'd recruited a mob.

Drinking like sailors and partying late every night, it was all Harden could do to have them ready for departure by sunrise. They arose hungover and irritable, snarling like dogs whenever Thon pushed them. With rifles slung and ammo crates stacked in the beds of pickup trucks, they were only ready to leave after Harden threatened to cancel Thon's contract.

The pale-eyed warlord literally bared his teeth at that, dropping a hand to the Colt revolver holstered in a cowboy belt on his hip. But what was he going to do?

Dead men can't pay.

Harden and the warlord led the column in Harden's Toyota Hilux. They bounced along pitted forest roads for two hours, winding back to Harden's base camp where the rest of his little army, his child captives, and the LRA uniforms waited.

That was when the wheels really flew off. Thon's men dismounted their vehicles the moment they arrived, colliding with Harden's men and throwing them to the ground. Spitting in their faces. Pointing their rifles skyward and dumping full-automatic fire into the forest canopy. Leaves and dead birds rained to the ground as the chaos snowballed—all while Thon laughed and chugged kassese.

Then one of Thon's soldiers whooped loud and long, and something like a hot rock dropped into Harden's stomach. The newcomers had found the palisade stocked with two hundred imprisoned children. With his rifle slung over his back, one of the gunmen was already climbing the chain link gate, drawing the attention of the others. Dropping to the ground on the inside of the pen, his hands went to his belt as he beelined toward a girl of maybe fourteen years old.

Then Harden shot him—twice between the shoulder blades from twenty yards away. The bullets zipped through the chain link and the guy simply froze. Dead stillness consumed the encampment even as gun smoke rose from the muzzle of Harden's Glock 17.

Then the body hit the dirt and all hell broke loose. Thon's men charged Harden—Harden's men crowded around him, rifles brandished in pitiful defense. An AK barked and one of Harden's men went down with a shriek, spurting blood from his gut. The guy next to Harden lifted his rifle, prepared to return fire.

Then Thon bellowed—an animal roar that was neither English nor any African dialect. He shoved through the crowd and reached Harden.

"What are you doing?" Thon shouted.

Harden's heart thundered, cortisol crashing through his body—but he knew better than to show it. He hadn't survived this long in so many murderous places by losing his nerve.

He stared dead into Thon's eyes. "The children are mine."

Thon didn't answer. The forest was silent except for the agonized moans of Harden's gut-shot soldier. Thon's jaw tightened and he didn't blink—Harden refused to blink, either.

Then Thon drew his Colt—so fast it surprised even Harden. The muzzle flicked right. Thon never took his eyes off Harden as hot lead exploded from the muzzle. He shot Harden's wounded soldier right in the face, driving his body into the mud.

Everyone flinched. Tensed. Took half steps back.

Thon only smiled. He returned the Colt to its holster with a grind of leather against gunmetal.

"Now we're even!" he said. "Ready to work?"

Psycho.

It was all Harden could think, and there was nothing to say. He holstered his own pistol and turned toward the hood of his Hilux without further comment. Thon shouted to his men in their tribal language, and the standoff melted.

Just another day in Western Equatoria.

At the Hilux, Harden drew a map from inside his plate carrier. Folded and covered in pencil notes, it depicted not only his base but every village in the vicinity—those he had hit and those he planned to hit.

But not anymore. Harden had a bigger, final target. One more brutal stroke, and then he could be paid, same as Thon. He could cash out and leave this pit permanently.

Not soon enough.

Thon swigged kassese as Harden traced a route southwest toward the Central African Republic—about sixty miles, he thought. Rough roads, but their light trucks could handle them. He thought the trip would take about two hours, three at most.

And then the killing stroke. Harden circled a spot about three klicks outside of Tambura.

"Here," he said. "We leave as soon as you're ready."

Thon leaned close and wrinkled his nose. He didn't seem to recognize the spot.

"That's just brushland," he said. "What's there?"

Harden pocketed the pencil. "An orphanage."

Thon's gaze flicked up. He stood motionless—seeming to measure Harden somehow.

Then a slow, evil smile stretched his face.

72

Juba, South Sudan
07:04 Hours, East Africa Time

Wing-Kei made it back to the city safe and sound.

The pilot didn't breathe a word the entire flight, which left Wing-Kei thinking that he'd observed more than he indicated. Upon departing the aircraft, Wing-Kei paused to unzip his pack. He withdrew ten thousand United States dollars and extended the roll without a word.

The pilot hesitated. He glanced around the airstrip to see if anyone was watching. Swallowed once.

Then he took it, because everyone always does. He nodded once and turned away.

Wing-Kei departed the airstrip in a cab. At the Radisson, he scrubbed himself clean under lukewarm water before settling naked into the lotus position for sixty minutes of silent meditation.

Focusing his mind. Reviewing each phase of what had already occurred, just to ensure that he'd made no mistakes. That he'd left no tracks.

And then looking ahead to what came next—the final phase.

At nine a.m. his watch chirped, and Wing-Kei dressed in slacks and a pale blue shirt—no tie. Ties were rare in Juba outside of formal settings, and Wing-Kei wanted to blend in. He departed the hotel with a compact leather satchel, only two items inside.

The Glock 26 and a memory card.

Another cab brought him to Juba's Kator district—a riverside blend of residential and commercial developments. Middle class, the population was a blend of African and Arab with a strong representation of outsiders—aid workers, traveling businessmen, and even expats.

Nobody would question or suspect an Asian seated at the open-air cafe across the street from St. Theresa's Cathedral. With his satchel close to hand and a pair of dark roasts on the way, Wing-Kei did his best to relax.

The weather was cool, nearly comfortable. Nobody paid any attention to the dusty black Mercedes that pulled up ten minutes after Wing-Kei's arrival. The newcomer—also an Asian—helped himself to the waiting coffee cup, sipping without a sound.

"You have it?" he said.

By way of answer, Wing-Kei withdrew the memory card from his satchel and slid it across the table. The newcomer slipped it into his pocket.

"Did you review it?" he asked.

"In full. Forty-six minutes spanning three days of travel. Much of it is useless. But seven minutes depict the..." Wing-Kei paused as a server passed by. Then he said: "The subject matter we need."

A soft grunt. "So you're done?"

"Almost. There was a complication with the journalist. He tangled with an orphanage and possibly some sort of outside security team. I'm unclear on the details, but I've tasked our contractor to erase any potential witnesses. Actually, this could be a good thing—quite the spectacle. It will make the news."

Just as that video makes the news, Wing-Kei thought. But he didn't add that. It was up to his boss to fine-tune the timing.

One more slurp of coffee. "I will commend you to Beijing, Wing-Kei. You'll have your choice of next assignment."

Wing-Kei ducked his head in humble acceptance. The newcomer rose, leaving the coffee. He half turned, then paused.

"This *security team*...we don't know who sent it?"

Wing-Kei shook his head. "The contractor reported it. Some of his men were killed."

"And we don't know the circumstances?"

Wing-Kei's stomach tightened with sudden anxiety. He should have expected the question—he should have been ready.

"Our contractor wasn't on site...He didn't collect details."

The newcomer squinted—but not at Wing-Kei. He was watching the waitress, focusing as she bent to distribute drinks. Wing-Kei couldn't tell if his boss was lusting or just lost in thought.

At last, he grunted once more. "No matter, the mission is complete. Well done, my friend."

Then he left, sliding back into the Mercedes. Leaving Wing-Kei feeling just a little uneasy.

73

Juba, South Sudan
09:20 Hours, East Africa Time

Jaxon Wilks spent all of the previous day sitting in a warm waiting room at South Sudan's Ministry Complex. In a sagging chair with a squeaking ceiling fan overhead, the hours dripped by in slow motion while Jaxon made periodic check-ins with Minister Abiem's secretary.

In every case he was invited to wait "just a while longer," and with the expectations of Jaxon's boss weighing heavy on his mind, that was exactly what he did. Sweating and tapping his foot. Playing games on his iPad and standing at the window overlooking a web of dirty, overpopulated streets. Chewing his lip, trying not to overthink.

And yet unable to shake the conviction that something was *very* wrong. Not just with Abiem and his illogical refusal to meet but with the desperation in Paul Morris's tone when he had pushed Jaxon to ram the deal through.

Offer them a battalion of United States Marines—tell them we'll wipe James Wani off the map. Just get this done.

Morris's office checked in with Jaxon about as often as he checked in with Abiem's secretary, but there was nothing to report. He couldn't *force*

Abiem to see him, and every time Jaxon pushed the secretary, he weakened his own bargaining position. Somehow the world's greatest superpower, not one of her weakest developing nations, was coming across as the desperate and needy half of this situation.

Was that Abiem's entire aim? Or was something deeper at play here?

The day ended without a meeting or any answers to those questions. Jaxon was ushered out of the waiting room by an only semi-apologetic secretary. He took his car back to the embassy and was *not* invited to dine with the ambassador's family. He ate another crummy meal from the cafeteria, slept poorly, and woke early to grind out an eight-mile run in the embassy gym.

After breakfast, as expected, Morris called. Jaxon was back in his private quarters, fussing with his tie and failing to get the knot right. He'd always struggled with ties, but his own frustration was exacerbating the problem. He kept tying it too short, then too long, then tangling the knot.

Jaxon snatched the tie off and looked to the phone, heart thumping. He didn't *want* to answer. Better yet, he wanted to answer and tell Morris to take a long walk off a short pier.

What would any of that accomplish? One misstep here and Jaxon's future with the State Department was history. All that hard work, all this misery in Africa—wasted.

So Jaxon calmed. He breathed deep and answered with a clear, confident voice.

"Good morning, Mr. Assistant Secretary."

"Sleep well?"

The snarled question felt like a harpoon. Jaxon took it on the chin but didn't answer.

"I want you back at the Ministry Complex. We're done playing Mr. Nice Guy. Inform Mr. Abiem that he has until lunch to meet with you, after which time the United States will be reevaluating the standing visas issued to both himself and his family."

Dead silence filled Jaxon's room. He blinked, his own stress evaporating in a moment of complete surprise, maybe closer to shock.

Had Morris *really* just said that?

"Mr. Assistant Secretary, with respect, that's a drastic measure. We're walking a tightrope, here, and we already look desperate after I camped out at—"

"Did I ask for your opinion?" Morris barked. "You're not paid to strategize, *Wilks*. You're paid to do what I tell you. Now get down there and tell that jungle mutt that he's got four hours to return to the table, or else his Vegas vacations are permanent history. If that's not scary enough, remind Mr. Abiem that I'm meeting with Congress next month to discuss the next round of aid for East Africa. Maybe South Sudan slips off the list for this cycle—maybe they don't get a dime. *That* should get him to the table."

Jaxon stood frozen, still in front of the mirror. He could see the crimson rising up his own neck even as his body tensed with increased blood pressure. Teeth gritted, he fought back a nearly undeniable urge to scream. To curse Morris until his throat was raw—to remind the assistant secretary that he had no *idea* what it was like to be there on the ground. That he couldn't read the room or judge the temperature from seven thousand miles away—that a brute force approach was likely to destroy any hope of a sustainable partnership.

He wanted to say all those things...but already knew that they would be wasted words. Something was eating at Morris, something had consumed all better judgment. He didn't just sound desperate, he *was* desperate.

Why? Jaxon had no idea. But he couldn't talk sense to a rabid dog. The best he could hope for was to keep Morris at a distance.

"I said, *is that clear?*"

"It's clear, Mr. Assistant Secretary. I'll update you directly."

Jaxon hung up before Morris could say anything further—or maybe before Jaxon himself could. He slammed the phone down and cursed. A loud, raw-throated scream that hurt his own ears. He was shaking all over, ready to put his fist through the mirror. Ready to throw himself from the top of the tallest building in Juba for *ever* assisting that Maryland charity with well-digging in Africa. For ever setting himself on this path of being *too good*.

Stupid, stupid, *stupid*.

Jaxon slammed his fist into a standing wardrobe, sending hangers jumping. From the desk beside his bed a phone rang. He knew it was the embassy security office calling, feigning a welfare check while really asking him to shut up.

Jaxon wasn't in the mood. He snatched the phone up and barked "*what?*" just to stop the ringing.

"Mr. Wilks? It's the front desk. I've got Minister Abiem's office calling for you."

Jaxon's heart skipped. He swallowed, suddenly short on breath and even shorter on words. He opened his mouth but nothing came out.

"Mr. Wilks? Should I put them through?"

"Yes," Jaxon managed.

The phone buzzed. Jaxon recognized the South Sudanese accent that greeted him—it was the same secretary that he had hounded the day before.

"Good morning, Mr. Wilks. I hope you slept well."

Jaxon licked his lips, still caught off guard but correcting quickly. He had Abiem's office on the line, and they were calling *him*. This was good.

"Great, thank you. What can I do for you?"

What the secretary said next was enough to send Jaxon's heart rate spiking again—the best possible thing she could have said.

"I was calling to check your schedule. Minister Abiem would like to meet with you at the Ministry Complex—as soon as possible."

74

Western Equatoria, South Sudan
09:33 Hours, East Africa Time

Harden's war party of one Toyota Hilux, three Land Cruiser pickups mounted with Dushka machine guns, and one Isuzu medium-duty truck loaded with gunmen arrived outside of Tambura in a tight column. Topping a final hill, Harden tapped his horn to signal a halt.

The column obeyed, but nobody dismounted. Turned broadside some four hundred yards from the complex, Harden lifted dusty binoculars and adjusted the focus, sweeping the premises. There was a core building constructed of block, three stories high with open windows and a flat roof. A mechanic's shed out front, and the corner of a pole barn barely visible behind the main structure.

But no sign of people, and no sign of any vehicles. Particularly no sign of any stolen Russian Ural.

"Well?" Thon barked from the seat next to Harden.

Ignoring the question, Harden momentarily questioned his intel on the orphanage's location. Everything *looked* right...but where was everyone?

"*Atem!*" Harden barked into his radio. "Check it out."

One Land Cruiser technical ground into gear. It bounced down the hillside, the muzzle of its Dushka swinging as a gunman clung to the grips. At two hundred yards from the complex, the vehicle generated a column of dust, impossible to miss. At one hundred yards, the Cruiser was within range.

But nobody fired. Nobody appeared on the rooftop or the windows. The technical raced right up to the main entrance, grinding to a halt. Two men bailed from the bed—the driver and the machine gunner remained in place. A quick search was conducted.

"You brought us here for an empty building?" Thon snorted.

Harden's teeth clenched, and he didn't answer. Lifting his binoculars, he swept the grounds once more. He watched as one of his men appeared on the complex roof, still wielding his AK-47.

Then the radio crackled. It was Atem, his captain.

"Nobody here, but this was definitely the place. Sleeping quarters on floors two and three—lots of small beds. Small clothes, also, in boxes."

Harden's blood turned hot. He wanted to punch the Hilux's steering wheel, but he knew that Thon was watching—probably scoffing at him. Mocking him.

"They can't be gone long," Harden snapped. "Search the grounds. Look for tracks!"

His men spread out on command. Harden adjusted the binoculars and watched, now chewing his lip. Biding his time.

Double his fee. He was *so close* to doubling his fee and being out of this pit forever.

"Americans." Thon swigged from a bottle of kassese. "You all think you know Africa...until Africa knows *you*. They saw you coming, heavy-footed fool. You do not *move* like Africa moves."

Harden withdrew his face from the binos. He locked gazes with the pale-eyed warlord, froth from the kassese still gleaming on the stocky man's lips. Harden didn't blink, he didn't budge. He stared until Thon broke first —looking away and muttering in some tribal dialect that Harden didn't know and didn't care to know.

Maybe, Harden thought, he could land even more than a doubled fee before this sweaty mess was over. Maybe he could land a bullet between Thon's dumb eyes.

"Kawaja!"

The radio crackled. Harden lifted it. "Go ahead."

"Two sets of heavy tracks. One leads southeast, toward the town. One leads north."

Harden pivoted the binoculars, tracing each path from the orphanage. The *town* would be Tambura. It lay three klicks away, and the tracks leading in that direction might represent fleeing orphans...or they might simply represent the Ural on its original approach.

The secondary tracks, meanwhile, led nowhere. North into...what? The empty bushlands?

"What's over there?" Harden pointed.

Thon snorted. "There is nothing over there. The town of Wau, if you go far enough. But in between? *James Wani.*"

Harden lowered the binoculars again. He dipped two fingers into the open tobacco pouch resting in the Hilux's cupholder and packed a wad into his cheek. He barely noticed the rush of nicotine as his mind worked in high gear, putting himself in the shoes of an elite American operative. Maybe several of them. Giving himself the task of dragging eighty-plus children to safety.

There was no safety in the brushlands, no safety near Wani's militia. But would Tambura be any better?

"They're in the town," Thon snarled. "Call your men back and we'll sack it—nothing but ashes by evening! It's a death pit."

A death pit, Harden thought. *And wouldn't an elite operator know that?*

He lifted the radio. "Atem! Move your men to Tambura and search for the Ural. Interrogate the locals if you have to. Radio back when you know."

Thon tensed in the passenger seat. Harden already knew what he was thinking—about the element of surprise, wasted. But Harden didn't really expect anyone to be waiting in Tambura. He keyed the radio again.

"Kuol! Take one technical and move north along the road. Radio if you see anything."

The only answer came as a pair of chirps from Harden's radio—he'd trained his men to respond that way, just as he'd trained the driver and the machine gunner to remain in place at all times. In seconds, one of Thon's

Land Cruisers was spinning south out of the orphanage while another turned north for the open road.

Or track. Or trail. It didn't look like much.

"Is this how they train you to fight in America?" Thon's voice hung heavy with condescension, but this time Harden didn't mind. He actually smiled.

"No. This is how they trained us to *hunt*."

75

Western Equatoria, South Sudan
10:52 Hours, East Africa Time

It wasn't driving at all—it was slogging at barely fifteen miles per hour.

Shortly after departing the orphanage, the awkward caravan of two vehicles and only one engine hit mud. Not just inches of it, but in some places, feet of it. Thick and goopy, sticking to tires and spraying as wheels slid. It filled ruts and washed-out basins between hilltops, turning what could barely be considered a road into little better than a trench.

The orphanage sat on high and sandy soil. The rain had drained away quickly, and the dust had returned. But here in the lowlands of Western Equatoria, slogging at barely a snail's pace, the land was *far* from dry. Hale kept the Ural locked into its lowest gear and wrestled the giant wheel as six gnarled tires tore the earth. Through his side-view mirror, he monitored the Mitsubishi bus as it lurched and jerked behind, sometimes becoming fully stuck before the Ural snatched it free again with a lurch.

The children were bouncing. Behind the steering wheel, Diko fought to direct the Mitsubishi, but was nearly helpless. The Ural dragged the bus as much as it pulled it. Nearly six hours had passed since departing the orphanage, and judging by the ticking odometer built into the Ural's dash, Hale and his convoy had made it barely fifty klicks—halfway, at most.

Inching toward the top of a low rise, Hale kept both hands on the wheel and planted his foot into the gas. Sweat drenched his face and his shirt clung to his chest—Hale had long ago removed his chest rig and only allowed himself to sip Hawkeye every fifteen minutes.

They could only carry so much. At this rate, he had no *idea* when they would reach the base...and he could only hope that water waited for them when they did.

Ten yards from the hilltop, the bus was stuck again. Hale looked into his mirror and found its back left wheel buried up to the axle. He added more juice and the Ural strained with an unearthly roar. The Mitsubishi moved, but only a little. Hale downshifted for torque, then depressed the accelerator again. This time the Mitsubishi broke free and the Ural yanked it to the top of the hill in one unbroken lurch.

That was when Hale heard the shouts. Rising from the back of the truck, accompanied by hands beating on the back of the Ural's cab. He mashed the clutch and the brake. The beating continued as Hale's gaze snapped toward the rearview mirror, heart thumping as he instinctively reached for the AK resting next to his leg.

But this wasn't that kind of threat. Joseph had already dropped out of the back of the Ural and was bent to look beneath the Mitsubishi.

Not good.

Hale applied the parking brake and dropped from the cab. The blazing African sun roasted his skin the moment his boots hit the mud—squishing and sticking. Damp elephant grass bent along his path, insects clicking amid the brush. Through the Mitsubishi's mud-caked windows wide-eyed children gazed out, looking half curious and half terrified.

At the bus's nose, Joseph lay on his side, stretched beneath the Mitsubishi's bumper. Hale already saw the problem. The bus was connected to the Ural with two chains, both taut, but the Mitsubishi no longer pulled evenly. It sat at an awkward angle behind the Ural, one end of the bumper twisted toward the Russian truck.

Hale squatted, swabbing away more sweat. Joseph shot him a look, keeping his voice low.

"We bent the frame. The front suspension is all twisted."

Hale leaned beneath the bumper. He saw exactly what Joseph described—a mess of twisted metal, with the front right wheel no longer parallel with its twin, and being dragged through the mud. The righthand chain looked ready to rip a chunk of the frame right out from under the bus. Another good hill, and it just might.

"What do you think?" Hale said.

Joseph took his time answering, twisting his head to examine various stress points, and then simply shaking his head.

"We'll adjust the point of hookup," Hale said. "Slow down if we have to. Let me reverse the truck."

Before Joseph could respond, Diko called from the open driver's seat window.

"Mr. Hale! Mr. Hale, *look*!"

Hale's gaze snapped in the direction of Diko's pointing arm—across rolling hills and beyond clusters of damp forest, maybe two kilometers behind them to a shallow valley barely visible between gentle slopes. The sun was so bright that at first Hale could see nothing—he shielded his eyes and squinted.

Then he realized that the glare *was* the object. It moved in a streak across the valley floor, bouncing a little, then vanishing around a curve. Riding the same road that they had traveled, it was another vehicle.

And it was coming in hot.

"Back in the bus," Hale snapped. "Everybody get down!"

Joseph must have detected the edge in Hale's tone—he scrambled from beneath the Mitsubishi, covered in mud. Hale grabbed his hand and hauled him up.

Then he was sprinting back to the Ural's cab, hauling the chest rig out. It landed over his shoulders with a thud of armor plates smacking his spine and sternum. He cinched the retention straps down just as Joseph caught up.

"What is it?" Joseph hissed.

"Small vehicle," Hale said, pulling the AK from the cab and checking the chamber. "About two klicks out."

"What do we do?" Joseph said.

Hale ignored the question, slinging the AK over his shoulder and reaching back into the Ural's cab. A moment later he emerged with both his range-finding binoculars and the British Lee-Enfield rifle, dusty and rusty. Hale drew the bolt and checked the load, dumping additional rounds into one cargo pocket. Then he put a hand on Joseph's shoulder.

"Re-chain the bus and get moving. I'll catch up."

Hale turned. Joseph caught him by the arm.

"What if you need help?"

Hale didn't hesitate. "If I need help, you'll need distance. *Don't stop.*"

Then he ran for the brush.

76

Hale's heart thundered as he stretched sore and exhausted legs to weave amid acacia shrubs, clusters of razor thorn bushes, and intermittent termite mounds. He reached the bottom of the hill the Ural had just climbed and wove north to circle the next.

He didn't want to run along the road. He wanted to swing alongside it, ascending a low rise with a bald top that offered a point of overwatch above the muddy track.

A sniper's nest? Not unless he needed it.

Hale accelerated, leaning low with the AK slapping. He could no longer hear the chug of the Ural or even the buzz of surrounding insects. The thunder of blood in his own ears deafened him as sweat coated his face in sheets, tasting salty between his lips.

Two kilometers. The vehicle had been too far away from Hale to determine its make or model, but he knew it was small, and it moved with much better agility than the Ural or its awkward trailer. Assuming the newcomer to be a technical moving at forty klicks per hour through the ruts and over the potholes, that left Hale with not more than three minutes to intercept before the vehicle drew within range of the stranded convoy.

Faster, Ian. Move!

Hale clawed his way up his target hill, slipping and nearly falling, catching himself with the butt of the Enfield. The weapon was four feet long and couldn't weigh less than ten pounds, as much a club as a rifle—but it was way more accurate than any AK.

Another hundred yards.

Hale gave it everything, the breath whistling through his teeth as his bare arms tore on passing thorns. One boot slipped and the other caught. He thrashed, nearly tripping over an African grass rat as the little mammal scurried for cover. Cresting the hill, Hale looked across a rolling valley with a forest lining the horizon and the sun beating down from almost directly overhead. He gasped for air and shielded his eyes, sweeping right. Sweeping left.

Then he saw it. Another glint bouncing across the South Sudanese wilderness, maybe four hundred yards distant but approaching Hale's position at an angle. Already it was starting up the last hill between its position and the orphanage convoy half a kilometer beyond. Hale could no longer see the bus or the Ural, and the moment the approaching vehicle crossed that hilltop, he would lose sight of it, also.

And he now knew—he could now clearly see—it was definitely a technical. The outline of another Dushka heavy machine gun was clear, a weapon that would shred the walls of the Mitsubishi bus like wet paper. Mary Grace and Diko and the children wouldn't stand a chance—Joseph would be lucky to pop off half a magazine before he was sliced down.

If the technical crossed the hilltop.

Hale hit the dirt, landing on his chest. The Enfield featured a fast-action bolt, and despite the age and abuse, the mechanism ran well. The moment Hale turned the handle, the bolt jumped back to grab the top cartridge from the magazine. A military surplus .303 round landed in the chamber with a smooth click, and the bolt locked closed.

Hale threw his left arm forward, resting the rifle's hand guard over the crook of his wrist. There was no optic on the Enfield, no scope or red dot or magnification of any sort. But the British designers who had fine-tuned the legendary bolt gun for use in the Second World War knew something about precision shooting. They had equipped the rifle with a flip up, adjustable rear sight aperture that ran along a vertical rail, with hash marks to indicate adjustments ranging from two hundred to thirteen hundred yards.

Hale jerked the binoculars from his leg cargo pocket and settled them on his target. He mashed the range finder button and allowed the laser only a moment to settle on the moving truck—the distance was now 480 yards, with less than a minute remaining before the technical crossed out of sight.

Hale dropped the binoculars and set the Enfield's sliding aperture at the five-hundred-yard mark. He swung his head against the stock and breathed deep, using the crook of his wrist as a swivel as he swung for the target.

A flash of dirty white. Distant silhouettes, a bouncing machine gun muzzle. Mucky orange tires and a filthy driver's side window. Hale's heart hammered as his body fought to recover from the sprint. His torso trembled even as he curled his finger around the trigger and inhaled once...then held his breath.

The technical was a hundred yards from the hilltop. A hundred twenty from disappearing. A hundred forty from engaging the Mitsubishi bus.

And a long five hundred yards from Hale—nothing but iron sights and a battered World War Two rifle resting in between. A moment of perfect stillness, like the moment the hand of God halted the sun in the sky.

Then Hale pressed the trigger.

The Enfield thundered, slamming into Hale's shoulder and bucking off his wrist. For a split second the world was gone, and even though he couldn't see, he *knew* he had missed. Hale tasted gun smoke as his vision cleared and already his right hand curled to pop the bolt on the rifle. It snapped back, rammed back in, and Hale blinked to clear his vision.

He was wrong—the first shot hadn't been a miss. It had been a dead hit, straight through the open driver's window of the technical and into the driver's torso. Hale didn't think the guy was dead, because his body thrashed, blood spraying the windshield as the technical turned directly toward Hale and bounced into a ditch. The engine raced—Hale could hear it from five hundred yards as he recentered the aperture and breathed and held and squeezed.

Another crack of British thunder—the windshield shattered and the tango in the passenger's seat was down. Blood coated glass and shouts carried over the African wind. Two guys bailed from the pickup's bed while a third—the guy behind the Dushka—finally returned fire. The machine gun spun, belching fire as an empty .303 casing cartwheeled over Hale's shoulder. His cheek hit the stock again. Russian lead shredded a nearby bush and whined over his head, dirt clouding the air from near misses.

And then another squeeze. The guy's head exploded and he pitched backward, the Dushka still firing as the muzzle shot skyward.

Three shots. Three hits. *What a rifle.*

Hale ran the bolt but didn't aim again. There was nothing left to shoot—the survivors had gone to ground, fleeing the sniper fire as they remained a threat to the nearby convoy. Hale had lost them...

But there was no way he was letting them get to the children. Slinging the Enfield over his shoulder and replacing it with the AK, he started down the hill.

77

Hale sprinted between the brush, mud squishing beneath his boots, the AK ready for short-range engagement. He'd already decided on an angle of attack that circled in from the north—between the tangos and the children. Hale needed to hit them in the mouth before they even knew what was happening.

Seconds ticked by and only the pounding of Hale's boots broke the silence of the wasteland. No thunder of the Dushka, no roar of an engine struggling to back the technical out of the ditch. No small-arms fire, either.

Were they hiding? Probably, and that made this entire situation so much worse. Lurking in the brush out of sight of the road, Hale's enemy held all the high ground. He couldn't afford to ignore them, but he'd be walking in blind if he went after them. If they had any sense at all they would simply lie in wait, allowing him to draw close and expose himself.

But these weren't US Army trained soldiers. They weren't even South Sudanese national military. They were just thugs with battered rifles, and they blew their own cover long before Hale was even in range.

The first chatter of full-auto fire burst from just beyond the technical in a blaze of muzzle flash. Bullets bit the dirt and tore the brush yards from Hale's position, but he didn't return fire. He kept running, circling ahead of the technical and right up to the edge of the road. Sliding to his knees behind an acacia bush and pivoting.

The tango was still firing, spraying the hillside in desperate sweeps. He'd seen *something*; maybe it wasn't even Hale. Maybe it was another African grass rat. Whatever the case, he was acting on impulse and fear. His weapon was heating up. He was running short on ammunition. Right on schedule the AK choked off.

Then Hale hit him—swinging just out of cover, firing and moving all at once. Hale crossed the road while dumping ten rounds straight at the clump of elephant grass where the tango had fired. He never heard the scream but blades of the grass shuddered under a spray of crimson. An AK-47 tumbled to earth, its magazine well empty.

Then the second guy engaged, just as Hale was reaching the east side of the road. He'd been smarter than his friend—he'd waited for Hale to expose himself, but even then he fired in full auto, dumping lead in a panicked spray. Hale was out of the far ditch and back into the grass without so much as a scratch. He turned south and wove around an acacia tree, passing the body of the last guy he shot before entering another thicket of thorn brush.

Then Hale stopped, because the brushlands had turned suddenly quiet. He felt the moment the change occurred—not just the absence of further gunfire but the absence of *any* sound. He couldn't hear the guy breathing. He couldn't hear the snap of an AK magazine locking into a matching receiver. He couldn't even hear any insects—all was dead quiet in the blink of an eye and on the battlefield that was *never* a good thing.

Hale lowered the rifle, just half an inch. A glint of metal caught his eye to the right, and he turned in that direction, his finger still tense around the trigger. He made it three yards, moving on the balls of his feet with elephant grass rising up to his shoulders on one side, thorn brush on the other, a clump of acacia bushes straight ahead. The glint grew brighter—it was metal. Hale aimed but wasn't ready to fire. Something in his gut bothered him. He moved another half a yard, tilting his head to block the sunlight. Obtaining a slightly better visual.

And then hurling himself into the elephant grass only a split second before the grenade went off. It had been wedged between the trunks of acacia bushes—that flash he saw was the moment a long string yanked the pin free. Hale hit the dirt just as the air cracked with the blast, shrapnel and bits of torn acacia blasting his legs and back. He choked on dirt and fumbled the rifle beneath his chest. He rolled face up just as a shadow exploded from the grass.

It was the last tango—the lone survivor. He was out of ammo and wielding his AK like a club, screaming and leaping like a crazed jungle cat.

Hale saw the AK's solid wood stock coming barely in time to dodge it. He yanked his head and got his hand around the grip of the TOPS Dawn Warrior just as the AK's stock slammed into the mud. The lunging tango landed on Hale's stomach with both knees, driving the air out of him, breaking his fall against the rifle. Already yanking it back up to strike again.

Then Hale drew the knife—one pop and it was free of its Kydex sheath. A second later he had it cocked away from his body, the point aimed at the exposed rib cage of the tango still riding his gut.

Then the knife bit—all the way to the hilt. Hale drove and kept driving until he'd punched through ribs and flesh and deep into vital organs. The guy choked and fumbled the AK. Hale snatched his hips left, rolling the tango into the mud even as Hale gasped for air. He landed on top and jerked the blade free. A feeble fist flew at his face while another flailed for the knife.

All too late. The blade ran up to the hilt once more, this time in the guy's neck. Eyes turned wide and his mouth opened, but he couldn't breathe. Even as Hale's breath returned to his lungs, the guy only choked. The knife snatched free but the damage was done.

Tango number five was down, bleeding out between Hale's knees. The body went limp as Hale leaned over him, still gasping for breath. Breathing in the stench of sweat and the dead man's body odor—but just happy to be breathing.

Hale gave himself barely five seconds before forcing himself to his unsteady feet, still dizzy. He plunged the Dawn Warrior back into its sheath without bothering to clean it, and stooped to recover his fallen AK.

It was covered in mud, so he worked the action to confirm function. Then he swept the grass, the brush, the bushes. Rifle up and listening while he continued to wheeze.

The insect noises were back, which was a good sign. Hale thought he detected a rustling animal also, and...was that a voice? A crackle of static?

Hale ran. Through the grass and across a muddy road to the gunshot technical. It rested nose-down in the opposing ditch, one dead guy in the bed and another in the passenger seat. Hale heard the crackle of static again and detected movement from behind the wheel. He circled from behind, the AK pressed into his shoulder. Moving on the balls of his feet, tracing movement in a dirty side-view mirror. Reaching the window and snatching around the doorpost with his finger on the trigger...

And finding the driver—the man Hale had shot first. He lay slumped sideways in the seat, his body covered in blood. The .303 round had ripped through his upper left arm, tearing through muscle before tumbling into his torso and obliterating his left lung—maybe other vital organs. The guy's face was pale and his eyes wide. His gaze traveled up to the window as Hale appeared, his lips parting.

But he didn't speak, he just died. His body turned limp...

And the high-frequency radio slipped from his grasp.

78

Somewhere over East Africa
11:00 Hours, East Africa Time

The first flight Shaw could find from Atlanta to sub-Saharan Africa was bound for Addis Ababa, Ethiopia. It was nonstop, lasting just over fourteen hours and flying through the night. With her carry-on bag jammed between her legs, Shaw spent the first seven hours dead to the world, catching up on all the sleep she had missed since Hale first landed in Juba. She didn't dream—she probably snored and drooled.

Shaw didn't care. She awoke to the golden kiss of sunlight piercing an airliner window, slowly drawing her way awake.

Then came coffee. Bad breakfast. A lot of spinning, stressful thoughts.

And eventually—her laptop again. Because Shaw had spent hours banging her head against a metaphorical wall, searching for any strategy to spirit fully a hundred people straight out of a war zone. Cashing in favors, promising future favors, and even begging had all failed her thus far.

Shaw was fully prepared to play dirty and shatter the rules, if necessary. But first she wanted to circle back to Nolan O'Rourke one last time. Not because the CIA would offer any air transport—O'Rourke had already made it clear that the Agency had no presence in Western Equatoria—but because the CIA just *might* be able to offer a line of communication with the government in Juba.

If Shaw could talk to Juba, maybe she could convince the military to dispatch a patrol to meet Hale on his way to their army garrison. It was an idea that had only just occurred to her as she emerged from sleep, and even if successful it might not be much help to Hale. Still, it would be better than nothing, and at least she might be able to reestablish communications between herself and the orphanage convoy.

That was worth a lot...*if* Shaw could speak with authorities in Juba.

Shaw linked her computer to the airline's overpriced Wi-Fi and fired up the Signal app on her computer. She didn't attempt to dial O'Rourke directly—the internet service was too weak, and he probably wouldn't answer, anyway. She messaged him instead, striking below the belt on her opening salvo.

To be clear, when eighty-two children, two South Sudanese nationals, and two Americans die in Western Equatoria, my statement to CNN will be that the CIA could have prevented this disaster...but refused to assist.

It was a brash statement—the kind that was sure to terminate whatever remained of Shaw's relationship with O'Rourke. But why should she care? O'Rourke wasn't her boyfriend. If he wouldn't be willingly useful, she might as well roll the dice on forcing him.

Chewing one fingernail, Shaw tabbed away from Signal and into her web browser. She scanned news reports concerning South Sudan—mostly about the downed UN flight and the five lives lost. International outrage was at a predictable high. Canada, Spain, and Italy had all issued statements condemning Wani's assumed aggression and demanding that the South Sudanese government take action...or else the United Nations should.

Useless. It was all Shaw could think, and she hated herself for being so cynical. But wasn't this all *useless?*

Words were so cheap in a place like Western Equatoria. What these people needed was real, concrete help. The kind Shaw desperately wanted to provide but—

Signal dinged, indicating an incoming message. Shaw tabbed back and couldn't help but smile. O'Rourke had called her a very ugly four-letter word—but he had responded.

There's still time to change that headline, Shaw wrote.

For the last time—the Agency has zero presence in Western Equatoria. I want to help you. I can't help you.

Shaw's teeth clenched. Her fingers jabbed at the keys.

I'm not looking for boots on the ground, I'm looking for contact with the government in Juba. My guy is moving the orphans to a South Sudanese garrison north of Tambura. I want Juba to know that he's coming, and I want them to dispatch a patrol to meet him. Can you handle that?

Long pause. Shaw chewed her thumbnail again. The European guy seated next to her shifted and shot her a dirty look—she ignored him.

Come on, Nolan. Be useful for a change...

I don't know anybody in Juba, O'Rourke wrote. *Sorry.*

That wasn't the answer Shaw wanted to hear—neither was it an answer she was prepared to accept. She jabbed at the keys again.

Fine. CNN it is, then.

This time the response was immediate—a repeat of the previous slur. Shaw's lips tightened in a humorless smile.

I just need a line to Juba. You get me connected with a government official and we're square. That's all I ask.

Another slow sixty seconds. Shaw shifted the laptop and shut her window to block out sunrise glare. She was getting a headache—she was smelling herself, also. The Bulldogs hoodie was rank with dried sweat.

O'Rourke wrote: *Where did you say they're going?*

Shaw's heart lurched. She tightened a fist and smacked her armrest, again startling the European guy before she could stop herself. She rattled out another reply.

South Sudanese military garrison on the road to Wau. It's just west of the Southern National Park.

Near Nagero?

Yes.

Okay. Hold.

Shaw's nail slipped back between her teeth. They were bitter with polish—cracked black and red, prepped for the upcoming Falcons/Patriots game in Foxboro. Shaw was planning to go, unintimidated by guaranteed taunts of *28 to 3*. She even had face paint and hair dye.

Now all those concerns felt like ancient history. Meaningless. Shaw tapped her foot. Shifted in her seat. Bit off another chunk of rigid nail and rubbery polish. Spat it onto the airplane's carpet.

That was too much for her neighbor. He sat up with a heavy sigh, eyes popping open. When he spoke, it was in a heavy British accent.

"I'm wondering, miss. Were you *born* this annoying, or does it require practice?"

Shaw met his gaze, hearing the words but barely registering them. Not really caring what he meant.

Signal chimed again and Shaw's attention snapped back to the screen. She scanned the message and blinked. She read it again and her heart slammed. The air turned thin in her lungs. The airplane constricted around her, the world slowing.

South Sudanese embassy confirms—Nagero garrison abandoned, James Wani in full control of region. Sorry. Your boy is on his own.

79

Western Equatoria, South Sudan
12:03 Hours, East Africa Time

Harden's handheld, high-frequency radio crackled exactly sixty-four minutes after he dispatched each of his scouting parties.

The first truck—the one bound south for Tambura—had already returned. In town they were greeted by petrified villagers who scrambled for cover at the sight of the incoming technical. One local policeman challenged them and he was shot dead in the streets, but after ten minutes of searching, they found neither the Russian Ural nor any sign of the missing orphans.

Harden had called the men back but refused to move from his hilltop. Growing impatient, Thon exploded out of the truck to drink and play cards with his men. Somewhere along the way a dispute arose, and now one of those men was dead—shot through the head with Thon's Colt single-action.

Animals.

Harden chewed and spit and waited, growing more irritable with every minute that ticked by without an update from his northern scouting party. He was beginning to wonder if something had gone wrong—if maybe the technical had become lost, or maybe his and Thon's men had simply abandoned their mission and their bosses with it. Maybe this wasn't the right place at all, and Harden's employer was wrong about the orphanage's location.

Harden wondered...and then his radio crackled.

"*Under...attack,*" an agonized voice panted. *"Help us!"*

80

Western Equatoria, South Sudan
12:48 Hours, East Africa Time

The first shot cracked as Hale bounced around a corner in the rutted trail. The captured Land Cruiser, running hard with wind whistling through a .303 caliber bullet hole in the windshield, had taken some effort to extract from the ditch. Hale literally stacked bodies in the bed to weigh down the rear axles and increase traction.

Tires spun and mud pinged against the undercarriage, but he got it out. He took the captured weapons and left the bodies. He ran hard in four-wheel drive for nearly six kilometers before catching up with the caravan, which rolled at an accelerated pace across a relatively smooth section of road.

Then came the pistol fire. It popped from the driver's side of the bus, just a blink of muzzle flash before a bullet ricocheted off the Land Cruiser's brush guard. Hale cursed and whipped the wheel left, bouncing off the road and through a thicket of thorn brush. The pistol popped again, but this time the bullet flew wide. Hale didn't even hear it. He laid on the horn, sticking one arm out the open window and waving.

Nobody stopped or even slowed. Hale upshifted and stomped on the gas, blasting through tall grass, hurtling alongside the Mitsubishi and waving again.

He could see Diko. The kid looked scared out of his mind, clutching the bus's steering wheel with one hand and a revolver with the other. Hale hurtled on, catching up with the Ural and blasting his horn once more.

Joseph saw him, and the Ural finally ground to a bouncing halt in a spray of mud. Hale whipped the Cruiser to a stop and left the engine running.

"What happened?" Joseph shouted.

"That fool kid of yours tried to kill me," Hale snapped. He marched right past the Ural toward the Mitsubishi. The bus was still trailing the Ural at a less-than-direct angle. As Hale approached, Joseph rushed to follow and Mary Grace tumbled out of the bus's sliding passenger door.

"Mr. Hale! What happened?"

Hale ignored Mary Grace, reaching the bus's driver's side window and snapping his fingers.

"Give it to me."

Diko looked petrified, his wide eyes dropping to the ground as he sheepishly produced the gun. Hale took it, glaring him down for a moment longer before addressing the weapon for the first time.

It was a Russian-made Nagant double-action revolver, about the same vintage as the Enfield rifle that rode in the back of the captured technical. Greasy and worn, the pistol looked like it had been through a half dozen wars already, with hash marks carved on the wooden handle to signify the obvious.

Hale bit back another curse. He turned away from the bus as Joseph and Mary Grace lectured Diko, tearing into him first about the origins of the hidden weapon and then his questionable use of it.

For his part, Hale wasn't even all that mad about being shot at. He wasn't mad in general. He was just overwhelmed—pushed to the limit, mind racing as he reevaluated his options based on the material at hand and reached the same conclusion as before.

Nothing had changed. The plan was still the plan. They just had less time now.

"Joseph," Hale snapped.

Joseph broke off his lecture and waded through the grass. Mary Grace followed. As they neared, Joseph looked sideways toward the parked technical.

Its bloody, gunshot windshield might as well have been a neon sign—the story was obvious.

"Scouts," Hale said. "My guess is they reached the orphanage and sent a truck in each direction along the road."

"How many?" Mary Grace whispered, her voice wavering for the first time since Hale had met her.

"Five."

"You killed them?" Joseph said.

"Not before they radioed base," Hale said.

Joseph's gaze fell and his eyes closed. Hale thought he might be praying. It was a good idea—the next good idea was just as obvious.

"We've gotta run harder," Hale said. "If we rip that bus apart, that's just what happens. We've got to reach that base before nightfall, or we're sitting ducks."

Joseph nodded. Hale turned to Mary Grace.

"I'll be in the pickup trailing one hill behind. If you hear a horn blast, put all the children on the bus's floor and keep their heads down, no matter what. Understand?"

She swallowed. Nodded.

"Okay, then," Hale said. "Let's roll."

Mary Grace headed back to the bus. Hale started out of the grass, but Joseph caught his arm.

"Ian...are you good? Were you injured?"

Hale shook his head. "I got the jump on them."

Joseph squeezed Hale's arm. He lowered his voice.

"Were they...LRA?"

Hale squinted, looking back down the road toward the distant battleground. Remembering. Then shaking his head.

"No...they weren't. Just guys with guns."

And that's bad enough.

Hale kept the last thought to himself. He tilted his head and Joseph jogged toward the Ural while Hale advanced back to the Mitsubishi and found Diko still shrinking in the driver's seat.

"Hey," Hale snapped.

Diko looked up. There was still a lot of uncertainty in his face, a lot of embarrassment. But there was some mischief, too.

Kids.

"You point this thing at me again and I'll kick your ass," Hale said. Then he rolled the revolver in his hand and extended it grip-first.

Diko hesitated, glancing over his shoulder. Maybe worrying about Mary Grace. He took the gun and it vanished beneath his shirt.

"Keep her on the road," Hale said. "And hang on."

Diko shot him a two-finger salute, and Hale ran for the technical. By the time he reached it, Joseph had the Ural back in gear. The caravan was moving again, jolting faster than before. Through the untied rear flaps of the truck's bed, Hale saw Ajok and Wal shepherding the kids, arms extended around them as the heavy vehicle bounced.

Wal made eye contact. He nodded once.

Hale slid back into the Cruiser's driver seat and dropped it into gear. A twist of the wheel and a mash of the gas and he was spinning around, headed for the back of the column.

Ready to stand as their last line of defense.

81

Juba, South Sudan
13:00 Hours, East Africa Time

Something was wrong—badly so.

Jaxon felt it the moment he arrived at the Ministry Complex. The secretary was there to greet him and she didn't smile. She didn't even speak—she just ushered Jaxon into the same waiting room where he had spent most of the previous day. He sat and tapped a foot, once more checking his watch.

Ten minutes. Then thirty. Twice he caught the secretary looking at him—both times the look was like ice, nearly hatred.

What happened?

It was all he could think, because this wasn't like the day prior. It wasn't like any moment since he'd arrived in Juba. Every instinct born out of years in diplomatic work warned Jaxon that this meeting, whatever it was about, wouldn't be positive.

At one p.m. on the dot, the secretary stood. She gestured and Jaxon rose. He adjusted his suit and smiled.

She did not smile back.

Down the hall and into a conference room. With the windows open, a warm breeze cycled through. Cars whirred outside. A pitcher of water sat, joined by two upturned glasses. Minister Abiem wasn't there, but Jaxon wasn't left waiting any longer. No sooner had the secretary shut the door than another door opened, and Abiem himself appeared. In full business attire, he was flanked by a man Jaxon had never met in person but recognized from the photographs of South Sudanese officials that he had memorized.

It was John Chol, Director General of South Sudan's National Security Service.

Not good. Not good at all.

The door shut. Abiem pulled a chair back and sat at the head of the table. Chol sat to his left. Both men stared—and then Jaxon Wilks seized the initiative, because he was still a diplomatic representative of the world's greatest superpower. He walked the length of the table, extending a hand.

"Minister, thank you for meeting with me."

Abiem ignored the hand. He stared into Jaxon's eyes, unblinking.

"*Sit,*" he said.

Jaxon withdrew the hand. He held the stare. Then he withdrew the chair to Abiem's right and sat. What else was he going to do?

"Okay," Jaxon said. "Clearly, there's a problem. How can I help?"

Abiem snorted—a harsh sound. "How can you help? Let's see, Mr. Wilks. How about if you tell me whether you recognize this man?"

Abiem extended his hand. Chol reached into a satchel and produced a printed photograph. Full color, it depicted a Caucasian male about thirty years old. Short-cropped blond hair and the deadest eyes Jaxon had ever seen. It looked like an ID photo, but the tone felt more like a mugshot.

Then there was the tattoo—a curling snake wrapped around the man's right arm.

Jaxon shook his head. "I've never seen this man in my life."

"Oh really? Are you sure?"

Jaxon slid the photo back. "Absolutely sure."

"Well, then. Perhaps further detail would assist your memory."

Abiem extended his hand. Chol passed him another document—this time a multi-page file. Abiem threw it down and Jaxon had barely scanned the headline before his stomach fell straight into his shoes.

TOP SECRET — INTERNAL PERSONNEL FILE, CENTRAL INTELLIGENCE AGENCY.

A smaller version of the photo was there, along with full details on a man named Marcus Garrick Harden—an Agency contractor, apparently. Jaxon legitimately had never heard of the man. He wasn't Agency himself. He only ever interacted with the CIA via field officers stationed at African embassies—and that was rare.

So what was this?

"I'm sorry," Jaxon said. "I still don't get it. I don't know this man."

"That's funny, Mr. Wilks. For the past three days you've been pressuring our government to sign a deal with your government. Security, security, security, you say. The United States will bring peace to Western Equatoria. And then...we find this."

Once more Abiem extended a hand. Once more Chol passed something to him—only this time it wasn't a document but a tablet computer. Abiem handed it to Jaxon, but even before Jaxon pressed play on the video, his stomach was on fire. His heart was thundering. He was watching hell unfold and the world fly apart, all at once.

It was a video captured somewhere out in the bush—a village on fire. Men in ragtag uniforms with patches on their sleeves storming from hut to hut, dragging adults into a knot and shoving children toward a truck. Jaxon's eyes stung when the gunfire began—the thunder of a machine gun mixed with wretched screams and tumbling bodies.

And then...there he was. Marcus Garrick Harden, tattoo and all. Calling commands.

"So you see," Abiem said, his voice barely above a growl. "Even while Washington offers troops to quell the unrest in Western Equatoria, who do we find *inflaming* that unrest? A resurgence of the Lord's Resistance Army..."

Abiem leaned close. He spoke through gritted teeth. "Led by a member *of the CIA*."

82

Addis Ababa, Ethiopia
12:03 Hours, East Africa Time

Laney Shaw spent sixty unbroken seconds in absolute silence after O'Rourke's message came through. She didn't move, she didn't tap her foot, she didn't bite her nails. She sat staring at the back of the seat as the dread closed in, the world shattering into a billion razor shards.

The garrison was abandoned...and without communication, she had zero way to warn Hale.

When the moment was over, Shaw blinked. Her fingers raced back to the keys. She started rattling off messages to O'Rourke, demanding assistance. Threatening CNN and leaked secrets from covert missions and phone calls to her congressman. She even threatened to disclose how she and O'Rourke met—that mission back in Vietnam that had gone sideways for Sentinel.

O'Rourke never replied, and after sixteen messages, Signal notified Shaw that O'Rourke had blocked her.

Game over—the CIA was out.

Shaw slapped her computer closed and spent the next two hours staring at the closed window, mind spinning. A career in the Army followed by a career in private contract security work had offered Shaw a plethora of opportunities to encounter wild, unchecked stress, but the last time she remembered feeling *this* desperate was...well.

The last time Mary Grace had been in trouble. When that Maserati flew off the road, when MG was rushed to an Atlanta hospital and looked unlikely to survive. The helplessness Shaw felt then was mirrored by the helplessness she felt now. The total *worthlessness*, so unlike her years in both the Army and Sentinel. At least then, when things went sideways, Shaw had some resources available to force a solution, however hackneyed it might be.

Now she was alone. She had nothing but favors to ask, and those favors had been refused. She was on a plane headed to Ethiopia with nothing at all to offer Hale or MG—Shaw couldn't even *get to them* to at least join the fight.

She was way up the creek. She was out of ideas.

Shaw closed her eyes and breathed hard and went to a very dark place. A place she'd only visited a precious few times in her life—like the time when MG wrecked her car. Or the time Shaw uncovered a conspiracy within her Army unit and was forced to report her commanding officer for extortion of innocent Iraqis. Or the time her own father, her best friend in the world, had finally lost the battle to ALS and was torn out of her life.

Shaw had gone to that dark, quiet place then. She ripped away all her safety nets and self-assurances and she begged for an answer. Hale might call that prayer—Shaw wasn't sure what it was. But she needed help. She needed something. She needed...

Her eyes opened. Shaw saw it, all at once. A wild, *insane* thought. So nuts that her mind almost spat it right back out, but as Shaw sat and spun it over and over again...she thought maybe...

Shaw was back on her laptop. By the time the plane landed in Addis Ababa with a slam, Shaw had fired off three more emails and had her phone ready. She stood just outside the terminal and made one phone call after another. It was her own bank that gave her the most trouble, which shouldn't have been a surprise. Security barriers stood like a wall of red tape in Shaw's path, but she forced her way through it all, not taking no for an answer until she at last obtained a green light.

Then she was rushing across the airport just in time to book the next flight into Kampala, Uganda. It was noon by the time she arrived, and everything she needed waited in either her email or the secure cloud storage drive where Shaw maintained her files. She paid a print shop inside the airport to run off a copy of one document and folded those pages into her bag. Then she rushed past a food court packed with every race and nationality of human to a Western Union terminal staffed by a very bored-looking French woman.

The transfer Shaw had ordered from her bank awaited her—seventy-five hundred dollars, which was the most she could transmit to Africa in a day. Combined with the seventy-five hundred Shaw had carried in cash inside her bag, that totaled a fifteen cool Gs of hard American currency.

Enough?

She could only hope.

Slinging her carry-on over her shoulder, Shaw chomped gum as she hit two more airport vendors, then she marched directly outside. A sprawling parking lot shuddered beneath her feet as jets screamed into the air overhead. Shaw chewed faster and kept marching all the way to a squat brick building marked *Charter Flights*, with a field of small aircraft parked beyond. She pushed through a glass door into a wash of lukewarm air conditioning and stepped right to the counter where a sleepy-looking guy slouched in a chair.

He was watching a soccer match. He didn't so much as look up when she entered.

"Excuse me," Shaw said. "I'm looking for a flight into South Sudan."

The guy blinked, very slowly. His gaze rotated toward hers. He scratched one cheek.

"Where now?"

"South Sudan?"

"You want to go to Juba?"

"No. I want to fly into Wau."

"Where?"

"It's in Western Equatoria."

He blinked again, seeming to wait for something. Maybe for Shaw to laugh.

Then he laughed instead, shaking his head. "Nobody going into Western Equatoria. They be killin' each other up there—shooting down planes, too. Forget it."

He bumped the volume up on his soccer match. Shaw's chest tightened and her heart thumped. She had the sudden urge to snatch the remote and ram it down his throat. Shake him by the collar—scream that she *knew* they were killing people. That was the whole *point*.

She remained calm instead. She reminded herself that she still held the trump card—specifically, fifteen thousand of them.

"Are you a pilot?" Shaw asked.

A grunt. She thought it was an affirmative.

"Are those your planes?" She tilted her head toward the back of the building.

"Boss man's planes," he said.

So you're making a fraction of what he does. Perfect.

"So how much would you charge me for a flight into Juba?"

He sighed—long and slow and laborious. He tore his gaze from the TV and lifted a pencil.

"You goin' by yourself?"

"Right."

"Any cargo?"

"Just my luggage."

"And you okay with a small plane?"

"Sure."

He scratched numbers, punching at a calculator in between. Then he grunted.

"Twenty-four hundred US dollars. Five percent fee if you use a credit card."

"Terrific," Shaw said, digging into her pocket for the Western Union envelope. "So let's say you book me a flight for Juba. I pay the twenty-four hundred. Then I pay *you* twelve thousand six hundred..."

Shaw counted the bills out slowly, one band of a thousand at a time, noting that the pilot's eyes were glued to the money the entire time. Soccer match forgotten, his body motionless.

Shaw looked up, meeting his gaze. "And you fly *me* to Wau."

83

Nagero, South Sudan
16:14 Hours, East Africa Time

A horn blast from the Ural was Hale's first signal that the caravan had finally reached their objective.

Half a mile back, parked sideways along a low hill with binoculars pressed to his eyes, Hale monitored the road behind for a distance of up to two thousand yards. The late afternoon sun was already sinking in the west, pouring amber glow over fields of low brush and outcroppings of forest. Near the horizon a herd of antelope grazed, appearing as little more than brown smudges even under the aid of the binos.

Hale's eyes burned. His whole body seemed to sag. He was sweeping yet barely noticing the wildlife, the vegetation, or the stunning beauty of undeveloped African frontier. The only thing he could think about was the bend in the road. That curve where his line of sight failed, and at any moment, a truck load of murderous militia could appear.

Hale could hit them with the Enfield at six hundred yards. He could rake them with the Dushka as they drew nearer. But how many could he realistically neutralize before one of the enemy fighters popped off his own lucky shot?

Get us to the base, Father. Just get us to the base, that's all I ask.

Then Hale heard the horn blast, long and low. It rang for a full four seconds, broke off, than rang again.

The signal.

Hale dropped the binos and yanked the Cruiser into gear. He bounced over ruts and around potholes, keeping his foot jammed into the accelerator until he hurtled around a corner and rejoined the caravan. They'd just reached a sweeping basin about four kilometers from the town of Nagero—a spec of a village with a population safely inside the triple digits. To their east the Southern National Park was marked by a distant outcropping of forest, highlighted gold by the setting sun. Directly ahead the road widened as it stretched toward the park.

But to their west, just beyond the nose of the Ural, a faded wood sign printed in both English and Juba Arabic featured an arrow and a two-word message: SSPDF GARRISON.

Bingo.

Hale flashed his high beams twice—the signal for Joseph to proceed. Lurching like a wounded elephant, the Ural turned off the worn road onto an even less maintained track. Winding between bushes, the path bore the ruts of heavy tires—maybe even tank tracks. As Hale hurtled along, he thought he could see the outpost—South Sudanese speak for what the Unit might have called a *forward operating base*—reflecting sunlight in the distance.

A fence, maybe a guard tower. A metal roof. All good things.

Hale passed the shuddering Mitsubishi and caught a toothy grin from Diko. The kid pumped his fist in the air and the children packed in behind him cheered. Hale indulged in a tight smile but didn't stop. He passed the Ural and took the lead, digging one hand beneath his seat to tug out a dirty white T-shirt he'd ripped from the body of a slain militiaman. It was stained red in one corner, but the remainder served well enough as a white flag.

Don't shoot.

Hale advanced a hundred yards ahead of the Ural and slowed to a less threatening speed. He could make out the guard towers now, each standing thirty feet off the ground behind a concrete and barbed-wire wall. Beyond a chain link gate, a handful of concrete buildings stood—barracks, maybe a command post.

Hale was half a mile out with the sun in his eyes, obscuring finer details. And yet as the Cruiser jolted on, he couldn't help but feeling that something was...missing. Or out of place.

The garrison felt altogether too quiet, somehow. He looked to the towers and didn't see any silhouettes. He looked to the open-faced sheds visible through the gate and didn't see the front bumpers of any military vehicles.

And, perhaps most concerning, he looked to the main building and didn't see any *flag*.

Hale glanced into the rearview and noted that Joseph had slowed. The Ural was two hundred yards back—maybe Joseph was getting the same bad feeling or maybe he was simply playing it safe. Whatever the case, Hale lowered the whipping white T-shirt and accelerated toward the base as the worry blossomed in his stomach.

By the time he was a hundred yards out, he knew. The story was painted as clearly as a neon sign—the tall grass growing beyond the fence told it, and the chain link gate hanging from one hinge underscored it. The empty guard tower and empty motor pool shed were the nails in the coffin.

Hale slid to a stop just outside the gate. He looked through the chain link...and saw no one. The place was vacant. With graffiti painted on its walls, grass growing chest high, and bullet scars marking concrete blocks, the outpost stood silent in the empty South Sudanese bushlands.

Abandoned.

Hale's eyes closed. He sat in the Cruiser, listening as the Ural ground to a stop some ways behind. He felt the warmth of the sun on his face, breathing sticky African air, and he knew in his very bones that they were alone. Parked on the edge of nowhere, limping at the last light of day into a military facility that was *supposed* to be a haven.

But this was no haven at all. It was an Alamo.

84

Kampala, Uganda
17:06 Hours, East Africa Time

His name was Kato, and he piloted the 1974 Cessna 206 like a cheap rental car with great insurance.

Exploding off the runway just past five p.m. local time, which was when the boss man left for the day, Kato hauled on the yoke with only one cup of his headset properly fitted, the other riding his skull above his ear so that he could still hear the dancehall reggae music pumping from a Bluetooth speaker taped to the dash.

Shaw rode shotgun, her pack stored in the back seat, her safety belt barely tightened before Kato was ramping up the throttle levers. The single engine had coughed a little on startup—Shaw's door barely latched also and vibrated at its bottom. Then there was the matter of the cracked windshield and the dark half of the instruments which were neither backlit nor appeared to function.

Whatever inspection regulations were practiced in Uganda, they clearly had overlooked a lot about 5-X-ray Apha Alpha Lima—the little Cessna's callsign. Shaw, never a great fan of flying in small aircraft to begin with, found her stomach flipping by the time the plane reached six thousand feet and banked north-northwest for Juba, their ostensible destination.

But Shaw had made her real target clear, and Kato held only two thousand of the promised twelve-thousand-dollar bonus. The rest was secured into Shaw's pack, and she would beat Kato with her own shoes if he attempted to swindle her out of it. If push came to shove, she'd even knock him out cold and attempt to pilot the plane herself.

Shaw had flown a couple times with pilot friends. She knew at least a little about the basic controls and the principals of multi-direction maneuvering. Navigation and landing would be the hardest two parts, but Shaw would risk her life to do both if necessary.

This mission was that important.

With the reggae bumping and the sun fading into the west, 5-X-ray Apha Alpha Lima zipped over the rolling green hills of northern Uganda. Kato flew lower than Shaw would have preferred, but she was even more ignorant about local aircraft regulations than she was about air navigation, so she kept her mouth shut. For the most part, her pilot followed suit. Munching plantain chips by the handful, he rarely used the radio after departing Kampala, except for once when another aircraft roared so close overhead that Shaw could feel the vibrations of its pounding engine in her skull.

"What the—"

"Hey, man!" Kato shouted. "You lost your mind?"

But he was laughing. He looked over his shoulder to watch the second plane fade, then shook his head.

"Old friend—total idiot."

Shaw was beginning to wonder if *she* was the idiot, but once more she kept her thoughts to herself. The landscape beneath them faded quickly with the setting sun, becoming so black that Shaw's only bearing on their altitude came from what shifty avionics equipment still worked. Kato thumped the attitude indicator from time to time, still munching plantains and bumping his head to the music, but the questionable instruments didn't seem to bother him.

It was only when they reached South Sudan that Kato's disposition changed, and Shaw only knew they had reached South Sudan *because* his disposition changed. Not only did he switch the music off, but he seemed interested in the passing landscape for the first time, piloting the plane with one hand while he monitored the sweeping ground. He made notes on a scratch pad strapped to his thigh and adjusted something on the dash. Finally, he keyed his mic and announced his present course and heading to some air traffic control authority, maybe in Juba.

The plane was still headed mostly north—Shaw could tell by the globe compass hanging from the ceiling.

"You know," Kato said. "I have lots of good friends in Juba. Many with planes. I am sure they would be better equipped to fly you—"

Kato's voice died as the cheap folding knife snapped open. Shaw had bought it from a vendor at the airport in Kampala. The blade was only two inches long and the handle was low-grade plastic, but the edge was sharp enough.

"You back out on me now and I'll slice you from eyeball to toenail, skip."

That was the end of the discussion. Kato banked the plane and they skirted Juba, turning for Western Equatoria.

Just a few hours more.

Shaw tried not to count the time as she monitored the horizon. It was illuminated only by dusty starlight—maybe a billion individual dots, but clouds covered more than half, dimming their glow. She couldn't see the ground at all. It might be rivers or towns of empty nothing passing beneath them. There could be an entire army, for all she knew, and she'd never see it.

But that army would see them. One glance over her shoulder and Shaw noted that Kato had killed the taillights—the wingtip lights were dead also. Gliding just above the lowest layer of clouds, the Cessna would be largely invisible to the naked eye and would be difficult to track even with night vision, but it *would* be audible. The engine was loud and there was nothing to do about that.

Shaw could only hope that whatever militia manned the anti-aircraft guns that had shot down the UNHAS plane were drunk out of their minds and passed out cold. She didn't want to meet them before her boots touched sticky African clay.

Another forty-five minutes. The Cessna throbbed and Kato made more notes on his thigh pad. He traced a folded map with his pencil and marked their location just southeast of South Sudan's Southern National Park. The ground was somehow even darker than before, but Shaw's eyes had adjusted well and she could identify rough features of the passing landscape.

Sprawling clumps of forest. Wide valleys and flat segments interspersed with low hills and mile after mile of what looked like fuzzy nothingness, but she thought it might be brush.

It was the African frontier, vast and largely forgotten...but maybe not empty. The Cessna was now flying across the same region where the UNHAS flight had been shot down. One glance left, and Shaw knew that Kato knew it, also. He was tense, his plantains forgotten. His gaze switched from the instrument panel to the windows and back to the instruments. He kept opening his mouth as though he wanted to speak—but he never did.

They flew another ten minutes, crossing the midsection of the park and breaking into clear African sky. A sliver of moon, hitherto obscured by the same clouds, gleamed from almost directly overhead.

Shaw looked out her window and found rolling brushlands interspersed with trees. A few passing huts and what looked like a bonfire—it glowed hot orange, and then it was gone. She thought she saw a road, maybe a truck.

And then she saw the shadow, and Shaw's stomach tightened as though it were clenched in plier jaws. It wasn't *a* shadow, it was *their* shadow. Cast by the moon and gliding over the ground at the speed of the plane. Impossible to miss from above, impossible to miss from below. A dead giveaway—they were silhouetted.

Shaw turned from the window, ready to call an order for Kato to navigate back into the clouds. Before she could utter a word, another sound interrupted. A distant snarl, a guttural thunder.

It was the voice of an anti-aircraft gun.

85

Washington, DC
11:14 Hours, Eastern Standard Time

When Jaxon Wilks's next update reached Paul Morris's office, the assistant secretary of state felt the impact in his chest.

Not metaphorically—literally. His heart burned. His left arm went numb, and his vision blurred. It wasn't the first time he'd encountered the symptoms of an impending heart attack, and it wasn't a surprise, either. Morris's doctors had warned him for years that a lack of exercise and a bad diet would catch up with him. It wasn't *if*, it was *when*.

Morris worried about that, sometimes. But not often, because pressures of the job and his own ravenous ambitions took precedence. Even as Jaxon's angry report boiled through the private phone line, punctuated by profanities and shouted questions, Morris didn't hang up and he didn't call for medical assistance. He simply fumbled with the emergency tube attached to his keychain, shaking out two nitroglycerin tablets and packing them beneath his tongue. He couldn't speak while holding them there, waiting for their sizzling effects to thin his blood and calm the tension in his chest.

That was okay, because Jaxon still hadn't stopped shouting. Morris had literally never encountered his young deputy this hot. Jaxon recounted his meeting with Minister Abiem and Director General John Chol. He hit the high points of the video recording and the resulting South Sudanese allegations that the United States was playing both ends against the middle—actively *instigating* regional violence and then offering to be the solution to that violence. Manipulating Juba into a better deal.

The absolute panic that Morris initially felt was the worst of his life, but in hindsight the chest pain was a miracle in and of itself. It kept Morris quiet long enough for him to realize that something huge was missing from Juba's allegations.

They talked a lot about this operator—Marcus *Harden*—but they hadn't said a word about James Wani.

"Shut up," Morris choked, the nitro still stinging beneath his tongue. "Just shut up and let me think."

Jaxon did—maybe because he was out of breath. Maybe because his world was shattering right before his wide eyes.

Whatever the case, the break was welcome. Morris swabbed sweat from his face and thought quickly. He recounted what Jaxon had said, what Juba alleged...and what was still missing.

"This Harden guy," Morris said, feigning like he'd never heard the name even though Nolan O'Rourke had called him with that name only one day prior. "You say the South Sudanese have his CIA personnel file?"

"Yep," Jaxon snapped.

"And how'd they get *that*?"

"I didn't ask. I was too busy doing everything I could to keep our entire diplomatic mission from being ejected forthwith."

Morris ran his tongue over his lips, breathing a little better as his chest loosened. The nitroglycerin was working its magic. He hadn't had a serious heart attack—maybe just a minor heart "event." He was still in this game, still in the fight.

"Mr. Assistant Secretary," Jaxon said. "Tell me *right now* that these allegations are groundless. That the United States is in *no way* manipulating the conflicts of South Sudan—"

"Just let me think!" Morris snapped.

He wiped his face again. He drained a mug half full of lukewarm coffee.

And then Morris knew what he had to do. Because this was totally unexpected, straight out of left field...but he had to confront it. If he didn't, far worse exposures may result.

"Of course it's not us," he said. "You think we're stupid enough to offer stability with one hand and be chucking hand grenades with the other? Grow up, Jaxon. You're smarter than that."

"So who *is it*, then?" Jaxon demanded. "The video was real, Mr. Assistant Secretary."

Morris thought. Chewed his lip. Then decided.

"It's Beijing. Got to be. They've been back-channeling negotiations this whole time, stringing Abiem along and keeping him from inking a deal with us. Now we know why. They were setting this whole thing up—sabotaging US-Juba relations. That's gotta be it."

Morris half believed his own theory. He'd been around long enough to know that this kind of thing was absolutely within the realm of Chinese "diplomatic" strategy—Beijing was as ruthless as it was crafty. But whatever the case, it didn't really matter who was responsible. For all Morris knew, Harden was a cracked nut acting on his own. Whoever had supplied Abiem with the CIA personnel file might simply have been exploiting an opportunity.

It only mattered that Jaxon knew and believed that the United States *wasn't* responsible. Because Jaxon was still on the ground, and it was now Jaxon's job to salvage this situation, whatever it took.

"We've got to massage this," Morris said. "Get back in touch with Abiem. Inform him that you've processed a report with your superiors and we are taking immediate action to uncover the truth of this situation. The United States is a stalwart ally of South Sudan—we would *never* manipulate them in any way. That's your message. Stick to it."

Jaxon didn't answer. Morris sat up.

"Did you hear me, boy?"

"Is it fake?"

"Is what fake?"

"The *personnel file*. Is Marcus Harden not actually a CIA contractor?"

Morris wasn't sure how to answer that. If he told Jaxon the truth—that Harden used to be a contractor but had subsequently been fired and blacklisted—then Jaxon would ask how Morris instantly knew so much about a random CIA employee. It wouldn't make sense.

On the other hand, Morris couldn't indulge the doubt.

"My next call is to the Agency's executive office," Morris said, his tone softening. "I'll find an answer, and I'll let you know. Okay?"

No reply.

"I need you with me on this, Jaxon. I need you dialed in one hundred percent. This is real diplomacy—your Super Bowl. Got it? The United States *needs* this partnership. We can't let it slip away. It's all on you."

More silence. This time, Morris gave Jaxon time. He waited.

Then Jaxon said: "Call me as soon as you know. I'll connect with Abiem's office."

"Good boy."

Morris slammed the phone down and snarled a curse, all his manufactured gentleness evaporated in a split second. His chest was tightening again, but this time it was just stress. Just wild disbelief.

How could this be happening? Of all the twists, all the bad luck...

No. Morris couldn't afford to dissolve into frustrated mental spirals. He needed to focus. He needed his cunning edge more than ever.

And he needed to call Nolan O'Rourke—because whatever happened in South Sudan, Juba could never be allowed to dig into the *real* truth of American involvement.

Seven thousand miles east, Jaxon Wilks stood alone in his embassy room staring at his phone...and desperately tried to buy what Paul Morris was selling.

Jaxon *wanted* to. He wanted to believe and maybe, when Morris called back after speaking with the CIA, Jaxon could believe. He could return to Abiem and explain everything—how Harden had never been an employee of the CIA, or even if he had, how this was all a big misunderstanding. How the CIA had nothing to do with instability in Western Equatoria and how the United States genuinely longed to help quell the violence.

Jaxon wanted to believe that he could still save this situation. Reverse course, undo the damage. But it's nearly impossible to prove a negative—the South Sudanese were holding what they believed to be hard proof of the United States' offenses. Minister Abiem was already threatening to bring details of those allegations to the attention of the United Nations.

The coltan deal, Jaxon knew, was cooked. Finished. History. Whether by the manipulations of the Chinese or bad luck or...

Or.

It was that last possibility that bothered Jaxon most. The scenario in which Abiem's evidence was exactly what it looked like.

And in that case...what was Jaxon going to do? With all his hopes and dreams burning to the ground...just what kind of diplomat was he *really*?

Jaxon wondered. He fought to bury the feeling.

And then at last he returned to his phone. He copied a number off his computer and dialed—another phone call around the globe, this time to Virginia.

Because one of Jaxon's Harvard classmates had also entered government service, not with the State Department but with the Central Intelligence Agency. A summer fling, hot and wild and doomed to be temporary, had nonetheless kept them in casual contact for years since. They had traded favors on occasion.

The favor Jaxon needed now might save his career or drive the final nail into its coffin. Either way, he dialed.

86

Western Equatoria, South Sudan
18:18 Hours, East Africa Time

Hale hauled open the gate and ordered the Ural, the bus, and all their occupants into the outpost despite its abandoned status.

What else was he going to do? They were at the end of a long day, the Mitsubishi was threatening to rip apart, and there was nowhere else besides the town of Nagero to go. Even smaller than Tambura with nothing in the way of fortifications or armed defense, Nagero lay right on the road to Wau and would be a dead giveaway if the LRA or the militia or whoever they were came roaring along.

Maybe Hale could hide the orphans in the garrison outpost. Maybe he could barricade the children inside the headquarters building and conceal the Ural and the bus in the dark. Maybe there would be weapons left behind by the South Sudanese army—at least there were the towers, which offered Hale a better opportunity to see incoming threats before they arrived.

It was all desperate optimism. Hale knew that. Very little about their situation had improved since leaving the orphanage, but for the moment, the children were still alive and Hale had at least captured a heavy machine gun with three or four hundred rounds of ammunition packed in the Land Cruiser's bed.

That was something.

"Put the children in the main building," Hale ordered Mary Grace. "Keep them out of sight and keep them quiet. Joseph, Diko, I want you to search the property for weapons or ammunition left behind by the army. Communications gear, also. Food and water. Whatever we can use."

Hesitation hung over the group like a cloud. Not even the children made a sound as they stared wide-eyed, their faces displaying a mixture of confusion and defeat. The adults, meanwhile, looked ready to drop. Exhausted from a long day with what just might be a much longer night ahead of them.

"Let's go," Hale said, a little sharper. It was enough to break the spell. Mary Grace, Ajok, and Wal shepherded the children while Joseph tossed Diko a flashlight and the two started off toward the main building.

"Ian," Joseph called over his shoulder.

"Yeah?"'

"Watch for snakes."

Right.

Hale started through the grass with the HK pistol drawn at his side. The moon's lunar light was shockingly bright in such a rural setting. Hale could see a hundred yards in any direction with reasonable clarity, and the glare of his SureFire Tactician drove back any persistent shadows.

He checked the open-faced sheds first. From a distance they already looked empty, but the hope of an armored vehicle or at least another pickup mounted with a heavy machine gun stuck in his mind. Beyond the grass he found nothing but empty fuel drums and oil-stained dirt. The electric lights and their copper wiring had all been ripped away.

Everything of value was long gone. This place had been abandoned for *months*. How had nobody in Tambura known that?

Hale swept the light along the perimeter of the concrete wall, finding it unbroken with razor wire still curled along its top. There was no second gate, and no rear guard tower. Only tall grass and clicking insects.

On his way to the outpost barracks, Hale scared up an adolescent warthog. The pig squealed and vanished into the dark, leaving Hale's heart hammering as his trigger finger constricted—but he didn't fire.

There was no need to scare the children. They had enough to eat, for the moment. Hale pressed on to the barracks, finding block walls scarred by small-arms fire, and a door hanging on one hinge. Hale couldn't tell why, but just the sight of the place felt vaguely menacing, like a graveyard at midnight. He didn't want to go in.

He went in anyway, leading with the pistol, turning the corner—and stopping cold.

It *was* a graveyard. Literally. Strewn across the floor and lying bent over bunk beds or twisted in corners, the skeletons weren't old but they'd long ago been stripped clean. Fragments of uniforms and military-issue boots remained behind—all else had been claimed by scavengers.

Hale's gut tightened, his gaze catching on a pair of skulls with bullet holes driven through their foreheads. About .30 caliber, with massive exit wounds blown out the back side.

Rifle rounds. Other skeletons featured shattered ribs and gunshot pelvic bones.

The last stand.

Hale pushed the door closed on his way out. He met Joseph and Diko halfway between the barracks and the armory.

"Main building is clear," Joseph said. "Just tables and trash. Plenty of room."

Hale nodded. "Keep the kids away from the barracks."

Joseph and Diko both cast glances toward the condemned building, but neither spoke. They followed Hale to the armory, where another door hung on one hinge. This time the blast marks indicated a direct RPG strike. Who needed keys, anyway?

The interior was hollow—empty rifle racks hung over a dusty floor. Hale scanned his light and found only an abandoned Makarov handgun with the slide locked half open. Momentary inspection revealed the reason why—there was a squib round stuck in the barrel. The pistol was useless. Hale tossed it to the floor and the weapon landed with a clatter...then an echo.

Hale's gaze snapped downward. The floor was concrete, but the pistol itself had landed on a rubber mat near the back corner—like a door mat, but heavier. Maybe a place to stand while performing maintenance on firearms.

Rubber shouldn't echo.

Hale crossed the floor and kicked the pistol aside. He tugged at the mat —it lifted easily, a three-by-four sheet. Beneath it Hale found a section of plywood cut with a finger slot.

"Hold," Hale said, passing off the light. Diko took it, leaning forward with wide eyes.

Hale sighed. "Diko."

"Yeah?"

"Hold it where *I* can see."

Diko quickly adjusted the light. Hale holstered his pistol and snapped the Dawn Warrior from his chest rig. The blade slid easily into the finger slot of the plywood. One quick flex, and the hatch was up, sliding free of its frame.

Diko extended his arm with the flashlight, and Hale bent to look inside. It was a vault—additional room for weapons storage, Hale thought, kept beneath ground for concealment or perhaps cooler temperatures.

Whatever the case, the auxiliary space hadn't been found by the militia that had raided this place. It hadn't been found by the local villagers who stripped away light fixtures and wire.

It remained buried—and not empty.

Hale bent, heaving the first item onto the floor with a clang. Long and tubular with a square metal base and adjustable legs, it was a mortar launcher. Judging by the Mandarin printed on its side, it was specifically a Chinese mortar launcher, compact and man portable. The cracked wooden case that lay in the vault beneath the launcher must have weighed sixty pounds. Hale had to heave with both arms to get it out. He used the Dawn Warrior to pry the lid off.

The case contained mortars, just as he expected. Half a dozen 60mm high-explosive rounds with accompanying fuses. Hale lifted one charge and rolled it in his hand, checking the butt for condensation or corrosion. It appeared clean—it was also marked in Mandarin. But Hale knew exactly what he was looking at, and one glance upward at Joseph, and Hale knew he wasn't the only one.

"What is it?" Diko hissed. "Is that a cannon?"

Hale ignored the question. Switching off the SureFire, he exited the armory without a word and looked east toward the road. As his eyes adjusted to the soft moonlight, he could make out individual clusters of brush bending in a soft breeze. The rustle of grass as some small wildlife—maybe that adolescent warthog—forced passage. The blink of more sinister eyes in a thicket of trees just beyond the fence.

The garrison was already surrounded. Hale's gaze switched from one deep pool of shadow to the next as he listened to the familiar sounds of children laughing in the main building. Ajok singing as she dispensed a dry dinner. Mary Grace chiding misbehavior while Wal directed the children away from the windows.

It was a lot of noise. Hale could silence some of it...but eighty children couldn't be forced into total quiet. They couldn't be fully concealed, either, and Hale couldn't drag them any farther north.

No. This was it, for better or worse. This was where their journey ended.

Joseph and Diko drew near. Neither man spoke as Hale completed his inspection, noting each possible angle of attack...

And formulating their best possible chance to repel it.

"Okay," Hale said. "Here's what we're gonna do."

87

Western Equatoria, South Sudan
18:50 Hours, East Africa Time

Kato spiraled into immediate panic mode.

Shaw saw it in real time—the moment his fascial muscles constricted and his free hand snapped around the yoke. His gaze turned down—through a dirty window to the torn brushlands. It wasn't hard to find the source of the incoming fire. Muzzle flash marked the spot at one thousand yards east and about two thousand yards beneath them.

Well within range.

Kato snatched the throttle rod. The aircraft roared, immediately gaining altitude as he hauled it into a harsh left turn—away from the gun.

Still strapped into the seat alongside him, Shaw lost sight of the muzzle flash. She clung to the handgrip mounted alongside her seat as the Cessna completed a 180-degree turn and pointed south once more.

Away from Nagero. Away from the road to Wau and the abandoned military outpost stationed somewhere along it.

Away from Ian Hale.

"Put her down!" Shaw shouted.

"What?" Kato shot her a wild look.

"Put her down!" Shaw repeated. "Land the plane there—on that flat spot."

Shaw pointed, flinching as an anti-aircraft shell detonated like a Fourth of July rocket only fifty yards from the plane. For a split second the sky was brilliant white—the ground beneath was fully illuminated. Shaw could see the wide, sandy patch of earth and she knew that Kato could see it too.

But he wasn't nosing down. He was still pointing the aircraft south, still lifting them higher into the sky.

"I said *put it down!*" Shaw shouted.

"I'm not landing here, you fool! They'll kill us. We should never have come here!"

Another near miss from the AA gun—this one closer than the last. The Cessna rocked left as the flash of white faded. Kato began mumbling in something other than English, his hands shaking as he yanked back up on the yoke once more, desperate for altitude.

But it was too late for that. The Cessna's stall alarm blared and Shaw watched the airspeed indicator plummet. A pause in the fire from the ground below might indicate the crew reloading, or it might indicate adjusted aim.

Whatever the case, Shaw knew that she and Kato had seconds, not minutes. They would never make it another hundred feet higher. There was no further time to argue.

It was now or never.

Shaw drove her left fist straight into Kato's crotch. The blow landed with a meaty thud and Kato gasped. His hands went slack and his jaw fell open. Shaw heard the shriek coming but she was way ahead of him.

She already had the starboard-side yoke in her own hands and was pushing down just as the next storm of AA fire exploded from just behind. Fireworks lit the sky and the Cessna's nose dropped. The stall alarm was still blaring, the engine was still thundering and Kato had just begun his shriek as the air speed indicator spiked.

"We're going *down*," Shaw said. "I don't really know what I'm doing and you can take over any time—but we're landing this plane!"

Shaw wasn't sure if Kato understood. The conversation was over, either way. Pointed toward the earth, the Cessna raced like a dart, shuddering with each subsequent crack of detonating anti-aircraft fire. The stall alarm ceased only to be replaced by another chime that Shaw didn't recognize. She instinctively reached for the throttle rod, ready to bleed back speed as the altimeter read five thousand feet—then forty-five hundred.

Here goes nothing.

"You crazy bi—"

Shaw hit Kato again, harder than the first time. Kato still hadn't closed his legs and took the strike with a choke—then he projectile vomited across the dash. The air turned putrid and Shaw closed her throat to keep from joining him.

Focus. Just get her on the dirt.

Thirty-five hundred feet. The air speed indicator still read 140 knots, and Shaw didn't need to be a pilot to know that they were moving *way* too fast.

"How do you slow this thing down?" Shaw shouted.

Kato gasped something, but the next detonating shell came so close on their tail that Shaw couldn't hear him. The plane jolted—the nose dove and Shaw pulled the yoke to compensate. She swept her gaze across the controls, searching for the landing gear lever before remembering that the 206 featured fixed landing gear...assuming they hadn't already been blown away.

"Slow us down, Kato!"

Shaw's contract pilot finally responded. With the altimeter dipping below two thousand feet, he retook control of the yoke. He mashed the throttle rod in, tears slipping from his eyes as his hands fumbled for an electric rocker switch labeled FLAP UP / FLAP DN.

Kato mashed the switch toward the downward position just as a shell detonated directly over their heads. The plane shuddered again and the nose lifted—speed decreased to ninety-five knots with barely thirteen hundred feet to go. Shaw looked through the shuddering righthand window toward a grassy plain that appeared a great deal less smooth than it had at six thousand feet.

There were acacia shrubs. Thorn brush. A small herd of panicked pigs that galloped off their righthand wing as the AA shells burst higher and higher over their heads.

They were under the guns now. They had some reprieve, maybe long enough to land.

"Get her down and keep the engine running. I'll bail and draw their fire —then you run for it."

Kato's watery eyes shot fire as he increased the flaps. He breathed in short gasps, his knees clamped together as the Cessna fell beneath a thousand feet—still moving at eighty knots.

Shaw closed her eyes, pressing her feet into the floor and her back against the seat. She breathed deep and thought about Super Bowl LI—because that loss to New England never failed to offer an angry distraction.

Twenty-eight to three...freaking twenty-eight to three.

She was just picturing that flutter of red-and-blue confetti raining from the stadium roof when the Cessna struck dirt, then bounced like a rubber ball. Kato shouted and the tail jerked sideways. Shaw clung on and cursed Tom Brady.

They hit again and stayed down a little longer. Bile exploded into Shaw's mouth but she managed not to spew. Dirt pinged against the fuselage and the propeller shredded brush—Shaw's eyes opened just in time to see an acacia tree rip past only yards from their left wingtip. They were spinning sideways, digging into the mud.

Shaw finally lost control of her airport lunch. An acidic spray and a smell that *again* reminded her of Super Bowl LI flooded the cabin. She slammed into the shuddering door and it popped open just as the plane shuddered to a halt, the engine still roaring.

Shaw's world spun. She spat bile and wiped her mouth with one hand. She gasped for air and fumbled for the belt—it unlatched with a heavy click just as Kato was turning wide eyes on her. Half stunned, half accusatory. Shaw wasn't interested in waiting around for him to find his senses.

She rolled out of the plane, landing on her feet and nearly falling. The outside air was thick with humidity, a hurricane of propeller wash blasting her in the face. Shaw bent and choked up more bile. She spat and wiped her mouth with the back of one hand.

Then Kato found his voice.

"You crazy—"

Shaw wasn't listening. She yanked her bag from the floorboard. One tug of the zipper and she found Kato's money—goodness knew, he'd earned it. She flung the bundle and shot him a two-finger wave.

"Good luck!"

Shaw stumbled through a thicket of thorn brush even as the Cessna's engine wound up again. One glance at the bumpy, semi-clear terrain stretching ahead of the aircraft and Shaw doubted whether Kato could get it off the ground.

She couldn't worry about that. She would offer a distraction and give him the best chance she could. Shaw stretched her burning legs and hurtled on through the brush. There was no wildlife—the plane had scared it away. She ran undisturbed for maybe two hundred yards, then hit her knees in a clearing and ripped the bag open. Toiletries and a little remaining cash spilled out. Shaw ignored both—only two items mattered.

The first was the folded document from the airport print shop. Shaw slipped that between her hip and her waistband, tightening her belt another notch to ensure its security. Then she scooped up the second item, another purchase from a vendor at the Kampala airport. Small and worn with only a single shot in its twelve-gauge barrel, Shaw cocked the pistol and pointed it dead into the sky. She pulled the trigger and a flash of hot orange light exploded from the muzzle. The projectile flare zipped skyward, illuminating the brushlands and marking the tail of Kato's plane just as it departed the ground and soared skyward.

He'd made it. In another three minutes he'd be beyond the range of the AA gun. He might even make it back to Kampala and his soccer match, his boss man none the wiser.

But not Shaw. She breathed deep as headlights appeared a thousand yards away. She didn't run as three technicals raced toward her. Dropping the flare gun, she raised both hands just before they surrounded her.

Shouting men bailed out. Heavy hands wrenched her arms behind her back. Shaw didn't object as a bag closed over her head. They hauled her to the back of a truck and threw her in, half a dozen voices shouting in an unfamiliar African dialect while only one spoke English.

"Who are you?"

Shaw didn't answer the question. As the speaker continued to shout, she would say only one thing.

"Take me to James Wani."

88

Western Equatoria, South Sudan
20:15 Hours, East Africa Time

Marc Harden drove his troops north, bouncing over ruts and through potholes large enough to swallow antelope. Riding just behind the lead technical, Harden himself piloted the Toyota Hilux while Thon chugged from his bottle and mumbled semi-inebriated threats about the dissolving mission.

The warlord wanted more money. He expected this mission to be already over—for the orphanage to be sacked and for his men to be enjoying the spoils of war.

Harden remembered the rumors of Thon's men engaging in gang rape and wondered just what *spoils* Thon was referring to. He knew he couldn't afford to care. If the last radio transmission from his northbound scouts was to be interpreted at face value, Harden was already losing more men and needed to press the assault while he had the chance. He would promise Thon more cash if necessary.

But as it turned out, the only motivation the warlord needed was a taste of fresh blood. The moment they reached the site of the northbound scouts' demise, everything changed.

The lead technical ground to a halt. Harden bailed out, sweeping the horizon to the north and west, and finding only darkened bushlands.

"Over here!"

Harden followed the shout to a ditch stained with blood...and holding five bodies. Most were shot through the chest and the face, while one of them had been stabbed in the ribs and neck. They wore the mismatched rags of Thon's uniformless troop—they were all Thon's man.

For a long moment nobody said anything. As Harden stared, Thon kneeled. He ran his fingers through congealed blood. It was mostly dry, but still sticky near cold flesh. Thon rubbed his fingers together, and then as Harden watched, the warlord ran his tongue over them.

Literally tasting the blood. Starting to quiver. And then standing.

Thon threw his head back and howled like an animal. He beat his chest with both arms and the men crowded around joined in. The shouts developed into an ear-piercing roar, mixed with the snarl of AKs fired into the sky. It lasted a full ten seconds, and then Thon bellowed something in a tribal language. Without further command, all his men rushed back to the trucks. Thon himself marched to the Hilux, taking the driver's seat before Harden could stop him.

Harden barely made it to the passenger's side before the tires spun. Mud rained in a shower over the very bodies Thon had just kneeled over. He hurtled past them, following the lead technical down a rutted hillside.

Clinging to the A-pillar grip, Harden's teeth crunched as the truck slammed through a pothole. He looked left to find Thon's pale eyes glowing like evil headlights.

And Harden knew—he'd lost control. The monster was out of its cage.

89

Western Equatoria, South Sudan
00:04 Hours, East Africa Time

Hale stood at the top of the guard tower and looked east.

It was peaceful in Western Equatoria, even if the bushlands were far from asleep. Under the aid of his binoculars, Hale could clearly see every shift in acacia bushes, every rustle of wildlife wriggling through tall grass.

There must have been ten thousand life forms littering the ground between the outpost and the road. Everything from crickets, termites, and scorpions to puff adders, monitor lizards, warthogs, and even hyenas. It was an untamed place—a true frontier. So unlike the Bob Marshall Wilderness of only a few days prior...and yet so much the same.

There was the same sense of savage balance—the same tick of an immeasurably complex timepiece wound by the very hand of God. Food chains and ecosystems; hunter, hunted, and those caught in between. A carousel of life and death so often thrown out of balance, and yet always reaching equilibrium again.

Truly, a masterpiece.

The tower shuddered and Hale glanced over his shoulder, expecting to see Joseph. To his surprise, he found Mary Grace climbing awkwardly in her patchwork skirt, a thermos hooked over her thumb.

"Easy there," Hale called. "The rungs are shaky."

Hale took the thermos and helped her into the tower. Mary Grace arrived panting, an awkward grin compromising her natural elegance for the first time since Hale met her.

"Wow—that's a workout!"

"Miss Dalton, it would be best for you—"

"Mary Grace," she said. "Or MG, if you like. All my high school and college friends used to call me that. I guess Laney's the only one now."

Mary Grace squinted, looking momentarily whimsical, or even sad. Then she shook her head.

"I brought you coffee. It's instant, but it's caffeinated. You must be exhausted."

Mary Grace poured from the thermos into its metal lid. The coffee steamed, and Hale wanted to step back—he was already sweating. But he was also exhausted, just as she said. He could use the jolt.

"Thank you."

Mary Grace smiled, watching him until he took a sip.

It wasn't half bad.

"Hawkeye water?" Hale said.

"The best in Tambura."

Mary Grace leaned sideways against the railing, arms folded. It creaked beneath her, but she didn't even flinch. Gazing toward the horizon with a gentle breeze playing with her hair, she seemed perfectly calm.

It was the most remarkable thing Hale had seen all day.

"There's an old-school water tower in Warner Robins with a walkway built around it," Mary Grace said. "Laney and I used to climb up there and look at the stars for hours. Just talking about life and boys and school and boys and our college plans and *boys*..."

Mary Grace laughed. She shook her head.

"I was the boy-craziest girl there ever was. Not, like, easy or anything. I just loved the attention. Laney had better sense—she was always getting me out of trouble. Hauling my drunk butt home and cleaning up the evidence before my parents woke up. Talk about a best friend..."

The smile faded. Hale forgot about the coffee, feeling that he could watch her all night. Not just because she was beautiful but because he saw a story in those distant blue eyes. A story so much deeper than water towers and high school nostalgia—a story he might like to know.

"Are you afraid, Mr. Hale?"

The question caught Hale off guard, but it was easy enough to answer.

"No."

"Why not?"

That question took longer. Hale tilted his head, deciding to deflect.

"Are *you* afraid?"

"No."

"And why not?"

Mary Grace's glacier eyes locked with his.

"Because I know why I'm here."

And there you go.

Hale sipped coffee, expecting Mary Grace to say something, but she didn't. When he at last met her gaze again, he found her crying.

Not a lot. One solitary tear slipped down her cheek as she relaxed against the rail as though she were posing for a magazine cover. It was so incongruous an image that Hale's mind descended into a bog. His lips parted but he didn't know what to say.

Then Mary Grace pushed off the rail. She crossed the guard tower and put her hand on his neck. Rising on her toes, she kissed him.

Long. Slow. Sweet.

"Thank you, Ian."

Hale's heart hammered. Before he could think of an answer, Mary Grace released him and started back down the ladder, just like that. She reached the ground and glided like an angel on ice all the way back to the main building where the children slept.

Hale watched her go. His mouth went dry and his hands buzzed. He barely noticed as the tower shuddered under a fresh pair of boots.

Not Mary Grace's. He *really* wished they were Mary Grace's.

Hale turned for the road and buried his face in the thermos lid as Joseph reached the top. A long moment passed, and Hale wiped his face with the back of one hand. He risked a sideways glance.

Joseph was smiling.

"You, uh..." Hale cleared his throat. "You good on the technical?"

Hale indicated the Land Cruiser pickup parked just inside the compound gate, which was now secured with the same chain they had used to tow the Mitsubishi bus. The nose of the Land Cruiser was pointed eastward, the muzzle of the Dushka supplied with a clear field of fire.

Just behind the Cruiser rested the mortar launcher. Staked and aimed toward the road with twenty-four high-explosive shells stacked nearby, it was a *lot* of potential death.

"It's good," Joseph said.

Hale knocked back the rest of his own coffee, then refilled the thermos lid and passed it to Joseph.

"What about Diko?" Hale said softly.

Joseph didn't answer immediately. He sipped coffee, his gaze passing beyond the truck to where the teenage South Sudanese sat behind a heap of sandbags. Legs drawn up to his chin, squatting a lot like Tito used to.

And staring at an AK-47 rifle.

"I spoke with him," Joseph said.

"And?"

"He's very strong. You know..."

Joseph trailed off, and for the second time that night, Hale glanced sideways to find tears. But these weren't like Mary Grace's tears—more than sadness, this was pain.

"I pray to God every day," Joseph whispered. "For six years I've begged my Maker not to let the old me return. I never again want to take another man's life. To pull that trigger..."

Joseph swallowed, allowing his tears to splash on his boots—then, slowly, his smile returned.

"I asked Diko if he was willing to fight. Do you know what he said?"

Joseph turned. Hale waited.

"He said: 'Was David willing?'"

Wow.

Hale shook his head, because there was nothing to say.

"Amazing, right?" Joseph said. "David and Goliath has always been

Diko's favorite Bible story. It's something to see a young man love the Word...It's something else to see him *understand it*."

The tower fell into thoughtful silence, and by default both men looked toward the road—breathing in the night air, listening to the night sounds.

And dreading the moment one of those sounds was man-made.

"They might miss us," Hale said. "If we make it through the night, I'll go into Nagero tomorrow and search for a satellite phone. We'll reconnect with Atlanta and...keep moving."

Joseph didn't answer. Hale knew what he was thinking—knew what he himself couldn't stop thinking.

If we make it through the night.

Hale had covered their tire tracks as best he could. He'd left the outpost looking just as they'd found it, save for the chained gate. He'd instructed Mary Grace to extinguish all lights and keep the children quiet. He'd prepped the mortar and the technical and drilled Joseph on the battle plan.

It was all he could do.

"Joseph," Hale said, his voice lowering.

"Yes?"

Hale chewed the inside of his lip, searching for the words. The questions swirling in his mind weren't new. They'd badgered him for years—since the moment that Army Black Hawk went down in flames, leaving him with a broken back and a medical discharge. He'd fought the resulting uncertainty with Sentinel—black boots instead of brown, contract missions instead of government missions. But still *something*.

Now Sentinel was gone. All that remained was busywork at Haleburg and elk hunts that could never fill the void of true purpose...and now Africa. A mission ready to fail despite all his best efforts.

Useless...why are you so useless?

"Do you ever think that God...forgets about people?" Hale said.

"What?"

Joseph squinted, and Hale already regretted the question. It wasn't really what he meant to say. The words just spilled out. He fought to retract them, to clarify his point—

And then headlights appeared on the South Sudanese highway. First a blink, then a sustained glare. Bouncing with the rough terrain, headed generally north toward Wao.

Hale snatched the binoculars to his eyes and zeroed on the target. It was too far away to determine make or model, but it was headed their way, and unless it turned, it would cross within a half mile of the outpost sometime within the next few minutes.

Hale and Joseph waited, silent and motionless as the moments ticked by. Soon, as the road curved, Hale would see the vehicle broadside for the first time. He prayed for the silhouette of a van—a bus. Some innocuous form of civilian transport, but what civilians would risk travel this late at night?

Thirty seconds. The vehicle began to turn. Hale's gut tightened...

It was a technical. Another small pickup mounted with a machine gun. Bouncing in the back was at least one gunman. Hale thought he detected two more shadows silhouetted by dash lights. The truck hurtled toward Nagero, and Hale prayed for it to *keep* going.

But just past the turn to the outpost, the technical braked. It ground to a halt, then reversed. Hale watched, not daring to breathe.

The technical stopped. Sat motionless. And then began to turn.

"*Down!*" Hale hissed.

He and Joseph hit the guard tower floor just before headlights blazed onto high beams, shooting toward the outpost. With his head twisted sideways and his face pressed against the mesh, Hale could no longer see the technical.

But he could see the Land Cruiser pickup he had parked just inside the chain link gate, and he could see its turn signals reflecting the incoming headlights.

One mistake.

The high beams died. The technical spun and started back the way it came, accelerating rapidly. In another moment it was gone, back over the hill. Hale and Joseph picked themselves up.

"They saw the truck," Hale said.

"Could be nothing," Joseph said. "Could be anybody's truck."

So why did they turn back?

Hale kept the thought to himself, playing out a predicted sequence of events in his mind. The scout returning to the main war party. Multiple vehicles and a *lot* of firepower crushing toward the outpost like a hammer swinging toward an anvil.

And caught in between? Nothing but Ian Hale, one jaded Sudan Civil War vet, and one shaken kid with a terrible sense of aim.

Impossible odds.

"The horse is made ready for the day of battle," Joseph said, speaking as though he could read Hale's thoughts.

Hale turned, squinting—and then remembering. An ancient word of wisdom. A truth as old as time itself.

"But victory belongs to the Lord," Hale finished.

Joseph nodded, and as Hale looked deep into aged and battle-weary eyes...he found a fighter.

"Let's lock and load," Hale said.

90

Western Equatoria, South Sudan
00:22 Hours, East Africa Time

The ride seemed to last forever.

Bound hand and foot with the bag nearly suffocating her, Shaw bounced in the back of a pickup with boots on every side. If she tumbled, they kicked her. If she attempted to sit up, they kicked her. If she made any noise at all—they kicked her.

The smell of body odor and homemade booze filled the bag and left Shaw choking, but she couldn't afford to panic. An accelerated heartbeat only consumed the air that much more quickly—she needed to be calm. She needed to focus her mind and consider every word of her sales pitch. If she fumbled—if she didn't nail this thing—she'd be far from the only one to suffer the consequences.

Music blared from the pickup's cab, some kind of regional hip-hop, but Shaw could still detect the crackle of nearby fires as the technical pulled into camp. Additional voices joined those of the soldiers that surrounded her, and the tailgate dropped with a slam. The fire she'd heard before was now much closer—she could feel its heat on her skin.

Were they going to throw her in?

It was a wild, irrational thought, but it was enough to spike the panic chemicals already fighting for control of her body. Shaw gasped as they hauled her out of the pickup. Her boots hit the mud but she never found her footing. They dragged her by her upper arms, sweaty bodies slamming into hers on every side.

Focus, Laney. Work the plan.

Another fifty yards. The sounds of more voices than she could count—glass shattering and music thumping. It was some kind of party. Shaw could smell the roasting meat on the fire, the faint odor of more homemade booze.

She had reached the hornet's nest. She was sure of it. Would she find what she'd come for?

They dropped her. Like a sack of potatoes, like a dead deer carcass. Shaw landed on her elbows as the breath exploded from her lungs. She twisted in the mud and gasped. A low voice in some tribal dialect muttered from not far away.

Then the hood was yanked from her head. Shaw blinked in sudden firelight glare—she was hauled to her knees, still bound, and cuffed across the face hard enough to draw blood from her lip. Shaw choked and spat. She nearly fell.

"Up!" a voice said. "You fall again, and I'll kill you."

Shaw found her balance and twisted just in time to see a shirtless black man, sweaty and muscular, step into view. He wore an AK pistol on a strap over his chest. He grabbed her by her hair before she could meet his gaze and shoved her face down.

"Look down! You look down before His Excellency."

Shaw obeyed—not because she was afraid but because she didn't have much choice. His fingers were still intertwined in her hair.

From beyond a crackling fire, a hinge groaned. Boots squished through the mud. A body descended into a creaking chair.

Then, in perfect English: "Let her go."

The fingers released Shaw's hair immediately. She sucked down smoky air and coughed. Then she looked up—because she wasn't afraid.

Shaw kneeled next to a campfire in the middle of a forest. Surrounding her on every side were men—no, not men. *Soldiers*. They all wore camouflage fatigues and most wore black berets. Weapons were everywhere—sidearms strapped to belts, rifles and rocket launchers stacked in tripod clusters. There were trucks also, large and small. A Russian-built T-55 tank, clearly broken down, and someways behind it in a small clearing another Russian war machine—a Mil Mi-24 attack helicopter, maybe not broken down.

There were tents and barbecue grills. Hammocks and outhouses. Most strikingly of all a fifth-wheel travel trailer, removed from its wheels, sat on concrete blocks only yards away. Shaw assumed that its door hinges were the hinges she'd heard groaning when somebody exited.

That *somebody* now sat just across the fire from her, dressed in a full military uniform adorned with both gold braid and a line of gold medals. He wasn't a big guy. Average height, average weight. He wore the uniform like a second skin, like he was born in it. His head appeared to be shaved but Shaw couldn't be sure because he also wore a black beret. On his belt hung a single weapon.

It was a Beretta M9 handgun—the same type of pistol Shaw herself had qualified with in the US Army.

"Who are you?"

The perfect English was marked by no discernible accent. The guy remained relaxed while somehow maintaining perfect posture—as though he were a veteran judge holding court.

"Laney Shaw."

Shaw kept her voice even, her chin held high.

"*Laney Shaw...*" the man repeated. He did not smile. "Why are you here, Laney Shaw?"

"I'm looking for James Wani."

No flinch, not so much as a blink. "And who sent you to look for James Wani?"

Shaw cast a glance to either side—she couldn't help it. The forest was so silent that her own breath sounded like a distant thunderstorm. Every eye was fixed on her, sweaty faces motionless in the dark. She felt like a steak laid out on a plate, circled by ravenous wolves.

Not lunging—not yet. But longing to.

"Are you Wani?" Shaw pressed.

The man in the beret tapped one finger against his bottle, staring through squinted eyes. Seeming to read her very soul—to pierce right through her body.

Then he said: "I am. Now answer my question, before I throw you to the hyenas."

Shaw breathed deep. "Nobody sent me. I came here on my own—I want to make a deal."

"A deal? What kind of deal?"

"The kind that makes you the wealthiest man in Africa."

A snort—instant, derisive, angry. She saw the fire flashing behind dark eyes like an erupting volcano. It came so fast she had barely registered it as Wani's head snapped right.

Then, before Shaw could so much as twitch, two men grabbed her by the elbows. They manhandled her around the dirt to Wani's feet—one of them planted a boot between her thighs while the second hauled her head back by the hair. A gleeful shout echoed from all around as Wani calmly handed off his water bottle, then drew the Beretta from his hip. He disengaged the safety with an oiled click, and Shaw's eyes caught on the receiver.

BERETTA M9 — U.S. PROPERTY.

Shaw blinked. Had she really seen that?

Before she could decide, the man who held her by the hair grabbed her jaw and forced her mouth open. She choked as the Beretta's muzzle was forced between her teeth.

"Let me explain something to you, *white woman*," Wani snarled. "You people come to my country with pockets full of American dollars, and you all think the same way—that Africa is for sale. That South Sudan is for sale. That *I* am for sale."

Wani's voice rose into a snarl, his teeth clenched as his finger wrapped around the Beretta's trigger. Shaw's eyes widened—she choked and tried to withdraw her head. There was no wiggle room away from the pistol.

"These men who stand around you are Azandes," Wani continued. "Bakas, Bongos, Avokayas—even Dinkas. Men who slaughtered each other in a former life but now fight together against a common enemy. Against a corrupt government in Juba, *bought and paid for*."

Wani's voice rose. His knuckles turned white around the pistol. Shaw's body turned rigid and she knew—she just knew. He was insane. He was off the rails. He was going to fire.

But instead, Wani calmed. Very slowly. And then he said: "Think carefully when I ask you again. *Who sent you?*"

Shaw gagged around the pistol. Wani withdrew it, not more than an inch but enough for her to breathe. She managed: "Nobody."

Wani snorted. Shook his head. Curled a thumb and cocked the Beretta's exposed hammer.

"Last chance, Laney Shaw. *Tell me the truth.*"

"Colt—" Shaw choked.

Wani squinted. "What?"

She gagged again. He eased the pistol back—its muzzle still rested on her tongue. Shaw jerked her head to free it and gasped. She spat blood and saliva before the fingers wrapped in her hair jerked her head around.

Wani was there, leaned low. Staring with wide, angry eyes.

"*What?*"

"Coltan," Shaw gasped.

"What's that?"

"Mineral ore," Shaw said, still panting. "A rare and highly valuable natural resource—the kind the whole world would beg you for. I didn't come here trying to buy you. I came here to offer you *real* power. Influence on a global scale—the kind not even America could deny."

Wani blinked—the first time. He looked to one of his captains but received no comment. As he turned back to Shaw, his eyes narrowed.

"Even America, you say?"

"Absolutely."

A snort—but Wani didn't look away. "So tell me. Where is this *vast* source of global influence?"

Shaw jerked her head, hard and fast. She tore her hair from the soldier's grasp—she lost some hair doing it. She twisted her bound hands to her left hip and lifted her shirt. She got a finger inside the folds of the sweat-stained printout from the Kampala airport and flipped it out into the mud.

Straight at Wani's feet. Then Shaw met his gaze.

"You're standing on it."

91

Western Equatoria, South Sudan
01:42 Hours, East Africa Time

Four vehicles—two armed with machine guns. That was what Hale identified via his binoculars as he lay prone in the guard tower, the Enfield resting alongside him, the distant road illuminated by four sets of headlights.

A technical arrived first, followed shortly thereafter by a Toyota Hilux, then a lumbering cargo truck, and finally another technical. They all stopped at the turnoff to the garrison, and shadows moved in the distant darkness as some soldiers dismounted while others remained in place.

There seemed to be some uncertainty, some reluctance. At half a mile, Hale couldn't tell for sure, but he certainly *hoped* that they were hesitating, maybe debating whether to risk a direct incursion toward the garrison.

Keep moving, Hale thought. *Just keep moving.*

But they didn't. They didn't send anyone to scout, either. Instead, the long snout of a Dushka machine gun pivoted atop the lead technical. It pointed directly toward the distant garrison, and it opened fire.

Hot lead tore across the brushland as Hale pressed his face to the tower's floor, making his body as small as possible. Beneath him he could clearly see Joseph and Diko crouched behind a mound of sandbags, only yards from the mortar launcher but safe from the bullets. They shriveled also, pulling a pair of AK rifles close to their chests as the Dushka's imprecise fire raked the ground, ripped through brush, and tore into the concrete wall. Closer misses zipped through the chain link fence, slamming into the parked technical's nose and shattering its windshield. Higher rounds pinged off the guard tower's legs, and one zipped through the metal roof over Hale's head.

But none found a human target. The thunder of the gun ran for a miserable twenty seconds—an eternity of fire. Then it stopped, as suddenly as it began, and Hale waited. His gaze switched back to the main building, where empty window cavities opened into a makeshift dormitory full of children.

Some teenagers. Some a few years younger. Some barely old enough to walk.

Quiet...not a sound.

Hale pleaded. He listened for the growl of an engine from the road, willing it into existence.

And then a child screamed. Like a tornado siren, starting out low and quickly growing into a desperate sob. It lasted only a couple of seconds before somebody clamped a hand over the child's mouth, but in the stillness of midnight Western Equatoria, the noise was as shocking as the Dushka.

Hale's attention snapped back toward the road. He didn't breathe.

Then a horn blasted from one of the trucks. An engine howled. The lead technical turned, hurling mud.

It bore straight toward the garrison.

"*Contact! Contact!*" Hale shouted, snatching up the binoculars. "Single vehicle, nine hundred yards. Man the mortar!"

Neither Joseph nor Diko hesitated. From the corner of his eye Hale watched them explode from behind the sandbags, rushing straight to the mortar launcher even as the oncoming technical opened fire once more—now straight at the gate. Bullets ripped the chain link and shredded the parked Land Cruiser's front bumper. Both front tires blew and air hissed.

But Joseph and Diko reached the mortar site. Sheltered behind the parked technical, they each took predesignated positions—Diko at the ordnance cases and Joseph at the launcher. With the weapon calibrated for six hundred and fifty yards—a short shot for a 60mm—Hale knew exactly what those high-explosive shells would land.

"HE quick!" Hale shouted. "Two rounds at my command..."

Diko dug into a mortar case and produced a round. Joseph tensed alongside the launcher, the high-explosive weapon held at its mouth but not yet dropped. Hale keyed the laser range finder built into the binoculars, and the readout numerals spun as the technical closed.

Eight hundred yards, still dumping lead.

Seven fifty, not slowing.

Seven hundred, pointed dead at the gate.

"*Fire! Fire!*"

92

Joseph dropped the round.

From the top of the tower, Hale felt the cannon-like blast as the high-explosive Chinese mortar struck the firing needler at the base of the tube, igniting the explosive charge that hurtled it right back into the air at breakneck speed. The air cracked with the blast, and even before the first shell landed, Joseph was dropping the second. Another popping *bang*—another weapon in the air. The technical reached six hundred fifty yards, dead on the mark.

Then the first shell landed. It hit the dirt maybe fifteen yards ahead of the oncoming truck, detonating with a blast five or six times as loud as the launch. Earth and smoke exploded into the air, an instant cloud of destruction only a moment before the second shell landed.

Right in the middle of the truck.

The technical went up in a fireball of detonated gasoline, shattered glass, and shredded metal. Hale watched through the binoculars, forced to squint in the glare. The guy in the bed was dead—blown apart by direct impact. One guy from the cabin was dead also, but the driver managed to tumble out of the cab, striking the dirt in a thrashing, burning heap. Hale touched the Enfield, but he already knew that he didn't have the time.

One sweep of the binoculars to the road and he found the remaining tangos on the move—the Hilux hurtling forward, the second technical fighting its way through the ditch, and the cargo truck spewing infantry.

"Good hit!" Hale shouted. "Add four hundred yards. Two rounds at my command!"

On the ground Joseph bent to adjust the elevation mechanism on the launcher, lowering the gaping muzzle for increased range. One thousand yards was a known quantity—Hale and Joseph had already marked the mechanism for quick adjustment. Joseph had the mortar ready for action within five seconds.

"Ready!"

"*Fire! Fire!*"

Two more back-to-back pops. The launcher belched mortars into a starlit sky even as Hale monitored swaths of infantry spreading along the road.

There were *so many*. Fifty, maybe sixty gunmen, several wielding what appeared to be rocket launchers or mobile machine guns. Already they were off the road and scrambling to the ditch. Already the HE rounds might be too late.

But then the first landed, smacking the road some twenty yards to the left of the sign marking the garrison. It detonated with another ear-splitting crack, hurling shrapnel and dirt across a five-meter kill radius and a twenty-meter injury radius. Hale witnessed at least one body flying to the ground amid the smoke before the second mortar ripped through the canvas-covered bed of the cargo truck and burst like a giant's hand grenade.

The truck was a diesel burner and it didn't explode, but a split second after the mortar detonated, the truck was burning, and by the time Hale got his binoculars pivoted to the point of impact, those flames illuminated the road in vivid detail.

Soldiers tumbling into the ditch—soldiers thrashing and bleeding on the road. The Hilux hurtling into the brush as its driver fled the impact zone.

"Good hit!" Hale said. "Fire when ready—let 'em have it!"

Joseph didn't need to be told twice. Diko passed him ordnance and Joseph fed that ordnance into the launcher's mouth, dancing backward to cover his ears before reaching for the next round. One high-explosive blast after another decimated the road, hurling dirt and shrapnel, shredding bodies and converting the gathered war party into a fragmented rabble running for cover.

But not all of them ran away from the garrison. Fully a dozen heavily armed soldiers ran forward, accompanied by the surviving technical, which now bounced through brush and termite hills to Hale's left. Its Dushka was dumping fire, and many of the men scrambling in and out of cover also engaged. A storm of copper-jacketed hornets slammed into the outpost's walls and zipped through the chain link gate, forcing Joseph and Diko back into cover—away from the mortar launcher.

Hale lifted the Enfield. He pulled the fast-action bolt and rammed a round into the chamber. He adjusted the rear aperture for six hundred yards and settled in behind the stock.

He set his sights on the militiaman standing behind the Dushka...and pressed the trigger.

93

Western Equatoria, South Sudan
01:48 Hours, East Africa Time

All hell broke loose in the blink of an eye.

Marc Harden heard the scream—the piercing wail of a brat child—and dispatched one technical to probe the outpost. The vehicle bounced down the drive, the tip of Harden's spear, already unleashing machine gun fire through the gate. Harden sat with a pair of night vision goggles strapped over his head, watching and waiting…

Then the first mortar fell. He didn't hear it launch—the Dushka was too loud—but everyone heard it fall. The blast was followed almost immediately by a second explosion, dead on target. The technical went up, fire lighting the night sky. Harden yanked the goggles away from his eyes, already knowing what came next and already screaming at his men.

"Off the road—"

The third mortar fell. Dirt and shrapnel ripped across the road and pelted the convoy. Harden's men bailed and scattered at will—Harden slammed the Hilux into gear and ran straight into the brush. The mortars were still falling, landing all along the road and smashing the medium-duty truck. A diesel fire burned—men screamed.

And everywhere, gunfire poured toward the outpost. It wasn't a coordinated attack or even a concentrated one. It was total chaos.

Harden threw his door open and bailed out, his heart pounding. He checked his AK and looked over his shoulder for Thon.

The warlord was circling the tail of the Hilux, walking upright with wild, pale eyes alight. He shouted to his men in some African dialect and whipped an arm toward the compound.

The command was clear. Harden scanned the developing battlefield and located his surviving technical halfway to the compound, its Dushka blazing.

Then that heavy machine gun *stopped* blazing as a body pitched sideways out of the bed. Harden marked the moment just as the blink of a single rifle shot caught his eye from the top of the outpost's guard tower.

Sniper.

Harden secured his rifle against his cheek and started into the killing field.

94

Western Equatoria, South Sudan
01:54 Hours, East Africa Time

Hale nailed the first gunner in the throat and flicked the Enfield's bolt. It ran better as it heated up, and Hale selected his next target—the technical's driver.

Five hundred and some odd yards. Nearly twice the range Hale had qualified at using an M4 with iron sights as a Ranger, but the Enfield was no M4. It was designed for a different time—an era of trenches and slogging conflict.

Hale aimed. He squeezed. The windshield shattered and the technical spun, slinging two more soldiers from the bed. Hale worked the bolt and fired again—a miss this time as his target scrambled.

Hale was rushing. He needed to slow down, but there were *so many*. Dispersed as individual gunmen instead of concentrated units, they were like a field of groundhogs. Too many to shoot, popping in and out of the brush before Hale could squeeze off a shot. He hit one in the leg and another in the gut—he missed on the next shot.

"Joseph!" Hale shouted. "Man the gun!"

Joseph and Diko were already scrambling into the back of the bullet-riddled technical parked behind the gate. Joseph worked the Dushka's bolt and Diko held the ammunition belt. Squatted low, they opened fire, sweeping the brush and shredding exposed bodies—driving others into desperate retreat.

Hale breathed. He worked the bolt once more and surveyed the field. One guy twitched, exposing half his body at three hundred yards. Hale didn't bother to adjust the aperture sight. He estimated the difference, held under, and fired.

Blood and a dropping body—no scream. Hale's fingers flew as his heart thundered. His breaths came in short bursts. He fired again—the Enfield was dry and Hale reached for a stripper clip preloaded with five rounds.

Then Joseph shouted. "*RPG!*"

Hale saw the flash. He rammed the fresh load into the Enfield's magazine just as the rocket-propelled grenade screamed toward the tower. It passed only a yard over Hale's head before vanishing into the night, never detonating. Hale found the shooter and aligned his sights. He held his breath, and suddenly he wasn't in South Sudan anymore.

He was back in The Bob. He was stalking his target—and this time, Hale didn't mind the unfair advantage of superior training.

The Enfield barked, and the RPG shooter went down. Hale reached for the bolt but already twin flashes caught his eye from both his left and dead ahead—more RPGs screaming in.

This time, they didn't miss.

The first struck the concrete wall at the base of the tower. It detonated with an ear-piercing blast, shaking the tower like a stop sign in a hurricane. Hale grabbed the railing just a split second before the second RPG struck the front left leg of the tower, only inches above the wall and some twenty feet beneath him. The blast sent shrapnel exploding through the expanded metal mesh that Hale lay on. It bit into his chest plate and stung his legs. He choked on the smoke—then he felt the shift. Heard the groan.

The tower was going down.

95

Western Equatoria, South Sudan
02:02 Hours, East Africa Time

Harden lay in a ditch just west of the road and directed the RPG fire via his radio.

"Hit the tower!" he shouted. "Bring down that tower!"

The first RPG missed. The second two struck, and dirt clouded Harden's night-vision-enhanced view. For a moment he couldn't see anything at all—just muzzle flash from the Dushka heavy machine gun parked behind the outpost's gate.

Then he heard the creak. The groan of collapsing metal. In what felt like slow motion, the silhouette of the tower's top appeared behind the haze—it was plummeting for the earth.

Harden slammed a closed fist into the ground and keyed his radio again.

"Good hit!"

A brief cheer was all Harden received in return. His gaze swept away from the tower, catching on the gate—the Dushka had gone silent, maybe distracted by the collapsing tower or maybe simply reloading.

Whatever the case, it was an opportunity Harden wouldn't miss. He keyed the radio again.

"All forces—converge on the gate!"

96

Western Equatoria, South Sudan
02:00 Hours, East Africa Time

Hale clung on as the tower leaned. For a split second he thought it might not fall—that the three remaining legs would hold.

But the shift in balance was too much. The legs were old, rusty, and sloppily constructed in the first place. Rivets popped like gunshots, and then he was going down. Swinging backward, clawing at the railing as the night sky flashed by.

"*Ian!*"

It was Joseph who shouted. Hale didn't have time to respond. He pulled his legs against his body as the Enfield flew from his grasp. Metal shrieked, so loud it obscured the pop of persistent gunfire. Then the tower smashed into the ground. Hale's grip broke and he slammed back-first into packed dirt. His head landed hard and stars spun overhead—he was stunned. Battlefield noises faded and Hale couldn't breathe. He was choking on dust.

Then a familiar face crossed into view—wide eyes and an open mouth. It was Diko.

"Mr. Ian! Mr. Ian, you dead?"

Hale blinked. The roar of gunfire resumed. He coughed and extended a hand. Diko pulled him upright, through the bent metal and into the outpost yard. The world swayed beneath Hale's boots, and he wanted to puke.

Once again, adrenaline and training took over. He pushed Diko behind the concrete. They both found cover in a squat, bullets whining like hornets through the chain link gate and landing with metallic pops against the already ventilated technical. Hale choked on dust and looked for his rifle—the Enfield was long gone, but he'd left an AK and two extra magazines at the base of the tower.

"Here, Mr. Ian!"

Diko passed him the rifle. Hale worked the bolt and spat dirt from his mouth. He rolled toward the gatepost and looked to the technical.

"*Joseph!*"

A hand appeared from inside the technical's bed. Joseph was squatting beneath the Dushka, its barrel glowing cherry red as no visible ammunition belt hung from its receiver.

Out of lead.

Hale's gaze snapped to the sandbags where Diko and Joseph had staged their ammunition—several crates still remained, but they were out of Joseph's reach…and every moment that Dushka remained silent, the wrath from beyond the wall grew nearer.

"Diko!" Hale grabbed the kid by his shoulder, shaking just hard enough to draw his attention. "You see that ammo?"

Diko's wide eyes traveled. He swallowed and nodded.

"Five smooth stones, Diko. You grab a belt and get it to Joseph. I'll keep Goliath busy. Okay?"

"O-okay." Diko started forward. Hale snatched him back, flashing a smile he didn't feel.

"Easy! Wait for my signal."

Hale pressed one shoulder against the gatepost and breathed deep. He risked a quick glance, mapping targets by their muzzle flash.

Dozens of them.

Hale lifted the rifle, planning the sequence in his mind. Right to left, targets at three, two, and twelve o'clock.

Fast and accurate.

"Now, Diko!"

Hale swung out and opened fire.

97

Langley, Virginia
19:10 Hours, Eastern Standard Time

"Fix this."

They were the last words Assistant Secretary of State Paul Morris snapped on his final private-line phone call with Nolan O'Rourke. Laced with venom and more than a little fear.

"*Whatever you have to do. This was your guy. Fix this.*"

Marcus Harden wasn't O'Rourke's guy. The two men had never met, and O'Rourke only recognized Laney Shaw's mention of a snake tattoo because the legend that was Marcus Harden's demise had been taught in every leadership class O'Rourke had ever taken with the Agency. As far as O'Rourke knew, Harden was a forgotten ghost. A cautionary tale to vet the psychological stability of contractors with better care.

But now this. Thanks to a leaked or stolen personnel file that did *not* mark Harden as terminated with prejudice, the South Sudanese and whoever was pulling their strings were one step away from convincing the world that America was engaged in forcing regime change—a sort of modern-day Iran-Contra Affair. It wasn't an allegation the CIA could easily disprove without delving into the entire sordid history of what a monster

Harden had become, and how they had paid him off to disappear instead of prosecuting him like they should have.

Worse still, if these allegations were allowed to boil into the public sphere, the resulting internal investigations and congressional hearings just might uncover something worse than Harden or his rabble of LRA wannabes—something Nolan O'Rourke absolutely *could not* allow to be known.

No, Marc Harden wasn't O'Rourke's man, but he was O'Rourke's problem. Like it or not. And this wasn't the kind of problem that could be swept under a rug with a seven-thousand-mile-long broom. So far out of touch with the situation on the ground, and yet so much at risk by it, the realization O'Rourke adopted while staring at Harden's picture on his screen was irrefutable.

He had to handle this in person. It was his best chance of weathering the storm.

Checking out of his office with nothing but a coat slung over one arm, Harden collected his Mercedes CLE Coupe from the Agency parking garage and zipped straight to his McLean condominium. As a mid-level officer with the Agency, powerful enough for people to sit up when he walked into the room but not nearly significant enough to justify access to Agency aircraft, O'Rourke would need to arrange his own travel. He deployed an AMEX to secure a first class ticket. The plane departed Dulles in eighty minutes—a nonstop Turkish Airlines flight to Istanbul. He would connect there for the final leg straight into Juba, another five or six hours.

With luck, O'Rourke could be in South Sudan by early afternoon the following day. He knew some people there who responded favorably to cash—people who had access to information from inside the shaky local government...and if necessary, untraceable firearms, also.

Yes, Nolan O'Rourke was going to fix this. One way or the other.

98

Western Equatoria, South Sudan
02:09 Hours, East Africa Time

Hale couldn't see the gunmen—only their muzzle flash, but that was enough. He dumped three rounds into each target before passing to the next. Not thinking, not hesitating, just moving and shooting as Diko sprinted across death alley to the ammunition canisters.

Some rifles went silent. There may have been a scream, but Hale couldn't tell—his ears rang from the hammer of his AK and the repeated RPG strikes.

"I got the bullets!"

Hale barely heard Diko's shout as his AK went dry. He rolled behind the wall and rocked the mag out, letting it flip to the ground. The rifle was hot—it was getting hard to hold. Hale latched in a fresh mag and worked the bolt. Already the hiss of incoming bullets concentrated on his position, some ricocheting off concrete while others bit the dirt.

"Joseph!" Hale choked. "*Let's go!*"

Joseph didn't answer—the Dushka did with a thunder of full-automatic fire. It raked the field in front of the outpost, shredding grass and bushes and chewing down a pair of soldiers as they broke from concealment to run for cover.

Too late.

Hale reengaged, placing more methodical shots as he mapped moving shadows. It was harder with the AK than it had been with the Enfield—the trigger group was loose and the barrel too piping hot for precision fire.

But the attackers were in retreat. Hale traced their silhouettes rushing for the road. The Dushka was ravaging them, leaving no safe place to huddle. With their own heavy machine guns either destroyed or abandoned, their only remaining option was space.

For the moment.

"Ian!" Joseph choked on smoke. "Last belt."

"Budget fire!" Hale shouted.

He withdrew from the gate and slung the rifle as Joseph's bursts constricted from six and eight rounds to three and four. Measuring the pop of infrequent return fire, Hale waited for a break. The pattern was random—impossible to predict.

So he went for it, sprinting across the exposure of open chain link. One bullet whizzed over his head and another skipped past his boot before he reached the shelter of the ventilated Land Cruiser. Hale slid to his knees alongside the mortar launcher.

"Diko!" he shouted. "Load me up!"

Diko squatted next to the sandbags with both hands clamped over his ears, nodded his understanding. He scrambled for a mortar case as Hale unlocked the launcher's elevation assembly. He didn't lock it down again on any particular range marker—precise fire was no longer the objective.

Now Hale wanted random fire—shells dropping all over the place, promising a game of Russian roulette for anyone stupid enough to remain behind.

"Let's go!" Hale called.

Diko was already on his way, dragging a case. He reached the side of the launcher, returning to his squat and lifting a mortar round. Before he could hand it off, Hale motioned to the tube.

"When I say you drop it, then snatch your hands back. Okay?"

"Me?" Diko blinked.

"No—King David. Who else am I talking to? Let's *roll*!"

The orders broke through Diko's haze. He pivoted to the mouth of the tube while Hale squatted alongside it, grasping the launcher with both hands to manually manage its trajectory of fire—an estimated, imprecise science.

But a great way to spread destruction in a hellfire hurry.

"Fire!"

Diko dropped the round, dancing back a split second before the launcher belched. The shell was gone and already Diko was reaching for another. Hale adjusted the launcher's angle by maybe an inch and called the next shot.

"*Fire!*"

Another belch, then the detonation of the first shell. The earth shook and the Dushka went silent as Joseph called reports from the bed.

"A hundred yards farther—a little to your left!"

Hale adjusted by hand. Twisted his head and shouted again.

"*Fire!*"

99

Western Equatoria, South Sudan
02:16 Hours, East Africa Time

Thon Jok's army was in full retreat.

From the ditch alongside the road, Harden monitored the fleeing soldiers through his NVGs as a swarm of moving green dots, scattered around the bushlands and ducking for cover with each thunderous blast of a falling mortar round. The shells rained from the sky like hailstones—not aimed, and most not detonating anywhere near a human target, but the random spread was terrifying in the same way a serial killer who hits random houses is terrifying.

Nobody could predict who would be next. Nobody was out of reach. The only logical option was to flee.

"Cowards!" Harden screamed, stripping the goggles from his head. "What are you *doing*?"

Nobody answered. Emerging from the brush in clumps of three or four, the men slid for cover in the ditch and covered their heads. Some bled—others limped. One was shot in the side and held the wound as he scrambled for safety. Maybe thirty gathered in total, just more than half of what Harden had arrived with.

The rest had been consumed inside of twenty minutes—torn down by a single machine gun, a single sniper, and a single mortar launcher.

"Get back out there!" Harden grabbed one man by the arm and shoved him away from the ditch.

The next mortar round landed within forty yards, detonating with a thunderclap that send both men stumbling to the ground. Harden landed on his side, gasping for air. When he scrambled back up again, he ran headlong into Thon.

The pale-eyed warlord looked no less bloodthirsty than before, but the falling mortar rounds seemed to have knocked some sanity into him. He squatted behind a bush, shouting at his men to stay down.

"Get them up!" Harden said. "They're no safer here than they are out there. We gotta breach that gate!"

"They *can't* breach it!" Thon sprayed spittle as he shouted. "We've lost our vehicles. We're out of range for RPGs. What do you expect?"

Another mortar round landed—they were coming more slowly, but this one fell close to the ditch, spraying shrapnel across a knot of sheltering soldiers. Two of them fell, thrashing and screaming. Harden grabbed Thon by the arm. He shook the smaller man, heedless of the Colt on his hip or how fast it could be drawn.

"Get your men out of this ditch before they're all killed! Split into two wings and advance from either side. We get into RPG range and blast the gate and their gun. Then we storm the place. Understand?"

Another exploding mortar, this one a few yards outside the ditch. More shouts were followed by scrambling bodies headed for the open brush-lands beyond the road—a further retreat.

Thon jerked free. "You want to blow that gate, you blow it! My men aren't taking another step until the mortar is gone."

With that, Thon pulled away. Bent low, he joined his men, circling the still-burning cargo truck and heading for the bushes.

Harden screamed a curse but nobody was listening. He looked back to the outpost and noted that the mortar launcher had fallen silent. The fleeing soldiers weren't yet out of range...

Was the enemy out of mortars?

They can't keep this up forever.

Harden slung his AK over his back. Stooping, he recovered both his NVGs and a fallen RPG launcher, already loaded.

Harden re-affixed the goggles to his head. He shouldered the launcher.

Then he sprinted into the shadows.

100

Western Equatoria, South Sudan
02:24 Hours, East Africa Time

"Mr. Ian! We're out!"

Hale looked through a haze of smoke, barely able to hear Diko's voice. The young man turned over empty crates, searching desperately for what wasn't there—another mortar, or even a belt for the Dushka.

Both weapons were dry.

"They're in retreat," Joseph called. "They're moving beyond the road."

It was the best news Hale had heard all day, but even as he pulled himself into the back of the bullet-ridden technical, he knew it was only a temporary reprieve.

Scathing cover fire had driven the untrained killers into a panicked retreat, but as the cover fire faded, so would the panic. Sanity would return...and maybe, so would they.

Hale lifted his binoculars from their tether. He scanned the road under the light of the burning cargo truck and noted only one moving shadow—a crawling man dragging a twisted leg.

How many others had survived?

"What happens now?" Joseph whispered.

He squatted calmly alongside Hale. Still looking through the binos, Hale was wondering the same thing. He tried to place himself in the shoes of his enemy, but logic and rationale were poor predictors of the actions of untrained men. For all Hale knew, they wouldn't stop running until they reached Congo.

Or maybe they would come back swinging with a better strategy. Worse-case scenario, what was Hale's greatest weakness? What would he try if he were in their boots?

"They don't know that we're out of mortars," Hale said, wiping sweat from his face. "And they'll still be worried about that Dushka. If it were me, I'd regroup the troops and take stock of my surviving force. Then I'd neutralize the gate, the technical, and the mortar before I launched a second attack."

"What do you mean, neutralize?"

The question came from Diko. Hale hadn't realized that the kid was so close. He'd slipped into the technical's bed and squatted just behind them.

Hale and Joseph both turned, thinking. But it was Joseph who spoke first.

"RPG," he said.

Hale agreed. A rocket-propelled grenade wouldn't be very accurate beyond maybe two hundred yards. Also, after the first shot, the shooter would be fully exposed, so he'd want to make that shot count. A direct hit on the gate and the nose of the technical could get the job done.

Given that strategy, anyone with even a microbe of tactical intelligence would want to slip in close before firing at all, using brush and mortar craters as leapfrog cover. With the guard tower destroyed, there would be no way for Hale to engage the incoming threat while remaining sheltered behind the walls.

One look at Joseph, and Hale knew that he was thinking the same thing.

"I'll go," Joseph said.

Hale shook his head. "No. This is my specialty. You take Diko and all the remaining firepower and get the children barricaded as far away from the windows and doors as possible. With any luck, I'll neutralize this guy before he ever draws within range...or maybe he never comes at all."

Diko, chewing his lip, looked between Joseph and Hale. The kid was still holding it together, doing remarkably well for a young man thrown headfirst into the deep end of the combat pool...but everyone has a breaking point.

"It's all right," Hale said. "We won the first round. Let's keep a good thing going."

He lifted his fist. Joseph tapped it first, fueling Diko's courage. Hale shot the kid a wink.

"You're pretty quick with a sling."

That brought a smile, however brief, and they exited the truck bed. In moments they had their weapons consolidated. Hale reloaded his AK. He secured it over his back and checked his sidearm, then his knife.

The Dawn Warrior would be quick and silent. If the guy died and nobody knew how...maybe that could be the end of this.

Maybe.

Hale turned back to Joseph. "If you don't hear any shots, that's a good thing."'

Joseph squeezed Hale's shoulder. "God be with you."

Then they broke. Joseph and Diko headed for the outpost's main building...and Hale turned for the wall.

101

Western Equatoria, South Sudan
02:39 Hours, East Africa Time

MARSOC taught Marcus Harden how to stalk.

As a member of the elite Marine Raider Regiment, Harden had specialized in stealth reconnaissance, a task which prioritized the ability to move undetected. He hadn't been the best at it—but heck, when you're a Raider at all, you're already one of the very best in the world. Even years removed from the Corps with a whole lot of nastiness in between, Harden remembered how to leverage bending shadows to his advantage. How to glide around brush and through grass without exposing himself. How to carry awkward equipment—even a long and cumbersome RPG launcher—without producing a hard profile that could be identified under night vision.

Of course, Harden wasn't immune to infrared technology. No man was—it was a risk for him to approach the outpost not knowing if a shooter lay waiting, marking his progress by the orange-and-red signature of his own body heat.

But what else was Harden going to do? A lot of money rode on this mission. More than he'd made in years—and Harden missed the hefty paychecks of his CIA days. Nothing but a dumpy apartment in some even dumpier South Asian city awaited him if he failed this op.

He might as well push his chips in.

Yards bled away in slow motion. Harden didn't get in a hurry. He already knew after reviewing satellite imagery that the compound had only one entrance, and that was clearly visible at four hundred yards down the access road. Nobody was leaving this place without his knowledge. With the mortar and the Dushka silent, Harden assumed that all occupants were hunkered down, maybe licking their wounds.

He had time. He could afford to slither like the snake wrapped around his arm, weaving ever closer to his target.

Two hundred yards—that was Harden's mark. He had some limited experience with RPGs and figured that was about the distance under which he could rely on a precise hit. One strike to the gate should be enough to blow it open, after which Thon's surviving army would enjoy a wide-open welcome mat into the compound...and they would take it. So help him, Harden would gut them with his own knife if they didn't.

Another football field melted away. Harden was breathing easily, using his core muscles to drive progress. He kept the gate in view without losing sight of his peripheral, passing twisted bodies and abandoned AKs from Thon's fleeing soldiers.

Cowards.

Just two hundred fifty yards remained. The parked technical was clearly visible, and Harden recognized it as the Land Cruiser pickup his northern scouts had driven the previous afternoon. Now the windshield and mirrors were blown away, the tires flattened, and the grill turned to shrapnel. The Dushka remained and might be operational, but there was nobody manning it.

Interesting.

Harden slowed, marking his final shooting position as a fresh mortar crater torn into the orange clay. It lay only twenty yards ahead, and he could spend as much time as necessary to reach it.

The gate was almost within range. With the hiss of a rushing rocket, the battle would resume.

102

Western Equatoria, South Sudan
02:50 Hours, East Africa Time

The guy was good—one of the best Hale had ever encountered.

In fact, if he hadn't made a single mistake, Hale might not have seen him at all. He might have closed all the way within striking distance, the first disclosure of his presence being the launch of an RPG.

But he did make a mistake—he used night vision goggles with exposed glass lenses, and as his head twisted in the darkness, moonlight glinted against them. The blink lasted no longer than a split second, but Hale didn't miss it. His gaze snapped to the spot as he crouched in the shadows just outside the wall.

Already the brushlands had returned to their normally scheduled program of gentle rustling and deep shadow. But the damage was done, nonetheless. Hale had a bearing on the intruder, and with enough focus and patience, he detected the minuscule movements that marked the attacker's approach. He mapped out the curving shadows, the gentle shift of brush and grass.

What was more, he estimated the stalker's trajectory.

Departing the wall, Hale bent low and moved easily. He took his time curving into the brush, keeping a steady screen of visual obstruction between himself and his target. That screen made it nearly impossible for Hale to keep track of the approaching shooter, but without the screen, the shooter would easily mark Hale's presence under the aid of his night vision.

Besides, Hale no longer needed to track him visually. He had the advantage of knowing both the enemy's objective and probable strategy. With that information, it was easy enough to predict an intercept point. Hale wanted to get there after the shooter dug in and focused on his target, but *before* he fired.

Another thirty seconds of stalking—Hale was moving past bodies and circling mortar craters. Even in the dark, this place was clearly a battlefield. The stench of blood and gunpowder was heavy on the air, all nocturnal voices silenced. It was as though nature herself was holding her breath, waiting to see which warrior would fall first...

But no. There was only one warrior here—and one child-snatching target.

Hale circled behind his enemy before turning back toward the outpost. He didn't like offering the guy a clear shot at the gate, but he wanted to neutralize him without alerting any other surviving combatants. That meant no gunshots, no scream. Hale would knife the shooter in the dark as soon as he reached his position of attack, and Hale already knew where that would be.

It was another mortar crater, a position just off the access drive and about two hundred yards away from the outpost's gate. A perfect shooting nest, and there, sliding into it, was the shooter.

He moved like an animal, like a reptile, nestling into torn clay. The RPG launcher rode his back, an obtuse shape amid the irregular blobs of brush. With his head pointed toward the outpost, he was blind to Hale. He rose out of the dirt just a little, giving himself a clear view of the gate. He reached for the launcher.

Hale accelerated, moving on the balls of his feet. He wove between the brush, keeping one hand on his holstered pistol just in case the shooter should suddenly turn. At thirty yards, Hale could clearly see his silhouette as the launcher tube settled over his right shoulder. He rocked his face behind the aiming reticle.

Fifteen yards. Hale's footsteps were so smooth that the gentle wind muted them. He was almost ready to release the sidearm and wrap his fingers around the grip of the TOPS knife holstered horizontally across his chest rig. The shooter reached for the launcher's pistol grip. Just a little farther...

Movement caught Hale's eye just as he crossed within ten feet of his target. It came from his right, a rustle of branches that moved contrary to the wind. Hale thought it was an animal, maybe another warthog or a monitor lizard.

But no. It was a human—one of the wounded attackers left behind, lying on his back but craning his head. Lifting a shaking pistol awkwardly across his chest, drawing not only Hale's gaze but the RPG shooter's as well. They both saw the wounded soldier—they both saw each other. Hale's fingers clutched the knife.

Then the wounded soldier fired.

103

The bullet cut through sticky African air and smacked Hale's leg just beneath his hip.

He felt it first as a hot pinch—like a bee sting. Adrenaline masked the pain and momentum carried him forward...

But the bullet struck *hard*—fast and sharp enough to knock Hale off-balance. Even as he was hurling toward the mortar crater, he fell too soon. He crashed to the dirt, tearing through brush.

And the RPG fired.

A whoosh of hot air exploded over Hale's face just as his head slammed into the dirt. The RPG detonated only a split second later, shaking the earth. Hale's hand was still wrapped around the knife even as he kicked his wounded leg against the ground and rolled right.

Into the mortar crater.

Hale hit the guy sideways. It wasn't a calculated approach or even a very logical one. It was just an instinctual reaction to the certain knowledge that he couldn't lift his head because of the wounded gunman who had already shot him, and he couldn't afford to waste time getting to the RPG sniper because that guy probably had a pistol and would be coming for him also.

Hale was right on both counts. As he tumbled into the crater, the wounded gunman shot again, dumping bullets at random over his head, and the RPG sniper abandoned his launcher, flailing for a handgun. Hale body-slammed him from the side, driving him into the dirt and knocking his night vision goggles loose. The Dawn Warrior snapped out of its sheath just as enraged curses exploded amid a rush of escaping breath.

An *American* accent.

Hale didn't think, he didn't hesitate. He grappled with his free arm and grabbed the guy by his chest rig, then jerked his own body up and over and on top. The knife flicked in his hand, pointing down in the glimmer of fresh firelight—the technical parked inside the gate was burning. Gasoline smoke boiled into the air and Hale looked into dark eyes and a snarling face—one muscled bicep wrapped in a brown-black snake.

Hale plunged with the knife, driving for the hollow spot between the guy's collarbones where an unprotected windpipe, brain stem, and several blood vessels lay exposed. The target was barely two feet away, the knife sharpened to a razor point.

But this guy was *fast*. His right arm struck like the snake wrapped around it—he didn't block Hale's hands, he just took the blade straight into the unprotected flesh of his outside forearm. It sank two inches through skin and muscle, sticking in place as Hale bore down, still driving for his throat.

The knife wouldn't punch through—it was blocked by bone. The snake man roared, bowing his back and kicking sideways. He was trying to throw Hale off, to manage him with his knife-stuck arm while his free hand flailed for a weapon of his own.

Hale saw the threat and released his own knife—he didn't have a choice. He swung his right arm to block the draw of another knife, making contact only just in time. A blade appeared for a split second, glimmering in the firelight.

Then Hale knocked it free. It spun out of the guy's hand and into the dirt. Hale lost control of the Dawn Warrior as the guy ripped his arm away, howling like a hyena and punching toward Hale's face.

The blow landed. Hale took it right in the jaw and flipped backward, his vision blurring as he once more struck the ground. His legs were still tangled with his target—the guy was flailing, jerking away. Somewhere in the background, Hale heard the chatter of small-arms fire. Bullets sliced overhead and peppered the concrete walls.

The attack was back underway. The RPG sniper didn't need to fire again—he only needed to escape. Already he was kicking his way backward, yanking the knife free of his forearm with a shriek, and then clawing at his hip. He was going for the pistol again.

Hale drew first. The HK cleared his holster and Hale twisted in the dirt. His finger found the trigger—the pistol was arcing upward. For a split second, he locked eyes with his target.

Hale saw dark blue pools illuminated by the burning technical. They opened like windows into a soul that reflected no anger. No battle lust. Not even any fear.

What Hale saw instead was sadness. Deep, chronic, lifelong...and then extinguished.

Hale shot him twice in the face, a double-tap stacked so tight together that it sounded like a single shot. The bullets smacked home, and the snake man hit the dirt.

104

Hale didn't have time to catch his breath. He didn't even have time to engage the wounded gunmen stretched somewhere to his right.

The assault on the outpost had resumed, with bullets whining past Hale's head as he staggered to his feet, the HK riding in a shaking right hand. Blood ran down his leg—he almost fell as he took his first step. From somewhere ahead somebody shouted, maybe Joseph.

Then twin strobe lights of muzzle flash blinked from just inside the shattered gate. Hale bent and half sprinted, half lurched straight for them. The flash continued, a snarl of full-auto fire that swept the fields to Hale's right and his left while leaving a narrow channel for him to hurtle down.

A hundred yards. He was breathing so hard his head went light. The pain exploding from his leg raced all the way up his spine, a hot river of misery muted by the adrenaline but not quite erased by it. Hale ignored the agony. He ignored the dizziness and the bullets clipping the dirt all around him. He didn't stop until he reeled straight through the RPG-shattered gate. The technical was still there, hurled sideways with its hood missing, a dying vehicle fire blazing from the cab.

Hale slammed into the toppled guard tower and nearly fell. Joseph appeared out of nowhere and caught him.

"Diko! Get the door!"

Hale leaned on Joseph and made it across the yard to the main building. Some ways behind him the gunfire continued, a maddened chatter unleashed by crazed attackers. They were still coming—they were totally unchallenged now.

Diko hauled the door open. Hale crossed inside with his right leg dragging—it had gone numb, and he couldn't tell how badly he was bleeding.

"Put the children in the back!" Hale shouted. "Go now!"

He landed in a chair with a crash. Somewhere amid streaking flashlight beams, small voices whispered while others cried. Ajok and Mary Grace herded the children while Joseph shouted for Diko to bar the door and Wal settled into a grunted kneel at Hale's side.

"I can't see," Wal said. "Somebody hold a light."

Joseph rushed in. Hale clawed the Benchmade from his pocket. It locked open with a snap and he passed it to Wal. Four seconds later a long cut opened in Hale's pants, and fingers probed his bloodied skin. Fresh pain pulsated under the pressure and Hale bit back a shout.

"How bad?" Hale snapped.

"I…I can't tell." Wal's voice trembled.

"Is it spurting?" Hale said. "Am I losing blood?"

"A little. It's not spurting—"

"Fine. Pack in some gauze. *Hurry!*"

Wal didn't need to be told twice. In another moment, raw cloth was shoved into the wound. Hale clutched the chair with one hand, then managed to jamb his pistol into its holster with his other.

Outside, the gunfire had ceased, and Hale knew that could only mean one thing. The attackers had neared the walls and were pausing to double-check for traps or snipers or whatever else before taking the final plunge.

The outpost had sixty seconds—not more.

Hale forced himself out of the chair and tugged the AK off his back. By muscle memory he found the safety lever, switching it off with a snap. Then he was sweeping his surroundings to find the children removed through a hallway and into a series of back rooms. He could still see some of their little bodies huddled in the shadows—there wasn't room for them all to hide.

In another ten minutes, it might not matter if they were locked inside steel vaults.

"Windows," Hale called. "Diko, you've got right. Joseph, you go left. I've got the door. Wal, can you shoot?"

The old doctor's hands shook, but he hefted a rifle and shuffled to an open window cavity alongside Joseph. He got the muzzle through and bent behind the sights—he didn't look like he knew what he was doing.

That, also, didn't matter.

Hale limped to the front door. He pressed his back against concrete and locked the rifle into his shoulder, muzzle pointed at the floor. He breathed through his nose, fighting an escalating heartbeat that would only force more blood loss past the sloppy wound-packing job.

Fast. Brutal. Accurate.

Hale repeated the old close quarters battle mantra in his mind, a reminder of the only three things that could save him—even though he knew they likely wouldn't.

It was still mostly quiet outside, with only the crackle of the burning truck to break the stillness. In the distance Hale thought he might hear voices calling to one another, maybe exchanging orders or strategies. Preparing for that final drive through the gate. The first half dozen wouldn't reach the building.

And after that?

Hale's gaze traveled the room, first to Wal and then Diko. Both looked shaken but working hard not to show it. Standing next to the window with his rifle in hand, Joseph drank from his belt canteen, wiping droplets from his lips and closing his eyes. Breathing deep. Probably thinking the same thing that Hale was thinking—that they all must be thinking.

This is the end.

"I lift up my eyes to the hills. From where does my help come?"

Hale's voice was soft in the quiet, but it filled the room. Despite the pain, his voice was steady. His heart beat calmed. He looked to Joseph and found tears sliding down dirty cheeks, but Joseph smiled.

"My help comes from the Lord," Joseph said. "Who made heaven and earth."

"Blessed be the name of the Lord."

The last words were Diko's. All eyes turned to him—he stood at his window with his chin up.

No tears. No fear.

"From this time forth and forevermore," Hale replied.

Then the next RPG struck the already mangled gate, and hell returned.

105

The gunfire came in torrents.

It exploded through the gate and ripped against the building. A howl of two or three dozen voices split the night and hot lead cut through the open window frames. Wal got off one shot and then took a round straight to his forehead, collapsing in a heap. Diko turned from his window, ready to take Wal's place, but Joseph and Hale were already on it. Brass rained over the floor as their rifles thundered in the contained space.

Hale could barely hear. His eyes and lungs burned with smoke. Shadows raced through the smog outside, clipping across his line of sight for only moments at a time. He engaged them the best he could, sending some bodies pitching to the dirt while others escaped.

Hale ran the AK dry. He rocked the mag out with mechanical routine and latched in another, still repeating the words of the Psalms in his mind —because they were good words, and they would be just as true in ten minutes as in ten thousand years.

A muted cry to Hale's left broke his focus. Joseph stumbled back from his window, clutching his upper right arm. Blood slipped through his fingers, but he was still firing one-handed with his AK, dumping rounds through a window. Diko ran to his side even as Joseph's rifle ran dry.

It was slow motion. It was sudden silence, and stillness, and absolute reality. Both Hale and Joseph saw the grenade flying through the open window—it arced across the room as a blink of dark metal, then clattered to the floor and bounced twice. It landed in place and spun—Hale heard the blood rushing in his ears and his mouth dropped open. He twisted from the wall, already shoving himself off. Already headed into a chest-first dive, that spinning black dot his bullseye.

He was on his way—but Joseph was closer.

The grenade detonated only a split second after Joseph's body landed on it. Concussive force struck Hale in the chest and drove him backward. He lost his footing and lost the rifle. He hit the floor and his head smacked the wall like a melon striking asphalt. The world blackened—the stillness of before was somehow so much deeper. Hale's whole body buzzed, and the room around him faded. He wasn't sure if he was breathing—he could no longer feel his gunshot leg or his battered body or even the throbbing from his skull.

But he still reached for the pistol. His hand found textured polymer and he closed around it. It snapped out of his holster as his ears rang. He could barely hear the pound of feet rushing toward the front door.

It was a vague drumbeat, like the gallop of ten thousand distant horses that were somehow still close enough to vibrate the building. Hale felt the shudders in his back, in his hips, really too strong to be feet at all. This felt more like a hurricane bearing down on the outpost...the final death blow.

Hale could only barely see the door, but he raised the pistol.

106

Western Equatoria, South Sudan
03:36 Hours, East Africa Time

"There!"

Laney Shaw stood next to the open side door of the Mil Mi-24 Russian helicopter, pointing through shredded night air toward the vehicle fire. It burned right at the gate of what looked to be a compound—the shadows were deep but Shaw made out a wall and a series of shadowy buildings.

The outpost was exactly where she expected it to be, just outside the town of Nagero. The burning vehicle marked the spot like a beacon while also serving as proof positive of exactly what was unfolding from six thousand feet below.

As if Shaw needed more convincing, she made out the muzzle flashes, also. Encircling one building, like distant fireflies, they were a sure indicator of the worst-case scenario, unfolding.

"Drop us there!" Shaw shouted, snatching up her borrowed M4 carbine and pulling the charging handle. Behind her, six men dressed in camouflage fatigues carried similar rifles, packed into a troop transport compartment barely large enough to fit them. Two pilots managed the chopper inside of separated, stacked cockpits, while an eighth and final passenger stood stooped in full dress uniform just behind the rear cockpit.

James Wani.

"Rockets," Wani said, jerking his head.

The gunship banked, bearing toward the compound. Shaw heard the command and her heart rate spiked. She clutched the overhead rail and jerked herself away from the door.

"No rockets! You'll kill my people."

Wani's glare snapped toward her, an expression Shaw was becoming accustomed to. She was no more impressed or intimidated than she had been when he'd shoved a Beretta into her mouth.

"Put us down outside the compound," Shaw said. "We'll hit them from the ground."

"And kill *my* people?" Wani said. "Think again."

He turned away. Shaw caught him by his gold-braided sleeve and jerked back. Behind her the men packed into the troop bay stiffened. She didn't care.

"We have a *deal*, Your Excellency."

Maybe it was the honorific, or maybe it was the venom in her voice. Whatever the case, Wani's eyes blazed but he didn't retort. He stared her in the eye a moment, then turned back to his pilot.

"Guns only. Mind your aim."

It wasn't what Shaw wanted but she didn't press further. Already the Mil Mi was ducking into its attack run, the bulbous nose pointed toward the earth with its flesh-and-armor-shredding machine gun pod spinning to action. The vibration shook the entire airframe, a buzz like a hundred thousand angry hornets streaking to earth.

Bullets hit the gate and the burning truck blew apart. Shaw stood windblasted at the open door and watched as a cluster of gunmen were blown in half and thrown to the ground. Everyone was running in separate directions as the chopper lifted, raced overhead, and then began its turn.

"One more sweep," Wani said. "Show me corpses."

The pilots didn't need to be told twice. The second pass was slower than the first and more methodical. Fire and fury poured in a river, but Shaw was no longer watching the fleeing gunmen or the toppling bodies—she was fixated on the building they had encircled. A rectangular block structure maybe twenty feet by sixty feet with hollow windows. She saw nothing but blackness inside.

"Set us down!" Shaw called.

This time Wani didn't argue. The Mil Mi thundered outside the compound and spun over a torn and rutted road. Even before it settled onto tripod landing gear, Shaw was bailing out. She ran with her head down, the M4 rifle held fast against her cheek—a weapon familiar to her from years of military service.

She passed bodies. She passed mortar craters and shredded brush. The air was rank with smoke and the flavor of burning fuel. By the time Shaw reached the gate, Wani's six soldiers were right on her heels. They fanned out and opened fire the moment they passed the burning truck.

Not toward the building—toward the survivors. Dead or playing dead, mortally wounded or only frozen in terror. All but one was shredded by 5.56 rounds and walked over like dead animals left to rot.

The final guy was short and stocky. He wore a cowboy-style gun belt and had stonewashed pale eyes. The Mil Mi had blown one of his legs off just beneath the knee. He was streaming blood and clawing his way backward, trying to escape. Babbling in something other than English. Reaching for a fallen Colt single-action but not reaching it in time.

One of Wani's men put a boot on his chest and drove the guy to the ground. Another placed his rifle muzzle in the guy's face, while a third keyed his radio.

"Your Excellency—I have the traitor."

Whatever would happen next, Shaw left them too it. She ran to the building, half tripping over trenches left by the Mil Mi's cannon. She was high on fumes—her head thundered as hard as her heart. Shaw closed on the door and found it open, a body stretched over the threshold.

"Ian! Are you there? Mary Grace?"

Shaw ducked her head but didn't lower her rifle. She edged closer to the door and stopped. She listened.

"Ian?"

A shuffling sound answered Shaw—just a scratching on concrete. She gritted her teeth and risked it, keeping her finger off the trigger as she charged through the door and straight into a pool of sticky blood. There were bodies everywhere, lying twisted on the floor and mangled by bullets or shrapnel. The air was thick with gun smoke—it was nearly impossible to breathe through.

But Shaw's eyes adjusted...and then she saw him. Leaned against the wall with one hand resting at his side, an HK pistol locked over an empty magazine still clutched in his fingers. Bleeding from his lip and sitting in a pool of crimson. Not moving.

Shaw ran. She hit her knees and dropped the rifle, sliding a hand around Hale's neck and feeling for a pulse. She shook him.

"Ian. *Ian.* Wake up."

A sound like metal scratching over rock rattled from Hale's lips. He twitched, just a little, then opened his eyes. He blinked, long and slow. Shaw's heart lurched.

"Ian. Thank God."

Shaw pulled him in. She wrapped an arm around his body armor plate and held him tight, still shaking herself. Both her eyes and throat stung.

But relief coursed through her chest. She didn't relax her hold until Hale pushed against her ribs. Shaw set him back against the wall. Leaden weight sank into her stomach again as she remembered—as she wondered.

"Where are they?"

Hale breathed slow. He didn't answer—his gaze just swept past her and across the room, deeper into the darkness.

Shaw looked but couldn't see. Hale took her hand and led it up his chest rig to a flashlight. She pulled it free as he slumped against the wall. Brilliant white light blazed down the hallway, driving back the shadows...

And revealed Mary Grace Dalton, standing crouched with arms spread in front of *dozens* of children. All alive and well.

The light slipped to the floor. Shaw sprinted across the room and wrapped Mary Grace in her arms.

107

Western Equatoria, South Sudan
03:55 Hours, East Africa Time

The rumble of the helicopter's cannon barely registered in Hale's mind. He recognized the sound but failed to assign to it any significance as the door exploded open and the first soldier through took four 9mm slugs to the chest and face, pitching sideways.

The next soldier likewise went down, only managing a pair of rifle rounds into the wall before death took him at the hands of Hale's HK pistol. Three shots, and then the VP9 locked back over empty. Hale's buzzing left hand clawed at his chest rig, searching for a replacement magazine even as his vision wavered.

He was choking on smoke. He got the empty mag out but fumbled it to the floor. He couldn't find it. He knew the next soldier had him—a sitting duck.

But the next soldier never came. The thunder of the chopper returned instead, a second sweep. The ground shook and ear-piercing screams tore the air outside. From the back of the building, children sobbed. Mary Grace prayed aloud. Hale's tongue was heavy with the flavor of death.

And then the fight was over, in a snarl of higher-pitched rifles and a blink of muzzle flash through the open windows. Hale slouched against the wall, gasping and weak. His leg was bleeding again and his head was going light—his vision tunneled.

But when Laney Shaw stormed in, her face tucked tight into the stock of an M4 rifle, he recognized her in an instant. He gritted his teeth against the pain as she pulled him into a hug. He passed her his flashlight and she found the children, Mary Grace Dalton, Ajok, and Diko. All shaken and filthy—in Diko's case, covered in Joseph's blood as he held his friend's body and sobbed.

But they were survivors. They had danced right through the jaws of death.

Hale's ears still rang, but as he caught his breath, that din began to fade. From outside the building, he heard shouts—an angry African voice barking in an unfamiliar dialect. Somebody else argued back in the same language, a gargling wet plea. Hale recognized the meaty thud of a boot driven into a gut. Somebody choked. The African voice barked something else.

Then a single pistol shot cracked, and a body hit the dirt. Hale swallowed on a dry throat and reached to the floor. His eyes still burned, but his vision clarified a little and he found the spare magazine. He managed to stand it upright on the concrete and drop the HK's mag well over it.

He dropped the slide just before footsteps reached the door, flashlight beams blazing in. Two men entered, both dressed in camouflage fatigues and black berets. They swept the room and one of them pointed an M4 carbine at Hale—they both carried M4 carbines and Beretta M9 sidearms.

"Drop weapon!"

Hale ignored him. He looked to the door as a third man entered, flanked by additional soldiers. Tall and muscular, with an iron jaw and piercing dark eyes. He wore a black dress uniform with gold braid and a chest strip loaded with medals. Another black beret rode his skull.

He looked dead at Hale, but didn't speak. His gaze continued across the room, over the body of Joseph and the still-sobbing Diko, who clutched it... and at last landing on Mary Grace. He approached without a word, boots crunching over dirt and fallen rifle brass. He stopped a yard away and looked to the children.

His gaze, already iron, hardened even further.

"You are the American missionary?" he said.

Mary Grace stood tall, but the fear was transparent in her eyes. "That's right."

A long pause. That angry hard stare crossed beyond Mary Grace to the children...then it turned back.

"I am James Wani, leader of the White Nile Liberation Army. On behalf of South Sudan, I thank you for your generous sacrifice. I have ground troops on the way bringing supplies and transportation to carry you back to Tambura—you and these children are now under my protection. You will not be harmed again."

With that, Wani turned. He and his soldiers left the building without another word...but as Wani passed through the door, Hale thought he saw the hint of a smile stretching tighter lips.

Hale lowered the pistol as Shaw returned to his side. The children were murmuring again. Mary Grace and Ajok were crying. Diko had fallen into shocked silence.

The haze of war, still heavy on the air, blanketed them all.

"A deal with the devil?" Hale rasped.

Shaw sat next to him and rocked her head back against the wall. She wore a Bulldogs hoodie stained with sweat, mud, and blood. She rested the M4 rifle across her lap, and Hale's gaze traveled up the stock. Past the forward assist, across a dusty receiver...

Then stopping on four words etched in bright English, visible even in the low light.

PROPERTY OF U.S. GOVERNMENT.

Hale looked up and Shaw met his gaze. She held it for a long moment, but she never answered his question.

She didn't have to.

108

Five Days Later
Juba, South Sudan
09:20 Hours, East Africa Time

Nolan O'Rourke was out of ideas.

He'd arrived in Juba with no precise idea of how to "fix" the situation. He knew he needed to find Marcus Harden and either buy him off or erase him altogether. He knew he needed to further compromise the video evidence supposedly proving America's plot to fuel instability in the region. Maybe engage in some counter-intel work, somehow poison the well...

He really didn't know. He just had to do *something*. Langley thought he was in Seattle looking after a mother dying of cancer. In fact, his mother *was* dying of cancer, but O'Rourke wasn't concerned with that. He wasn't even concerned with salvaging his and Paul Morris's scheme to land an exploitation contract with South Sudan.

Nolan O'Rourke was *only* concerned with covering his tracks. With making sure nobody ever found out what the Agency—or at least one member of it—had actually been up to in Western Equatoria. Because if they did, O'Rourke would be forced to stay in third world dumps like Juba for the rest of his life...or else return home and accept the handcuffs.

O'Rourke wasn't interested in prison. He'd rather swallow a bullet—so he hit the streets. He worked local Agency assets, mostly paid informants who were needy, demanding, and only semi-reliable. He mined what information he could from inside the South Sudanese government and worked the angles to determine just *who* had fed Juba the personnel file on Marcus Harden. He needed to know so that he could discredit them, but as it turned out, nobody was really thinking about Harden or an LRA resurgence or even an American conspiracy.

They were thinking about James Wani—because the warlord was *all over* local news media. Reports streaming out of Western Equatoria documented the recovery of over two hundred kidnapped children held in a compound buried in the forest. Nobody knew for sure who had captured them or why, but Wani sprang on their rescue like the PR gold mine that it was. He launched statements through regional media outlets condemning the administration in Juba for enabling a state of lawlessness and endangering so many young lives. He swore an oath to the people of South Sudan to protect their children from a reckless government—he championed his own militia as defenders of freedom and security.

And then came the *real* atom bomb. The earth-shaking blast heard across Africa. Wani called a press conference in Wau and appeared in spotless dress uniform. He stood in front of a dozen of the skinny children he'd rescued from the woods—orphans, now. He looked dead into the cameras and he announced to the world...

A coltan deposit. A billion dollars' worth of rare mineral ore, priceless to America and China and any country who depended on the tantalum extracted from coltan to produce high-performance capacitors used in every electronic device from smartphones to computers to medical equipment and military technology.

Especially military technology. It was a natural resource that, Wani claimed, lay right beneath his boots. He brought documents from a British mining exploration firm to prove the deposit's existence, and further accused Juba of concealing this gold mine with plans of auctioning off South Sudan's wealth for their own enrichment.

"I claim this blessing from heaven for the people!" Wani shouted, raising a fist. "Not one scrap nor cent shall be sold out from under us—we will defend it with our *blood*!"

O'Rourke watched the broadcast and could only stare. Could barely think. The world slowed around him and his heart beat heavy and he knew—it was over. It was done. The entire messy scheme. If he could get out alive, he should count himself lucky.

All that money, all that power...slipping right through his fingers.

Then the hotel phone rang. O'Rourke's gaze snapped to the bedside table and he hesitated. Sudden anxiety consumed his body.

Who was calling?

O'Rourke lifted the receiver, but he didn't say a thing.

"Nolan O'Rourke?"

The voice was male, young, and crisp. O'Rourke didn't recognize it.

"Who is this?"

"My name is Jaxon Wilks. I'm a deputy assistant secretary of state working under Paul Morris. I believe you know my boss."

O'Rourke froze.

"I'm aware that you're here in Juba, staying at the Crown Hotel," Jaxon continued. "I'm also aware of the reason for your visit. If you don't want my next call to be to CNN, then I think you and I should meet."

O'Rourke's mouth went dry. He looked instinctively to his door as though he expected Jaxon to be standing outside. One shake of his head drove the thoughts away as his paranoia was subjected to saner rational.

"I don't know what you're talking about."

"I'm talking Wani, Mr. O'Rourke. James Wani...and the people he calls friends."

The words landed like an artillery shell, and before O'Rourke could even contemplate an answer, Jaxon Wilks spoke again, as calm as before.

"Da Vinci Restaurant. You have thirty minutes."

109

Juba, South Sudan
09:45 Hours, East Africa Time

Hale's leg still throbbed.

With the slug removed and the skin stitched, everything that could be done to counteract the damage of the whizzing pistol round had been done. No artery had been cut—no major ligaments torn. Mostly, it was a flesh wound, albeit a deep one.

Rehydrated, showered, and with fifteen hours of unbroken sleep to his credit, Hale was back on his feet. He was moving slowly—but he was moving. Because Mary Grace and her children were safe, but the mission wasn't yet complete.

Hale and Shaw sat at a table on the open-air patio of the riverside restaurant. The tablecloth was lime green, the overhanging tree limbs still thick with foliage. A warm breeze carried off the White Nile, smelling of mud and fish and a lot of pain.

Or maybe that was just the aftertaste of Western Equatoria lingering in his mouth. Hale sat reclined in his chair, his right leg extended to minimize pressure on the wound. Dressed in canvas pants and a loose cotton T-shirt, his pistol was concealed but well within reach. As Hale sipped water from a bottle, neither he nor Shaw spoke.

There was nothing to say—at least, not yet.

Jaxon Wilks arrived first, looking like the recently fired coach of a winless team. Dark bags hung beneath his eyes, his suit wrinkled and his open collar sweat-stained. He didn't wear a tie—he didn't greet Hale or Shaw. He simply sat and ordered a triple Johnnie Walker Black on ice. The drink came and Jaxon knocked half of it back. He closed his eyes and his fingers tightened around the glass.

He looked ready to smash it, but just like Shaw and Hale, he didn't say anything. Enough had been said over the last three days. All that remained was to throw their cards on the table.

Nolan O'Rourke appeared six minutes later, which was three minutes past his deadline. Dressed in an untucked shirt that clung to his sweaty skin, Hale noted the hardened edge of a concealed pistol and slid his right hand beneath the table, close to the grip of his own weapon. He didn't expect to need it—but then, he hadn't expected this meeting, either.

O'Rourke hit the patio and stopped, scanning the tables. He seemed to be focusing on those with only one occupant each, but there were only two such exhibits and neither of them included Jaxon Wilks.

Observational skills of a hawk, Hale thought. He raised a hand and O'Rourke's gaze landed on Jaxon. It flicked to Hale—it stopped on Shaw.

And hardened, instantly. O'Rourke didn't move and Hale chugged more water. All three of them waited until he at last approached. Jaxon kicked back an empty seat, but O'Rourke didn't sit.

"Hello, Nolan," Shaw said.

A tendon in O'Rourke's jaw flexed. His gaze flicked to Jaxon.

"What is this?"

Jaxon swallowed the rest of the Johnnie Walker. He chewed ice, his own gaze hard.

"Not half of what it should be, Mr. O'Rourke. Now *sit down*."

O'Rourke looked over his shoulder, maybe checking to see if the cab he had arrived in was still there. It had already pulled off—there was no obvious escape.

And besides, Hale thought, *he couldn't afford to run*.

O'Rourke sat. The waiter returned and Jaxon ordered a refill. O'Rourke wanted nothing. The guy shuffled off and O'Rourke threw up a hand.

"Okay. You got me here. What do you want?"

"It was the Chinese," Jaxon said.

"What?"

"The Chinese provided Abiem with Marcus Harden's personnel file. They also supplied the video of him rounding up kids in Western Equatoria. I don't know it for sure and nobody ever will—the Chinese are great at covering their tracks. My guess is not even the South Sudanese know where the evidence came from. But I have confirmed that Beijing is the only other serious contender for a mineral exploitation contract in Western Equatoria. Seems that it was always going to be either us or them...the South Sudanese were leaning our way. And then Harden."

Jaxon's voice was clipped, his iron stare piercing O'Rourke like a blade. Hale had only known the deputy assistant secretary for a few days—he couldn't be sure what his regular disposition was or if he always came across this angry.

But Hale didn't think so. He thought this was a side of Jaxon Wilks that maybe nobody had ever seen.

"So how do we prove it wasn't us?" O'Rourke said. "How do we *fix this*?"

"Well," Jaxon said, rattling the ice in his fresh Johnnie Walker, "I suppose we *could* find Harden. Strap him to a board and dump water in his face until he cracked and gave us his employer. Although, now that I think of it, that won't be possible. What were you saying about Harden's condition, Mr. Hale?"

"That he was shot in the face," Hale said, perfectly monotone.

"Ah, right. Shot in the face. Twice, wasn't it? So I guess he won't be ratting anyone out."

O'Rourke squinted at Hale. "Who *are* you?"

"He's my guy," Shaw said. "The one I sent into Western Equatoria, and you recommended that I extract...because of *James Wani*."

The words landed and Hale could actually see the gears spinning behind O'Rourke's eyes. He was flailing for a solution—some kind of escape hatch. This guy could already feel the walls closing in on him, and the punchline hadn't even landed yet.

"Here's what we know," Hale said, seizing control. "Earlier this year a massive deposit of coltan, an extremely valuable mineral ore, was discovered in Western Equatoria. That discovery was made by a British exploration firm, leading to a domino effect of corrupt businessmen and politicians scrambling to seize control."

Hale didn't mention that one of those businessmen had been his old boss at Sentinel, or that one of the politicians was a Massachusetts congressman. He didn't mention that he himself had been entangled in the heart of that conspiracy and had shot his way out.

Those were facts that Nolan O'Rourke didn't need to know.

"The South Sudanese didn't know about the coltan deposits until after word of a conspiracy leaked," Hale continued. "At that point they terminated any pending contract negotiations until they could determine the actual value of aforementioned deposits—which, as I'm sure you know, ranks somewhere around the billion-dollar mark."

O'Rourke didn't move. Hale remained slouched in his chair, one hand only inches from his pistol.

"Eventually," Hale said, "negotiations were reopened. Countries and large corporations were invited to bid on an exploitation deal, seeing as South Sudan lacks the ability to mine the resources herself. The US was extremely interested, as were a number of major nations, but the South Sudanese asking price was high—much higher than the US or really anyone wanted to pay. Negotiations stalled. That's when Mr. Wilks was deployed into South Sudan as a special emissary, ready to clear the clutter and get the ink on the page."

Jaxon lifted a finger off his glass in acknowledgment of the point, but didn't otherwise interject. Hale continued.

"I guess it was sometime just before Jaxon arrived that China decided to play dirty. The situation in Western Equatoria, so far as security is concerned, was already bad. They must have known that the United States was offering military assistance as part of the purchase price of the exploitation contract. I guess they thought that if they could prove that the US was actively *inflaming* regional instability to improve their own bargaining position, they might kill any deal between Washington and Juba altogether...which, of course, would dramatically improve Beijing's bargaining position."

"Quite the checkmate," Shaw said. "Really, very clever."

O'Rourke didn't answer. He was twitching, his gaze shifting. Hale could read his eyes like a newspaper headline, so transparent that he wondered how this guy ever landed a job at the CIA.

He was thinking: *Do they know?*

"So Beijing wanted to set us up," Hale continued. "They decided to use Marcus Harden, a disgraced former CIA contractor with a bloody history that the Agency was *very* interested in concealing. This is all rumor, of course, but sort of an accepted truth inside Langley. We know, because Jaxon went to school with a woman who now works in the operations directorate. They're still buddies—she doesn't mind sharing gossip."

O'Rourke was getting edgier. Hale kept his gaze locked on him and didn't blink.

"So anyway, the Chinese found Harden and hired him to kidnap children while pretending to lead an LRA resurgence. He sacked villages and killed a bunch of people. They sent a guy named Lado Bakumba out into the bush to film him doing so, then they took that film and paired it with Harden's personnel file—maybe stolen, maybe manufactured—and supplied it to the South Sudanese. Proof of the CIA's interference and manipulation in Western Equatoria...a fatal blow to US–South Sudanese relations."

"It's all a lie," O'Rourke said. "We can prove Harden was fired. The Agency had *nothing* to do with him."

Hale rocked his water back. Drank half of what remained. Cleared his throat.

"It's tough to prove a negative, O'Rourke. Even tougher to rebuild trust...especially when the allegations are *true*."

O'Rourke blinked. "What? You just said it was a setup."

"Sure, Marcus Harden was a setup. But James Wani? Not so much."

All the color drained from O'Rourke's face. His gaze snapped back to Jaxon and then to Shaw. He seemed to be looking at everyone for a way out but nobody was giving him any room.

Hale sat forward for the first time. "You gave Wani the guns, O'Rourke.

Hundreds of M4 rifles and Beretta M9 handguns—firearms that are being phased out of the US Army as we speak. They were probably slated to be destroyed, but you found a way to funnel them into Africa, to dump fuel on Wani's fire. Twelve months ago he was nothing but a rampaging maniac—then, suddenly, he has all these weapons, all these resources. Heck, he even managed to acquire an *attack helicopter*, and people who knew how to fly it. Fuel and equipment to maintain it. I mean, this guy is really taking off. The violence in Western Equatoria is skyrocketing. The South Sudanese military is abandoning garrisons and beating a retreat. They're desperate. They need *help*...and there we are to give it to them. For the right price."

"It's almost funny, isn't it?" Jaxon said. "The Chinese thought they were setting us up...and there we were, guilty as sin the whole time."

Silence. A red current rose slowly up O'Rourke's neck. One look into his eyes and Hale knew—it was all true. Every word of it.

But slowly, O'Rourke relaxed in his seat. He folded his arms and shook his head.

"That's absurd—and you can't prove any of it."

"Maybe not," Hale said. "Jaxon's been digging ever since Shaw and I first approached the embassy with information about Wani's US-stamped equipment. He's got instincts. Maybe he'll find something."

"You'll end your career," O'Rourke snarled, addressing Jaxon.

The deputy assistant secretary didn't reply. He remained frozen, one hand wrapped around his glass, the rage boiling just behind his eyes.

"Thousands dead, Nolan," Shaw said. "Tens of thousands displaced. Wani's war has torn Western Equatoria apart—all so that *you* could negotiate a slightly cheaper deal on a pile of metallic dirt. Do you have any concept of how depraved that is?"

O'Rourke's hand tightened into a fist. He looked back to Jaxon.

"You know what? I don't have to deal with this. You don't work for me and I don't work for you. If you've got a complaint, call your boss."

Jaxon smirked, just a little. "Funny you should mention Morris—I already called him. He shut me down before I even got to the part about the rifles. Kinda makes me wonder...am I the only man left in Washington with a *soul*?"

That was too much. O'Rourke exploded out of his chair, jabbing a finger at Hale.

"You're in way over your head—all of you. There are forces at work here bigger than any of us. You can throw yourself on the train tracks and be flattened like—"

"Or we can throw James Wani on the tracks," Shaw said.

O'Rourke stopped. He squinted. "*What?*"

"You're a mean chess player, Nolan," Shaw said. "But just this once you're two steps behind. I met with Wani myself. We had a long, illuminating discussion about his complaints with the South Sudanese government. The guy is a psychopath and an egomaniac and a wannabe dictator, but he's not wrong about how corrupt Juba has become. They sell off their nation's precious natural resources to the highest international bidder, growing rich off the proceeds without any concern for their impoverished citizenry. It's happened with oil for decades—next up was the coltan deposit...but not if *Wani* has anything to say about it."

O'Rourke's lips parted. White-hot fury contorted his face.

"*You*," he said. "*You* told Wani about the coltan."

"I did more than that. I provided documentation from the British exploration company who discovered it—enough for Wani to validate his claims to the international community. He'll have Juba by the throat, after this, and Washington also. Backroom deals are dead, Wani will make sure of it. It'll keep him in power."

"You're *insane*," O'Rourke snapped. "Do you have any clue what you've done? That man is—"

"Your partner in crime?" Hale cut in.

Silence. Dead and cold. O'Rourke straightened.

"It's over," Jaxon said. "All of it. Your hope for a cheap deal—my hope for any kind of deal. Wani's war is over, too. Thanks to your back-channel support, it would have been hard to eradicate him, but the guy is just smart enough to know that he can't go on killing people with the eyes of the world watching. Now this is a diplomatic tightrope, and God only knows how it will end. Maybe with another civil war. Whatever the case..." Jaxon rose. He stepped around the table and spoke in a snarl. "*Your part is finished.*"

O'Rourke looked like he might explode—like he might draw his pistol and try to shoot them all. He'd be dead in the blink of an eye if he tried. Hale already had his own fingers wrapped around the HK beneath the table.

But O'Rourke never drew. He simply turned and marched away, back to the street. He lifted a hand for a cab—then he was gone.

Another rat vanishing into a hole.

Jaxon returned to his chair, snarling a curse. He finished his second glass of Johnnie Walker, staring at the table with his gaze lost in space.

He might be thirty years old, but he looked fifty. He looked beaten and battered...and really fed up. Twisting his hand, he flung the remnants of his ice over the concrete, snorting.

"You see that?" he said. "That's my career."

Hale and Shaw said nothing. Jaxon stood and dropped two twenties on the table.

"Nice meeting you," he said. "I hope we never meet again."

Then the deputy assistant secretary left, and Hale watched him vanish just like O'Rourke. Maybe not a rat—or maybe he was simply a better actor.

"You think he was involved?" Shaw said.

Hale only grunted. The thought had occurred to him—he really didn't know.

"They'll get away with it," Shaw continued, her voice dropping.

Yep, Hale thought. *But Marcus Harden didn't.*

He finished his water, his neck aching as he rocked his head back. He crumpled the bottle and left it on the table next to Jaxon's twenties. Then he stood and looked out over the White Nile.

Slow, lazy, timeless. A churn of muddy water just slipping by, relentless and unchanging.

"You know something," Hale said.

"What?"

Hale met Shaw's exhausted gaze and shook his head.

"You *do* owe me."

Shaw blinked. Her mouth opened but she didn't answer—then she laughed. Low and dry. Hale laughed, too, and extended a hand. He helped her out of the chair, and they both turned for the street.

110

Western Equatoria, South Sudan
16:50 Hours, East Africa Time

With the threat of Wani's anti-aircraft fire removed—the warlord-turned-revolutionary still claimed his innocence with regard to the UNHAS flight—Hale and Shaw were able to charter a plane to fly them into Tambura.

A four-door Land Cruiser waited to carry them from the airstrip to the orphanage—a gift from his most gracious excellency. Scattered around town and along the bumpy highway, Hale counted fully three dozen men in camo fatigues and black berets, all carrying M4 rifles and M9 sidearms, many saluting the Cruiser as it passed. They were Wani's security force, the promised protection for the orphanage, and Hale couldn't help but marvel at the strategic genius of their deployment.

Wani was *smart*. He did indeed feel the eyes on the world bearing down on coltan-rich Western Equatoria, and he was exploiting every moment of that attention. Some day soon, he might succeed in his ambitions of displacing Juba. He might become South Sudan's dictator.

But that was tomorrow's problem. Western Equatoria still had more than enough challenges to occupy its present attention.

Long before the Cruiser reached the orphanage, Hale could see the cargo trucks gathered in its front yard, local men unloading freshly airdropped supplies. Not only from Resurrection Mercy Ministries, many of these shipments came from the very same governments and NGOs who had refused to assist Shaw with emergency flights only a week prior.

Circumstances changed quickly, it seemed, and while Bill Carpenter and Mary Grace Dalton were nobody's fools, they also understood the value of capitalizing on the moment. The food in these trucks would last the orphans for *months*...and that was good, because two hundred fresh mouths were already on site, awaiting the construction of a new facility that Wani promised to build in Wau.

Maybe Wani would deliver. Hale doubted it.

The Cruiser stopped and a mob of children, sweaty and covered in fresh finger paint, swarmed the vehicle. Shaw laughed awkwardly and patted heads while Hale scooped up a kid on each hip and strolled into the orphanage as though it were home.

It kind of felt that way.

"Mr. Hale! Mr. Hale! Did you see how many Skittles they brought?"

The mention of the candy brought Joseph to mind, and Hale's chest tightened. He thought of the sock puppets on the roof. Tito squatting on the table, conducting backflips for the children. Wal's humble smile, as gentle and as steady as an African sunrise.

Good people.

They ate dinner at the pole barn with overflow seating spread across the yard. The meal was a mix of hastily warmed canned goods from the airdrops. Ajok had done wonders with a pinch of this and a dash of that sprinkled into the pots, but Hale didn't have much of an appetite. He sat at the head table avoiding eye contact with anyone and trying not to think too much about all the little things that had slipped through the cracks.

All the snakes that had slithered away.

With a half-empty plate, he excused himself and walked to the edge of the brushlands where a newly constructed picket fence surrounded a patch of clay about a hundred feet square. Wooden markers, pending the construction of stone ones, were planted at the heads of three graves.

The earth was fresh over each, looking rusty in the fading sunlight. Hale stood just outside the fence with his hands in his pockets, just staring at Joseph's marker and remembering the old warrior's quiet demeanor. His steady confidence.

The loss hit Diko harder than anyone. Mary Grace said that she found him crying himself to sleep two nights in a row...but on the third night, Diko appeared at dinner with Joseph's milsurp canteen strapped to his hip. He sat at the dinner table in Joseph's seat. He asked permission to bless the food.

And he didn't cry anymore.

"It never gets easier."

The gentle voice caught Hale off guard. He turned to find Mary Grace standing in her patchwork skirt just a few feet behind. She had slipped up, and he should have heard her.

Maybe he was still exhausted.

"Losing people like these," Mary Grace clarified. Her blue eyes, reflecting the setting sun, glimmered more than they should. She stepped nearer and placed her hands atop the picket fence.

They stood side by side, Hale's gaze traveling back to the marker. Then, after a long moment, he dropped his head. He breathed out, long and slow. He twisted and settled onto the ground with his back to the fence, his gaze traveling to the swarm of children at the pole barn.

Nearly three hundred. All parentless. All destitute. But listening to them, you wouldn't know it. There was a lot of laughter...a lot of childlike hope.

"I wish I was like that," Hale said.

Mary Grace smiled, very softly. Then she eased herself to the ground and sat beside him.

"Why do you think we lose it?" she said.

Because the world hits us in the face, Hale thought. *Because we watch people die, and maybe we cause people to die. We suffer pain and we inflict it. We see that brokenness all around us. We grow up.*

He knew it was the truth, but he didn't need to say it. Somehow the quiet of the evening felt too perfect to be shattered by jaded cynicism.

And yet he couldn't help but think, sitting there on the grass...

"My father was in the Army," Hale said.

Mary Grace faced him, cocking her head. But she didn't answer. She just watched.

"My grandfather was in the Navy," Hale continued. "His father was a Marine. All the way back to the Revolutionary War, my family has served in uniform. It's something that just...follows you. Like a crowd of ghosts, all watching you."

"Expecting you to fill their shoes," Mary Grace whispered.

Hale looked up. He nodded.

"Yes...exactly like that."

He trailed off. His gaze drifted again. A column of termites marched its way between his boots and circled beneath his knee, some carrying fragments of wood or dead grass. Hale looked at them but wasn't really watching.

"I just..." He shook his head. "I just don't understand why I failed."

Mary Grace squinted. Hale blinked, and saw fire. He breathed, and he heard the thunder of an exploding jet engine.

Echo Niner-Eight, going down.

"I broke my back falling out of a helicopter and the Army let me go. I fought my way through rehab, fought my way back to physical fitness... They still wouldn't take me. I worked in private security just to do something. Then that blew up, too. And it's just like..."

The words left him. Mary Grace's voice filled the gap, as soft as the African breeze.

"Like you're a hammer looking for a nail," she said.

He turned. The tears had returned to her eyes.

"I know," she said. "I've known ever since I woke up in that hospital fighting for my life. This overwhelming feeling that I was supposed to be doing something more—that I was failing."

"How..." Hale hesitated. "How did you find that? How did you know that *this* is what you're supposed to be doing? That this is your fight?"

Mary Grace laughed. It was a short, humorless sound. She looked at her hands and played with a grass stalk, winding it around one finger. Unwinding, then winding again.

"Honestly?" she said. "I don't know. I'm just doing the next right thing."

The words landed hard, like a missile strike. But in some weird way, they landed strong, too. Accurate and meaningful. Like a hit on target.

Mary Grace breathed deep, wavy hair raining down her back as the last rays of the sun faded behind them. From across the yard a child laughed, a bright and melodious sound.

Like wind chimes, Hale thought. Mary Grace smiled and Hale leaned against the fence, shoulders loosening. More young voices joined in the melody, and Hale's eyelids drooped. For the first time in maybe weeks, he pushed the storm from his mind and just listened to those laughs.

It was an amazing sound.

Price of Allegiance
Ian Hale Book 3

Deceived. Pursued. Trapped behind enemy lines.

Ian Hale is back in the private military game—but this time, he's calling the shots.

Fresh from a brutal mission in South Sudan, Hale and partner Laney Shaw have established themselves as elite operators. But reputation alone doesn't keep the lights on. Pressed for cash, Hale takes a high-stakes contract with Diedem, a tech giant crippled by cyberattacks. The mission: escort two executives into Belarus, pay off the hackers, and secure critical data. Simple enough.

Until everything falls apart.

When a gunshot cracks and one executive topples, Hale realizes he's been set up. Betrayed and hunted through hostile territory, Hale discovers that Diedem has a dark secret—a conspiracy linking the corporation to Moscow's brutal regime. Now, with ruthless Russian assassins and relentless Belarusian forces closing in, Hale must fight not just to survive, but to expose the truth.

He didn't start this fight, but he's determined to finish it.

ABOUT THE AUTHOR

Logan Ryles was born in small town USA and knew from an early age he wanted to be a writer. After working as a pizza delivery driver, sawmill operator, and banker, he finally embraced the dream and has been writing ever since. With a passion for action-packed and mystery-laced stories, Logan's work has ranged from global-scale political thrillers to small town vigilante hero fiction.

Beyond writing, Logan enjoys saltwater fishing, road trips, sports, and fast cars. He lives with his wife and three fun-loving dogs in Alabama.

Sign up for Logan Ryles's reader list at
severnriverbooks.com

Printed in the United States
by Baker & Taylor Publisher Services